THE BABY DOLL MURDER

Cliff Tierney was trained by M[illegible] carny. Then Holly entered his li[illegible] Markham had Tierney stomped. But that was months ago. Now Tierney is back, and Markham wants him to handle a blackmailer for him. Ann should be easy. She's in love with Cliff. But then Markham brings Holly back into the picture, and the set-up becomes complicated. Because Holly's father is the eminent Dr. Thad Ross, who not only controls the town but is involved in Ann's blackmail scheme. And Holly, well she's just as dangerous as her father, and more than a match for Tierney's carny skills.

KILLER TAKE ALL!

Tony Pearson knows he is no match for Steve Locke, Fern's new husband. Locke has the charm, the drive and the physical prowess he doesn't. He also has Fern. But as a failed golf pro, Tony doesn't have that many options either, and takes Locke up on his offer to work for Tony's boss, Max Baird. Max is a reformed gangster trying to fit in. He even bought a Rembrandt to show off his class. But now he needs the bucks more than the art, and Locke calls in an expert to appraise the painting. That's when they discover that the painting Max owns is a forgery. And who gets framed as the fall guy? Why, Tony, of course.

FRENZY

After the plan to snatch the boss's girl and some of his casino profits backfires, Norman Sands rails it back to his hometown to lick his wounds. His brother Matt lives there, and Laurie, who used to be his girl, now engaged to Matt. But with Matt and Laurie's help, Norm knows there is a killing to be made here, if he can just figure the angle. When he meets up with the town's movers, he realizes that Murdoch is the real power here. And when he meets Shannon, he knows he has found the perfect match—she's as greedy as he is. But Shannon is Murdoch's girl, and Murdoch isn't giving up *anything* without a fight.

James O. Causey Bibliography
(1924-2003)

Novels:
Killer Take All (Graphic, 1957)
The Baby Doll Murders (Gold Medal, 1957)
Frenzy (Crest, 1960)

Short Stories:
The Statue (*Weird Tales*, Jan 1943)
Legacy in Crystal (*Weird Tales*, July 1943)
Hammer of Cain (with Bill Blackbeard, *Weird Tales*, Nov 1943)
Death Song (*Detective Story Magazine*, June 1945)
Seventh Round Homicide (*Detective Story Magazine*, Nov 1946)
Vengeance from the Tomb (*Detective Story Magazine*, Dec 1946)
Obeah Kill (*Detective Story Magazine*, March 1947)
I Thought I'd Die (*New Detective Magazine*, Sept 1947)
Teething Ring (*Galaxy Science Fiction*, Jan 1953)
Exploiter's End (*Orbit Science Fiction*, June 1953)
Inferiority (*Science Stories*, Apr 1954)
School Days (*Science Stories*, Apr 1954)
Felony (*Galaxy Science Fiction*, July 1954)
So Lovely, So Lost (*Orbit Science Fiction,* Nov-Dec 1954)
Inhibition (*If*, Feb 1955)
Competition (*Galaxy Science Fiction*, May 1955)
Snakerdworp (*Other Worlds Science Stories*, July 1955)
Big Horse Coming (*Fast Action Detective and Mystery Stories*, March 1957)
Deathmate (*Manhunt*, March 1957)
I Watch Lisa Die (*Playtime*, 1958)
The Gentle People (*Spaceway*, Jan 1969)

THE BABY DOLL MURDERS

KILLER TAKE ALL!

FRENZY

BY JAMES O. CAUSEY

Introduction by Nicholas Litchfield

STARK HOUSE

Stark House Press • Eureka California

THE BABY DOLL MURDERS / KILLER TAKE ALL! / FRENZY

Published by Stark House Press
1315 H Street
Eureka, CA 95501, USA
griffinskye3@sbcglobal.net
www.starkhousepress.com

ISBN-13: 978-1-944520-51-9

Book design by Mark Shepard, SHEPGRAPHICS.COM
Proofreading by Bill Kelly
Cover art by Roy Lance from *Killer Take All!*

First Stark House Press Edition: August 2018

Contents

Causey's Fast, Frenzied Trio of Killer Novels

By Nicholas Litchfield

James Oliver Causey Jr. (1924 - 2003) was an American novelist and writer of science fiction and crime stories, with the brunt of his work published in the 1940s and 50s. His literary career was surprisingly short, particularly considering the quality of his writing. It began in 1943 when he placed several stories in *Weird Tales*, an influential pulp magazine focused on the horror and fantasy genres that ran from 1923 to 1954. After putting his writing on hold for a couple of years to serve in the military during World War II, he turned his attention to crime fiction, placing four stories in Street & Smith's long-running *Detective Story Magazine*, the first pulp magazine to devote itself entirely to crime fiction.

In the 1950s, his focus switched to science fiction. Several of his stories appeared in *Galaxy Science Fiction*, one of the most important science fiction digests in 1950s America—it published the likes of Ray Bradbury, Robert A. Heinlein, Isaac Asimov, Frederik Pohl, and Theodore Sturgeon. His other pieces were published in *Science Stories*, *If*, *Other Worlds Science Stories*, and the short-lived digest *Orbit Science Fiction*.

Either Causey decided to move away from science fiction writing after 1955 or he found trouble placing his work. The January 1969 issue of *Spaceway Science Fiction*, which ceased publication the following year, marks his last sci-fi publication credit.

Of all his work, he had the most success as a writer of crime fiction. His story "Deathmate," published in March 1957 in *Manhunt*, the popular magazine devoted to hardboiled crime fiction, was twice adapted for TV under the same title, both times as episodes of *Alfred Hitchcock Presents*. Best-selling author Bill S. Ballinger, who was predominantly a screenwriter but also hugely successful as a mystery and suspense writer—one of my favorites, in fact—wrote the teleplay to the 1961 episode, and an updated version of the story was made in 1987.

Causey also wrote several successful novels, each favorably reviewed in *The New York Times* by the noted book critic Anthony Boucher. The first, *Killer Take All!*, was published by Graphic Publications in January 1957. The cover of the Australian edition, released by Phantom in 1959, offers a strong indication that the novel did well domestically and internationally, advertising it as having sold 1.268 million copies to date. As for critical reception, Boucher had positive things to say, calling it an adroitly plotted novel that is "sharply economical and furiously paced."

Brisk and entertaining, it has a breezy tone that sets it apart from the author's later novels, and the dispirited, "chip on each shoulder" narrator, Tony Pearson, is an inspired choice of hero. He is a high school and city golf champ who cracked under pressure while on the PGA circuit and then returned to his former job as assistant pro at Briarview golf club feeling like a failure, with tattered dreams of glory.

Six months earlier, while he was on the tournament trail, seeing his drive falter and his name plummet off the leaderboard, his tall, pretty fiancé, Fern, a woman who can belt a golf ball like few others, suddenly married a dashing stranger, purportedly just to spite him. When he notices her on the driving range, her swing as faultless as always, her presence stirs up old passions and he winds up in a rough spot when her husband, Stephen Locke, suspects something going on between them.

Locke, a duplicitous rogue, is the perfect foil for the hapless Pearson. Strong, handsome, wealthy, and popular with the ladies, he has an indefinable charm and is utterly invincible when he wants something. He incessantly outshines Pearson, even bests him on the golf course. When he unexpectedly offers Pearson the well-paid position of head pro at the exclusive Point Rafael, an upper-crust country club near Laguna, Pearson jumps at the offer, unaware of Locke's ulterior motives.

Once at Point Rafael, surrounded by shifty characters like owner Max Baird, "a ruthless amoral gangster with the wistfulness of a child," the plot develops quickly, and Causey allows an aura of violence to waft over the proceedings. What begins as a dryly-amusing romance rapidly turns into an exciting tale of robbery, adultery, murder, and deception, with Pearson becoming the prime suspect in a murder investigation, on the run from the police, and striving to clear his name.

The swift pace and the likable, unpretentious main protagonist help make it a pleasurable read, and the opulent, country club setting, with its lush fairways and glittering blue lake, give it added appeal.

Causey's second novel, *The Baby Doll Murders*, which came out in October of the same year, has the distinction of being a Gold Medal Books original from Fawcett Publications. Unlike Pearson, the central character, Cliff Tierney, is a tough, unbreakable sort of guy who is rugged and resourceful. Disappointed with his lot in life, he's actively striving for something better. He is also an orphan, a drifter, and a "grifter," much the same as the main protagonist in Causey's subsequent novel.

At the start of *The Baby Doll Murders* Tierney is working as a blackjack dealer in the Trails, a small club on West Fremont in Las Vegas that is described as "a haven for losers, for those defeated dregs of humanity sweating out their last blue chips." His hot temper, which got him dismissed from a club the previous month, proves his undoing once again when he is fired for brawling with a patron.

Immediately, a sly, slippery crook named Tom Markham, whom Tierney has known since he worked for a traveling carnival at age fourteen, approaches him with an assignment. Markham is a specialist at controlling people to further his own ends. When Tierney returned from serving in Korea, Markham employed him as a bouncer/troubleshooter at his gambling house in Paloma Beach. Restrictive gambling laws had allowed Markham to buy the place cheap, and he then used his silent partner on the city council, Thad Ross, a prominent physician, to reinstate the casino license. He continues to partner with Thad in order to run a highly profitable black market baby operation on the side, and uses the doctor's wistful and wild daughter, Holly, to keep Tierney in his employ.

Having always considered Markham his "mentor and guide, the father he had never known," Tierney has come to realize that he is nothing more than a useful tool to Markham. Now, he no longer wants to work for the man. He also wants to distance himself from Holly, for his own mental wellbeing. Although passionate about her, with dreams of them raising a family, her drastic mood swings and deep emotional problems have made their stormy relationship untenable.

Unfortunately, neither is willing to let him go, and their emotional hold over him is so strong that he doesn't seem able to escape them.

Markham's interest in him is purely business. He needs Tierney to re-establish relations with Ann Childs, one of Tierney's former girlfriends, and recover some especially damaging documents that she is using for blackmail purposes. Tierney knows Ann well enough to suspect it's a cock-and-bull story, and sure enough, there's much more to the plot than mere blackmail.

The *New York Herald Tribune* had no complaints about the book, other than its misleading title, considering it the sort of taut, harsh and compulsive tale you might find in *Black Mask* magazine in its heyday. Like *Killer Take All!*, it is another fast-action crime thriller, but with a darker tone, a more intricate plot, and a less sympathetic lead.

For all his faults, Tierney seems like a saint compared to the author's next central character. *Frenzy*, Causey's final novel, was published by Fawcett Publications in February 1960, this time under its Crest imprint. Boucher described it as "a violent, ugly, and believable story of evil in action," with an irredeemable main protagonist who is possibly more vicious than those created by preeminent crime fiction authors Charles Williams and Jim Thompson.

Indeed, the narrator, Norman Sands, is a tough, womanizing, conniving thug who doesn't have many likable qualities. He describes himself as a "two-bit grifter," a pilot fish who desperately wants "to become a killer shark." It's an apt description.

A restless and moody boy, he developed a reputation for wildness, mixing with the wrong crowd and picking gang fights with the Mexican kids. At sixteen, he ran away from home, convinced he had killed a boy in a street fight, and subsequently became a street hustler in L.A., working pool halls and cheating at cards, before graduating to blackjack tables.

Frenzy begins when he is in his late twenties, working as a ringer at a casino. Punished for messing around with the boss' girlfriend, he then tries to steal from his boss, run off with the girlfriend, and land the man in jail. When his plans go awry, he flees town and eventually winds up in his hometown of Mason Flats, drawn back there in the hopes of scrounging money from his younger brother whom he last saw twelve years earlier. Feeling like a big deal in a little, jerkwater town, and benefitting from his brother's initial help, Norm finally has the opportunity to become the killer shark he always wanted to be.

Shortly after arriving, he hits on the idea of oil lease acquisitions, and it isn't long before he has moved on to other lucrative operations, everything from dope running to racketeering. He is willing to swindle anybody and everybody, his brother included, in order to make a bundle of cash. It doesn't seem to bother him who gets hurt or the sort of dangerous gangsters he finds himself up against. He sees every resident and mom-and-pop store as a potential income source, and whatever moneymaking enterprise he comes up with, he sticks with it until the bottom falls out. Hardened and unrelenting, Norm is a man who thinks big and lives big and doesn't stop at murder to achieve his ambitions.

As vile and despicable as he is, you can't help but admire his business acumen and his devotion to the pursuit of money. Cunning, unafraid, with no qualms about cheating those closest to him, his only real weakness is his determination to succeed.

Those around him are no better, making his cutthroat behavior seem unremarkable. In fact, the residents of Mason Flats, a small town in southern California with a population of 9,318, have an impressively large percentage of lying, cheating, backstabbing folk. Of those who work closely with Norm, "a nimbus of violence hovers about them." Even his brother, a do-gooder he nicknames "Galahad," is prepared to put a bullet in his back in his fight for justice.

What's most impressive about Causey's frenetic, hardboiled tale is that even though Norm might not endear himself to the reader, you can't help but become engrossed in his adventure and interested in finding out how it ends.

Considering the mass popular appeal of Fawcett's paperback originals, as well as the favorable critical reviews *Frenzy* and *The Baby Doll Murders* received, it seems likely that these two novels sold comparatively well. With that being so, it is slightly strange that no subsequent novel by Causey saw the light of day. For whatever reason, *Frenzy* marked the end of his crime fiction endeavors and was to be his last significant work of fiction.

Whether there were other thrilling stories of murder and deception that were overlooked or, simply, he had told all the tales he wanted to tell, I have no idea. What I can say for sure is that Causey left behind a fine trio of expertly plotted, fast-paced crime yarns and a memorable lineup of scheming card sharps, venomous crooks, and disloyal associates that, roughly sixty years later, still have the power to intrigue, startle and entertain.

—March 2018
Rochester, NY

THE BABY DOLL MURDERS

BY JAMES O. CAUSEY

CHAPTER 1

They found Tierney in Las Vegas, dealing blackjack at the Trails. It was three in the morning, and Tierney was tired. He dealt the cards with a fatalistic patience, hoping his relief man would come before the drunk opposite him started swinging.

Too many fights occurred at the Trails lately. It was a small club on West Fremont, with the bar done in Old West motif, much wood and dark leather and no chrome. Bar whisky was thirty cents. You could shoot craps for anything from a dime to five hundred dollars.

Tierney thought of the Trails as a haven for losers, for those defeated dregs of humanity sweating out their last blue chips. Slow death by attrition.

That, thought Tierney, would be a dilly. Hang a longhorn skull over the baize with a sign, *Losers Only*. The house would love that.

"Hey, friend." The drunk stared at Tierney with a wild smile. "You gave the lady my card."

The card was a five. Tierney kept his expression bland.

"Sorry, sir," he said. "You left your chips on top of your cards. No hit, sir."

The drunk sat breathing hard, his jaw muscles bunching. He was a big sallow man who had doubled his bets doggedly the last four hands, losing each time. He had three hundred dollars riding on this hand.

Tierney flipped over his own cards. "Pay eighteen," he announced, turning over the cards of the other players. The big man had stood short on sixteen.

"Don't touch it," the drunk said. He stood up, weaving slightly. "By rights that five was mine. You owe me three hundred bucks. Cough, mister."

The other players sat motionless. Tierney froze in the act of raking in chips. Jungle instinct told him to call for Charley, the pit boss. He felt a vague kinship with the drunk, and a touch of pity. Here it comes, he thought. He's going to reach for the house money and you'll grab his hands. Then he'll take a swing at you. You'll chop him in the throat over the carotid artery, just like you did last month at the Aladdin, the night they fired you. A good dealer needs control, and you've stopped caring.

Tierney reached for the chips with a faint smile, waiting for it to happen.

Then he saw Markham.

Markham was standing unobtrusively next to the drunk. He was a sparse gray man with that prosaic look that belongs to bank tellers and mailmen.

But Tom Markham was no bank clerk. He had been hunting Tierney for several days, and had no intention of letting some drunk cheat him out of his prey.

Markham smiled at him, both hands resting lightly on the edge of the table. Once in a carny brawl outside Fresno, Tierney had seen him break a rube's spine with those small, clever hands.

When the action came, it was an explosion. Afterwards, no one could quite agree on what happened. No one except Tierney, and his word didn't matter.

The drunk made a grab for Tierney's wrist, and simultaneously screamed, clutching at his groin as he crashed over the blackjack table in a welter of cards and chips. One belated punch grazed Tierney's temple as the big man went down, writhing.

Other house men converged on the scene. They worked with weary, practiced efficiency. Inside of two minutes the blackjack table was standing upright with fresh cards and chips and a new dealer. Markham, naturally, had vanished. Two house men were talking soothingly to the drunk in a back room. Tierney was in another back room being fired.

"Please save it," Charley said. "Four people saw you spear him in the gut when he grabbed you. Nobody saw a little gray man. Charley was the wizened pit boss. He had ulcers and was a very good house man.

"His name's Markham," Tierney said. "He's from the Coast—"

"You got sixty dollars coming. Here."

He took the money. There was no point arguing.

"You and your temper," Charley said uncomfortably. "I got to pass the word, Cliff. I got responsibilities to the other houses. You understand?"

Tierney understood. It meant he was washed up in Vegas. Nothing kills a dealer more quickly than a reputation for temper. He shook hands with Charley and left, not looking back. Charley frowned after him, thinking it was a damned shame because Tierney was the best dealer he had ever seen.

At three in the morning Fremont Street is a golden cascade of neons, luring sucker and high roller alike to rape the bright goddess of chance. Tierney walked slowly, not looking at the glittering marquees. He had nothing but time. There was no point in running, because Markham would inevitably find him. He turned into a bar and grill, where he ordered black coffee and sat waiting.

Within five minutes Markham came in and sat beside him, a calm icicle of a man dressed in gray sharkskin. He said, "Hi, Cliff," and ordered coffee and brandy.

Tierney looked at him. Without sound he asked the question.

"You weren't at Del Mar or Gardena," Markham shrugged. "Your Spanish is lousy, so that ruled out Ensenada. It had to be Vegas."

He's a God-damned robot, thought Tierney, looking at the little man. Like the Tin Woodman, Markham must have lost a leg once, and had metal substituted for it. He liked the metal so well he changed the other leg. Then the arms, and finally the whole body. His neural ganglia were spun platinum. He moved with the remorseless logic of a machine and never made mistakes.

"You've got a proposition," Tierney said. "That play at the table was designed to jar me into a receptive mood."

"Very good." Markham savored the laced coffee. "Your end will be five grand. Plus your old job back."

"Dirty?"

"Very dirty."

Rule out cards, thought Tierney. He can thumbnail four aces in three seconds flat, and he's better than you at cold readings. That left only one talent open.

"A woman?"

"Right again."

"*No.*" Tierney's knuckles, gripping the coffee cup, were white. When Markham spoke again he was going to get that cup right behind the ear. The little man sensed this. With the instinct of a professional, he could gauge the intensity of violence, could block it with the right words, softly spoken.

"Holly's in love with you."

Tierney felt a slow sensation of drowning. "You're a liar."

"Honest to God. She's been a nun these three months. You wouldn't know her. She keeps a picture of you in her bedroom—"

"Shut up!"

"Five grand and Holly." Markham said it like soft music. "For thirteen years I taught you, man and boy. You owe me this, Cliff. Last year didn't I pay you fourteen grand?"

"Sure," Tierney said through his teeth. "And then you had Valdez kick my face in." He spoke with a raw intensity, the words hurting him. "In the carny all you wanted was a stooge. Then at Paloma Beach I was strictly a hammer, somebody to break the opposition's heads. Faithful slob Tierney, who would have jumped into a fire if you'd snapped your fingers."

"I warned you about Holly." Markham's voice was a cold knife. "My orders were to have you rubbed—"

"But you had me stomped instead. Thanks! See these front teeth? Porcelain. They cost me six hundred bucks and three visits to the dentist. My ribs healed fine, but my kidneys still ache on cold nights." Tierney stood up, and now his voice was even. "Stay away from me, Tom, or I'll kill you."

Even as he walked away, Markham set the hook deep into him. It took only two words.

"Holly's here," Markham said.

Tierney kept walking like an automaton, feeling the numbness spread inside him. He was at the door, now he was outside, staring at the bright neon web. But he had stopped walking. He wasn't going any place.

Markham came up alongside him. "She wants to see you, Cliff."

Tierney said blindly, "I'm going away."

"Where? You're broke, or you wouldn't be dealing. You don't have a stake and you're too tired to run."

He's uncanny, thought Tierney. Somewhere in that carny they taught him to read minds. He took a slow deep breath and said, "All right, Tom. Let me think about it."

"Fine. You've got two hours to think about it. We're staying at the Flamingo."

Watching him walk away, Tierney decided that hate has a taste. It is a rusty, acrid taste, like iron filings.

Tierney's room was three blocks off Fremont, on a quiet side street. He paid twenty a week for the converted bachelor apartment which consisted of one small bedroom and bathroom. In the bottom bureau drawer, hidden between two undershirts, was a hundred and eighty dollars.

My stake, Tierney thought sardonically, putting the money into his wallet. He stood thinking about Reno, and his chances of getting a job as dealer. But Reno was out, because in that town he would stand out like a fighting cock among barnyard hens. They would easily find him. So it meant Chicago or Philly, and he needed traveling money. This time he would start a new life, fresh and clean.

For just a moment, Tierney lapsed into his favorite dream. The dream he had never shared with anyone but Holly, and she, being high at the time, had laughed hysterically.

There were variations, but basically the dream was this:

He was parking in a garage driveway, and getting out of his car. The house was a clean white frame, with red shutters and trim. Across the lawn, two boys were throwing a football. Two blond, husky, laughing youngsters, that saw him and yelled and started a mad dash to see who could reach him first. The race was always a tie, with him scooping up both boys in his arms and tousling their hair as they squealed with delight and started the inevitable romp that ended with him stretched out flat on the grass pleading that he had had enough. Then, of course, he would show them how to really throw a football.

They would call him Dad. No Father, or Pop, but Dad. His wife would come out on the front porch with a quiet shine to her smile and tell them it was time for supper. So into the house they would go, Tierney and his two sons. He would kiss his wife thoroughly and tell her about the new promotion, the raise. She would tell him about going to the doctor that morning, and how he was definitely going to be a father for the third time.

He would kiss her with a wild burst of happiness, hoping it might be a girl this time. She, of course, would want another boy...

At this point the dream splintered and fell apart. Tierney looked into the mirror with contempt.

You're a hustler, he told the mirror image. You're broke, and you haven't a friend in the world. Except for that stint in Korea you've never done an honest day's work in your life. You can do cold readings but you're out of practice. You're very good at cards. You can even do a one-armed *planche*. You've got talent with women, on account of this beautiful damned face.

He had blond hair over very blue eyes, and good cheekbones. The nose was finely chiseled, the mouth strong and brooding. It was a face which combined sensuality with power, and which the majority of women found irresistible.

He turned off the lights, thinking how sour his luck had been since he had left Holly. Outside, he walked fast, toward Fremont. You need at least a thousand, he thought. Play percentages. Don't get greedy.

He went into three casinos before he found the right one. They stood a silent three-deep around the crap table. Cigarette smoke curled like blue fog over the baize. He could smell that choked tension which meant some high roller had gone wild.

Tierney nudged expertly through to the table and bought chips. The high roller was a bald, elfin man in shirt sleeves. The pass line was littered with hundred-dollar chips.

"Five straight passes," a woman whispered. "And he still hasn't dragged."

In that moment, Tierney's brain became an analogue computer, calculating house odds. The high roller's point was nine. Tierney bet fifty dollars on the come line.

Craps goes fast.

Ten minutes later Tierney had nine hundred dollars in front of him. The high roller had sevened out, losing everything. He stood fingering a lone pink chip, his face pearled with sweat. Tierney gazed at him with the empathy one damned soul feels for another. The man's name was Dunbar, and he made a living by being a casino shill for ten dollars a day.

A year ago Dunbar had been a prosperous Chicago dentist with a wife and three children. He had stopped in Vegas overnight on his way to the Coast, and had lost fifteen thousand dollars. Subsequently he had lost every dime he owned, trying to recoup the fifteen thousand. Somewhere in the process, he had lost his wife and family. Like Nick the Greek, Dunbar was a Fremont Street legend. A few weeks ago he had created a mild furor on the strip by parlaying nine silver dollars into eighteen thousand, and losing it all before sundown.

It's a disease, Tierney thought, watching the red cubes bound against the backboard. It's a fever worse than typhoid or opium or liquor. But you don't want to win, really. Down inside it's that old moth-flame relationship, a corruption of the death wish. Like me and Holly.

He concentrated on the chant of the stickman and counted his chips. In two hours he could be on the plane. Once in Philly he would change his name. A new life. He shifted his bet from the field to the pass line.

An hour later he stood fingering his last pink chip. He tossed the chip on the pass line. The shooter crapped. He walked away from the table with one hand groping in his pocket for change. It took him less than five minutes to feed the slots his last quarter.

While he was doing this he was aware of a redhead staring at him from the bar. Her name was Florence and she danced at a downtown floor show. Because she looked like Holly he had taken her out once, a few weeks ago. After that she had called him repeatedly until he asked her to leave him alone.

"Cliff."

She had come up behind him. He smelled the softness of her perfume, and shivered.

"I won tonight," Florence said tremulously. "Let me stake you, honey. Please?"

Markham's right, he thought. You've only got one important talent. He turned, giving her his very best smile, watching her blush.

"No thanks, Florence," he said. "Let me take a rain check."

As he walked toward the glass door he saw that it was almost dawn. Time for vampires and gamblers to return to their caves.

He went to see Markham.

CHAPTER 2

"Her name is Ann Childs," Markham said. "She's twenty-four, a Senior at Vardon University. Sociology major. A while back she quit college and did a year in China with the Red Cross. Very dedicated girl."

Markham paced the plush Flamingo suite with his hands locked behind him, the way he always did when outlining a score. Tierney sat in a white contour chair, chain-smoking.

"She used to stop by the Pink Barrel in the evenings," Markham said. "She'd play dollar lowball, remember?"

Ann had been intense, blue-eyed, vital. Once, Tierney had taken her home. He had made a routine pass which she had casually blocked. Next day he met Holly and forgot all about Ann.

"Nice kid," Tierney mused. "Working her way through college. What about her?"

"She's blackmailing a friend of mine."

Tierney considered it. "Who's the friend?"

"That's not important," Markham said gently. "Two weeks ago this friend receives a photostat of certain names and addresses by registered mail. But no demand for money, just those damned photostats."

"A nice touch," Tierney said, liking it. "Letting him sweat until she's ready for the shakedown." He knew better than to ask the nature of the photostats. It was a routine assignment, and he was a specialist in such assignments. Although Ann had hardly seemed the blackmail type.

Markham stopped pacing. Behind his back fingers coiled like small restless snakes.

"You worked for me three years, Cliff. What do you know about our connections?"

Tierney shrugged. "You've got a silent partner on the city council. He heads off the reformers when they start screaming about the Pink Barrel. You've also got a sideline operation—"

He hesitated. "Go on," Markham said.

"It's not joysticks or women," Tierney said slowly. "I used to wonder about it, but you never confided in me and I didn't ask questions."

"Very good." Markham relaxed and sat down. "You always were a professional, Cliff. Ann's a vulnerable, confused girl. And she's got a yen for you. I used to see her watching you across the casino. She'd ask casual questions about Cliff Tierney. You can take her, no hands."

Tierney tasted nausea. He thought about getting up and clipping Markham in the throat. The only trouble was, Tom was fast. A doctor had once tested the little man's reflexes and told him his neural synapses short-circuited through his spine. Tom was very proud of his reflexes.

"So move in," Tierney said with contempt. "Rough her up like you did me. You're good at that."

"Ann's a fanatic," Markham said thoughtfully. "I know the type. You could use red-hot pincers on her and she'd laugh at you. We've already tried one approach that's failed." He resumed pacing. "This needs finesse, the Tierney touch."

"I lost it," Tierney said. "Remember?"

The little man's face was expressionless. Suddenly a vein jumped on his forehead.

"I want the original of those photostats, Cliff. You're going to get it."

Tierney sat very still, hating himself. Then he thought about Holly. After a moment he started asking the calm questions one professional asks another. Markham had all the answers. He was telling Tierney what a simple operation it was when the door opened. Holly Ross came in.

Tierney stared at her numbly.

"Hello, darling," Holly said.

She had cool green eyes a man could drown in, and a smile that burned him halfway across the room. In the silence, Markham chuckled. It was a flat metallic sound, the sound a computer dial makes when registering the correct total. He was at the door, saying, "I'm sure you two have a lot to talk about. I'll be downstairs in the casino."

He and Holly were alone.

Her hair was soft flame in the lamplight as she walked toward him, shrugging off the mink stole.

"Three rotten months without you." Holly's eyes were shining wet. "Why, Cliff, *why?*"

He looked at her, feeling the storm grow inside him.

Without sound he said, You bitch. You faithless tramp. But nothing changed. He was still in love with her.

"I was in the hospital three days," he said harshly. "You never came. You didn't give a damn."

"I needed time to think, Cliff."

She went over to the sideboard and mixed him a drink, making it a ritual. She handed him the glass, surrender implicit in every line of her body. "Irish on the rocks, remember?"

"Where's yours?"

"I've been on the wagon. Do I look different, darling?" There was a new demureness about her. Her auburn hair was done in a chaste bob, and the pink evening dress made her look like a wistful child.

"Very touching." There was a tearing constriction in his throat, but his voice was brutal. "How many times did Markham have you rehearse this?"

Holly's smile deepened. Then her right hand was a snake striking and whisky slashed into Tierney's face.

"You're filthy," she choked. Tears flashed in her green eyes. "Tom told me you were in Vegas, that was all. I wanted to give us a second chance! We could go to Mexico where they can't find us—"

"They'll find us." He wiped his face wearily. "Besides, we wouldn't last two weeks together."

"We can try." Holly knelt by the chair. Her fingers traced a lingering design on his cheek. "Honestly, I've changed, darling. I'm off alcohol, off weed. Let me prove it—"

"Then start by telling the truth instead of taking your damn clothes off. What's Markham got on you?"

"N-nothing. All I know is that he's worried. So is Daddy."

"Thad Ross?" He frowned, not getting it. Holly's father was an austere, silvered puritan who was head of the city council. Thad spearheaded charity drives, and had once helped close the Pink Barrel down before Markham took over.

Before Markham took over.

"The honorable Doctor Ross," Tierney said softly. "Tom's silent partner. What's Ann got on your father?"

Holly's eyes were clear and innocent. "You're not making sense, darling."

It made deadly sense. Holly was the bait and he was prize rube of the year. Suddenly she leaned over for a kiss, her breasts full and taut under the pink evening dress. He tried to tell her to stop, but her fingers were deft lightnings on his shirt buttons, and her palm was sliding inside his shirt with the old warm urgency.

"Let it go, Cliff. These three months were a bad dream."

She moved, and bright hair spilled across his lap as he fumbled blindly with the zipper at the back of her dress. For three months he had hated her, desired her, and to hell with memory. Holly was an expert destroyer of memory.

The zipper was halfway down when his fingers paused.

"Hurry, darling." Her soft breath tickled his ear.

It was the hardest thing he had ever done in his life, taking his hands off her, letting out a long sigh. "Remember the last time, baby doll? That afternoon you were in the shower and asked me to scrub your back?"

"Oh, good," she breathed. "That's very good." She stood up, and her shoulders writhed as the pink evening dress whispered to the floor. There was just a hint of the old Holly in the quick surety of her fingers as she undressed and stood splendid and white before him.

"Count to fifty." Her eyes were misty with desire. "Then come in."

She went into the bathroom. In a moment he heard the hiss of the shower.

He needed time to think, and there was no time. The need for Holly was a consuming flame. He fumbled for a cigarette. The pack was empty. Holly's handbag lay on the floor. He rummaged through it, thinking how wonderful it could be if Holly were telling the truth, if she had really changed.

He found two cigarettes in her handbag.

Two large brownish cylinders wrapped in tissue. Two tickets to cloud seven.

He sat staring at them, feeling tired, and the sound of the shower was a mounting scream.

"Cliff," Holly called from the bathroom. "Come in and scrub my back, will you?"

He replaced the sticks carefully in her handbag. In that moment the professional part of Tierney took over. The bleak emotionless hustler, whom Markham had fashioned during eight long years on the carny midway.

"Hurry, darling!" Her voice was a siren call.

Tierney got up and left the suite, closing the door softly behind him. He found the stairs at the end of the corridor, and took them three at a time.

At seven in the morning, play was desultory in the casino. Markham stood at the crap table fondling a stack of blues. His intent frown deepened when he saw Tierney.

"She's sleeping," Tierney said, repressing a yawn. "Thought I'd play for a while, see if my luck's changed."

The little man gave him a strange look. "Didn't take you long to reconcile things, did it?"

"Not long." He let the smugness show. "Give me some chips."

Markham stared at him, reading him. Tierney had a tomcat look of surfeit, and he hadn't bothered to wipe off the lipstick. He was hooked, but good. The little man shrugged and gave Tierney a stack of blues. When the dice came around, Tierney crapped twice, then threw four straight passes.

A few minutes later Markham went to the men's room. Tierney promptly cashed in eight hundred dollars' worth of chips. By the time the little man came back to the table Tierney had found a cab in front of the lobby and was three blocks away, telling the cabbie to step on it.

It was seven-fifteen when Tierney left the Flamingo. By eight o'clock he had packed and checked out of his room. By eight-thirty he had paid four hundred dollars for a fifty Ford coupe the used car dealer assured him had been owned by a retired judge. By nine, Vegas was twenty miles behind him, and he was doing a steady seventy along the burning desert highway.

Tierney was back in business.

In his Flamingo suite, Markham had stopped pacing.

"Tell it again." He was implacable. "Every detail."

Holly told it with a patient venom. "Fixer Markham," she said sweetly. "We were going to lead him back by the nose, remember?"

"You goofed, Holly. Hurry up and dress."

She dressed with an uncertain smile, appraising her body in the full-length mirror. "But I was the perfect ingenue." She was talking to herself, not to him. "And I was *sincere*. I really would have gone away with him, did you know that?"

"Sure," he said, amused. "But I could have blocked it. Right now, you hate him."

Holly nodded, staring into the mirror. She whirled, suddenly imperious. "Tom, look at me! How did I goof?"

He looked at her body without emotion. An ivory-and-gold princess, shaken by her first male refusal. "It wasn't you, baby," he said gently. "It was Cliff. It was a good gamble, but we lost."

This one gamble he could not afford to lose. A feeling of weariness swept him. He had always been able to probe beneath the surface mask, to see the secret motivations hidden from the world. But Tierney had just tricked him. He sighed, considering the strength of Tierney, and how it would now be necessary to destroy him.

"Get packed," he said. "Hurry."

Holly was at the sideboard, making herself a drink. She tossed it down with a cynical defiance.

"Come here, Tom," she said.

Tierney wiped sweat from his eyes and squinted at the dash. The Ford was beginning to heat up. He was ten miles from Baker when he saw the filling station and stopped for water. He was out in back drinking a Coke when Markham's charcoal Lincoln went past at ninety miles an hour.

CHAPTER 3

Tierney hit Paloma Beach at ten o'clock that night. The Ford's fuel pump had conked out around noon, and he had lost four hours walking back to Barstow to find a tow truck. He was sunburned and tired.

He drove slowly down the coast highway, past gleaming glass-and-stone motels and new drive-in theatres. A few blocks down he saw the familiar neon shimmer above a huge pink quonset hut. A nostalgic lump rose in his throat. He caught himself involuntarily counting the cars in the big lot, telling himself it was an off night, an easy night to spot the hustlers. He smiled sourly and turned left on Broad Street, three blocks later.

He had no definite plan. There was only a cold bitterness, a resolve still unformed. The thought of Holly was still an open wound, but he could consider her objectively, and that, at least, was something.

He parked on a quiet side street and hesitated in front of a bar. The thought of a drink was tempting, but first he needed food. He had not eaten since Barstow, and was going on thirty hours without sleep.

He wolfed three hamburgers at a café, and almost fell asleep while drinking coffee. A block from the café he registered at a small hotel, and once in his room, discovered that he could not sleep.

He chain-smoked in the darkness, thinking about Markham. In a sense, Tom had created him.

Tierney had run away from the orphanage at fourteen and found a roustabout's job with a traveling carnival. It was Markham who had adopted him, had gotten him the pitchman's slot and shown him the mechanics of shortchanging rubes—Markham, grizzled and wise, who did cold readings and owned a piece of the carny.

Tierney loved the midway glitter and excitement. He learned to reel off a grind that dragged the marks into the freak show like flies. He enjoyed milking them for that last dollar inside the bally tent. *See the unveiled mystery of sex, only one dollah, women and children not allowed, sorry, ma'am.*

On his seventeenth birthday Markham had taught him cold readings. "Look for reactions," the little man said. "The twitch of a mouth, the blink of an eyelid. Watch their hands."

Markham was his mentor and guide, the father he had never known.

There were women. Flora, statuesque and golden, whose impotent husband threw knives at her each night while the marks goggled in awe. Sal, a vital dark belly dancer. Sex was an act of friendship, like shaking hands.

Markham noted Tierney's casual success with women, and filed the fact for future reference.

At twenty-two, the Korea draft took him. He saw action at Punchbowl Ridge, and had his thigh torn by shrapnel. They gave him a Purple Heart, which made him inordinately proud.

He came back from Korea with a fierce unnamed restlessness. Markham was no longer with the carny. He had sold his interest six months before. But he left a brief letter for Tierney. *After Korea you'll be bored with the hanky-panks. Look me up in Paloma Beach.*

Then Paloma Beach, and the long talk with Markham in his office at the Pink Barrel. It was a nice office, paneled in oak and leather. Markham sat behind the refectory desk saying, "A rube town, eating itself to death with taxes, watching Newport and Laguna get all the tourist gravy. Three years ago a smart operator named Kilian built this place. You know that cute California law that bans stud, but permits lowball and draw poker?"

He nodded. "You work for Kilian?"

Markham grinned. "The bluenoses closed him down in six months. For two years he tried to reopen, civic petitions, everything. He finally gave up and sold out. To me."

Tierney nodded with disbelief, and Markham told him about his silent partner. The councilman who had financed him. About the tax angle to placate the reformers. Half the profits went into the municipal treasury.

"I need a troubleshooter," Markham said. "Somebody to spot the grifters. I need smooth muscle I can trust. You'll get six hundred a month and bonuses."

The little man had told him, not asked him. But Tierney had obeyed him like a son for eight years, and this was even better than the carny.

Any poker palace attracts certain night crawlers. Floaters, mushroom-faced hustlers who work in teams. Tierney developed a sixth sense for spotting them and showing them to the door. If they returned, he used stronger methods of persuasion....

The reformers bothered them that first year. An impassioned spinster jurist made anti-gambling speeches at P.T.A. luncheons and civic league meetings. One night Markham arranged for Tierney to meet her at a country club benefit.

She was pathetically easy.

During a long weekend at Ensenada, he sublimated her energies into more natural channels. Thereafter she stopped crusading.

Tierney felt soiled. But Markham's praise was a shining medal. Three months later the little man called him into his office. "We've attracted an undesirable element to Paloma Beach. Herzog's in town."

Tierney had heard of Herzog. He was big time and played for keeps.

"He's importing a string of girls this weekend," Markham had said. "If the cops close him down he'll make a stink about having paid us for protection. We can't afford adverse publicity."

"Clever of him." Tierney thought about it. "No cops?"

"No cops."

"I'll take Valdez with me."

"Fine." Markham gave him the address.

Herzog and his boys left town that night, never to return. But Tierney was a month in the hospital with one arm in a cast and sixteen stitches to close the knife wounds. Markham paid him a bonus for that one.

That second year, Markham expanded. He set up distribution centers for booking the football cards. The Vardon campus, only eight miles inland, provided excellent revenue, as did Newport and Balboa. Come football season, everyone bets the cards, give or take points. You pick only three teams and the odds are so wonderful you hardly mind losing.

During the third year, Tierney became aware of a great emotional fatigue. He discovered that he was an insecure, lonely man. He wanted roots. A wife, children. He told Markham about it, and the little man's scorn was a branding iron. Afterwards, he kept his dream to himself.

Then he fell in love with Holly Ross.

Holly had hair like flame and a body of molded ivory. Her Newport studio apartment was filled with tortured abstractions in clay and stone. Her sculptures were brilliant, but undisciplined. Once her father had given her an exhibition at Laguna. The critics had spoken darkly of form and warped power. She was wistful and wild.

The night Tierney first saw her in the casino, Markham murmured, "Leave her alone."

"Why?"

"Her old man's a civic wheel. Mr. Bluenose himself. Besides, she's a madball. Stay away from her."

Tierney nodded, and ten minutes later was shilling at Holly's table. A few hours later he took her home. It was dawn when he left her apartment.

Next afternoon he phoned her and she hung up on him. Bewildered, he sent flowers. She returned his note with an obscenity scrawled across it. Furious, he drove out to her apartment and found her high on weed.

He took her, violently, and afterwards she cried. She begged him to go away. She told him about her father's perverted jealousy. About her last affair, when she was nineteen. She did not tell him that her father had performed the abortion, and kept her in a sanitarium for two months afterwards. It had broken her, completely.

Tierney held her very close and talked of love. In the end, she went away with him.

They had three days at Catalina. The first day was wonderful, the second good, and the third nightmare, with Holly's moody silences alternating with drunken, emotional storms. At first her lovemaking had been akin to a sharp sweet pain; now she was listless and uncommunicative. She told him there was no point in caring, since there could be but one ending.

The end came on the fourth day, after they had gone back to the mainland. Tierney took her home, then went out to buy cigarettes. On returning, he found a reception committee. Valdez and Garth. They worked for Markham, and their talents were as specialized as his own.

While they worked him over, Holly did not scream. She watched with a bright impassivity, smoking a long brownish cigarette.

He was in the hospital three days. Markham came to see him, and told him sadly that it was a matter of discipline, and that his old job was still waiting for him. He cursed Markham with a broken fury, and the little man went away.

When he got out of the hospital, he went to see Holly. Her landlady told him she had gone to Acapulco for a few weeks, with her father. There were no messages.

He went away like a hurt animal. It was not Holly, or the beating. It was the bitter realization that to Markham he had been no son, only a useful tool. He had saved six thousand dollars, and it took him less than a week to lose it over the Vegas gaming tables. Thereafter, he drifted.

Now he lay awake, staring at the ceiling. Trying to plan, he became confused. He fell asleep around midnight, thinking about a wife and children. Only it became nightmare, with Markham kidnaping the children and holding them for ransom.

Tierney got up at noon. He shaved and dressed with extreme care. The shirt was Egyptian cotton, the slacks gray flannel. Hand-tailored loafer jacket, burnished moccasins. He was a college boy with a mission.

He opened the dresser drawer and took out the short-barreled .32. He hefted it thoughtfully. Markham had given him the gun two years ago, yet he seldom carried it, and had never used it. He shrugged, and dropped the .32 back into the drawer.

He ate ham and eggs at a beachfront restaurant. Afterwards, he drove along the ocean boardwalk, remembering how once Paloma Beach had been a sleepy coast town. Two miles of salt-white beach, half a dozen motels. But he and Markham had helped change that. Now it was a smart town, a money town. The tourists came, the merchant fishermen, the summer vacation crowd, and Paloma Beach clipped them with loving care.

He turned inland at the intersection, and drove through the hills toward Vardonville. It was a clear October Friday. The sunlight splashed molten orange on the hillside shrubs, and painted the tree foliage ocher and old gold. A crisp, windy day, ideal for a family picnic.

He felt emotion, and cursed. Then he let the professional part of him take over, and it was easy. He knew exactly what to do.

Besides the university, Vardonville consisted of a new housing tract, and a few main street stores. The college was small, enrollment about four thousand. Tierney parked in the student's lot and walked across the campus toward the red brick faculty building. With his blond crew cut and relaxed smile, he was another Senior, cutting classes.

He tried the student's lounge first. It was a venerable hall with leaded windows that stained the late afternoon sun a rich amber. The chairs were leather, the tables weathered mahogany. He watched the students reading, talking, playing bridge. Nowhere did he see Ann.

In the faculty office he told them he was Ann's cousin, just in from the East. The counselor was very polite. Ann had a two-thirty lab which was just letting out. By the time Tierney found the science hall, the bell rang, and a mob of students engulfed him at the door. He searched the crowd with a taut fear that he was too late, and then he saw her.

She wore a blue cashmere and tweed skirt. A tall, leggy girl, with clear blue eyes and a good-boned, exciting face. When he saw who was with her, his carefully laid plans went smash.

The man had that pale olive skin possessed by some Latins. He was built like a wrestler, and his face was startlingly lean and intense. It was Eddie Valdez.

As he tried to blend with the crowd, Ann saw him and waved. They came over. Valdez was carrying Ann's books.

"Dig that crazy Joe College." Valdez' grin was hard and amused. "We heard you had gone West."

"Just passing by," Tierney said awkwardly, trying to adjust to the shock of seeing them together. "You look good Ann."

She studied him with a cool reserve. "Eddie's taking me into town for some shopping, Cliff. We're going to see the game tonight, Vardon and State."

"Fine," he said. "Maybe I'll see you there."

Ann said she hoped so. She said it without coquetry, and Valdez winked at Tierney as they walked away.

He stood with a sick bewilderment. He had hoped to find her alone, to strike some remembered chord of contact, but she had been with Valdez. Lithe, clever Valdez, who was equally deft with cards or women, and who never took a girl out unless he first possessed her.

Ann must have made a deal with Markham. Or else Valdez was operating on his own. Behind the Latin's lazy smile lurked cruelty, and a sharklike mind. Within hours Markham would know he was in town.

Which meant no time for an elaborate buildup. Time only for direct action, a thing at which he had always excelled. Tierney walked faster, toward the parking lot. In three hours it would be time for the big game between Vardon and State. Ann didn't know it, but he had a date with her.

And with Valdez.

CHAPTER 4

It was the second quarter. Vardon was fighting the favored State team to a standstill, and the home rooters had gone wild.

Tierney had waited patiently at the crowded turnstiles, and followed Ann and Valdez into the stadium, unnoticed. He now sat three rows back, watching Valdez put his arm around Ann's shoulders.

She sat stiffly passive. Tierney thought she shivered. Now Valdez was taking a bottle out of his overcoat. He offered it to Ann. She shook her head. Valdez laughed and finished the bottle. He began to paw her.

Etched in the white blaze of gridiron arcs, the Vardon players were darting, red-jerseyed dolls. They smashed through scrimmage and trapped the State back on his own thirty. He threw a long desperation pass. The Vardon tailback intercepted on the fifty. He shook off two tacklers and streaked down the sidelines, going all the way.

As the entire stadium roared, Tierney got up like a great golden cat. He hurdled the benches in front of him. Ann was trying to pull free of Valdez. Their benches were in darkness, and no one around them noticed or cared. Now Valdez had her arms trapped. He was laughing when Tierney hit him.

Long ago, Markham had taught Tierney that only rubes broke their knuckles. He used a slicing palm chop, a spearing elbow, and Valdez was on the concrete, spitting blood. Ann's scream was swallowed up in the thunder as Vardon scored.

Valdez got up, lunging. Tierney twisted, and took the knee on the outside of his thigh. He moved in close, using his hands carny style, and Valdez took it in the throat and plexus before he went down again.

Tierney had Ann's arm, and was dragging her toward the exits. Then he wasn't dragging her any more. She was coming with him.

When they were outside the stadium, Ann said, "You're breaking my arm, Cliff."

"Sorry." He released her.

Ann rubbed her arm. Twin spots of color glowed in her cheeks. "It was unnecessary, Cliff, and a little brutal. For all you know, I was enjoying it."

"Were you?"

She didn't answer. They walked toward the lights of the parking lot. There was a distant roar from the stadium. Vardon had kicked the extra point.

"You followed us," Ann said with a cool seriousness. "Why?"

Direct, Tierney thought. Open and above board. He still couldn't picture Ann as a blackmailer.

"Because I know Eddie Valdez," he said. "You're in trouble, Ann."

"From you or from Eddie?"

They reached his car in silence. Tierney helped her in, and slammed the door. He went around and got behind the wheel. Ann wore a strange smile. "It was beautifully timed, Cliff. Now I'm supposed to fall all over you with limp gratitude and trust, is that the idea?"

The Ford's tires screeched as they whipped out of the lot. Tierney found the main highway and turned toward Vardonville. "Sorry I interrupted him," he said savagely. "You and Valdez were obviously made for each other. I'll drop you off in town."

Ahead, he saw the crimson flicker of traffic lights. They were coming into Vardonville. He sensed Ann's hesitation, and inner conflict.

"Stop the car, Cliff." She did not look at him.

He pulled over to the side of the road, wanting to hit her. Instead, he took a deep angry breath and told her about Markham, about Las Vegas. He told her nothing about Holly. Ann listened in silence, and finally said, "You think Thad Ross is connected with Markham, is that it? And I'm blackmailing him?"

"Stop it," he said wearily. "I'm trying to help you—"

"Listen, Cliff. During the summer I worked in Ross's Clinic as a receptionist. Three weeks ago he fired me for snooping in his private office." Her voice was very calm. "The snooping happens to be a personal matter. But it doesn't make me a blackmailer."

He punched the starter viciously. "I'll drop you off in town, Ann. It's your business. And Markham's."

Ann touched his arm. "Do you remember that night you drove me home from the Pink Barrel?" She had sidetracked him again. He wondered what she was getting at. "You told me some night we'd really do the town. Only there wasn't a next time. Next day you met another girl. Then you went away."

This one is dedicated, he thought. She's worse than Holly. *She's got a yen for you*, Markham had said. And Markham was an oracle.

He turned hard at the intersection, taking the highway toward the Coast. "All right," he said softly. "Tonight we're on the town. No talk about Markham or what kind of game you're playing with Valdez. Is that the way you want it?"

"That's exactly what I want, Cliff." She turned on the car radio. There was the soft throb of Cuban drums, and a fantastic October moon limning the countryside. Tierney felt suddenly, unaccountably good.

They arrived in Paloma Beach at ten-thirty. He took her first to the Mariner. It was a quiet, expensive place, with a glass dining wall overlooking the Pacific. They sat near the flagstone hearth drinking stingers, and Ann's profile was meditative in the firelight.

"Talk to me, Cliff. About carny life."

She was astonishingly easy to talk to. Over Chateaubriand and sparkling burgundy, he told her about the bally grinds. He made it light and casual, interjecting humor into the subtleties of midway life, and Ann's laughter was unforced and free.

Over benedictine, Tierney said, "Fair is fair. Tell me about Ann Childs. Your father was, no doubt, a missionary?"

She looked up, blue lightnings in her eyes. "He was a missionary, Cliff. A very special kind. He was a country doctor that didn't care whether he got paid in promises or potatoes, just so the patient got well. In your book he'd be a—rube—is that what you call them? There are only three kinds of people, aren't there? Rubes and carnys and cops."

She had him pegged nicely. It irritated him that he could not fit Ann into either category.

"He died five years after my mother did," Ann murmured. "I was sixteen. I got a job waiting tables and went to night school. I wanted to be a famous surgeon, only it didn't work out that way." She bit her lip and stared at her brandy. "Do you remember Zoe Miller?"

"Zoe?" He frowned. "Used to be a house girl at the Barrel?"

Ann nodded, intently. It seemed terribly important to her.

He remembered Zoe as lush, blonde, vapid. She spent half her salary on voice and drama lessons and dreamed of being a singer. Once she had borrowed fifty dollars from Tierney to have a strawberry birthmark removed from her right cheek. She had been positive the birthmark was all that stood between her and a studio contract. Ultimately Zoe married a sleek character who claimed to be a Hollywood agent. By the time she discovered he was a phony and left him, Zoe was three months pregnant.

"She dropped out of sight for a while," Tierney mused. "I heard her baby died. Later, they picked her up in Balboa for pushing horse. She got eighteen months in Corona."

"Correction," Ann said evenly. "The baby didn't die. And Zoe wasn't the narcotics type. She happens to be my cousin."

He stared at her. "You think Markham framed her? Look, Tom runs a poker house. He runs it clean. What could Zoe possibly have had on him?"

"Possibly she wanted her baby. Tell me something, Cliff. Your grudge with Markham is personal, right? If you happened to see him—kill someone, would you call the police?"

He shifted, uncomfortably. "Depends on who he killed."

"Someone like Eddie Valdez."

"Probably not," he said slowly. "I'd bleed him white, instead."

"Because you'd be violating a basic carny ethic by calling the police?" She was baiting him, now. "Carnys settle beefs in their own way. Right?"

"That's right." Confusion fought with anger. "Let's not play analyst, Ann. If you don't want my help, why did you go out with me?"

"Did you ever read about Lady Chatterley?"

He recalled the book vaguely. Ann's smile turned clinical. "Lawrence makes the premise that a man's body is a separate entity. Lady Chatterley despised her lover's mind. He was banal, proud and stupid. But she loved his body. Did any girl ever tell you that you resemble a great tawny stallion?"

A slow pulse thundered in his eardrums as he stared at her. The brandy was beginning to hit them both. That, and the firelight, and Ann's smile. He paid the check and said in a voice not his own, "Let's get out of here."

Outside, in his coupe, Tierney pulled her to him roughly and found her mouth. It was a long kiss. Yet he still felt reserve in her, a taut barrier. Ann stirred against him with a husky laugh.

"Too soon, Cliff. Much too soon. Take me to the Owl Club."

The Owl was six blocks down, a small place with a loud juke and sawdust on the floor. If you liked barroom brawls with merchant fishermen, if you wanted your fun fast and rough and expensive, the Owl was the place to go. As Ann preceded him through the alley entrance Tierney wondered why she had picked this particular bar.

Inside, he stopped wondering.

Eddie Valdez was lounging in a corner booth, talking with two other men. He looked at Ann with mock surprise as Tierney escorted her to a booth. Now he was coming over.

"Galahad and Elaine, I believe." He smiled, white flash of teeth against the tan. Tierney started up, and Ann's hand was on his shoulder.

"Don't, Cliff. Please."

"Beat it," Tierney said.

Valdez' mouth was puffed and he had a mouse over one eye, but it didn't seem to bother him. Ann's face was pale with strain as he slid into the booth beside her.

"We've got personal things to discuss, honey," the Latin said blandly. "But Galahad might be shocked if he heard us. We don't want that, do we?"

Ann was fighting for control. All the sparkle had gone out of her, and her dark eyes were tragic. "You'd better go, Cliff."

"Let him tell me," Tierney said. His right palm was stiff and he was staring hungrily at the bridge of Valdez' nose.

"Please." Ann was on the ragged edge of hysteria. "It's—business, Cliff. I'll be all right."

"She'll be fine," Valdez said, his tone of voice begging Tierney to hit him.

It was something personal, something between Ann and Valdez. He couldn't help her, and she didn't want him around. Tierney spun out of the booth and looked down at her.

"You knew he'd be here," he said harshly. Statement, not question.

Then he turned away, not looking back. Ann hadn't answered him. She didn't have to.

As he walked out of the bar, he failed to notice that the two men who had been sitting with Valdez were no longer in the corner booth. It was a tactical blunder. Normally he had a professional awareness of such things. But he was too angry to care, and Valdez had counted on that.

He took perhaps a dozen steps through the dark alley before they hit him. White pain splintered the night as he fell, rolling by instinct into a tight ball, avoiding the kick in the groin, sensing the swish of brass knuckles past his ear. His groping hands found a foot and twisted. There was an agonized grunt, the thud of flesh hitting concrete. Someone giggled. The foot came swinging out of the darkness and crunched into Tierney's neck. He fell sideways, retching. They were methodically kicking him in the kidneys.

Then he came to the end of pain.

CHAPTER 5

Several blocks away, the lights shone in a fourth-story office suite. It was a doctor's office, moderately pretentious, decorated in walnut and gray frieze. Six men sat in leather chairs talking quietly of civic elections. One was a municipal judge. Two were city councilmen.

"It's late," the judge said, yawning. "We've resolved the main campaign issues, gentlemen. But the opposition still intends to make great noises about gambling. Suggestions?"

"But it's controlled!" protested one of the councilmen. "Practically a city enterprise."

The other councilman stood up. He was a tall man, with a voice of modulated power. His name was Thaddeus Ross. When he spoke, a respectful hush swept the room.

"Four years ago, Sam, I helped close Kilian down. I was, and am, against legalized gambling. On the other hand the revenue from those tables has helped build a new library and add a wing to the city hospital. But there's been talk. Hints of organized vice. I'm not going to preach about cutting off your right arm if it offends you. But I sincerely believe we should revoke their franchise for six months."

There were nods, murmurs of dissension. The phone rang. Ross answered it.

"I'm downstairs in the lobby," Markham said. "Get rid of them."

"Is it important?"

"Very. I'll be up in five minutes."

"All right, dear," Ross said, hanging up. "My wife, gentlemen." He looked wry. "It's almost midnight. Have we settled the important issues?"

At the door, he shook hands with each of them, a lean, silvered man of integrity. When the last one had gone, he went over to the sideboard and splashed brandy into a glass.

He felt tired, hemmed in.

There were too many pressures.

There was Madge, his wife. An early menopause made her listless and shrill by turns. She made violent demands upon his body, leaving him shriveled and tired. Where money was concerned, she was insatiate. There was the new station wagon, the club luncheons, the mink stole he had given her for Christmas. He thought of her as an aging mantis, devouring his body and his mind.

Blaine, thank God, was no problem. In his third year at Stanford, Blaine was an honor student, soft-spoken and grave. Although that girl last spring had cost a thousand dollars. Little tramp, he thought. Bitch. He wished Blaine weren't such a chip off the old block.

There was Holly.

Her desire to go to Paris had become an obsession. She had a wistful dream that in the city of light she would learn new techniques, a fresh purity of line. At first she had pleaded. In the last few months he had sensed a sly withdrawal. She was punishing him. The wildness was banked, waiting to flare. At the thought of losing her, his mouth went dry.

There were those damned photostats.

He sat hating Ann Childs. But Markham could fix it. Markham could fix anything.

Perhaps, after this election, he could take Holly to Paris for a while. She needed his strength to take care of her, to protect her from men. They followed her always, filthy animals in heat. Thinking about Holly, he made rapid calculations on a pad. Abruptly he crumpled the paper into a tight ball.

It cost him five thousand a month just to live.

He could cash out the blue chip securities, the oil stock. Thirty thousand dollars.

He had a momentary vision of a Left Bank artist's studio, with Holly smiling redly at him while her white fingers modeled his bust in clay. He felt a sudden giddiness. Six months with Holly ...

Markham opened the door and said dryly, "Good evening, Doctor."

As always, he was struck by the little man's faceless personality. Markham was utterly functional, a gyroscope that kept the Pink Barrel in precarious balance.

"I told you never to call me here," he said, standing. "I don't care how important—"

He stopped short when he saw his daughter. She followed Markham into the office and shut the door. She was wearing a green knit dress that fitted her like a second skin, accenting her lush vitality. She crossed to his desk in four angry strides and said, "Give me a hundred dollars, Daddy."

Ross stared at them. Understanding came, and quick fury. "She's been playing again?"

"And losing," Markham said. "Tonight she got sore because I wouldn't cash a check."

"Holly," he said in a scalpel voice. "I have forbidden—"

"Don't make a production," she said lazily. "Not now. Just give me the money." She moistened her lips, savoring the next words. "Indirectly, I've been working for you the last two days. Chalk it up to expenses."

He stared at her, not getting it, not even when Markham said, "Tierney's in town."

"Tierney?" His lips curled in recollection. "The lover? You were going to make a deal with him. What happened?"

"We found him in Vegas. Holly flubbed it."

"Holly?" Ross's voice was suddenly strained. "You took her with you?"

"Certainly. I needed a gimmick—"

The slap came without warning, like a pistol shot. Markham stood with a faint smile, blood trickling down his chin.

"God damn you," Ross whispered.

"Relax, Daddy." Holly touched his arm. "Nothing happened. I promised three months ago, remember?"

He stared down at her, feeling his temples pound. Slowly the rage drained out of him, leaving a tired void. Holly gazed up with a virginal innocence. "I'm giving up my studio next week," she said softly. "I'm coming home. If you want me, Daddy."

"If I want—" He swallowed, painfully. "Don't lie to me, my dear."

"You'll have to be patient with me," Holly murmured. "Sometimes the clay goes sour. Then I want to smash things. The craving for excitement is like a disease. You told me that two years ago at the sanitarium, remember? When you kept telling me how sick I was, how badly I needed treatment. When you aborted me, Daddy."

"*Holly*." He was livid.

"Yes, Daddy?"

"It was a miscarriage. Don't ever forget that."

"Of course, Daddy." Green depths of mockery in her eyes. "Call it sublimation. Gambling is such a safe diversion, don't you agree?"

Markham watched, his thin face impassive. He had always considered himself beyond good or evil. But what he was witnessing now was the essence of corruption. Holly, looking up into her father's face, her smile a crimson wound. Thad Ross, very pale, reaching for his wallet and giving her money without counting it.

Holly stood on tiptoe and kissed him. She went out without looking back.

"We've got problems," Markham said.

"What?" Ross roused himself like a man in a dream.

"Last night Tierney registered at the Dunes. This afternoon he was spotted on the Vardon campus. Right now he's with Ann."

"So make a deal with them." Ross's hands shook as he poured another brandy. "But no violence. It's too close to election."

Markham looked at him with pity. "No violence, he says. You just don't understand the spot we're in, do you?"

"Tom, that's an order!"

"Valdez tailed Ann yesterday. She went to DeWitt Smith's newspaper office. She probably told him about the Miller baby."

"You're lying!" Brandy slopped on the desk. "She wouldn't—"

"Pick up the phone. Ask him."

He stared at the phone, livid. He started to touch it, and then just sat. Markham stood over him, the words hitting like hail.

"She doesn't want money. I tried to tell you that three weeks ago, but you were too scared to listen! Now it's too late, even for a deal. She wants Zoe sprung, and she wants your hide, understand? Tierney's with her. So we do it my way, Doctor. *My* way."

Ross nodded, miserably. Markham stood looking at him. He said, "Not to change the subject, but I've got a line on two new clients."

"Oh, God."

"They live in Bel-Air. The husband makes thirty grand a year from Standard Oil. The wife is thirty-nine. Their daughter died last year of polio, an only child. They're ripe, doctor—"

"Shut up. Please."

He got up blindly, turning away. Markham watched him cross to the far wall with his hands clenched behind him. There was a terra-cotta figurine on the wall shelf. It was abstract, tortured, phallic. Without turning, Ross said, "About the girl. Tierney. Do you have to—"

"It's already been arranged. Tonight."

"Why?"

"Because Tierney's a sleeping giant, and Ann might awaken him. Him alone I can handle. Not the girl. She's a fanatic. Together they could smash the whole apple-cart—"

"All right, Tom." His voice was modulated, tightly controlled. "All right."

Markham went quietly out and closed the door. Thad Ross stared at the twisted figurine. Holly had dedicated it to him last month. She had titled it *Hate in Three Octaves*.

CHAPTER 6

"Up. On your feet." A gruff voice, sardonic. Tierney came up from dark waters of pain. Strong hands helped him erect, guided him toward the red neons in back of the Owl Club.

"You're lucky tonight," the voice said. "A minute later and they roll you, maybe cripple you. Did you see their faces?"

"Real lucky," Tierney said, touching his kidneys. "Tonight I'm drawing all straight flushes. No, I didn't see them."

Then he was standing under the neons looking at deep-set gray eyes in a lined Irish face. A cop face. He saw the shock of recognition and the eyes hardening as he said, "Hello, Lennox."

"I wish I'd been five minutes later," Lennox said with soft regret. "What are you doing back in town, grifter?"

Joe Lennox was fifty-two. He would always be a plainclothesman. Once he had been fiercely outspoken about legalized gambling. Now the bitterness was a quietly festering wound. Last Christmas Markham had sent him a case of twelve-year old Scotch, knowing how Lennox would methodically smash the bottles, one by one.

"I asked you a question, grifter."

"Just passing through," Tierney said.

"Stand over there. Hold still."

Lennox braced him. Tierney kept his face stoic as the hard hands slapped his kidneys. Long ago he had learned the strict carny etiquette of dealing with fuzz.

"Too bad." Lennox kept his face close to Tierney's. "If you weren't clean I could jug you."

"You could vag me."

"I might. I just might." Lennox regarded him with a mastiff wariness. "Three months ago I heard you fell out of bed with Markham. They schlammed you, and you went away. So now you're back in town fighting in alleys. Angle?"

"No angle," Tierney shrugged. "Maybe I came back to find a job. Since when is getting rolled in an alley a felony?"

Lennox's breath whistled softly between his teeth. "Three quiet months," he said. "Civic elections coming up, and all the filth whitewashed so it doesn't show. After a while you start pretending it's really a quiet little town, a friendly town. Then you smell filth and remember. Right now I'm off duty. Tomorrow morning if you're still in town I'll vag you. Understand?"

Tierney said he understood. He was used to the abstract cruelty of the law. But this was a personal thing. Lennox hated him.

"Good night," Lennox said, and walked down the alley, bull-shouldered and erect. Tierney looked after him, feeling the dull ache in his kidneys, and then he remembered.

A year ago Lennox had almost been broken for assault charges against a private citizen. The citizen was Lennox's son-in-law. The son-in-law was a weak-chinned youth who worked at a Newport tuna cannery and fancied himself a sharp hand at poker. Every Friday night he lost half his paycheck at the Pink Barrel. Lennox's daughter finally left him and went home to Mother. By that time she had two children.

"Lennox." The cop turned at the alley mouth. Tierney said gently, "How's the family?"

Lennox stood, a stone man. Tierney felt a sudden stab of guilt. Then he reminded himself that gambling was one of the five freedoms and you could take it or let it alone, and it angered him that he was finding it necessary to justify the Pink Barrel. He went into the Owl Club. He wanted a drink.

Inside, the juke was blaring and three merchant fishermen were arguing noisily at the end of the bar. Tierney ordered a double rye. Drinking it, he saw Ann.

She was sitting alone in the corner booth, smiling. As if she had been waiting for him.

He went over to her booth and sat. Ann said, "You're late."

"I got detained."

Ann nodded, looking at his split lip, the purpling bruise over one eye. There was a new brightness about her, a sense of relief.

"I'm sorry, Cliff. But I had to be sure."

It took a moment, then the anger was breaking apart inside him, spilling through his lips in hot shrapnel fragments. "You bitch," he said. "You thought that rumble with Valdez was for effect, that I wanted to get into your brain through your pants, is that right? So you let me walk out of here cold turkey to see if I was working for Markham? Trust costs six broken ribs, is that it?"

"Yes." Ann spoke slowly, spacing each word. "Now I trust you."

"Enough finally to answer some questions?"

"Perhaps."

He almost threw the drink in her face. Instead he said, "I know another girl like you."

"Really?" Her eyes were dark, almost luminous.

"She's prettier than you, and wilder. She wants something that doesn't exist, that no man can give her—"

"Especially Cliff Tierney?"

He blinked. Damned if she hadn't put him on the defensive again. The waitress drifted over and Ann ordered two coffees. When the waitress was beyond earshot Tierney said, "The night Thad Ross fired you for snooping in his office—did you find what you were looking for?"

"No." Her gaze was unflinching. "But they thought I did. Two weeks ago Valdez approached me. He said I had something that belonged to a friend of his, that he wanted it back. I told him I didn't know what he was talking about, and he grinned, nasty and knowing. He started talking about Zoe, an accident—" She shivered. The waitress brought coffee, scalding and black. Tierney sipped his gingerly.

"Accident," he said. "You mean in prison? Scalded under a hot shower, something like that?"

"He's got friends in prison," Ann breathed. "Inmates that hate stoolies. At first I thought it was some wild joke. When I saw that he was serious I was terrified. Then tonight, he told me he'd made a mistake. To keep my mouth shut and forget the whole thing."

Tierney nodded. The cool detached part of his mind told him Ann was telling the truth. But Markham had gone to a great deal of trouble to find him in Vegas, and there were the blackmail photostats Ross had received by registered mail. He said, "*What* were you looking for in Ross's office?"

"It's not your fight, Cliff. I don't want you involved."

"It is and I am," he said bitterly. "And here's something for free. Valdez doesn't have any friends in Corona. He was bluffing."

The words penetrated slowly. Ann's head came up as if he'd slapped her. He got the impression of a steel blade withdrawing from its scabbard as she stood up, lithe and tall.

"Will you play chauffeur for me, Cliff? Just for an hour?"

He looked at her steadily, asking the question without sound. And he saw the slow answering smile, and her breasts quicken with her breathing. Desire smashed a velvet fist along his loins as he got up and paid the check.

Outside, as they walked down the alley toward his parked Ford, Ann's hand found his. It was a natural gesture, asexual, promising nothing beyond the fact of their being together. He felt a dry shaking anger at her objectivity. She was a dedicated female, intent on her own purposes, and she was using him. Later, in his arms, making the soft wild cry of love, she would still be using him.

In the Ford, he said, "Where to?"

"Laguna. Take the highway straight out."

Once on the dark beach stretch into Laguna, Ann turned on the car radio. He reached out and turned it off.

"Last chance," he said tightly. "You can't fight Markham alone. *I* can, if you'll let me—"

"Why should you?"

The question came like a whip, catching him off balance, and he said slowly, "It's something I have to do, that's all."

"I know, Cliff. But your reason is personal. Mine isn't."

He thought about it, and after a time Ann turned on the radio again.

The Laguna address turned out to be a white stucco office just off the main highway. Cracked gilt letters on the plate glass window, *The Laguna Enquirer*. A light shone dimly from in back. "I'll be five minutes," Ann said.

"Please wait in the car."

She got out quickly and went inside. Tierney watched her walk past two long tables to a wooden railing bisecting the office. There was a man on the other side of the railing. He was a big man, tired. He was balding, with a bad complexion. Now Ann was arguing violently with him.

Restlessly, Tierney lighted a cigarette. All his life he had been able to read people. But Ann baffled him. Somehow she had discovered Markham's connection with Ross. She had clumsily traced that lead, and had been trapped. Yet tonight, after two weeks of pressuring her, Valdez had suddenly let her off the hook. Why? Had he discovered the real identity of the shakedown artist?

Tierney threw away his cigarette. He got out of the car and went to the office doorway. Ann and the big man were completely oblivious to anything but each other.

"Please, Witt!" Ann's voice was a quiet flame. "You can run an editorial tonight—"

"Sorry," Witt said doggedly. "Not without proof."

He went over to a desk and sat down. Ann followed him, her blue eyes stormy. "Their name is Lackland. They live on Aspen Drive, in Santa Ana. They've had the baby a year—"

"I won't do it, Ann. That's final."

"Witt, look at me!"

His head came up slowly. Sweat diamonds sparkled on his forehead.

"Remember two years ago, Witt? When I gave you back your ring?"

"When you discovered I was a human being instead of a God-damned white knight?" His mouth twisted. "Why are you still determined to martyr me?"

Ann just looked at him. Witt stared at his hands, kneading them painfully. Tierney followed his gaze and saw how a small tornado had passed through the office. He saw the gutted file cabinet, the papers spilled about, the printer mats strewn on the floor.

"They came twenty minutes ago," Witt murmured. "Two of them. First they wrecked the office. Then they gave me a genteel beating. No marks on the face, just the short ribs and kidneys." He touched his stomach and grimaced. "They said it was so I wouldn't get any ideas about crusading."

"Please." Ann's eyes were brimming. "We could start fresh, darling. You could take that foreign correspondent's berth. We could be married. I'm giving you a chance to cleanse yourself, to regain your manhood—"

"I keep my manhood in the side drawer. See?"

"Stop it!" She slapped the bottle out of his hand. "I'm sick to death of your whisky platitudes, your drunken self-pity! Two years you've waited for this chance, and now you're afraid to take it—"

She broke off, seeing his expression change as Tierney came into the office. She whirled. "Please wait outside, Cliff."

"Your five minutes are up," Tierney said.

Ann swung back to the big man. "I'm begging you, Witt—"

"No. Who's your friend?"

"Cliff Tierney," she said wearily, "meet DeWitt Smith."

"Hello," Tierney said. "Those two visitors of yours. Was one of them a short stocky blond?" Smith nodded. "Garth," Tierney said. "He works at the Barrel."

Smith stared at him with a bloodshot recognition. He got up from the desk. "You used to work for Markham?"

Tierney nodded and Smith swung viciously, without warning. Tierney rolled with the punch, absorbing it high on the cheek, and expertly tied up the big man in chancery. Smith grunted and thrashed. Tierney released him as Ann darted between them, very pale. "No," she cried. "Stop it!"

"You son of a bitch," Smith said thickly. He was shaking with an impotent fury. "Take him out of here, Ann." He turned away and started to clean up the office. Ann tried to speak but no sound came. Tierney took her arm. They went outside.

He drove silently down the coast highway. Beside him Ann sat with her head back on the seat, eyes closed. She was a spent woman. He felt a bleak bewildered hurt. In the past hour he had met two men, Lennox and Smith. Both hated him. He tried to rationalize his depression and felt tired. "You two used to be engaged?" he asked.

"Three years ago," she murmured. "I thought he was some kind of god. He edited the Paloma Beach *Sentinel.* One of his editorials won the annual Southland news award."

Tierney frowned, recalling Smith's vitriolic editorials against the Pink Barrel, and Markham's deadly reprisal. Abruptly the *Sentinel's* advertising slumped. The publisher, no fool, fired Smith.

"He went on a six-month drunk," Ann said listlessly. "He changed—horribly. He'd go on long crying jags. Once he tried to kill me. Now he edits a weekly throw-away and sops up his conscience in alcohol. He claims advertising is really the only important function of a newspaper."

"So he adapted," Tierney shrugged. "Why condemn him for that?"

"I don't. Only—"

"Only what?"

"Nothing. Take me home, Cliff." She gave him her address in Vardonville.

He turned left toward the inland foothills, and for the next ten minutes concentrated on his driving. Then he said, "Shall I tell you why you hate

Markham?"

"But I don't hate him."

"Stop rationalizing," he said brutally. "You hate him because he framed Zoe, but most of all because he made you realize you were incapable of a deathless love for Witt—"

"That's not true!"

"You can't forgive a love defiled, made small and shallow and transitory. You look at something that used to be a man and you blame Markham. I don't think you ever loved Witt as a person, only as a symbol. But we'll pass that. You want Markham and Ross behind bars, right? A nice tidy conviction according to your sense of justice."

"That's right," Ann whispered. She kept her eyes fixed on the highway.

"Me, I'm just a hustler. I'd be satisfied with bleeding him, no help from the law. So that puts me in the same league with Tom. Doesn't it!"

He said these things goadingly, but Ann only nodded. She would not look at him.

Tierney squinted into the rear-view mirror, at the unwavering headlights half a mile behind. He veered sharply over to the shoulder and sat, tensed and waiting. The headlights slowed, then picked up speed. The car roared past, a red Pontiac. Tierney exhaled slowly, then grinned. "Shall I tell you what you're really thinking?"

"What?" She couldn't care less.

"You're wishing Witt was more like me. That he had half my strength—"

He saw the slap coming and moved inside it, hands hard on her shoulders as he pinned her against the far seat. Ann's face was contorted, her nails clawing at the back of his neck. Then she went passive, lips slack as he ground his mouth down on hers. He understood. Earlier tonight he had helped her, and she was repaying the debt in her most basic coin.

He straightened up and slid behind the wheel. His hands were shaking, partly from anger. "Tomorrow morning I'm driving into Santa Ana. I'm looking up a couple named Lackland—"

"They'll tell you nothing!" But Ann's face was white.

"We'll see."

He drove the ten miles to Vardonville in a frozen silence. It was one-thirty when he parked in Ann's driveway.

"End of the line," he said. "Good night."

Ann hesitated, hand on the door handle. He saw the ghost of a smile in her eyes. "You're not—coming in?"

"Why? I want a woman, not a human sacrifice."

Ann got out quickly and slammed the door. She ran up the steps, fumbling for her key. Tierney burned rubber backing out of the driveway, then jammed on the brakes so hard the Ford almost turned over. He was staring at the white Olds parked down the street under the palms.

"Ann!"

She had the key in the lock. She would not look at him.

The Olds parking lights snapped on. It began to move.

Tierney was out of the Ford and up the duplex steps. He had Ann by the arm, and she saw the Olds moving faster now, as she understood. She ran after Tierney and climbed into the Ford, too late.

There were the headlights blinding them and the whimper of tires as the Olds whipped in diagonally, pinning them to the curb. Tierney fumbled with the ignition. His thoughts were utterly calm and technical as he gunned the Ford. The little coupe shuddered. Then its tires clawed the curbing and Ann cried out as they sideswiped the Olds with a tearing of metal. Then they were careening down the sidewalk at thirty miles an hour.

The Ford demolished two sidewalk hedges before it slewed wildly back into the street. As they turned the corner Tierney had one backwards glimpse of the white car. It was completing an angry U-turn.

Five minutes later, Tierney parked on the dark side street and reached for a cigarette. His hands were sweating as he took a long drag, handed the cigarette to Ann. "They've stopped playing games," he said. "Is it finally beginning to soak through?'

Ann sat numbed with the shock of reaction. "They wouldn't—dare."

"Tom's a patient man. But once his mind's made up, the devil couldn't change it. For the last time, what have you got on him?"

"N-nothing I can prove—"

"That wasn't what you told DeWitt Smith."

Her lips tightened and he felt a blazing anger at her stubbornness. But he kept his voice grimly objective. "You can't go back to your apartment. Have you got some other place to spend the night?"

Ann shook her head. He snapped on the ignition and drove toward the main highway. Ann said nothing all the way into Paloma Beach, not even when he parked a block from his hotel and got out. She just looked at him with the question in her eyes.

"You can have my room," he said roughly. "Come on."

She came slowly, a girl in a dream. He took her arm as they went into the lobby, and said, "I'll be back in about six hours. Don't answer any knocks on the door or telephone calls. Understand?"

She came awake all at once, her blue eyes wary. "Where are you going, Cliff?"

"I'm not sure," he said honestly. "I need a lever, some gimmick to use on Tom, You won't help me; I'll have to dig a little."

Ann digested it as they went up the steps to the second floor. Then they were standing in front of his hotel room. Ann's lips were moist, parted. He chuckled, handed her the key.

"See you at ten," he said, and turned down the hall. Ann looked after him a moment, then went into the room. Tierney was starting down the lobby stairs when he heard her muffled cry.

He ran back down the hall. Ann was leaning against the doorjamb, biting her fist. When Tierney saw what was in the room, he pushed her inside and closed the door behind them.

The room was a shambles. The mattress lay gutted on the floor, the dresser drawers were open with clothing strewn about. Lying across the mattress was Valdez. His head was bent back at an impossible angle as he stared blindly at the ceiling.

CHAPTER 7

Once, in Korea, Tierney had returned alone from a night patrol. He had returned with a thigh full of shrapnel, moving like an automaton. An hour earlier his sergeant had screamed and died next to him. In that moment, Tierney had felt no tearing loss, no fury. He had dived for cover and lain immobile while bullets from the gook pillbox ripped the brush near his face.

Later, in the field hospital, he brooded. He had liked the sergeant. It would have been so easy to lob a grenade at that pillbox. Instead he had figured the percentages and survived. Ultimately he decided Markham was right, that emotion was strictly for rubes and a smart operator never felt anything except cold impassivity during a crisis.

Now he moved slowly about the hotel room, frowning at the overturned nightstand, the gutted bureau drawers. Ann stood rigid against the wall. He waited for hysteria, hoping he would not have to slap her. Instead Ann whispered, "What were they looking for?"

Tierney shrugged. "Whatever it was, they didn't find it. Looks as if one of them was disappointed."

He bent over Valdez. The Latin lay on his side. The bullet had gone through the back of his skull and blood from the ruined forehead was coagulating on the mattress. A crumpled pillow lay near the corpse. Tierney fingered the dark splotch of powder burn on the pillow, the small black hole.

"Very professional," he said, showing her the powder burn. "It muffles the shot."

Then a cold thought struck him, and he rummaged through the bureau drawers. He felt panic. His snub-nosed .32 was gone.

Nice, he thought bitterly. That really ties it. And he could see it happening in retrospect, Valdez and friend coming to his room with a passkey. The frantic search. The friend scenting a cross. The friend finding the .32 and giving it to Valdez from behind.

He looked at Ann, remembering her bright sense of relief an hour ago when he had found her alone in the Owl Club. Ann met his gaze squarely. Color was returning to her cheeks. "You think I had something to do with it?"

"Who, then?" He was all ice. "Markham? Your friend Smith?"

"I don't know. Here, help me with the mattress."

He helped her reposition the mattress on the bed. Abruptly Ann went into the bathroom. He thought she was going to be sick. Instead she returned with a damp towel. He watched her scrub ineffectually at the mattress. His smile was wooden.

"You're going to help me dump the body?"

"You helped me, Cliff. Now I'm helping you."

"We're wasting time," he said. "Whoever did it phoned the cops. They'll be hammering that door down any minute. We're leaving, right now. By dawn we can be in Tijuana—"

Her blue eyes were clear and direct. "How far would we get?" She had him there.

It took them ten minutes to clean up the room. Ann folded the blood-stained towel and pillow slip and put them in her handbag. "Now what, Cliff?"

"You're really something," he said, studying her. "You and your sense of duty. You know what the rap is for accessory? Twenty to life."

Ann's chin set stubbornly. She leaned on the bedstead for support, and he saw the dark fatigue circles under her eyes. He thought, Maybe there's something to this duty thing after all. He went to the window and opened it, looking down at the dark alley, at the soft fine rain that had begun to fall. Then he gave Ann the keys to his Ford and told her to bring it around to the fire escape.

The Latin's body was heavy. Tierney managed to hoist him in a fireman's hold and get him out to the hallway. The fire escape windows were at the far end of the hall, and there was one agonizing moment when he heard a creak on the lobby stairs that sounded like footsteps. He juggled the window latch, and it stuck. He thought about smashing the windows. But when he nudged the jamb with his shoulder it gave.

Lugging Valdez down the fire escape, he realized how far he was out of condition. He was drenched in sweat when he reached the second landing.

In the alley, the headlights blinded him. He made frantic motions and Ann cut the lights. He worked Valdez into the back seat and slid behind the wheel, gasping. "What kept you?"

"I got sick," Ann said matter-of-factly, "the minute I got out of the lobby. I'm sorry, Cliff."

A thin drizzle filmed the windshield as he nudged the Ford out of the alley and turned right on Broad Street. Beside him, Ann was shivering uncontrollably, her teeth clenched. He parked near a liquor store, said, "Be right back." Ann nodded, eyes closed.

In the liquor store he bought a pint of bonded bourbon. The lush blonde matron behind the counter gleamed at him in recognition. "Hi, Cliff."

He grinned at her, cursing his luck. Marie was a typical weekend poker addict. She played with the quiet frenzy common to many housewives, and she usually won. Once in a four-eight draw game, he had dealt her four kings.

"We've missed you down at the Barrel," Marie said expectantly.

"I've been in Vegas." He felt taut, nerve-naked. "Don't bother to wrap it, Marie."

"No trouble," Marie said. She took her time making change, complaining how sour her luck had been lately, and Tierney told her she didn't know what hard luck was.

"I'm closing in twenty minutes." She gave him a wistful look. "Thought I'd stop by the Barrel. You going to be there?"

"Maybe," he said, stuffing the change into his pocket. "See you around, honey."

A customer came into the store, and Tierney left, thinking what a dandy witness Marie would make at the trial. By now Valdez's killer had certainly phoned in an anonymous tip. The police would be in his room by now, and they would be very thorough indeed. They would spot the hastily made bed, the blood on the mattress. Ultimately they would find the bullet, embedded in floor or wall.

The rain came down hard as Tierney ran toward the Ford, half expecting to see a white Olds nearby, or better still, a prowl car. "Here." He slid behind the wheel, handed the bottle to Ann. "Take two stiff swallows."

Ann swallowed and coughed. He felt admiration for her, and pity. "You don't need this," he said. "I'll drop you off at a motel—"

She handed him the bottle. "Drive, Cliff."

He had a triple shot that burned going down. He drove carefully through the rain, glancing into the rear-view mirror. Nerves, he thought. You've built Tom into some kind of implacable force. The avenging father-image, remote and deadly. He took the inland highway to Vardonville and drove at a cautious forty. Not that precautions mattered. If Markham were trailing him, he'd never know.

"There's a grove of eucalyptus," Ann murmured. "Three miles north."

The highway was black and shining wet and the only sound was the swish of the windshield wiper blades. The headlights punched twin yellow tunnels through the rain. He said, frowning, "You figure helping me makes us even, is that it? A favor for a favor?"

"No." Ann moved closer. He felt the warm pressure of her thigh. "I've stopped fighting alone."

It was her hopelessly weary tone, and the meaning of it pounded through him like wine. He said, "You're going to tell me about Tom's sideline operation, his tie-in with Ross?"

"Yes, Cliff. Only promise me one thing?"

"What?"

"Don't use it for personal gain. Please."

She really thinks I'm something, he thought bitterly. Cliff Tierney, grifter extraordinary.

"First let's get rid of—" She couldn't say it.

"All right," he said.

The eucalyptus grove was a quarter of a mile off the highway, on a shallow hill slope. Tierney found the side road that led off through the trees, and drove slowly, bumping over ruts and chuckholes. He killed the motor and they sat listening to the drum of rain on the canvas top.

"I'll be ten minutes." He lighted a cigarette, handed it to her. "Any farther and we'd risk tire marks. Scared?"

Ann said yes. Tierney grinned at her as he got out on his side. She sat very still, watching him move across the headlight beam with Valdez across his shoulders. He looked back at her once. Just a look, and she almost cried.

She tried to tell herself it was that beautiful damned face of his, that he had no real soul and his morals were those of a mink, but it did not matter. And she hated him for knowing that it did not matter. Then he vanished in the rainswept darkness, and she felt desolate and alone. The warmth of the liquor expanded inside her. She felt a heady recklessness. Your strengths are not his strengths, she thought. You expect too much from him, the way you did from Witt. But you're strong. You can mold him. For a brief daring second she dared to think how it could be, and she felt almost giddy. Then she remembered what was in her handbag.

She jumped out of the car and hurried into the woods. She buried the bloodstained towel and pillowslip carefully, scattering leaf mold to obscure all traces. When she went back to the Ford she saw the blurred outline of the white Olds, parked ten yards behind.

Markham stood by the Ford. His smile was almost paternal. Next to him stood a blond stocky man. Garth.

"No more games," Markham said. "Let's go quietly. Please?"

She made the mistake of trying to scream.

Tierney heard it. He straightened up from the shallow grave, and emotion wiped out instinct. He moved quickly through the dripping trees and stopped short when Markham said, "That's far enough."

Tierney slowed to a walk. He saw the white Olds, and Garth sitting behind the wheel. He did not see Ann anywhere. Markham was a black silhouette against the Ford's headlights. He moved toward the silhouette, looking for the precise juncture of throat and carotid artery. His right palm was poised, stiff. When he was a yard away, Markham chuckled. He said the four words calculated to stop Tierney cold.

"She lied to you."

Tierney stood motionless. "Keep talking."

"She's a first-class freebee artist," Markham said softly. "Want proof?"

He handed over a slip of white paper. "Read that. I got it by special delivery four hours ago."

Tierney squinted at the letter, handed it back to the little man. "Suppose you read it."

"Sure." Markham read calmly. "Consider the enclosures, and the effect of a grand jury investigation. At nine-thirty tonight, drop fifteen thousand dollars off the Carleton freeway underpass. Small bills, paper bag preferred."

He paused, smiling at Tierney. "It's typewritten, no signature. But it really doesn't need one, does it?"

Tierney said numbly, "How about the enclosures?"

"You wouldn't be interested."

"I want to see the enclosures," Tierney said.

"No," Markham said as Tierney moved in.

Later, Tierney decided it was the whisky that had blurred his reflexes. He threw a lightning palm chop, but Markham was no longer there. Two blows hit Tierney simultaneously, plexus and nose bridge. The pain was blinding. Markham hit him twice more as he crumpled. Then he was lying in the mud, hands jerking spasmodically as he tried to rise. Markham motioned to Garth, who got quickly out of the Olds.

"Take a look," Markham said gently, indicating the woods. "See who he was burying."

Garth vanished into the trees. He was gone less than five minutes. When he returned he walked up to Tierney and kicked him in the side.

"Easy," Markham murmured. "What was it?"

"Eddie," the blond man said tightly. "Cliffie boy scragged him. He had the grave already dug."

Markham shook his head, lips pursed. He did not seem surprised. "That's a shame. Eddie had a great deal of talent. Cliff must have gotten excited."

Garth nodded, cynically. "He always did have a temper. You want—"

"No," Markham said. He seemed to be considering it. "Go wait in the car."

He bent over Tierney. His voice came from a far distance, distorted by rain.

"You know why you really came back to Paloma Beach, Cliff? Because all you wanted was an excuse to return to the fold! Guys like you need somebody to belong to, and that somebody is me. Do you know what you're going to do now?" Markham asked gently. "You're going to lie here a while thinking how right I am and hating that tramp for conning you. Tomorrow afternoon you'll walk into the Pink Barrel, understand? You bumped Eddie, so you're replacing him. You've been away for a while, son. Now you're coming home."

Tierney lay still. After a time the voice stopped. He heard the growl of the Olds' ignition, and the swish of tires. Then there was only the rain.

When he finally got up and lurched over to the Ford, the ignition keys were gone. He said "son" the way Markham had said it, and hit the dashboard with his fist. He groped for the pint and found it on the floor. He killed the bottle, not tasting it. Then he started down the slippery path toward the main highway.

Tom really laid it out for you, he thought. And he's right, he's always right. Tomorrow night you'll be back where you belong. You'll be dealing lowball, and sometime after midnight you'll see Holly. She'll come in wearing that tight green dress, smiling at you slow and easy. And that's the way it's going to be. Thinking about Holly made it better.

He kept walking, and hit the main highway. Almost, he felt grateful towards Markham for taking the ignition keys. Tom had known that a walk in the rain would be good for him, it would clear his head. The last three months were a bad dream. He had gotten emotional, and like a small boy he had returned to smash things, to get attention. Well, he'd gotten the attention.

Ann had read him. Intuitively, she had known he would use Ross's tie-in with Markham to worm his way back into the fold. A smart girl, Ann. Only she hadn't been quite smart enough.

Ann had lied to him. He held onto the thought as he slogged along the muddy highway shoulder. She had tried a shakedown and gotten caught.

Wait a minute, he thought. That doesn't explain Valdez. Ann didn't do that. She's not cold enough to lure a guy like Valdez to your hotel room and leave the body. Is she?

Well, how about DeWitt Smith, then? A bitter man, weak and dangerous. But Smith isn't the type, he thought. Although he seemed awfully eager to get rid of Ann tonight.

Forget it, he thought. Focus on Holly, how it's going to be. You're Tom's adopted son, and you got out of line and he spanked you, but that's over and done. From here on out it's going to be cream and velvet. Only the trouble is, Tom's operators have really got to be perfect. Just one slip and you're done. Next month, or next year perhaps, you'll make a very small error, just one minor flaw in strategy, and Tom will sadly tell your replacement what a sharp boy Cliff was, too bad that we lost him.

The car came hissing around the curve and almost hit him. It swerved aside at the last second, tires crying on the slick asphalt, and stopped fifty yards ahead.

Tierney kept walking, not seeing the car. He kept trying to concentrate on Holly, but Ann kept popping back into his mind. The way she had stubbornly helped clean his room and gotten sick afterwards. The way she had confronted DeWitt Smith, angry and tearful and dedicated. And he thought wearily, this is a state of shock; you're not being rational. But you're going to start analyzing again and get sucked in, sure as hell. It's happening right now and there isn't a damned thing you can do about it....

The car was backing up. In the front seat were two boys and a girl. They were Vardon University cheerleaders and had been celebrating Vardon's two-touchdown victory over State.

"Look at him," the boy at the wheel said. "He's been hurt."

"Hey," the girl called, rolling down the window. "You need a lift, mister?"

"He doesn't even hear us," the driver said. "Look at his face."

"Did you have an accident, mister?"

Tierney looked at them blankly. He was thinking about Ann, adding up the score. No matter how he totaled it, the score was zero. Yet he was making the biggest decision of his life.

The girl shivered and moved closer to the driver. She whispered, "Drive on, Sam."

The Chevy moved reluctantly down the highway. Tierney stared at the dwindling red taillights; then he turned back toward the eucalyptus grove. He began to run.

It took him fifteen minutes to find the hill path, to reach the Ford. By then his breath came in whistling gasps and there was a raw pain in his throat. The first thing he did was turn off the headlights. Then he crouched under the dash, fumbling with the ignition wires, tearing and splicing. Finally he punched the starter. The motor coughed and died.

He got out, frowning at the Ford. Wet plugs or a dead battery, and it didn't matter which. It was fate and you couldn't fight it. He kept telling himself he was a fool as he disengaged the emergency brake and canted the steering wheel. He went around to the front bumper and heaved. The Ford shuddered backwards and stopped as a rear tire found a chuckhole. Tierney heaved again. His feet flew out from under him and he landed in the mud. He got up and strained at the front bumper. The Ford rocked stubbornly, but refused to budge. He set his teeth and grunted. The second time he fell he cracked his face against the fender.

He got up dizzily, spitting blood. This won't do, he thought. This won't do at all. If you keep on like this you're going to fracture something. He stumbled down the path into the woods. When he came back he was carrying an armload of dead branches. He surveyed the right rear tire clinically, and started experimenting with leverage factors. Then he went back to the front end and began rocking the Ford back and forth. One last gut-wrenching effort and the car quivered free. It took him another five minutes to guide it sideways and reverse the angle of turn. He slid behind the wheel as the Ford coasted down the hill path, five, ten miles an hour.

Just before he hit the main highway, Tierney snapped the gear shift into second and disengaged the clutch, praying.

There was a torturing interval of jerks and sputters, then the motor caught with a roar. Tierney wiped rain and sweat from his face. He squinted at the dash clock. The time was four-fifteen. He drove toward Paloma Beach at seventy miles an hour.

CHAPTER 8

In the hour before dawn, a peculiar hush creeps into the Pink Barrel. Less than half the casino tables are occupied. The players glance feverishly at the wall clock, at their dwindling hoard of chips. One hour till closing time.

It is the get-even hour, the time of sweating out that last card for the open-end straight, when a winner's smile can needle a loser into bloody violence. House men stalk nervously among the tables, watching for focal points of action.

Holly sat at a lowball table. She felt languorous, sated. Since midnight she had won three hundred dollars. An hour ago she had excused herself from the table and gone to the women's lounge. When she returned she wore a dim smile. The scent of clover hung about her like a cloak.

Now she glanced abstractly at her cards and passed. Lighting a cigarette, she saw Tierney.

At first she hardly recognized him. He stood under the arched entrance to the coffee lounge. It was a shock; he was a pale, uncertain stranger. She gathered her chips into her handbag and went over to the cashier's window. When she went into the lounge Tierney was gone. She felt momentary panic as she hurried to the outside entrance. Tierney stood under the concrete overhang, gazing at the parking lot. The cars shone like toys in the misting rain.

"Waiting for me, Cliff?" He started and looked down at her. She saw the bruises and touched his cheek. "What happened?"

"An accident." He sounded remote, tired. "Where's Markham?"

"He left around midnight," she said softly. "Remember forty-eight hours ago, darling? You ran out on me, remember?"

"You lied to me, Holly."

"You wouldn't accept the truth," she said.

He looked down at her in the neon dimness, at the tight green dress, the perfect body, the shining glory of her hair. His nostrils twitched as he smelled the clover sweetness. "Still on the sticks route?" The pain was naked on his face.

"It's a substitute," she giggled, "like gambling." Then her face was composed, green eyes limpid. "Come home with me, Cliff. Right now."

He gave her a preoccupied smile. It was the smile of a shill in a dice game, the professional mask of the pitchman short-changing the rubes outside the bally tent. "I can't," he said. "Is Garth inside?"

"To hell with Garth." And she moved expertly against him in the darkness, feeling his quick intake of breath and his hard hands on her shoulders as his face came down to hers. She kissed him with a wild exultation. "You love me," she said.

"No choice," he said bitterly. He was thinking of Ann.

Holly searched his face. She said in a different voice, "You look different, darling."

"I've been walking in the rain," he said. "You find out all kinds of things about yourself when you walk in the rain."

"Are you in trouble, Cliff? With Markham?"

"No," he mused, holding her close. "I'm just like a son to Markham."

Then, astonishingly, he was pushing her away. He was staring at the white Olds parked at the far end of the lot.

"I'll see you sometime today," he said. "At your place. Wait for me, baby doll."

He kissed her, then disappeared inside. Holly's first reaction was rage. Then she laughed. She walked through the rain toward her Porsche. She was still floating in the backwash of weed.

Cliff would come to her apartment by noon. She thought about it, tasting it, thinking of the peace afterward, the heavenly calm. Afterward, she could work again. Last week at the quarry she had bought a cube of pink marble. A madonna lay imprisoned in that stone, waiting to be freed with hammer and chisel. Holly drove home through the rain, moistening her lips. She was thinking about the pink madonna....

In the lounge Tierney drank two black coffees. He closed his eyes and felt fatigue singing along his nerve ends. He had taken a hot shower in his hotel room and changed clothes, but he still felt tired. Then his thoughts became purely technical, focusing on the immediate problem. He flexed his fingers. They felt like shards of ice.

He went to the archway and studied the casino. Garth was shilling at a five-ten table. Tierney turned quickly into the men's restroom. There he turned on the hot water tap, letting it run over his hands until they felt scalded. He kneaded his fingers as he returned to the casino and approached Garth's table.

Four men sat at the table. One was lean, nervous, sandy-haired. He had four hundred dollars' worth of chips in front of him. The other two were big men, bleak and unshaven. They played with a quiet desperation, fingering their chips. Both were tuna fishermen. Tierney recognized one of them as a man named Bisbee. Bisbee weighed a solid two-fifty, none of it fat. He played a reckless brawling style of poker, and hated to lose.

"Looking for company?" Tierney sat down on Garth's left.

There were hostile nods from the two big men. Garth just stared, his square face impassive. He had a great deal of control.

Tierney bought fifty dollars' worth of chips.

It was a grudge game, an angry game. The sandy-haired man was winning. Garth was even. Bisbee and the other fisherman brooded sullenly over their cards.

When his deal came Tierney managed to thumbnail three aces. It was an action hand, with Tierney passing and Garth raising the sandy-haired man and being re-raised by Bisbee. Garth won the pot with a full house. Bisbee swore and bought more chips.

Garth regarded Tierney thoughtfully. An hour ago Tierney had been lying in the mud, beaten. Now he was smiling softly at Garth over a deck of cards. It didn't figure.

Garth frowned, wishing Markham were here. Markham could handle situations like this. He glanced at the wall clock. Five-thirty. Half an hour till closing time. He caught the eye of a floating house man and covertly indicated Tierney. The house man nodded. He sat at an adjacent table. Presently another house man drifted over to join the first. Garth relaxed.

In his own field Garth had talent. He was stolid, unimaginative, and very good at taking orders. He was brilliant at figures, and with one glance at the evening crowd, could estimate the casino's take within five per cent. He had one flaw. Two or three times a year he would become edgy, irritable. A dull shine would appear in his eyes. Markham would observe him keenly at such times and send him away for a long weekend.

The stocky blond man would go down the coast alone. Usually he visited the tenderloin of Los Angeles, the Flower Street alleys where cops walk in pairs. Sometimes he went to the dives of Tijuana. He would drink for hours, alone. Then he would find a woman, the uglier the better. He would start to make love to her. Invariably he would fail. Then he would hurt her, sometimes terribly. But when he returned to Paloma Beach the dull shine would be gone from his eyes. For the next few months he would be very calm and efficient.

Only Markham knew that he was impotent because of an incident which had occurred when Garth was sixteen, or what would happen to him if he were denied his periodic release.

Tierney looked across the table at the blond man. He thought about Ann, alone with Garth. He felt his palms grow moist. He almost dropped the cards.

"Deal," Garth said.

Tierney dealt.

Fifteen minutes later Garth was winning three hundred dollars. It disturbed him. He wanted to leave the game, but it might make the two fishermen unhappy. He smelled violence like a deadly nimbus over the table. Yet Tierney sat bland and utterly relaxed. He had not won a hand.

Garth considered the situation logically. It occurred to him that Tierney was punchy, that Tom had hurt him very badly indeed. Perhaps Tierney was one of those persons who enjoyed pain. The blond man tried a gambit.

"Some guys like losing," he said. "They keep coming back for more."

Tierney gave no sign of hearing. His smile was fixed at a point somewhere above and beyond Garth's right ear.

"They never know when they've had enough," Garth said.

Bisbee stopped dealing. "You needling me?" he asked in a dangerous voice.

"No," Garth said.

"I don't like the needle," Bisbee said.

He resumed dealing. Tierney picked up his hand. It was a spade flush. "Pass," he said and threw his cards in.

Garth won the pot with three queens, beating Bisbee's two pair. The big man threw down his cards viciously. "Let's have a fresh deck. This one stinks."

"Blondie doesn't think it stinks," Tierney murmured.

Garth flushed. "How do you mean that?"

"Listen to him," Tierney told the giant fisherman. "He wants to know how I mean it."

Garth bit his lip and let it lie. He signaled for a fresh deck. Tierney exchanged decks with the house man. While doing so he managed to palm the ace of diamonds from the old deck.

Two hands later it was his deal. When Garth picked up his cards something stirred in his eyes. He opened. The sandy-haired man called. Bisbee raised. Tierney and the other fisherman passed.

"Cards?" Tierney inquired.

Garth took one card. The sandy-haired man was pat. Bisbee took two cards. Garth bet ten and Bisbee raised. Garth re-raised. The sandy-haired man looked ready to cry.

"Call?" Tierney asked Bisbee.

The big man was memorizing his cards. His face was a granite mask of strain. He called. Garth laid down his hand. Three aces and the joker.

Bisbee made a choking sound and started to rise. As Garth reached for the pot, Tierney's hand clamped on his wrist.

"Hold on," he said. "Let's look at the discards."

Garth turned his head slowly. "You dealt the cards."

"And you cut them."

The silence was like thick cold syrup. The table became a nexus, with the silence oozing in heavy waves outward through the casino. The two house men got up from the adjacent table.

"Let go of my wrist." Garth's nostrils were white.

Bisbee slowly sat. He was looking at Garth. "Let's look at the discards."

Tierney flipped over the discards. "See?" he pointed. "A duplicate ace of diamonds. *My* discard."

Everyone looked at Garth's hand. One of his cards was also the ace of diamonds.

"A slickster," Tierney said affably. "He palms an extra ace for emergencies. You're a shill, aren't you, chum?"

Understanding came to Garth, too late. He moved sideways, coming out of the chair fast as Bisbee reached for him. The house men closed in. One of them grabbed Tierney. The other made the mistake of grabbing Bisbee. The big man doubled up a fist like a small ham, and swung. The house man went backward as if catapulted from a slingshot, his arms flailing as he caromed off one table and crashed into another, overturning it. A woman screamed. The sandy-haired man was running toward the exits.

The other house man had a stranglehold on Tierney from behind. Garth came at him like a small blond bull, and hit him twice in the groin before the other tuna fisherman hit Garth with a crunching right. Garth seemed to melt behind the table. Tierney finally freed himself.

Bisbee was methodically overturning tables and wrecking furniture. He had a frozen grin on his face and was enjoying himself thoroughly. Three more house men came running from the cashier's cage. The other tuna fisherman picked up a chair and threw it, fast and low. Two house men went down like ninepins.

Tierney was on hands and knees, crawling under tables toward the exit. Some of the patrons had left when the action started. Most of them were spectators, fascinated by the vortex of action in the center of the casino. When Tierney was near the arches he stood up, brushing off his clothes. Nobody paid him any attention.

The brawl had shifted to the far casino wall. The other tuna fisherman had gone down and Bisbee stood alone, swinging his chair like a hatchet. Two house men circled him warily. Garth was crawling toward the exits. His face was bloody, contorted. Tierney moved into the open so that Garth could see him. The blond man stood up, weaving. Tierney smiled politely and moved through the outside arches.

Outside, the rain had stopped. It was almost dawn. Tierney walked leisurely among the parked cars, not looking back. There was a patter of footsteps behind. He turned behind a gray Buick and waited.

In a moment Garth came stalking down the car aisles. He moved slowly, his breath a broken sob. Something glittered in his right hand.

He saw Tierney a fraction of a second too late. The knife slashed upward in a disemboweling arc, but Tierney had drifted sideways like smoke. His palm sliced down twice, and Garth was on his knees, quivering. Then he pitched forward on his face.

There was a skirl of sirens. Two highway patrol cars screeched into the parking lot and stopped in front of the casino. Three troopers got out of each car and ran inside. Tierney stood listening to the sounds from inside the casino. His expression was that of a music critic appraising an opening-night concert. He dragged Garth toward the white Olds parked six cars away.

Ten minutes later Garth awoke with a sensation of drowning. It took him a moment to realize that he was propped up on the outside of the Olds with his head sticking through the window. The window was open six inches from the top, leaving his neck wedged securely between the glass and top frame. It was a thoroughly uncomfortable position.

"What the hell?" Garth said.

Tierney sat behind the wheel, smoking. He was gazing abstractly at the landscape, at the gray dawn mist over the surrounding tomato fields. They were parked in a clump of palms a hundred yards from the highway. Garth saw the tomato fields, and estimated they were somewhere south of town. His nose throbbed like fire. He wondered if it were broken.

"Hey," he said. "Whatsa idea?"

Tierney turned his head, as if seeing Garth for the first time. His expression was friendly, almost warm. "Drag?" he inquired, extending the cigarette. Garth took the drag gratefully. Outside the car, his left hand was groping for the door handle.

"Don't do that," Tierney said.

"Why not?"

"You'll be uncomfortable."

"I'm uncomfortable now," Garth said.

"Where's Ann?"

Garth went right on fumbling with the door handle, Tierney sighed. He flicked the electric windowlifts on his side, and the window hummed up against Garth's throat. Garth's fists hammered weakly against the glass. His face was purpling. Tierney flicked the switch again. The window hummed down two inches. Garth coughed, gulping air.

"Where's Ann?"

"I don't know. Honest to God, I don't know."

The windowlifts hummed. Garth shrieked.

"See?" Tierney said pleasantly. "We're wasting time." He depressed the switch. Garth was swearing in a cracked monotone.

"You don't need this. Why not make it easy?"

"I can't breathe," Garth moaned.

"You can breathe. Watch my fingers."

Garth watched Tierney's fingers hovering over the windowlifts. His eyes were terrible. "All right," he choked. "All right."

"I'm listening."

"We took her to a big house on Shane Drive," Garth said rapidly. "A white colonial, with pillars, like. I don't remember the address. Markham told me to go back and run the casino, he'd call later."

"You're doing fine."

"That's all there is, honest. They drove away in Tom's car. A black Lincoln."

"They?"

"Tom and the girl. And a thin guy. Tall, white hair, real distinguished-looking."

Tierney thought about it. To Garth, in the gray half light, he resembled a calm, smiling satan.

"Remember Zoe?" Tierney asked.

"Sure." Garth sucked air. He felt that he could never again get enough air into his lungs. "What about her?"

"She got a year for possession. You framed her, didn't you?"

Garth started to shout a denial, then changed his mind. "Tom said she was trouble. He told me to plant the caps in her car and then call the fuzz. I don't ask Tom for reasons, you know that."

Tierney decided this was true. "What happened to her baby?"

"Hell, who cares?" Then, quickly, "Tom said it died."

Tierney tried another tack. "Around midnight, you clobbered me outside the Owl Club. Then you visited DeWitt Smith, in Laguna. Now take it from there."

Garth gnawed at his lip. "Tom said to rough up Smith. He said it was some kind of insurance. I took Feeney along." Feeney was one of Markham's minor operatives. "Then we drove back to Vardonville and staked out in front of the dame's pad until you brought her home." He grimaced. "Tom was sore because you got away. He told Feeney to stay at the casino. Then he came with me. We spotted your car outside the hotel and tailed you." He began to sweat. "That's all there is."

"You're forgetting one thing. Valdez."

"Eddie?" Garth looked bewildered. "Hell, *you* sank Eddie—"

"I didn't."

"Then it was the girl. We saw Eddie around midnight, at the Owl Club. He said he had a real heavy date, and he'd see us later."

Tierney lighted another cigarette, weighing it. If Garth was telling the truth that left only two possibilities: Markham and DeWitt Smith. He leaned forward, said distinctly, "Lackland. Does the name mean anything to you?"

Garth thought so hard he squinted. "No."

It went on like that for ten minutes, and Tierney finally gave up. The blond man knew nothing about Markham's sideline operation, or where Ann had been taken. Tierney depressed the windowlifts all the way, and Garth was abruptly free, rubbing his neck and not believing it. The Olds rocked toward the highway in a cloud of dust, and turned north toward town.

It was seven o'clock when Tierney parked in front of Markham's bungalow on Orange Street. It was a small white frame, with blue shutters and a manicured lawn. It looked like the residence of a conservative bachelor, which Markham basically was. It took Tierney a moment of prowling outside the windows before he decided nobody was home.

It was five after seven when he turned into an all-night drive-in and ordered ham and eggs.

Eating breakfast was a mistake. He realized it when he spilled coffee on his coat. His fingers were trembling in tiny spasms. You're getting old, he thought. Once you went sixty hours without sleep because Tom wanted you to do a job for him. He tried to remember what that particular job had been, but his memory was a bit hazy. He finished the coffee, holding the cup carefully with both hands. Then he paid the check and went over to the phone booth.

In the local directory he found Thad Ross's number. The address was on Shane Drive. He dialed and waited.

"Ross residence." It sounded like a colored maid.

"Is Thad there?"

"Mistuh Ross not home. He left on a business trip early this morning. Who's calling?"

Tierney hung up and went back to the Olds. His eyelids felt hot and granulated. He sat for a moment with his eyes closed, then it came to him that what he needed at this point was a shave and cold shower. He drove back toward town.

It was seven-forty when he parked in front of his hotel and walked into the lobby. The first thing he saw was Joe Lennox, sitting in a corner, dozing behind a newspaper. Waiting for him.

He did an about-face and went outside. He got into the Olds and burned rubber for fifty feet, thinking that Lennox was a very vindictive cop indeed. Then the thought came that Lennox wasn't waiting merely to vag him, that he was waiting for a very special reason, involving a corpse named Valdez. A corpse which had left blood traces on Tierney's mattress.

You'd better snap out of it, he told himself. You've got all the statistics you really need. You were a high-class operator once, there's no reason why you can't come up with some answers.

He thought about the anonymous demand for fifteen thousand dollars which Markham had received last night by special delivery. He thought about Zoe's frame, and about DeWitt Smith.

Then all at once something clicked and he found himself driving east, toward the county seat. It's just a hunch, he thought; it doesn't mean anything, one way or the other, but let's see what happens.

The county hall records opened at eight-thirty. Tierney arrived a few minutes early, and sat on the stone steps watching the sparrows play hide-and-seek in the red tile eaves. The sun burned down through the torn fleece of cumulus.

It was going to be a hot day.

CHAPTER 9

Tierney found the office of vital statistics on the second floor. It took him half an hour of browsing through the steel-jacketed file records to find what he wanted, and then it was a vast disappointment.

Zoe's baby had been born fourteen months ago, at the Paloma Beach City Hospital. Doctor Thad Ross had been the delivering physician. The baby had been named Michael George Miller, and there was no subsequent record of death.

Tierney slammed the folder back into the cabinet. The clerk at the desk jumped and glared. Then he saw the expression on Tierney's face and went back to his filing.

There's got to be more, Tierney thought, gazing at the file cabinets. You've got the answer right in front of you, the whole key to Markham's sideline operation and Valdez's murder, only you're too dumb to see it. Too dumb and too tired.

He concentrated on Ann. Last night, in DeWitt Smith's office. The way she had pleaded with the drunken editor to run an editorial. She had mentioned a couple named Lackland—

Tierney flipped open another cabinet and began searching. He had to go back four years, but he finally found it. The Lacklands lived in Santa Ana. Four years ago, Mrs. Lackland had given birth to a boy. The child had been named Paul Terrance, and had died at the age of two.

Tierney gently closed the cabinet. He thought about Zoe Miller, remembering her pathetic ambition to be an actress, her foolish pride. He felt pity for Ann, and a quiet hatred for Markham. Only Tom could dream up an operation like this, he thought. You've really got to hand it to him.

But it was too wild. It was like a professional prizefighter running a lingerie shop on the side.

Wait a minute, he thought. Supposing that lingerie shop paid real money, more money than the fighter would make for a main event at the Garden? That changes things, doesn't it?

There was one way to find out.

Tierney walked downstairs slowly, his heels echoing on the cement steps. Halfway down, the steps seemed to undulate, and he grabbed the railing for support. He held tightly to the railing, hands slippery with sweat. He had perhaps two hours left before he passed out from fatigue. But if he had guessed right, two hours would be enough.

On the ground floor he found a phone booth opposite the utilities office. He dialed information and asked for DeWitt Smith's home phone number.

Five rings. He counted them, abstractly staring across the hallway at the utilities office. White-bloused girls were busy at filing cabinets and adding machines, and people were lined up in front of cashiers' cages. He wondered how it would feel to live in a world where you paid your utilities promptly, where you went to civic league meetings and complained about higher water bills and taxes. On the sixth ring, Smith answered the phone.

"Hello?" The editor's voice was fuzzy, thick.

"This is Tierney. I was with Ann last night, remember?"

Smith's breathing was harsh over the wire. "We've got nothing to talk about." Smith hesitated. "Is Ann there?"

"Markham's got her."

"You're lying!"

Tierney said coldly, "He wouldn't have her if you'd run an exposé on him, as she's been begging you to do for the past month."

"What kind of exposé?" Smith sounded very tired.

"Black-market babies."

If he'd guessed wrong Smith would laugh at him and sang up. But Smith didn't hang up.

"There's no proof. Even if there were, it's not my fight." Smith spoke heavily, with great effort. It occurred to Tierney that he was drunk.

"It's your fight now," Tierney said.

"Ann can take care of herself! She's an idealistic and sometimes foolish girl. I don't know what your angle is, mister. But I know what you are, and I want you to stay away from Ann. Have you got that? Does it register?"

"It registers fine," Tierney said. "There's just one thing."

"What's that?"

"Markham thinks Ann's trying to shake him down. She's not. But I think she's protecting the real shakedown artist. Because she knows he's a sick man, emotionally castrated. He's afraid to fight Markham in the open because he tried it once and got destroyed—"

Smith cursed him, slowly and bitterly.

"You'd better run that editorial today," Tierney said. "The lid's coming off within a few hours, and one way or another, you'll get full credit."

"You're crazy!" Smith was frantic now. "If you're talking about Zoe Miller, she gave up her baby willingly. She didn't want it—"

"But later she changed her mind, didn't she? That second or third month a lot of them decide to keep the baby after all. Only in Zoe's case it was very unprofitable for Markham."

"Did Ann tell you all this?" A cunning note had crept into the editor's voice.

"Some of it. Understand, I still need more facts—"

"Brother, you don't know how many facts you do need." Smith sounded relieved, and it disturbed Tierney. It implied there was a great deal more, and he was running out of time.

"For now," Tierney said nastily, "go back to your bottle. Think about Ann with Markham. If you think about it hard enough, maybe you'll write a great editorial, the kind that gets you a Southland news award posthumously—"

There was a broken sound and Smith hung up. Tierney stood looking at the receiver, rubbing his forehead. You scored that time, he told himself. The only trouble is, you're bluffing. But Tom taught you the advantages of bluff in a situation like this. You get enough people frightened and the action starts. Any hustler thrives off action because he can use it, divert it to his own ends, although sometimes the hustler gets caught in the middle and squeezed flat.

Then he remembered Ann, and his weariness fell away like a cloak. He leafed through the phone directory until he found the Lackland residence on Aspen Drive. He went out into the hot sunlight and got into the Olds.

The house turned out to be a ranch-style redwood, with a circular flagstone drive bordered by a low rustic fence. The lawn was a vivid green carpet and the white trellis by the porch was covered with rambler roses. A year-old station wagon was parked in the garage. From in back came the sound of hammering.

Tierney sat appraising the house, feeling sorry for the people who lived here. The husband, he decided, was in the twelve grand a year category, but no snob—he does his own gardening. Those are really fine roses, and you can see how that redwood trim sparkles in the sun. I'll bet he used three coats of oil. Taxpayers, good substantial citizens.

Then he realized he was stalling. He got out of the car and walked up the drive, mentally rehearsing his pitch. It was going to be a cruel pitch, fast and rough. He hated it, but it had to be this way. If he barged in with awkward questions the door would slam in his face.

He touched the doorbell and heard chimes within the house. The door opened. The woman wore a blue housecoat, and he noticed her figure was on the plump side. Dark hair with streaks of gray. She stared at him out of anxious brown eyes and said, "Yes? What is it?"

"Mrs. Lackland?" His smile was smug, knowing.

She nodded uncertainly.

"I'm a friend of Zoe Miller's."

"I'm afraid I don't understand—"

"It's about the baby. Can we talk inside?"

Something died in her eyes. Wordlessly, she opened the door. He walked inside.

There was sea-green carpeting, and a limestone fireplace that stood out like snow from the charcoal cork wall. Candy-pink drapes framed sliding glass doors to the outside patio. A warm room, designed for family living.

The playpen stood against the far wall, by the fireplace. In it was a baby, sound asleep. Tierney sat in the green womb chair, staring at the baby's cheek. He saw the livid strawberry mark which had once made Zoe so ashamed. He exhaled in relief.

"Poor little guy looks beat," he murmured. "Is he teething?"

"Never mind that," Mrs. Lackland said in a flat voice. She stood rigidly by the sofa. "What is it you want?"

He leaned back with a soft smile. "Let's just say I'm a friend of Zoe's. She's in trouble. She really needs help."

He was playing this by ear, but it was working fine. Markham would have been quite proud of him in that moment. Mrs. Lackland closed her eyes. Then she looked directly at Tierney. Her expression made him a little sick.

"How much?" she asked. "How much this time?"

Tierney kept his smile bland. "How does two thousand sound?"

The woman sat bonelessly on the sofa. "It was three thousand the time before. You people said it would be the very last time."

"I wouldn't know about that." Tierney was diffident. "I'm new on this route."

Mrs. Lackland just nodded, and a warning bell clanged in Tierney's mind. She was taking it too calmly.

"You're clever," she whispered.

He made a depreciating gesture.

"So very clever. First it was six hundred to get the baby, and that was fine. Then it was seven months of nursing it, loving it, and realizing you're a whole woman again. Seven good months, while the love hook sinks in deep, then you come back telling how the mother wants her baby back, but you can maybe buy her off for three thousand dollars."

"Are you sure it was three thousand last trip?" He was gazing abstractly at the playpen.

"Cash," she said bleakly. "He wouldn't take a check."

"Who wouldn't?"

"Your polite Spanish friend. He said he was Zoe's husband. We halfway believed him."

And that, thought Tierney, caps it. Eddie Valdez made the collections. Markham was obviously the broker, the go-between. He cleared his throat and said, "Why didn't you go through the state adoption board?"

"I'm thirty-nine." She made a screaming face. "The age limit is thirty-eight. But of course you know that."

Tierney nodded solemnly. He couldn't take much more of this, but in a moment he could tell her it was all over, that she had made her very last installment payment to Markham.

"We've had the baby for ten months." Mrs. Lackland stood up slowly. "The adoption papers don't finalize for another two months, and any time within that first year the mother can kill the adoption. Even if we proved her unfit, she could still have the baby taken away and put in some state home. And we haven't *got* two thousand dollars, understand?"

Now she was walking like a somnambulist toward the bedroom. Tierney swallowed and said, "Please sit down a minute. I've got something to tell you—"

She didn't hear him. The bedroom door closed behind her. From outside, the hammering rose to a shrill crescendo. Tierney got up and went over to the sliding glass doors. Past the translucent fiberglass overhang he saw a red-haired man building a latticework on top of the redwood fence. The man was applying himself with great determination, and Tierney felt a warm empathy for the Lacklands, anticipating their faces when he told them that it was finally over, there would be no more collections.

The bedroom door opened. Mrs. Lackland came out holding a gun. It shone small and black and deadly in her pudgy fist.

"Sit down," she said thickly. "Over there, by the fireplace. I don't want you near the playpen."

Tierney sat, looking at the gun. It was a .22 target pistol mounted on a .38 frame. Mrs. Lackland held it competently, as if she knew all about guns.

"Listen, I'm not really—"

"Be quiet. I want to tell you something." Her nostrils were white and pinched; her breath made a curious whistling sound. "Since we were tapped for that three thousand, I've been expecting something like this to happen. When I was thirty," she said harshly, "I spent six months in Camarillo, the state mental hospital. You didn't know that, did you?"

Tierney shook his head. The gun kept making tiny concentric spirals. It pointed now at his face, now at his abdomen.

"They said I was the schiz type." Abruptly her voice was calm. "I almost went over the edge. But they finally released me. Then I met Fred. He was wonderful. We had six good years, and then the baby came. It almost killed me. I had a hysterectomy afterwards, but that didn't matter. We had Terry. For three years we had him; then he died of pneumonia, that quiet gentle kind that steals them in the night. I almost went back to the sanitarium."

"I'm sorry—"

"Just shut up," she said. "I want you to understand what this baby means to me. I want you to realize that I can't possibly afford to lose it." She moved quickly to the pink drapes. "Fred!" she called. "Could you come inside a minute?"

The hammering stopped. It was very quiet in the room.

Tierney stared numbly at the gun, thinking, this sort of thing doesn't happen—a plump housewife with a target pistol. But it's for real, and she's not a housewife any longer; you've turned her into an animal protecting its young.

There were footsteps on the patio and Fred came in, wiping his feet on the mat. He was big, raw-boned, freckled. The rimless glasses gave him a meek look. He saw the gun and said, "What the hell, Alice!"

"He says the baby's mother sent him." Alice was holding the pistol in a death grip. "Just like the last time, Fred. Now, they want two thousand dollars."

"Oh no." Fred looked at Tierney.

Tierney said desperately, "I'm not really—" The pistol swung up and he stopped talking. Fred came into the room and sat down.

"Alice, will you please put that thing away?" He was trying to be calm. "We can work this out—"

"What's to work out?" Alice was shrill. "We haven't got two thousand dollars! And if we let him walk out of that door, the mother puts in a complaint and they'll take the baby!"

"Nobody's going to take him," Fred said grimly. He turned to Tierney. "See what you've done? She was like this for six months after Terry died. When we got this child it was as if she was born again, a new woman. She's fighting for her life right now; can't you see that?"

Tierney could see it quite clearly.

"I've got an idea," Fred said, looking decisive. "We could slap a second mortgage on the house—"

Alice threw back her head and laughed. Then the laughter stopped cold. "I'd really like to meet the mother. Just once I'd like to meet the sort of woman who'd—"

"She's in prison." Tierney got it out too quickly for Alice to shoot him.

"How do you mean?" Fred blurted.

"I mean Zoe Miller has no connection with the people that are bleeding you. She wanted her baby back, six months ago. So they framed her for narcotics possession. Nine months in Corona."

Alice's smile was mirthless. "You're a liar."

Tierney started talking faster than he had ever talked in his life. It was no use, Alice wasn't buying it. And when he mentioned Thad Ross he drew a complete blank. Neither Fred nor Alice had ever heard of Doctor Ross. Tierney tried another tack. "Do you know a girl named Ann Childs?"

Alice nodded tightly. "She came here two weeks ago, asking questions. I told her the baby was legally adopted, but I don't think she believed me."

"She's a news reporter. I was only trying to verify—"

"See?" Alice wailed. "You hear him, Fred? They're going to print it in the papers, they'll name names, we'll lose the baby regardless—"

"We won't lose it." Fred stood up, stolid and tall. "Give me the gun, honey."

Fred extended his hand, palm up. Alice looked at Tierney, her mouth twitching. In that moment Tierney thought about Ann, and how he had to contact Markham immediately and tell him it was stalemate, the game was over. As Fred passed in front of Alice, he moved.

It was a mistake.

Alice cried out, and he was at the front door clawing at the knob when the .22 went off. It was like a bomb exploding in the confines of the room. There was a stinging jolt in his left shoulder. Alice fired again, squinting along the barrel with intense concentration. Plaster spurted inches from Tierney's face as the door flew open. Then Fred grabbed the gun and Tierney was outside, running fleetly toward the Olds. He was behind the wheel, fumbling with the ignition. From inside the house he heard the frightened screams of the baby.

Fred stood uncertainly on the porch, staring after him. Now Fred was hurrying down the flagstone drive. The ignition caught, and the Olds's tires clawed the pavement. Tierney was doing fifty by the time he reached the corner.

For a time he drove without volition, feeling the numbness in his shoulder become a stabbing pain. He touched his coat, and his hand came away wet and sticky. You really bungled that one, he thought. You wanted information, so you went after it like pulling teeth; only you forgot that sometimes they shoot the dentist.

He drove south, toward Paloma Beach. He gripped the steering wheel tightly, but the Olds had a tendency to waver all over the highway. It bothered him. In a few more minutes shock would set in, and he could lie down under the dash and take a nap. He looked down at the seat cushions and winced. It was a shame about Garth's upholstery, but it really couldn't be helped.

Then he remembered Ann, and his driving became less erratic.

He badly needed the services of a professional. But the only professionals in town had a direct pipeline to Markham, and that wouldn't do at all.

Wait a minute. There was Pop Stroot.

Tierney's hands ached on the steering wheel. He flexed his shoulder gingerly, and decided no bones were broken. That was a break of sorts. He was getting all manner of breaks lately.

Pop Stroot could help him. Providing he hadn't died of cancer by now, and of course providing Pop was in the right mood.

CHAPTER 10

It was eight-fifteen when Thad Ross parked Markham's Lincoln in his basement garage. He took the elevator to the fourth floor, and walked slowly down the gray-carpeted corridor to his office.

This morning he did not go past the reception desk. He unlocked the side door to his consultation room and sat at the desk for a moment, eyes closed. He had been up since three, and the headache was a quiet flame in his temples.

He thought about a drink, moistening his lips. Or coffee, he thought despairingly, laced with rich dark brandy. But that, of course, was out of the question.

Out in the reception room several young matrons in varying degrees of pregnancy would be waiting for their appointments. Elizabeth would be sitting at the reception desk, crisp and efficient in her white starched uniform. He got up, still moving with exaggerated slowness, like a man walking under water. He went into the adjoining bathroom. He shaved carefully, trying not to observe the bloodless face in the mirror, the eyes like dark wounds. Watch your hands instead, Doctor, and the deft surgeon's fingers, moving with beautiful white precision.

He toweled vigorously and combed his silver hair. The silver of leprosy, he decided. Carcinoma of the soul, tertiary stage. Immediate amputation recommended.

He thought about Ann, and shivered. The stubborn, vicious girl. "She's a fanatic, doc," Markham had said three hours earlier. "There's only one way to cure fanatics."

There was Valdez.

A dead man complicated things. But Markham would handle everything. He held onto that thought with a quiet desperation as he went back to his desk and flipped the intercom switch.

"Good morning, Elizabeth."

"Good morning, doctor." She was cool, serene.

"I had an emergency hospital call at seven." The small lie made him feel guilty. "How many are waiting?"

"Five, doctor." She ticked off the names and appointment times. Thank God all were routine examinations. "Who's first?"

"Mrs. Timken."

He sighed. "Send her in."

He hated Mrs. Timken. She was a frail blonde hypochondriac who whined about imaginary backaches and morning sickness. This was her third child and she would probably have five more.

"Look at my hands, Doctor," she demanded as he took her blood pressure. "Isn't there a slight swelling?" Her great aunt had died of uremia.

He scowled at her hands, told her she was fine, that she had the constitution of a horse. This invariably made her unhappy. He prescribed an iron prescription and she brightened. He indicated a slight anemic tendency and she beamed. When she left, she was a grateful woman.

It was like that for the next hour. He hated the interminable complaints, his own unctuous mask of reassurance, yet it was necessary. Necessary to keep up his farce of a practice, just as it was necessary to spend every Friday afternoon—for free—at the county hospital polio clinic, and to attend charity luncheons, civic league meetings.

Then it was nine-thirty, and he was alone at his desk, massaging his temples. The intercom buzzed.

Wearily: "Yes, Elizabeth?"

"The county hospital called. Doctor Quinn would like to know if you'll be available at the children's clinic Wednesday afternoon."

"Of course," he said. Doctor Thad Ross, crusader, public citizen.

The next call came ten minutes later, on his private desk phone. It was Tom Markham. "You'd better come out here right away, doc."

"*Why?*" He fought rising panic. "You said you'd handle it—"

"She's in a coma," Markham said.

"You fool," he whispered. "You sadistic fool."

"She's stubborn. That's my fault?"

"Listen, I can't possibly come—" Inspiration came. "The Santa Ana hospital just called. Emergency—"

"This is a bigger emergency," Markham said. "I don't like her color, or the way she's breathing."

He wanted to scream.

"Coming, doc?"

"Yes," he said listlessly. "How did it happen?"

"She tried to make a break. I hit her. She stumbled and fell."

"Concussion?"

"We'll find out. Bring your little black bag, Doctor."

He hung up, tasting fear like a thick bile. He buzzed Elizabeth and told her she could leave by noon, and to cancel all late appointments.

Once, Thad Ross had enjoyed the half hour drive to Pineview. But this morning he felt only a savage depression as the Lincoln sped down the lonely beach stretch towards Newport.

It was a warm day for October, and the Pacific was curdled jade in the sunlight, as he swung inland towards the green Irvine hills. Inevitably those hills reminded him of a long-dead dream, the good years when he had been an interne. The very good years ...

The long hours in an operating room, scrubbing up, the feeling of hot water on his hands, the warm tang of steam from the sterilizer, standing under the operating lights. The silent commands, the gestures. The array of forceps, scissors, the scalpels clean and shining. The first threadlike incision, the swift rhythm of white fingers, the clean sure knots.

"You've got good hands, Thad. Your knots go in nicely."

"Thank you, sir."

And he was a god in a white operating smock, the dream.

Ultimately the dream died. It died of starvation during the depression years, the very bad years. He was a general practitioner in San Diego, and his office was a shabby frame house near the waterfront. His patients were dirt-poor, navy-poor. In their fifth year of marriage Madge was pregnant and hysterical over bills. So many bills.

He remembered the first abortion.

It happened two years before Pearl Harbor. The girl was young, desperate. She had pleaded, a trapped lovely animal. He had refused. But in the end he had done it—because the girl was Madge's friend.

The following week he received a special-delivery envelope. Inside the envelope were two hundred-dollar bills

So then it was started, and next time was much easier He made a great many house calls during the war years and performed his special operation in the privacy of the home, sometimes on the kitchen table.

Then the war years were a forgotten sickness, and he had money. He came to Paloma Beach. He bought Madge the white colonial on Shane Drive. He opened his own office. He worked hard, and gradually his practice expanded. He attended civic league meetings, donated Friday afternoons to social work. He even ran for councilman, and it was a shock when he was elected.

He became a crusader.

A man named Kilian was operating a poker establishment called the Pink Barrel. Thad Ross sparked the petitions for license recall, ultimately the Barrel closed down.

Life was good. Some day he would have his own maternity hospital. Holly was growing into exquisite young womanhood, and Madge was reasonably content with her club activities, her church luncheons....

One day a small gray man walked into his office. A man named Markham, who spoke of Thad's civic influence, and how under the proper management the Pink Barrel could mean a great deal of tax revenue for Paloma Beach.

He ordered Markham out of his office. The little man smiled at him, pityingly, and began to speak softly and terribly of his San Diego practice. He named dates, clients, fees.

Thad had considered killing Markham.

But in the end, he had no difficulty persuading the council to grant a new license. He pointed out how the revenue from the Barrel could add a wing to the city hospital. And then it was Markham running the Barrel, a smooth operation.

Unfortunately, Markham's talents required other channels. That second year, he bought Pineview. Ross argued futilely, but there was no real choice. And like all of Markham's enterprises, Pineview proved profitable.

Markham screened the prospective parents with loving care. Invariably they had money, wanted a baby quite terribly, and could not meet the strict requirements of the state adoption board.

Zoe Miller had been an unfortunate mistake. But Markham had taken care of that....

Thad Ross drove through the inland hills, chewing the inside of his cheek and thinking about Zoe. He passed orange groves and terraced hill vineyards, with an occasional white farmhouse dotting the landscape.

Abruptly he turned down a graveled road bordered with scrub pines and eucalyptus. He came into the five-acre clearing which had been a vineyard before the war. The house was sprawling Spanish stucco and red tile. There was a strip of lawn in front of the screened patio, a white gravel parking square, a weatherbeaten fence with the sign *Pineview Rest Home*.

He parked, and sat gazing at the rolling green foothills beyond the valley. He tried to tell himself that it was strictly nerves, that Markham had everything under tight control. Then his mouth twisted. He got out of the Lincoln and walked around to the patio.

Two girls sat in wicker chairs reading magazines. Both were young and pretty, both in their eighth month of pregnancy. They glanced up and smiled.

"Hello, Doctor Albertson," one said.

He smiled a warm hello and went into the foyer, down the linoleum hall to the wrought-iron staircase. On the way up he nodded to a white-jacketed orderly.

The room was at the end of the hall on the second floor. He knocked twice, then remembered this particular room had soundproof cork walls. He stabbed the button on the jamb and the door opened. Markham looked at him, drawn and tired.

"Try her pulse," Markham said, closing the door behind him.

Ross crossed to the hospital cot and looked down at Ann. Her face was puffy, discolored. She breathed heavily through her broken mouth. Ross's hands were quite steady as he took out his stethoscope. Only his cheek twitched as he listened to the strong heartbeat. He pulled back Ann's eyelid and examined the pupil.

"Was this necessary?"

"You're forgetting that note she sent," Markham said. "Tonight we drop fifteen grand off the Carleton freeway, remember?"

Ross took a deep grinding breath. "Supposing it's not her? She kept denying—"

"Remember the night you found her going through your desk? That previous day we had an argument over percentages, and you just *had* to see it down in black and white, names and amounts. So I give you the breakdown and you're satisfied. So satisfied you leave it in your office so this bitch can lift it!" Markham was pacing the room, and his voice was a ratchet file. "If I knew she was in it alone we could handle it, quick and clean. But she's not that stupid. She's got a friend somewhere."

"Who?" Ross found his voice. "Tierney?"

"No, she doesn't trust him." Markham looked thoughtful. "But she loves him. Feature that." Then he stared at Ann. "I'll be damned," he said as the idea struck him. "Look, I'll wait in the car. Before you go, see Louise."

"What about?"

"A new girl, out of state. Name's Fay Thompson."

Ross nodded. Out of state were always better, with less chance of the mother changing her mind.

Markham went out quietly, closing the door behind him. Ross stared at Ann for almost a full minute. His face was pearly white with sweat as he took out the hypodermic.

Five minutes later he came out into the hallway, carrying his black bag. He went downstairs, to the office at the head of the corridor.

It was a small office, with fluorescent lighting and gray metal furniture. Louise Rucci sat white-haired and prim behind the desk. "Good morning, Doctor," she said, and he saw that she was playing it straight. Then he noticed the other girl in the room.

She was eighteen at the outside, at least five months pregnant. Blonde, with stormy dark eyes and a sullen mouth.

"I'm Doctor Albertson." His smile radiated sympathy, understanding. "I understand you'll be with us a while. Did Mrs. Rucci give you an application—"

"I'm not signing anything." The girl was openly suspicious. Her eyes were hard. "Just what kind of place is this, Doctor?"

"A rest home, Fay. For girls like yourself, girls that need help." He cleared his throat, and Louise, with monumental discretion, went out into the hall.

Abruptly Fay was confused. She had expected an inquisition, but everybody was so darned *polite* here. And this doctor, so tall and distinguished-looking, with his kindly gray eyes and gentle voice that said he really wanted to help her.

A month ago she'd been frantic. She'd considered sleeping pills, razor blades, or a walk along the pier some dark night. But finally she had gone humbly to State Welfare. Her interrogator had been a fat man, bald, with horn-rimmed glasses. He had asked those damned questions, looking at her as if she were diseased, and finally shaken his head. "Sorry, Miss

Thompson. We can't help you unless we know who the father is. Why don't you try a private hospital?"

And he had mentioned Pineview.

Now this Doctor Albertson was saying, "Who recommended us, my dear?"

"Some bald guy at State Welfare," Fay said bitterly. "He wanted to know who the father was."

Ross nodded. Retaining Joe Vaught had been Markham's idea. Markham paid him a flat hundred for each girl he sent to Pineview.

"Naturally," he said, "the state has to determine paternity in order to assess the father for hospital expenses. Some girls don't wish their parents to know; they'd rather go away by themselves—"

"But it costs money, is that the idea?" Fay was contemptuous, now.

"Not much." His smile was a benediction. "Mrs. Rucci's a fine woman, and she doesn't ask questions. If there's a financial hardship she'll let you earn part of your keep by helping in the kitchen or laundry. Including the delivery fee, you shouldn't pay over—" he hesitated, while Fay stared at him, not breathing—"six hundred dollars. How does that sound?"

Hope died in her eyes. "Sounds fine, if you've got it. Sorry I've wasted your time, Doctor."

"Of course," he continued, not looking at her, "you wouldn't necessarily pay the six hundred."

"How—do you mean?"

"It's customary, Fay, for the adopting couple to pick up the tab in cases like this." A delicate pause. "Or had you planned on keeping the baby?"

It sank in slowly.

"No," she said. "No, I hadn't planned on keeping it." Then she was fighting to get the words out, hardly daring to hope. "But I don't want it to wind up in some home—"

"You'll meet the adopting parents yourself, I promise." Which was hardly true, but at this point they seldom cared. "Louise Rucci keeps in close touch with several adoption agencies." He smiled ruefully. "My time here is gratis. I classify Pineview the same as my social welfare work—"

Fay crumpled, then. The tears came in a scalding flood. She told him it had happened five months ago when she was a waitress in San Diego, how the father was married with three children, a wonderful man who loved her, but his wife refused to grant a divorce. After the baby she would go home to her folks in Phoenix and start a new life. The old, sordid story.

Louise, with adroit timing, came in and took Fay in tow. Thad went out into the hall. He walked slowly down the corridor. When Louise came in, five minutes later, he was staring out at the pines.

"You handled it nice," Louise said. "What's with the new girl upstairs?"

"She's under sedation." He did not turn his head. "Keep her door locked all afternoon."

Louise understood. "Did you want to look at the Knox girl? She had her first pains an hour ago."

"But she's not due for six weeks—"

"I promised her you'd look in, doc."

The Knox girl's room was at the end of the hall. She was a raddled blonde who was subject to crying spells. He gave her a cursory examination and told her she was just fine.

"I'll send Louise in with a codeine," he said, patting her hand. "All you need is a long nap—"

"No, Doctor." She stared listlessly at the ceiling. "It's gonna happen soon, real soon." She bit her lip and clutched at her abdomen. "Right here. It comes and goes so quick, like—"

"I'll be back by six," he said softly. "You haven't a thing to worry about."

"Promise, Doctor?" She clutched his hand like a drowning woman.

He promised before he left the room.

Louise was waiting for him at the end of the hall. "How is she?"

"No signs of dilation," he said, frowning. "Give her a codeine, keep her quiet. Did you check her history?"

"Nothing unusual," Louise shrugged. "She told me she almost fainted with abdominal pains when she was six weeks along. But that could have been the quinine she tried. Think we ought to send her to a public hospital?"

"I'll let you know tonight." He paused, recalling how the Knox girl had clutched at the upper right area of abdomen. An ectopic pregnancy? No, impossible. And yet—"I'd have her prepped, Louise. Just in case."

"We'll shave her right away." Then came Louise's insinuating chuckle. "See you tonight, doc."

Filth, he thought as he walked outside. Louise was a hateful, white-haired millstone which Markham had placed about his neck. But she was a reliable and competent woman. Markham had chosen her carefully, at a time when her career as a madam was being jeopardized by infrequent raids from the Los Angeles vice squad. Louise had one great talent. Whether a girl was whore or unwed mother, Louise could keep her in line.

Thad walked across the white gravel and stopped as he saw that Markham was not in the Lincoln. He walked around to the side of the house and swore.

There was a large kennel with a sliding mesh door. Markham had the door open, and was scratching the Doberman behind the ears. The Doberman was huge, black, magnificent. He grinned wetly up at Markham, red tongue lolling.

"When you can tear yourself away," Thad said acidly, "I've got a noon appointment."

The Doberman growled. Markham patted him and stood up, letting the door fall. "Nice pooch," he said. "So long, boy."

The Doberman woofed farewell as they got into the Lincoln. "Dogs like me." Markham smiled, punching the ignition. "It's a gift. How's Ann?"

Soft, casual, like inquiring about the weather. "Exhaustion," Ross said, rubbing his temples. "Possible shock. She'll sleep all afternoon."

They drove down the hill road in silence. Abruptly Markham said, "Tierney caused a ruckus last night at the Barrel."

"Go on!" Thad's cheek was twitching again.

"I called Garth an hour ago, told him what to do. Will you relax? It's being handled—"

"Like you handled Valdez?" Ross said through his teeth. "And Ann! What are you going to do about Ann?"

"Use Tierney to make a deal. You want the details?"

"No, I just want him taken care of. He's unpredictable, crazy! Why not call the police. An anonymous phone tip—"

"Sorry, Doctor. No fuzz."

"But he killed Valdez—"

"So what?" The gray lines deepened about Markham's mouth. "We're both carny, Tierney and me. We don't use fuzz to settle personal beefs. But aside from that, I don't want Valdez found."

"I'm pulling out," Ross whispered. "The Barrel closes down, you can have Pineview. Find yourself another doctor—"

"We've got seven collections coming up next month," Markham said inexorably. "At three grand a collection. Within a few months you can build that maternity clinic you're always yakking about! Now will you let me do the worrying? Will you?"

He went on pounding at Thad's defenses until they were well past Newport. Finally Thad wiped his forehead, said in a calmer tone, "You're sure you can handle Ann?"

"Positive. I'll be at the Barrel all afternoon. You'll be at the club?"

"Yes," Ross said. "I'll be at the club."

They reached Paloma Beach in silence. Markham dropped Thad off on a side street, three blocks from his home. Thad got out of the car without a word. Markham drove away frowning.

Inevitably, Thad would crack. It would not be pleasant. At times like this Markham felt like a chess master dealing with psychotic knights and pawns. He parked in the Barrel's asphalt lot, and got out of the Lincoln.

It was five minutes till noon when he walked into the casino. He noticed with satisfaction that half the tables were already occupied. It would be a good Saturday. He went into the coffee shop and ordered a club sandwich and a glass of milk. When he went back to his office he called Jerry, the head cashier. When Jerry came in with last night's receipt tally, Markham glanced at it and said, "Where's Garth?"

"He left half an hour ago, with Feeney. Said you'd know where they were going." Jerry was very sensitive to Markham's moods. "Anything wrong?"

"Everything's fine," Markham said. He felt a brief regret for Tierney.

Jerry nodded briskly and shut the door. Markham smiled at the tally sheet and yawned, leaning back in the leather chair. Within minutes he was asleep....

The interior of Thad's house was dark and quiet. He walked into the cool dimness of his study, and saw a note on his desk, written in Madge's angular scrawl, telling him she had taken the station wagon, she had gone shopping in Laguna, and would be home by nine. Damn her, he thought, she left me her convertible, and she knows how I hate convertibles.

He smiled sourly and went over to the sideboard. He mixed a double brandy and sipped it, thinking about the Knox girl. The smart thing was to have her removed to a hospital, it was best not to take chances with prematures. He finished the brandy and sat drumming on the desk with his fingertips. His mind was a feverish computer, adding up the blue-chip securities, the savings account.

He reached for the phone and dialed his stockbroker. Norm argued, after the fashion of stockbrokers. He pointed out several factors of long-term capital gains versus straight income tax. Finally Norm shrugged verbally and said of course, he'd sell immediately.

Thad hung up, moistening his lips. He dialed Holly's number.

"Holly, dear? It's Thad."

"Oh, hello, Daddy." She was cool, distant.

"How would you like to go to Paris? Say, next weekend?" He waited, while his smile slowly congealed.

"But I thought—"

He was silent, listening.

"You and me," he said quickly. "A long vacation, six months at least." A pause. "*By yourself?* No, absolutely not. As your father, I forbid it—"

Shock gave way to fury. "Holly, you're lying to me! It's that—Tierney isn't it? He's back in town, and you're seeing him!"

Another pause, while the veins almost burst in his forehead. "You promised," he said wildly. "You promised that was all over with. He's filth! All right," he said, choking. "No, I won't get excited."

He hung up feeling shriveled and old.

Before leaving the house, Thad made one final phone call.

He took out his handkerchief and placed it over the mouthpiece while he dialed. "Hello," he said into the handkerchief. "Police headquarters?"

He paused, savoring it.

"I wish to report a murder. A man named Valdez—"

CHAPTER 11

It was almost ten-thirty when Tierney parked the Olds in an alley near the boardwalk. His shoulder was beginning to stiffen and throb, but the bleeding had finally stopped.

Getting to Pop Stroot's would be a problem. Pop's boardwalk concession was only two blocks away, but in the shape he was in it might just as well be two miles. While Tierney was considering the situation objectively, his head slumped against the wheel and the horn blare shocked him rudely awake.

He yawned.

Then he got out of the Olds and locked the car doors. He took off his coat and carefully folded it over his shoulder. Not bad, he decided. The trick is to keep your shoulder hunched so they don't see the left side of your shirt.

He walked down the alley, feeling lightheaded and giddy. At the alley corner he stood staring across the street at the huge concrete arch over the boardwalk steps, with the neons sparkling *Fun Zone*.

A couple walked by holding hands. The girl was blonde, and moved with a self-conscious hip strut in her tight red bathing suit. The boy wore yellow trunks and a glittering satin jacket with *Rogues* emblazoned across the back in purple script. He held the blonde's arm with a fierce possessiveness, and glared at Tierney as they walked past.

Tierney looked away, down the alley. A hot-rod artist, he thought. A cool stud out with his chick for some sunburn. Now they're crossing the street at the intersection. The stud's staring back at you. He sees the blood on your shirt.

Tierney turned, keeping his left side toward the alley. When he looked again, the couple had vanished under the concrete arch. He exhaled sharply, then jaywalked across the street, ignoring the outraged horn squalls. From the top of the steps he could see the boardwalk, stretching two hundred yards toward the pier. The strand was dotted with bathers, and the asphalt parking lot was filled with parked cars.

He seemed to float down the shallow steps toward the sand. You're doing fine, he told himself. Just one more block and you're there. Don't look at anybody. Look preoccupied and tired, it's a hot day and you're carrying your coat. Hug the left side of the boardwalk, look straight ahead. He passed a shooting gallery, a hot-dog stand.

Then he was at Pop Stroot's.

It was a dusty little shop sandwiched between the hall of mirrors and Madame Zarak's palmistry arcade. The sign on the door said, *Magic Tricks, Novelties. Amaze Your Friends!*

He walked inside.

Pop was behind the glass counter, giving a fat customer his usual melodramatic spiel. He gave Tierney one raking glance, then redoubled his efforts on the customer.

"Only three ninety-five." Pop's voice was molten honey. "It's an auto bomb to end all auto bombs. It whistles and smokes and explodes *twice*, get it? Really kills them. Full satisfaction guaranteed or money back, friend."

"I don't know," the fat man said. "That's pretty steep for what I got in mind." He brightened. "Lemmie see that one there. No, the one marked four bits."

"We're out of stock on those," Pop said suavely. "Can I order one for you?"

The fat man said he'd think about it. Tierney leaned dizzily against the wall. His shoulder was bleeding again. Pop darted another glance at him and lowered his voice to a confidential whisper.

"Look at this one," he told the fat man. "Only one sevenny-five, and you can reload it over and over again."

The fat man leaned over the counter. "How does it work?"

"You slip the load in here and adjust the lever. Then drop it, see?"

There was a small explosion, a puff of black smoke. The fat man jerked back, rubbing his eyes. "What the hell!"

"Only one sevenny-five," Pop beamed.

The fat man left in a huff. He did not even glance at Tierney as he slammed the door.

Pop was around the counter like a lean shaggy terrier. "Easy, Cliffie boy," he said. "Easy does it. Back this way."

He led Tierney to the rear of the shop and propped him on a chair. "Incidentally, you owe me three ninety-five. I had him hooked when you come in."

Tierney grinned feebly. "Look at the shoulder, Pops. Give me an estimate."

He leaned back and Pop ripped his shirt open. "Very clean," Pop said, inspecting the wound. "It went right on through."

"Fix me up, Pop. I got a long way to travel."

Pop peered closely at him, and Tierney caught a whiff of port. "How long you been without sleep, Cliffie?"

"Fix me up," Tierney said.

Pop sighed. Tierney's blue eyes were bloodshot and his blond hair was mussed. His face was the color of salt, and he was obviously a stretcher case. But there was no point in arguing.

"Back to the donniker," Pop said. "Come on."

Tierney followed him to the bathroom and docilely submitted to the warm water, the liquid fire of iodine. Pop's fingers were surprisingly gentle as he cut lengths of surgical tape and bandaged the wound.

"You'll be fine," Pop said. "Providing you can turn invisible for the next few years."

"How do you mean?"

But Tierney knew the answer.

"You're incendiary, man. The word came out this morning. Tom wants you, bad." His grin flickered. "You know what it means to do Tom a favor in this town?"

Tierney knew. He fumbled in his pocket and held out a fistful of bills. "No favors, Pop. Enough?"

Pop leafed through the money and bit his lip. In that moment Tierney could read the old man clearly. Pop was thinking about Markham, and what would happen if Markham discovered Pop had helped him.

Then Pop folded the bills neatly, held them between thumb and forefinger. He made a solemn pass and the money vanished. "Enough, Cliff," and his voice was strictly clinical, now. Tierney was just another customer. "What else do you want?"

"A clean shirt. Thirty-four sleeve, sixteen neck."

"What else?"

"A benny, or a double maltadrene. Something to keep me awake."

Pop frowned and reached into the bathroom cupboard. "This is better, man. Utterly whaling."

A bottle of white port.

Tierney said no thanks, and watched Pop take a long swallow, his Adam's apple jerking convulsively. He felt shame and pity for Pop. A year ago the old man had been a very competent professional. Markham often retained him on a free-lance basis. Then Pop had gone to the hospital, where they had found a malignancy and removed half his stomach. They gave him two years.

Pop subsequently discovered that port was an excellent anodyne for the pain that racked him. Unfortunately, five bottles a day does not make for professional dependability. Six months ago Pop had visited the Pink Barrel, and Markham had thrown him out.

"How's the stomach?" Tierney asked tactfully.

"Bad," Pop said sadly. "The last operation was four months ago." He hiccuped, then grinned. "But I'm still swinging high, man. So far."

The front door opened and Pop said, "Sit tight. Be right back."

Tierney was alone in the bathroom. He leaned against the basin and took out a cigarette. Then he opened the bathroom door an inch, and listened.

"Hi, Ruthie," Pop wheezed. "How's tricks?"

"Lousy." The girl's voice was a plaintive whine. "Pop, I'm flat. I need it on credit."

Pop chuckled. "That's what I like about you, honey. Always making with the yaks. Always a sense of humor."

"I'm hurting, Pop. Please—"

"Honey, there's a panic on." Pop's voice was soft regretful. "My source is dried up. Maybe next week—"

"*Please*, Pop."

"You got bread, girl?"

"I need a gram," she said. "I got to have a gram."

"I can maybe let you have two caps. For bread, honey."

They argued while Tierney listened, unaware that his mouth was tightening. He tried to analyze the sudden dislike he felt for Pop, and felt confused. Six months ago he would have paid no attention. He had seen horse bought, sold, and used. They had to have it, and if you didn't deliver, someone else would. He believed in the simple economics of supply and demand; it was the code by which he had always lived.

But at the moment he disliked Pop Stroot intensely. He tried to tell himself it was rube thinking, but that didn't help. He took a long bitter drag from his cigarette and ground it out on the floor.

Out in front Ruthie and Pop completed negotiations. Ruthie finally scored for a gram and screamed at the price. When the door slammed Pop came back and said, "Feeling better?"

Tierney closed his eyes, considering. He would have liked very much to lie down on the floor and sleep for a month, but there was a job that had to be done first, although at the moment he could not remember precisely what the job was. But if he stayed awake, it would come to him.

"Pop, do you remember Zoe Miller?"

The old man looked blank. Then he brightened. "Peroxide-type blonde? Used to work at the Barrel a coupla years back?"

Tierney nodded.

"A small habit," Pop said dimly. "She used to stop by once in awhile. They come and they go. Sure you don't wanta sleep a while?"

Tierney said he was sure, and Pop shrugged. He left the bathroom and returned with a glass of water. "Here."

Tierney blinked at the small red pill. "This a benny?"

"Better. I tried one and couldn't sleep for a week."

Tierney swallowed the pill.

"Be back in five minutes with your shirt," Pop said.

The front door slammed and it was very quiet in the shop. Tierney stood braced against the basin, feeling the numbness creep from his shoulder down to his belly.

Pop had been too eager to help him.

A dying hustler is a pitiful, broken-toothed old wolf, craving the security of the pack. The one thing Pop dearly wanted was the sense of belonging to a strong organization, of having a man like Markham owe him a favor.

Suddenly the room dissolved into gray mist.

The floor wavered up gently, and Tierney was on hands and knees, shaking his head. He clawed at the washbasin. His body weighed a ton. His breath was a sharp hiss in the silence as he drew himself level with the basin. He grabbed at the cake of soap and forced it into his mouth, chewing frantically, swallowing.

He chased the soap with warm water.

Then he vomited.

The hazy outlines of the room cleared. Tierney staggered out toward the glass showcase as Pop came in the front door.

"You're a sick man," Pop said. "Better lie down for a while—"

"The shirt." Tierney's lips were numb. "Where's the shirt?"

Pop said nothing, just looked compassionate. When Tierney kept coming he tried to grab him. Tierney swung his right arm. It felt weightless, like a huge feather. But Pop skittered along the glass counter and hit the floor. Tierney staggered out to the boardwalk.

His body was a lurching automaton, without sensation. Yet his brain was keen as winter starlight.

Pop fed you a goofball, he thought. A special, quick-acting goofball. It took him maybe five minutes to phone the Barrel. Add another seven or eight minutes for Garth or Markham to get here. Which gives you maybe two minutes to hide. You can't possibly make it back to the Olds. They're probably here right now.

Plan, he thought desperately. You got to have a plan.

He lurched around Madam Zarak's palmistry arcade toward the beach strand. The ocean shimmered a hundred yards away. Over to his left the pier was a shifting black outline that jutted far out into the surf. Beyond it was the parking lot where the boardwalk ended. Tierney shambled along the rear of the concessions toward the pier. Twice he stumbled and fell.

The second time he lay in the sand. No one noticed him. He was just another sunbather with no shirt on. The shoulder bandage was caked with sand. After a time he began to crawl on hands and knees.

At the end of the boardwalk was a hot-dog stand. In the rear was a pay telephone booth. Tierney slumped inside the booth, fumbling in his pocket for change. He dialed with wooden fingers.

"Hello." Holly's voice was deliciously fogged with sleep.

He tried to speak. Nausea came in a black wave and he doubled over, retching.

"Hello? Is anybody there?"

"Yes," he said after an interminable time. "I'm here."

"Cliff, what is it? What's the matter?"

"Holly," he said, choking.

"Cliff, are you drunk? Answer me!"

"Sick," he said. "Goofed, and high. I need you—"

"Say that again," she said. "I want to hear that again."

"I need y—"

He clenched his jaw tight against the stomach cramps.

"*Cliff* "

"I wan' you to drive to the Paloma Beach boar'-walk," he mumbled. "The big parking lot, by the pier. Wait there for me, you got that? Wait for me."

"Yes, darling. Oh, yes. The parking lot by the pier."

He squinted at the parking lot. "The one with the palms," he said.

"I understand, darling. Are you hurt?"

The receiver clattered against the side of the booth. He got up blindly and stumbled toward the pier.

By now, certainly, they had reached Pop Stroot's. They would be moving efficiently down the boardwalk, combing the sidewalk concessions, very precise and methodical. Feeney, he decided. Possibly Garth. Garth would be very eager to find him.

He started toward the pier. His teeth were chattering. Once a redhead in a black bathing suit stared, and decided he was drunk.

Then he was under the pier, leaning against the pilings. It was dark and cool, an excellent vantage point to see if he were being followed.

He squinted from behind a piling and saw two distant figures strolling down the boardwalk. Garth and Feeney. They moved slowly, patiently checking each concession. They paused at the shooting gallery. Now they cut across the sand toward the pier.

Tierney dropped flat in the wet sand. He wriggled farther under the pier where the pilings were shored with granite boulders. He smelled kelp and rotting fish. The tide was coming in.

It's nice here, he thought drowsily. So very nice. But you mustn't sleep. Without conscious volition his hand groped in the damp sand. It found a barnacle shell and squeezed. He felt the pain and jerked erect, listening to the slap of waves against the pilings.

Then he heard the voices, ten feet away.

"I tell you I saw him," Feeney insisted. "He cut for the pier."

"Sure you saw him," agreed Garth. "He's a seagull with white wings. He flew right on over the pier and out to sea."

"We wasted time checking those concessions," Feeney said regretfully. "He cut across the parking lot. Come on."

"First let's check the pier."

"What's to check? I see three fishermen up there. You see anybody else? Maybe he's hiding under the water, is that the idea?"

"Stop bugging me," said Feeney. "He's right around here someplace. Maybe under the pier—"

"I said we'll check out the lot." Garth's tone was soft.

Feeney grunted, and the voices faded. Tierney lay with his face buried in damp sand. Without transition he was asleep. When the first wavelet licked at his shoes he did not feel it. The second wave drenched him, and he came awake gasping.

It's a trick, he thought. They're waiting on top of the pier for you to come out. Of course you've got a choice. You can drown. He peered at the distant parking lot. The sand undulated with heat waves, and the palms were green explosions over the asphalt. He thought he saw a small pink dot—Holly's Porsche. He blinked, and the dot vanished in a rainbow blur.

Well, he thought. Let's see what happens.

Getting up, he banged his face against a piling. There was no sensation whatever. He started across the sand.

It was a timeless journey. There were the white gulls swooping overhead, and the blue ocean in back of him, and the parking lot shimmering like a black mirror in the noonday heat.

This, he decided, is some kind of dirty trick. You've blundered into the hall of mirrors by mistake, and they keep shifting the sand like an escalator. Or maybe, he thought, it's the Sahara Desert, that's why nobody looks at you. Keep those legs moving. If you fall down again you won't get up.

But there that pink Porsche, sparkling in the sun. Let's hope it isn't a mirage.

Then there was no more sand, he was walking on hard asphalt. He was moving toward the Porsche. It expanded, grew real. He could see Holly, jumping out and opening the side door for him. The sun struck sparks from her red-gold hair, and she was crying.

Now there, he thought judiciously, is a lovely girl. A bit wild, but dependable. She's right there when you need her.

"Here, Cliff," Holly whispered. "Let me help you, darling. Oh God, look at your shoulder."

She was helping him into the front seat. Then he was leaning back, eyes closed. "Tired," he mumbled. "So tired."

"Don't talk," Holly said. "Everything's all right now, Cliff. Just don't talk, darling."

The Porsche slanted up the steep grade, then swirled out into the highway traffic. Holly drove fast, and they turned on all the green lights for her, all the way to Newport.

When they whipped into her apartment driveway, she had to shake him viciously before he came awake. Even then it was a project, getting him up the steps to her doorway.

But she got him inside and steered him to the bedroom. He collapsed on the silken coverlet, a straw man. The last thing he heard before the darkness closed in was the phone ringing.

CHAPTER 12

Holly woke him at two-thirty.

For two hours she had worked feverishly on the cube of pink marble, driving off the outer layers with adze and chisel. At first she had seen the madonna clearly imprisoned within the stone. Now she frowned and bit her lip.

She picked up her preliminary charcoal sketch, studying it. Abruptly she crumpled the paper into a ball and resketched the madonna in bold black strokes. Her face felt flushed, hot.

Damn him, she thought, glancing at the bedroom door. It's happening again. You went to a great deal of trouble in selecting this stone. A warm, pure cube that you couldn't possibly befoul.

But you're befouling it now. You're making a mockery of something that could be clean and beautiful. You'll turn it into a subphallic horror like that terra cotta glaze last week, or the Swedish granite bust in the corner.

But there's one way to cure this, she thought. A quick, effective way. You've tried it before, and it works every time. Holly threw down her adze and went into the bedroom.

Tierney's breathing was a sharp rasp in the silence. He lay on his back, arms outstretched. There was a reddish clot of dried blood on his shoulder where she had changed the bandage. Looking at him, she felt a warm burst of tenderness. The poor, hurt darling, she thought. He's in trouble with Tom, and that's the most terrible kind of trouble there is. Look at him. He needs sleep wretchedly, you can tell by the way he's breathing.

Holly took a long shuddering breath as she reached for the glass of water on the nightstand. Deliberately, she poured the water in his face. He awoke, gagging. She shook him and he groaned.

"Please," he muttered. "No drowning."

"Wake up!" she commanded. "Cliff, look at me."

He saw her as a distorted pale shadow, pulling the green dress over her head, throwing the covers back and slipping lithely in beside him. Her body was a warm shock, and at first it was a dream, languid and slow.

Then it was pain, exploding in a twisting storm of violence.

Afterward, she dressed and went into the kitchen. Tierney lay spent, nerve-shattered. He was almost asleep when Holly returned with a pot of coffee.

"Drink it, darling." Her voice was calm.

He drank a cup, choking. She gave him a lighted cigarette. "What time is it?" he husked.

"Almost three. Go back to sleep, my dear."

He shook his head doggedly, trying to sit up. His muscles were quivering in uncontrollable spasms. He reached for the coffee and poured another cup, scalding his hand in the process.

Holly was no longer in the bedroom. From her studio, he heard the ring of steel on stone.

Tierney finished the pot of coffee and smoked another cigarette. He got to his feet and stumbled into the bathroom. He turned on the cold water in the shower.

In her studio, Holly was using the adze with swift sure slashes. Her green eyes were luminous, face tranquil. Within the stone the outline of the madonna was a clear silhouette of light. Tierney was forgotten. He was an instrument she had used to cleanse herself, nothing more.

Smiling, she remembered her Laguna exhibition, a year ago. Van Meter himself had seen her work—Van Meter, the stooped, bearded giant who was a legend in his own time. He had smiled sadly at her and shaken his head.

"*Ach*, that it should be given to a girl. A great gift for a naughty child."

But he had liked one of her figurines. A child, done in cold green marble. "You must burn out the nastiness," he told her brutally. "Go to Paris, Rome. Work, create, purge yourself. Work and learn."

For months afterwards, she was a dedicated woman. She tried clay, stone, bronze. Her conceptions were brilliant. But the finished statue would show a sly distortion, verging on the obscene.

Her studio was a fusillade of color. The ceiling was ice-green, the floor pink terrazzo. Charcoal sketches lined the ebony wall shelves. The figurines were veined marble, bronze, granite. All showed an elemental power—until you observed them closely.

But this madonna would be serene. Delicately, she rived the stone away—and stood frozen, staring in horror at the dark jagged splotch on the madonna's flank. She chipped again. The splotch widened.

From the bathroom, Tierney heard her cry out.

By the time he had wrapped a towel about him and reached the studio, Holly was smashing the statue into pink shards of rubble. Her lips were drawn back from her teeth and her eyes were wild. Tierney reached her in three quick strides, grabbing her shoulders. She tried to bite him, then burst into tears.

He held her close, patting her shoulder while she sobbed heartbrokenly about the vein of rottenness through the heart, how she was predestined to failure, and damned.

"Easy," he murmured. "All that fuss over a hunk of stone?"

"You'd never understand." She tried to smile through her tears. "I'm unclean, Cliff. Everything I touch turns rotten. But it's all right, darling. Very soon—we're going to Paris."

"We?" She felt him stiffen.

"Daddy called, right around noon. He's finally broken down, Cliff. Only he plans on going to Paris with me." Unexpectedly, she giggled. "Want to know what I told him?"

Tierney went over to the chesterfield and sat. "I'm afraid to ask," he said tiredly.

"I told him you were here, in my bedroom. Oh, he didn't believe me, but the idea made him furious. Ultimately, he'll realize I'm no longer a child, and let me go alone."

Tierney stared at her. "But you're taking me along, is that the idea?"

"Yes, darling. I'm taking you along."

"You don't love me, Holly."

"I need you," she said.

"For how long?" he asked with the old bitterness. "Two, three months?"

"Perhaps less." She was gazing reflectively at the broken madonna. "Until I find myself. But by then it won't matter, can you understand?"

He understood very well. And he could see it happening, Holly and himself in Rome, in Antibes, his sweet inexorable destruction.

"Yes," Holly said, reading him. "That's the way it's going to be, darling. Because it's what we both want. Isn't it?"

She was moving toward him with unbearable slowness, and he could see how her green knit dress stretched to the bursting point over her deep breasts, how her face seemed to expand as she bent over him.

Then she was on his lap, her hands snaking around his neck, lips hot and devouring.

She's being perfectly logical, the hustler core of him said. You two deserve each other. And she'll be faithful to you, after her fashion, for a little while.

Until she discovers she's searching for something no man can give her. Who cares how long it lasts, or what comes afterwards? You've got to have this woman, there's nobody else, ever.

Not even Ann?

No, especially not Ann. She's dedicated, remember? She's the respectable white house with the steady paycheck and the night feedings and the PTA meetings. She's the antithesis to everything that's Cliff Tierney, and the final proof is that she never trusted you.

Wait, there's something else. Something about a dead man lying in an eucalyptus grove. You never did finish burying him, did you?

"Cliff," Holly whispered. She was moving, her fingers unknotting the towel from his hips.

He moved suddenly. Holly sprawled on the floor, bright hair in tangled disarray. He strode past her into the kitchen. The wall clock said five after three. Holly was furious until she saw how his face was pinched and drawn.

"What is it, darling? Tell me!"

"I've got to go out for a while," he said. "I'll be back tonight."

She moistened her lips. "Tom?"

"Tom."

"You can't fight him! Please, don't try—"

"I've got to." His voice made her shiver. "There's a stakeout at my hotel; I need some clothes. Will you go out and get me a shirt and a pair of slacks?"

She began to laugh, helplessly. Then the laughter stopped and she went into the bedroom. She came out in five minutes wearing a different dress, her entire attitude businesslike. He gave her his shirt and slacks size and said, "How long?"

"Half an hour; there's a men's shop down the street." She stood at the front door. "You're—going to Paris with me?"

"Yes," he said. "I'm going to Paris with you."

The front door closed, and he went into the kitchen, smiling and shaking his head. She was much woman. She hadn't asked any questions. He wondered how Ann would react in a similar situation, and his smile vanished.

In the freezer he found steak, and fried it over the electric range. He made another pot of coffee, and drank three cups, black and corrosively strong. Then it was three-twenty, and he sat in the kitchen, chain-smoking. His body was tired, but his brain at last was clear.

He went over to the dinette phone and picked up the receiver. He dialed Markham's private desk number, which could not be found in any telephone book. Tom answered on the second ring.

"Hello?"

"Tierney."

"Well," Tom said gently, "how's the boy?"

"How's Ann?"

For a moment Tom said nothing, and Tierney felt a painful throbbing in his temples.

"She's not doing too well," Markham said. "But that really can't be helped, can it? She's stubborn—"

"I went to see the Lacklands this morning, in Santa Ana." Tierney was gripping the receiver hard enough to break it. "They told me the whole story, Tom. You're through."

"I don't get it," Markham said in a different voice. "Suppose you lay it out for me."

"First you sell them the baby. Then you milk them for all the traffic will stand. Even if they prove the real mother unfit, she can insist on the baby's being taken away from them and placed in some state home. She can do that any time during the first year, before the adopting parents get their final papers." He was silent, listening to Markham's soft laughter over the wire. And the professional part of him said, "Now you talk. Tell me what I missed."

"That's better," Tom said. "Sure I'll tell you what you missed. One, Zoe delivered the baby to the Lacklands of her own free will. Two, the Lacklands don't even know I exist. Three, Eddie Valdez tagged them for three grand a few months back, but where's Eddie now? Where's your proof, Cliff?"

Tierney opened his mouth, but no words came out. Finally he said, "Garth told me he planted the caps in Zoe's car."

"So what?" Markham sounded bored. "Did you know she was a user? Did you know she was on probation when they picked her up, that they proved addiction? Hell, Cliff, I only did the fuzz a favor by turning her in."

"I'm going to kill you, Tom."

"No, you won't. For Ann you'll make a deal."

"I'm listening." Suddenly the steak and coffee roiled in his stomach, he wanted to throw up.

"I want those photostats. You've probably guessed what they are by now."

"Names," Tierney said dully. "Payoffs, actual amounts. Couples that are buying babies on the installment plan."

"Brilliant, Cliff. I want you to come over to the Barrel. You can make Ann talk. Understand?"

"I thought you said she was a fanatic."

"She also loves you. See the possibilities?"

Yes, he thought. I see all kinds of possibilities. You're really a professional, Tom. A true-blue competent professional. He hedged, saying, "Afterwards, what happens to her?"

"Now, Cliff, let's not go into that." Tom sounded regretful. "After all, she can't be trusted. Besides, I thought you had it for Holly. What's Ann got that you want?"

"Nothing," he said. "Nothing at all. But let's not be messy. If she comes up missing you'll have trouble with Smith."

"Witt Smith?" Tom chuckled. "Not hardly. He's got rabbit blood."

"Remember when you broke him, two years ago? He's never forgotten, and he hates your guts for it." Tierney spoke in a calm, controlled voice, while the sweat ran down his chin. "Ann's trying to protect Smith. She stole those records from Thad's office last month, turned them over to Smith to run a newspaper editorial. Instead Smith decided to bleed you—"

"You just might have something there." Markham thought about it. "It fits, after a fashion. But Smith I can handle—"

"Let me handle it. Tom, I can bring you those records inside of two hours."

"You can?"

"In return I want Ann, safe and unharmed. Deal?"

"Deal. You've got until five-thirty. Cliff, if this is a stall—"

"It's not. But even if it is, you've got Ann, haven't you?"

"That's right," Markham said. "I've got Ann. Incidentally, I wish you hadn't gotten emotional at the Barrel last night. You're lucky Garth didn't find you on the board-walk."

"Yes," Tierney said. "I'm a very lucky guy."

"Don't press your luck," Tom warned him. "See you in two hours."

Tierney hung up, wiping his face. You've stalled him, he thought tiredly; you've bought Ann's safety for two hours. But supposing you guessed wrong about Witt Smith, or worse still, suppose you can't find him? But you've got to find him.

He dialed Smith's home phone, and hung up on the fourteenth ring. He tried the Laguna newspaper office and the girl who answered informed him Mr. Smith had worked late last night, he would be in around five.

He hung up and went into the living room. He was sitting on the chesterfield when Holly came in loaded down with parcels, and kissed him behind the ear.

"Is it bad trouble?" she asked tremulously as he tried on the slacks. "With Tom, I mean?"

"We made a deal," he said bleakly. "I'm doing a very routine job for him."

"Thank God," she whispered. "Promise you'll be careful?"

He nodded abstractly, buttoning the new slacks. They were custom flannel, a perfect fit. The shirt was tailored raw silk, the jacket soft luxurious suede. He went into the bedroom and found his shoes. His old slacks were a ruin, sandy and torn. His wallet was empty. He had given Pop Stroot his last dollar.

"Can you lend me twenty, Holly?"

She flashed a gamin grin and opened her purse, handing him two tens. She almost made a remark about kept men, but caught herself in time.

"I'll mix the drinks," she said, going into the dinette. Tierney was on the point of telling her not to bother when it occurred to him that he needed to ask her a few questions. He went into the living room and was studying the warped figurines on the mantel when she came in with his highball.

"That sandstone piece on the end, Cliff. Like it?"

He sipped his drink, frowning at the figurine. "Hideous."

"It's Daddy," she said in a frozen voice. "He gets his jollies out of having me sculpt him. Especially when he's drunk—"

"Why do you hate him, Holly?"

Her throat worked convulsively. She sat on the chesterfield, looking down at her glass.

"I was fourteen, darling. It was my first date. After the movie, the boy walked me home. A nice boy, shy and uncomplicated. He kissed me good night on the front porch." Her eyes slitted in recollection. "Then the door flew open. Sometimes I still dream about it, Daddy standing tall in the doorway with that animal look on his face. I thought he was going to kill us both. The boy ran. Daddy took me inside and whaled me with his belt. It wasn't the beating, it was the way he talked. I was filth—"

She picked up her drink and finished it, her eyes closed. "It was my last date for three years. Thad sent me to a strict private school in Carmel. When I was home on vacations I'd notice a strangeness about him. I'd catch him glancing at my legs across the room. When I was nineteen I met Gideon. I met him at the Laguna Art festival. He was a tall blond god who could paint like Michelangelo. We fell in love—" Her face crimsoned. "I was pregnant, but it didn't matter. We were going to elope. We had it all planned. But somehow, Daddy found out. The next thing I heard, Gideon was in the hospital. Two men had crippled him in an alley. Daddy sent me to a private sanitarium for two months. To this day he swears I had a miscarriage there." She exhaled softly. "But it wasn't a miscarriage, Cliff. Let's not go into that."

Tierney felt pity for her, and a sharp disappointment. He had hoped she could give him some lead, something tangible to use on Thad Ross. He asked, "How did you first find out about Thad's connection with

Markham?"

"That time in the sanitarium," she said simply. "I saw Markham. Daddy was furious because he had come there. I overheard them talking about the Pink Barrel, and how Tom wanted Daddy to make sure it stayed open."

"Was there anything else? Think hard, Holly."

"N-no. Cliff, why are you looking at me like that?"

"Where was the sanitarium located?"

"Somewhere in Irvine Hills. Pineview, I think they called it. Why?"

"Your father's tied in with Tom Markham much deeper than the Pink Barrel," he said, watching her flinch. "A cute, profitable operation. Black-market babies."

After the first reaction, Holly's smile grew crooked and hard. "Am I supposed to be surprised? Now tell me you're involved; that's all I need."

He saw that her smile was a prelude to tears, and went over and took her in his arms. "No, I'm not involved. Wait up for me tonight?"

"Of course." He felt her body quiver in relief. "On one condition."

"What's that?"

"Save your strength, darling." This time her smile made him dizzy.

She did not kiss him good-by. She stood at the doorway, watching him walk down the block toward the intersection. He flagged a passing cab, and told the driver to take him to the Paloma Beach boardwalk. At this point he badly needed a car, and Garth's Olds should still be parked in that back alley....

Holly closed the door and went back to her studio, her shoulders drooping like an old woman's. She was gazing at the smashed madonna when she heard the door chimes. She hurried back to the front door, thinking Cliff had returned.

Instead, it was Thad Ross. He came in quickly, slamming the door behind him.

She saw that he was very drunk. His face was the color of old ivory, and his eyes held a terrifying emptiness. Before she could speak, his backhanded slap knocked her sprawling.

CHAPTER 13

It was midafternoon when Joe Lennox parked the squad car in his driveway. For a moment he sat with a bemused smile, savoring the past two hours. He got out of the car and walked across the parched Bermuda lawn, noting absently that, he would have a renovating job next February. Normally, this thought would have bothered him. But he grinned as he opened the front door.

From the kitchen he heard the clatter of pans, and Gail calling, "Joe?"

"Uh-huh. Lunch ready?"

And not hearing her reply, went into the hallway and picked up the phone. He dialed the Dunes hotel and told the desk clerk, "This is Lieutenant Lennox. Room two-twelve, please. One long ring, one short."

The switchboard crackled and Tate's voice said cautiously, "Hello?"

"Lennox. How'd you make out?"

"We found a thirty-two slug embedded in the wall plaster," Tate said. "Cordite traces on the pillow, fresh bloodstains on the mattress. Did you find him?"

"Smack in the eucalyptus grove. One bullet through the back of his head. The M.E. fixes time of death at midnight, give or take an hour."

"Are you at the station now?"

"No, I'm home." Lennox hesitated. "I haven't eaten yet, Sergeant. Suppose I relieve you around four."

"Fine. We got a statement from the night clerk, such as it is. He recalls Tierney coming in around midnight, but doesn't recall him leaving."

"It's enough," Lennox said. "We called in the report from Vardonville; there's a general fugitive warrant out for Tierney right now."

"You know," Tate said, "I've got an idea about that phone tip." Tate had made sergeant last month and was still eager.

"A rival syndicate, maybe?" Lennox grinned at the phone. "Gang killing?"

"It figures." Sarcasm was wasted on Tate. "After all, Valdez worked at the Pink Barrel. Wouldn't you say it figures?"

"I smell lunch burning." Lennox wrinkled his nostrils. "See you at four, Sergeant."

He hung up and went into the kitchen, where Gail was busy over the steaming skillet. Her face was flushed and her blonde hair damp with perspiration, but he thought she had never looked more desirable. He caught her in a bear hug and she squealed.

"Joe, it's burning! Hand me that platter on the drain."

He got the platter. "Swiss steak," he said, beaming. Usually he hated swiss steak. Then he saw Gail had been crying.

"Hey, what is it, baby?"

"It's Fran." She dished up the steak grimly. "She's gone back to Roger."

Lennox blinked. He went into the dinette and sat at the table. "When did all this happen?"

"At noon. I wouldn't even let him in the house, but he insisted on seeing her. Tears and reconciliation and promises. He swears he's got a good aircraft job in San Diego, that he hasn't gambled in three months."

"Well," Lennox said uncomfortably, "they've got to make their own way."

Gail came in with the platter. "But she'll come back inside of a month, you know she will!"

Her lip was trembling, and he knew what was coming next. A ten-minute tirade on what a slob her son-in-law was, how Roger was a no-good lush who gambled away each paycheck. Lennox chewed his steak without tasting it, and finally said, "If she's not back by spring, what say we sell the house? Get us a single apartment on the beach front."

Gail said she wouldn't hear of it, and Lennox sighed, thinking of the lawn renovation next spring, and how the outside of the house needed a fresh coat of paint, and how much he detested painting.

Wisely, he changed the subject. "Remember that Tierney citizen? The one I almost gagged this morning?" Gail sipped her coffee. "What about him?"

"He killed a man last night. A local hood named Valdez."

"Oh." Gail set down her cup. "Have they got him yet?"

"Not yet. And I hope they don't for a few hours."

"I don't understand, Joe."

"I'm going to try something," he said. "A squeeze play. I'll tell you about it tonight."

In that moment, Gail realized something. Her husband never talked about a case. When he even mentioned one, it implied a great deal. Looking closely, Gail saw something in Joe's face she had seen only twice in their twenty-four years of marriage. A stranger sat opposite her, wearing Joe's Irish face. A bleak stranger, with a hard, wet sheen to his eyes that frightened her.

"The Lennings asked us for bridge tonight," she said nervously. "I'll tell them you're working. Shall I wait up, Joe?"

"I'll call you tonight," he said, giving her a perfunctory peck on the cheek. She watched him walk down the drive with that old cocky stride and get into the squad car. In that past year, she could not remember his walking like that. He had walked tiredly, and his face was old. Their daughter and her two children in this house had not helped matters. Gail had a leaping premonition of disaster as she gathered up the dishes. Then she thought fretfully of Fran, and how long it would be before her daughter left Roger and came home for good.

Lennox parked in back of the Pink Barrel shortly after four. He went in through the side arches, firmly adjusting his hat. The casino was a quiet surf of sound. The cashiers were busy in their glass cages and house men marked game openings on a giant blackboard. Unnoticed, Lennox walked along the roped aisle toward Markham's office. When he was three feet from the door a sallow, blue-suited man materialized at his elbow. "Can I help you, sir?"

"Is Markham in?"

"He's in conference," the sallow man said earnestly. "Hey, you can't—"

This last in a snarl as the stocky plainclothesman shouldered him aside and opened the door. He made the mistake of grabbing Lennox's collar. Almost casually, Lennox elbowed him in the plexus.

Markham frowned at them from behind the refectory desk.

"It's all right, Wilbur," he said. "Shut the door, please."

Wilbur had sagged against the door jamb, his face gray. He straightened with an effort and closed the door, not looking at Lennox.

"I'm honored," Markham said with soft mockery. "You're grinning at me, Joe. Obviously the jig is up. You have just picked up some poor hophead, who under the stimulus of a rubber sap has admitted that I'm the West Coast overlord for prostitution and gambling."

Lennox chuckled and sat. "Keep talking, Tom. It sounds so good when you stop."

"I've stopped," Markham said coldly. "These visits of yours are getting rather monotonous, Joe."

"Does Eddie Valdez work for you?"

"Valdez?" Markham looked distant. "He used to be one of my house men. But a while back I found he had a prison record and had to terminate him. This is a respectable place, Joe. We can't afford adverse publicity."

"How about Tierney? You fired him too, I suppose."

"No, Tierney quit, three months ago. Why?"

Lennox just waited, cop fashion. Markham was toying with a pencil. The tension built like a soundless scream.

"Look, Joe, I'm a very busy man—"

"You won't be, come Monday. You'll have nothing but time. You're finally closing down, Tom."

Markham waited.

"An hour from now," Lennox said, watching him. "I'm feeding a statement to the Southland Press. 'Gang Killing. In Paloma Beach.' How does it sound?"

"I'm frightened," the little man murmured. "I'll make a full confession now, Officer."

"Last night," Lennox said, "I see this Tierney getting clobbered in an alley. I tell him to vag out by sunup, but he don't vag. Instead, he takes Valdez up to his hotel room and kills him. Next, he dumps the body in the woods and comes back to town. For a finishing touch he wrecks your place, around four this morning."

Nothing changed in Markham's face. But suddenly he seemed older, grayer. "Go on." His voice was inaudible.

"You see where I'm leading?" Lennox asked cheerfully. "See how it builds?"

A vein jumped in Markham's forehead. "Tierney confessed to all this?"

"He will when we pick him up. He'll probably involve you, Tom. You've got an alibi for last night, naturally."

"Naturally." Markham's voice was cold acid. "I was playing poker with friends. I've got witnesses—"

"Reliable, paid witnesses? Oh, I almost forgot. I just called the civic league. For your information, they're already circulating a special petition to have your license revoked as being detrimental to the public interest. The city council has to act automatically on such petitions. By Monday, you've had it."

It was a lie, but Lennox was enjoying himself thoroughly. Look at him, he thought. He's really smooth; nothing shows. But it's hurting, you can feel the sympathy pains as you shove it in. A cop lives for moments like this. You take their crap, you let it fester inside you, knowing you can't touch them, and finally a crack appears in the wall. Dig away at that one crack, and the whole structure collapses.

Markham cleared his throat. "Remember three years ago, Joe? When Paloma Beach incorporated, and they picked a police chief? You were senior lieutenant, working out of the county. You were in line for chief, as I recall."

Lennox remembered very well.

"But they imported somebody from Los Angeles, didn't they?"

"That's right. Chief Sloane. What about it?"

"Sloane's due for retirement come January."

It hung softly between them, and Lennox laughed a short hard laugh. "Thanks for that much, Tom. It makes it so much better."

Markham toyed with the pencil. "Why do you hate me, Joe?"

"Because you're no better than a pusher." Now it was all business between them. "Worse, maybe, because you hide under the cloak of legality. Those mill hands, those merchant fishermen out there are diseased, just like a dope addict. They can't win, and ultimately the house butcher gets them. You make it off the little guy, the poor slob who thinks he can get something for nothing and winds up losing the Friday paycheck. To make it worse, you attract other kinds of vermin—"

"That's not true, Joe."

"But it sounds good," Lennox said sweetly. "In the papers it'll sound real good."

The door closed. Markham sat motionless. There was a sharp crack, and he looked down at the broken pencil. Wilbur came into the office.

"Get Garth," Markham said.

Wilbur withdrew, and Markham sat at his desk, brooding. It finally catches up with you, he thought. It takes such a little thing to upset the applecart. Like a chess game against children. Only one of the children makes an accidental move, a random move, and abruptly there's a fool's mate staring down your throat. This particular fool's mate demanded a sacrifice

Garth came in. His eyes were red-rimmed and tired.

"Get Potok," Markham said. "Get him over here right away."

"Gee, Tom, Potok wouldn't—"

"You'll probably find him at the Turf Club, playing shuffleboard. I want him here in ten minutes."

Garth left without a word. Markham sat brooding in the gray silence. He picked up the phone and dialed the Paloma Beach Country Club. "I'd like to page Doctor Ross, please. Yes, very important."

He waited, and there was no answer to the page. Doctor Ross had left the club around three-thirty.

Garth brought Potok into the office fifteen minutes later. Potok was a tall, pale man with a quiet look of dedication. He wore a dark flannel suit. His brown eyes were kindly behind rimless glasses. At first glance, many people mistook him for a priest.

"Sit down," Markham said.

It only took him five minutes to explain it, and Potok understood perfectly. But it was a little heavy for Garth.

"But why Smith?" Garth asked. "He's nothing—"

Potok glanced at him and Garth shut up. Potok often had that effect on people.

"Take Garth along," Markham said. "He knows all the addresses. Questions?"

"You want Smith to look like an accident," Potok said. "Tierney simply drops out of sight."

After they left, Markham sat thinking sadly about Tierney. It was a shame, considering they had made a deal earlier this afternoon. But that particular deal, as such, was no longer important. It was now part of a much larger issue, which could be settled only in one way.

Before leaving the office, he called Pineview. Louise was in foul humor. The Knox girl was violently in labor, and Louise was damned if she'd play midwife again this month; it wasn't her job. Markham sighed and promised her a hundred-dollar bonus. Louise subsided, sullenly.

"How's our special patient?"

"Not a peep all afternoon."

"Good. I'll be there inside of an hour. We're removing her."

Louise asked no questions.

Markham got up and paced the office. He considered using Potok to take care of Ann, but it would be best to handle that particular detail himself. As a matter of fact he would enjoy it. But it was really unfortunate about Cliff. He wondered if Tierney had ever heard of David and Absalom.

Lennox sat patiently in his squad car, smoking. It was five minutes after four. He had driven around to the front lot and parked behind a gray Buick. It was an excellent vantage point to observe the Barrel's front and side entrances. Yet he felt mildly ridiculous, sitting there. He tried to tell himself that he knew a great deal about human behavior patterns, that in dealing with a high-grade operator like Markham, logic was futile because you were hopelessly outclassed, that it took cop instinct and determination to get results.

Then it was four-fifteen, and he felt depressed. There is, he thought, nothing more pitiful than an old cop who thinks he's doing a job. It's strictly wish-fulfillment, nothing's going to happen. You've rationalized this thing into the one big break you've been waiting for these past five years, and it's so important that you've lost all perspective.

He thought about Tate, alone in that hotel room, and he remembered Tate had not yet eaten lunch. He was about to turn on the ignition when he saw Garth and Potok walking through the side entrance. His memory file clicked, and he thought about Potok, who had been arrested half a dozen times, and how the charges had been dismissed because of lack of evidence. Lennox sat up straight, and his eyes brightened.

Five minutes later, Garth and Potok came out of the side entrance. Lennox watched them get into a blue Pontiac and drive away.

He made no attempt to tail them. With the squad car, it would have been amateurish. Instead, he drove six blocks to the Dunes Hotel. When he went up to Room Two-twelve he rapped sharply on the door, twice. The door opened. Tate sighed and put away his gun.

"What the hell kept you?"

"I was goosing somebody," Lennox said dreamily. "What happens when you get goosed, Sergeant?"

Tate blinked, and took it literally. "I'll bite, Lieutenant."

"You jump, Sergeant. And sometimes you come down in a more vulnerable position."

Tate passed that. He went to the door, said, "What makes you think Tierney will come back here, anyway."

"Just a hunch. He left all his luggage and clothes. I'll call you at headquarters if I decide to leave."

The door closed and Lennox sat alone by the window, watching the traffic. Sometimes waiting gets on a cop's nerves, but Lennox felt only a pleasant anticipation.

CHAPTER 14

By midafternoon, the Paloma Beach Country Club was jammed. White-shirted foursomes straggled in from the eighteenth green, complaining listlessly about the heat. Bar and locker room were a soft bedlam. The glass dining terrace above the pool had a *Reserved* sign on the door. Inside, five men were arguing around the oak dining table.

They had discussed the rezoning ordinance, the water bond issue. Now came an awkward silence. Judge Canfield cleared his throat.

"Where's Thad?"

"At the bar," Tripp said. Tripp was the youngest councilman.

"Again?"

"I'll go get him." As Tripp got up, Thad Ross came in, pale and impassive. He held the frosted cocktail glass as if it were a part of him.

"This rezoning thing, Thad. Would you explain just why we should hold it in abeyance until after election?"

"Certainly." Thad walked around the table, stood looking out at the pool. "If we open the west end to heavy industry, the next thing is fish canneries and oil wells. The opposition's been waiting—"

"You see?" The judge turned to the others. "Any questions?"

They looked glumly at their briefcases. Each was waiting for the main issue to be mentioned. Tripp fiddled with his pen. Judge Canfield cleared his throat again. Thad stared at the exploding sunlight flashes on the pool, at the blonde who was practicing gainers from the high board. She resembled Holly.

"About the Pink Barrel," Tripp said bravely. "I hear there was a brawl there last night. A barroom brawl," he said, liking the sound of it. "What do you think, Judge?"

The judge ignored the question. He was looking at Thad's back. The silence grew, until Thad said without turning, "It's a small thing, isn't it?"

"The kind of small thing the opposition likes."

"That's right," Tripp said, "they could parlay it into—"

"A public nuisance," said another councilman, jumping on the bandwagon. Tripp shot him a resentful glance as Thad turned, facing the table.

"We've got a choice, gentlemen?" He let it reverberate, and smiled. "You can be tolerant of filth just so long. Then you smash it—"

"You mean close them down?" Tripp was incredulous.

"I mean there is no compromise," Thad droned, and the judge saw how very drunk he was. It was in the slurred voice, the too-careful movements, the glazed eyes.

"Very good." Tripp scribbled on his pad. "I'll include this in the minutes, if you don't mind."

"Then we issue an injunction," Judge Canfield said carefully, "on the grounds that the Barrel is detrimental to public interest. We'll take the play right away from the opposition. In fact, we can use it as a campaign blurb, Keep Paloma Beach Clean, something like that."

"Oh good," said Tripp, and there was only the scratching of his pen.

Thad set his empty glass down with a click. He walked out of the room with precise metronome steps. Five pairs of eyes swiveled, followed him.

"By God," Tripp said, "he's taking this hard."

"He voted to renew their franchise last month, remember?"

"But the civic take. Think about that."

"We can't afford to."

"But we're in the red," Tripp said, biting his pen. "They'll make a big play about that."

"Let them. We're doing the right thing."

"How about Gardena? They've got a half dozen poker clubs—"

"This isn't Gardena," Judge Canfield said, taking command. "By election time the city treasury will be in the black, we can get along without their revenue."

"Let's get out a special petition," Tripp said. "Seconded?"

The motion was unanimous....

Thad Ross stood at the crowded bar. Across the way he could see two women and a man in the corner booth, laughing over highballs, sated in their animal stink of relaxation. One of the women had red hair. Now she threw back her head and laughed. Full, rich, red laughter that went through him like a knife.

Like Holly, over the phone.

The bartender came and Thad ordered brandy. When his drink came, he signed the check and turned from the bar, walking out by the pool. He sat in the lounge chair, staring at the girl on the high board.

A tall girl, bosomy and nubile, diving out of the blue sky into the water. Defiling the green mirror of pool surface, smashing the water into a prismatic brilliance of gold and jade. Surfacing in lace foam, white shine of smile as she stroked toward the edge of the pool. Bronzed lifeguard sitting by the ladder, grinning at her. Girl removing bathing cap, gold tumble of hair, shaking the water droplets from her like an animal. She-animal in heat. The knowing smirk of the lifeguard.

Holly.

Thad reached for his glass and found it empty. He frowned at it, and stood tall and strong. Walking with clockwork precision around the pool, through the flag-stoned pillars toward the parking lot. Getting into the convertible, turning on the ignition. Thrum of motor, spurt of speed down the long concrete ribbon toward town. Hearing the wind hiss against the windshield and ricochet against his face. Then, without transition, he was coming into town. The traffic signal flashed green, welcoming him. There was no conscious memory of the last five miles of highway.

Back there, the minor godlings had held council. They had sat respectfully awaiting his verdict. And he had given them the truth. That evil must be destroyed. They had nodded, made sibilant sound of approval. He had gone, to do what he had to do.

And reaching her street, turning. Parking beneath the sheltering palms. Glancing at the chronometer on his wrist. The time was three-thirty.

You must be fair, he told himself. Perhaps she was playing a cruel joke. She is a moody child, full of hate. But some things you cannot forgive. The cold rage grew, became panic. He did not wish to know. He sat frozen, watching the apartment door across the street. Watching it open, and Tierney come out, tall and blond. Walking fast toward the corner intersection.

Thad closed his eyes, retching.

Then he was opening the car door, walking across the street. The panic was gone, there was only an icy calm. He punched the door chimes. The door opened. He went in quickly, slamming it shut behind him as Holly recoiled. He stood watching her face, seeing the guilt and the fear.

He struck a savage, backhanded blow. She sprawled, bitch legs akimbo, dress flaring above silken thighs.

Then he turned into the bedroom. The bed was rumpled, as he had known it would be. A pair of men's trousers were draped over the chair. Wheeling back to the living room, he saw two cocktail glasses on the end table. Holly whimpered, scrabbling to her feet as he followed her.

He followed her inexorably as she fled past the kitchen to the well-remembered room with the pink floor and ice-green ceiling, and the leering statues in the corner. He caught her, as she darted towards the side door, smashing a fist to the base of her skull.

He bent over her as she crumpled, placing the avenging fingers about her throat, watching the green eyes distend, pleading.

He heard the spasmodic kicking of her heels on the flooring, saw the red mottling of bitch face, and too late sensed the feral movement of her right hand, and felt jagged lightnings rip through his skull and white agony dissolving in darkness....

Holly stood up, her breath an hysterical sob. She stared at the pink shard of marble in her fist, then bent down, listening for a pulse. Thad's breathing was harsh, irregular. She hurried back into the bedroom and took a suitcase from the closet. She packed swiftly.

In the garage, she threw the suitcase into the back seat of her Porsche, and slid behind the wheel, gnawing her lip. She had no place to go.

CHAPTER 15

The alarm woke DeWitt Smith at one-thirty. He came awake with a headache, and sat on the side of the bed holding his face. He got up and went into the kitchenette. The fifth of rye was on the dinette table, half full. He had been in process of opening that bottle when Tierney called him that morning.

Smith filled a water glass, spilling the whisky. Then he winced and set the glass gently on the tile drain. He picked up the phone and dialed Ann's apartment. After a time he hung up and went into the living room.

It was a bleak room, sterile. Green frieze furniture, no pictures on the walls. A monk's cell, aseptic and spotless. He went into the bathroom, where he splashed cold water on his face.

Hatred, he thought wryly, can take many forms. Some people, like Markham, are too big to hate. Markham was an implacable gray force, a machine. Thinking about Markham brought a sick, warm loosening of his sphincter muscles.

But Tierney was a man. His hatred for Tierney was a shining blade.

He finished shaving and went into the hallway. He found the Belgian .38 automatic on the second shelf, wrapped in oilskin. As he unwrapped it, he saw the ebony and gold plaque back on the dusty shelf. The Southland News award he had received three years ago.

His giant-killing days, he thought wearily, when he had expanded in the bright sun of Ann's adoration. The acid editorials, his by-lines, were so many trophies to lay at Ann's feet. He was forty-two, old enough to be her father. Yet he had needed her, that blue-eyed-urchin who believed passionately in the eternal verities.

It could not last. At heart he believed in nothing except the inherent invulnerability of the fourth estate. He was too much the aging cynic, Ann the idealist. Her love had a mystical shine which angered him.

Once they had quarreled. He had accused her of an Electra fixation and she had cried. Afterwards, she'd made love with a forced violence, trying to prove something that he knew she could never prove.

It is so easy to break a man, to smash his small idols.

Markham had broken him casually, like swatting a fly.

He had gotten another job, on the San Diego *Wire*. Copy desk, guild rates. They had fired him the second week for coming in drunk. That was when he went on a six-month binge, savagely rejecting Ann's efforts to salvage him. It had taken rare talent to make her return his ring. It took a great deal of whisky, tantrums, and finally a beating. She cried with a raw whimpering sound, a cry identical to the time he had tricked her into sleeping with him. She had gone away.

Ultimately he drifted into the editorial job on the *Enquirer.* A door-to-door throwaway, a glorified handbill, with a front-page spread consisting of chamber of commerce squibs and the grand opening of a supermarket.

Advertising is the only important function of a newspaper....

Smith hefted the .38 and checked the clip. He went back to his bedroom and dressed, slipping the gun into his coat pocket. When he went to the kitchen he picked up the glass of whisky, hesitating.

What are you trying to prove? he asked himself in contempt. That you're not a lush? That this particular day you don't need it for breakfast?

He left the glass on the sink, and fumbled in the bread drawer. Breakfast was stale danish and black coffee. Afterwards, he called the paper and told Bonny he would be in by five-thirty.

"Gee, Witt," she protested. "You promised I could get off early today—"

"All right," he said. "Any calls?"

"Old man Arvin called, mad as a hornet. Says he won't pay for that quarter-page spread. You omitted his big special, corned beef at forty-nine cents a pound—"

"I'll call him," he said. "That new ad salesman—Jacobs. Has he shown?"

Bonny said no, and would he be there by five, sure? Smith said probably, and hung up, remembering that Jacobs was not due to start work until Monday. The small lapse bothered him.

It was two-thirty when he left the apartment.

He drove out 101, and took the inland cutoff to Vardonville. It was almost three when he parked in front of Ann's duplex.

He knocked on the door, then tried the knob. The door swung open. He went inside, staring at the ruined living room. White cotton batting exploded from the slashed sofa pillows. The wine broadloom was rolled against the wall, and chairs were overturned. He went numbly into the bedroom, seeing the open bureau drawers, clothing scattered about.

He bent down and picked up the broken shoe. A black suede pump with the heel wrenched off. On her dresser he saw a forlorn pearl earring. He smelled the faint scent of lavender cachet. Ann was here, all about him, in this torn bedroom.

In that moment, he shivered at the dull pain in his kidneys, remembering how Garth and Feeney had come into his office last night. They had struck him in the same place, again and again. "Just for nothing," Garth had said. "Just to discourage the crusading instinct."

Smith grimaced, and opened Ann's closet. On the floor, he found Ann's portable typewriter, lying on its side. He picked it up tenderly, replacing it in its case, and carried it out into the dinette. He took two sheets of bond paper from the case, and sat, inserting them into position.

He sat motionless for almost ten minutes, staring at the blank paper. When he finally began to type, it was in sharp angry bursts. For the first time in two years, there was no more fear....

It was almost five when he drove into Paloma Beach and parked near the Dunes Hotel. The gun felt heavy in his coat pocket as he walked across the street and into the lobby. The desk clerk glanced at him and went back to the afternoon headlines.

Smith climbed the steps to the second floor, remembering last night, how easily Tierney had handled him, how Ann had taken Tierney's arm as she left the office. How she had looked up at Tierney with that special shine in her eyes which had once been reserved for a drunken newspaperman named Smith.

Inevitably, a man had to make a stand.

But this isn't really a stand, he told himself as he walked down the corridor. It's more of a dying gesture. And don't pretend you're doing this for Ann. Tierney's a grift artist, with the morality of a snake.

He stopped in front of Room Two-twelve and knocked, boldly. The door opened. A stocky man stood framed in the doorway. His eyes were hot and bright.

"Come in."

Smith sucked air painfully. "I'm afraid there's some mistake—"

"I said come in."

Smith walked into the room. Lennox took out his wallet, flashed his badge. "Lieutenant Lennox, Paloma Beach police. May I see your identification?"

Smith took out his wallet, handed it over. Lennox glanced at his driver's license, frowned, returned the wallet. "Now raise your arms, Smith."

"What for?"

Lennox sighed, and spun him hard against the wall. He braced Smith, found the gun.

"Got a permit for this?"

"Yes, I'm editor of the *Enquirer*—"

"Where's your permit?"

"At home," Smith said desperately. "Sometimes I—"

"Carry large sums of money, that the idea?"

Lennox stood in a balanced crouch, and Smith had the premonition the man was going to hit him. Instead, Lennox looked vaguely disappointed. "Witt Smith," he mused. "You used to work on the *Sentinel* a couple of years back. I used to read your editorials. They were good, had guts. Whatever happened to you?"

"I sold out," Smith said evenly. "Like the Paloma Beach police force."

"You son of a hitch." Lennox's mouth worked. He went over to the bed and sat. When he looked up his face was unreadable. "What kind of business did you have with Tierney?"

"It's about a story," Smith improvised. Those typed sheets of bond felt very warm in his pocket. "Last night Tierney stopped by my office. He said he had something big, a story about local graft—"

"Go on."

"That's all he told me. Said it would cost me five hundred bucks—"

Lennox chuckled. He was examining the gun. He came up from the bed effortlessly, walked over to Smith. "I'll give you a chance to tell it over again," he smiled. "Why you really came here. Go ahead."

Smith swallowed. This bull-shouldered little man was playing a game with him. A game which certain types of cop love to play. Soft talk, then the sudden knee to the groin, the elbow smash to the throat, and you talk feverishly, babbling through a red ecstasy of pain.

"No," Smith tried to keep his voice steady. "That's exactly why I'm here, Officer. Is Tierney in some kind of trouble?"

Lennox looked pensive. He seemed to be making some sort of decision. Then, amazingly, he was handing the gun back, saying, "I'll check on your permit. Where will you be this evening?"

"At my Laguna office." Smith shook his head, not believing it. "Is Tierney—"

"We've got a fugitive warrant out for him. Call the station house at eight; they'll give you a news release."

"Thank you," Smith said, not daring to hope. "Is that all?"

"That's all. If you decide to leave town, please call us."

He almost laughed aloud at the dazed look on Smith's face. The door closed, and Lennox was alone. He grinned and went over to the window. Below, Smith crossed the street and got into the green coupe. He looked back once, scratching his head. Then he drove away.

Lennox called headquarters. Sergeant Tate was still out for supper.

"I'm leaving for a while," Lennox told the desk sergeant. "Tell Tate to stick around; I'll call in by six." He nodded, blunt fingers caressing the phone. "That's right. I got a lead."

He hung up, and carefully adjusted his hat. When he left the room, he was whistling....

It was ten minutes after five when Smith walked into his office. He reached the wooden railing, and stopped dead. Bonny was not at her desk. Tierney sat by the filing cabinet in the corner.

"Where's Bonny?"

"She had a heavy date." Tierney smiled faintly. "She thought I was Jacobs, your new ad salesman. She told me you'd be in any minute, that I could wait."

"I'll fire her!"

"No, you won't." Tierney got up, came toward him. Then he paused, looking at the .38. It trembled in Smith's hand.

"Come around the railing," Smith said. "Real slow."

Tierney came around the railing.

"Now sit."

Tierney sat.

"Where's Ann?"

"Markham's got her," Tierney said. Smith saw how pale he was, pale and tired. "Look, Smith, all I came for are the photostats—"

"What photostats? You think I'm blackmailing Markham?"

Tierney's smile almost made Smith pull the trigger. Instead he took out the editorial, tossed it at Tierney. "Read this. Now tell me I'm blackmailing him!"

Tierney read the typewritten pages and looked up, unbelieving. "You're going to print this?"

"In the Monday edition!" Smith's hate made him feel eight feet tall. "Unless you tell me where Ann—"

"Pineview," Tierney read aloud. "A haven for unwed mothers who sell their babies—" He stopped reading as it came to him where Ann was, where she had to be.

"You poor bastard," he said. "Ann gave you those records to run an expose on Markham. But you didn't have the guts to run a news editorial, instead you tried to shake Tom down. Only Valdez found out and you had to kill him. So now they've got Ann and you finally develop a conscience—"

"Shut up!" Smith was livid. But his gun hand had stopped shaking. "Did you know there's a general fugitive warrant out for you, a police stake-out at your hotel right now!"

They glared at each other like animals, and Tierney suddenly grinned. "How'd you find my hotel?"

"I called all the hotels in Paloma Beach this afternoon," Smith said in a calmer tone. "I went there to kill you, but now I've got a better idea. Unless you tell me where Ann is, I'm turning you over to the police."

Tierney shrugged and handed the editorial back. As Smith reached for it, the papers dropped from Tierney's hand. Smith started to bend over, and checked himself too late. Tierney's foot was a blur, and the gun clattered on the floor. Smith stared at his numbed wrist. "Don't," Tierney said sharply, but Smith was beyond caring. He dived for the gun and, regretfully, Tierney kicked him in the side. Smith huddled into a tight ball and made noises.

Tierney bent down and grabbed him by the coat. Smith weighed two hundred, but he came up like a feather.

"The photostats," Tierney said, and drove three stiff fingers into Smith's plexus. Smith tried to butt him, and Tierney let him fall against the desk, cracking his head as he fell. Smith grunted and tried to rise. Yet fear was gone. There was only fury.

"Get up," Tierney said, not liking it, then he turned quickly toward the door.

Garth and Potok came in.

Tierney recognized Potok immediately, and he was puzzled. He measured the distance to Smith's gun, over by the filing cabinet. Wisely, he did not move.

"I don't believe it," Garth said. "Both of them together. It's too easy."

"It happens like that sometimes," Potok said, watching Tierney. He stood by the railing, hoping Tierney would move, waiting him to move. But Tierney just stood. Smith wavered to his feet, holding onto the desk.

Garth had closed the door and locked it. Now he was closing the Venetian blinds across the front window.

CHAPTER 16

For Tierney, there was no other person in the room but Potok. He had seen Potok operate once, two years ago. It had been an assignment which he had refused, and Markham had not spoken to him for days afterwards. He stood by the railing watching Garth close the Venetians, then turn, smiling at him.

"Can I ask one question?" Tierney said.

"Go ahead," Garth said.

"Does Tom know about this?"

Garth just grinned, and it was answer enough. Tierney felt no anger, just a technical curiosity. Forty minutes ago, he and Tom had made a deal, and Tom always kept his word. Unless—

"I see." Tierney was thinking aloud, putting himself in Markham's position. "They found Valdez."

"I'm glad you see." Garth's grin expanded. "That makes it so much better. Incidentally, where's my car?"

"Three blocks from here," Tierney said, keeping it light. "You owe me for a tank of ethyl."

Garth started to laugh, then stopped. "Potok," he said.

"Not here," Potok said, watching Tierney. "Outside, in the car."

Smith shook his head weakly, while his eyes focused. In that first moment he thought Potok was a cop. Then he recognized Garth, and involuntarily rubbed his kidneys. But fear was gone. He took a deep breath, wanting one more try at Tierney. Tierney gave him a lazy smile and that made it worse.

"Let's go," Potok said.

Tierney leaned on the railing. He shook his head.

"Maybe he didn't hear you," Garth murmured.

"He heard me." Potok's dark eyes turned dreamy. Then he was holding the gun. "You want it here, is that it?"

Tierney straightened up from the railing. In that moment the office became a small, deadly arena. There was Smith, hanging onto the desk, still unaware of what was happening. There was Garth, who was incompetent at best, and there was Potok who was a craftsman. There was Smith's gun, lying by the filing cabinet.

It was, Tierney told himself, a very delicate equation. Once outside, in the car, you won't have a chance. So it has to be here, and you've got to concentrate on Witt Smith, maneuver him into position.

Potok's nostrils flared. His gun tilted. He was going to shoot Tierney in the kneecap.

"Wait a minute." Tierney looked utterly relaxed. "Garth, I want you to read something." His glance flicked to the editorial on the floor.

"I don't feel like reading anything right now," Garth said politely. He was enjoying it, hoping Tierney would crack.

"But it's why you came." Tierney grinned nastily at Smith. "Read it, you'll see what I mean."

"You stinking bastard," Smith choked. He started around the railing, and a motion of Potok's gun stopped him.

Garth frowned at the editorial. He picked it up, started to read. His eyes widened. "My God," he said.

"It's about Tom's sideline operation," Tierney explained. "Mr. Rabbit here knew all about it, but he didn't have the guts—"

It was the smirk in his voice and the rabbit reference that broke Smith. He came around the railing with a strangled sob and hit Tierney.

It was the last thing that Potok expected. For one fractional second, Smith intercepted his line of fire.

Tierney moved.

His right arm was a lever, his left a hatchet, and Smith was a broken doll hurtling towards Potok. The gun went off as Smith crashed into him, and Tierney was diving across the railing toward the file cabinet. Garth made the mistake of going after him.

Across the street, Lennox was sitting in the coffee shop, in the booth next to the window. He had been sitting there for almost five minutes. His squad car was parked half a block away, in a side alley.

At first he had congratulated himself. That was when Garth and Potok had parked in front of the newspaper office and went inside. But when the blinds closed across the windows, Lennox scowled. He lighted a cigarette, wondering if perhaps he weren't playing this too close to his vest after all.

He heard the first shot and jumped, spilling hot coffee down his shirt front. He was halfway out of the diner when he heard three more shots, blending into a savage drum of sound. Then the silence was a club.

Lennox was halfway across the street when the office door flew open. Tierney stood there, a gun in his hand. Without breaking stride, Lennox yanked out his police special and fired. The shot went wide, smashing the door glass. The door slammed shut immediately, but Lennox kept going and hit the jamb hard with his shoulder. The door held. Cursing, he reached around and fumbled with the inside latch. He heard the distant patter of footsteps, a back door slam. Then absolute stillness.

The latch gave, and Lennox was inside.

Witt Smith lay face down by the railing. Garth huddled against the file cabinet, moaning softly. Potok was on hands and knees, his face wrenched into an agony of strain as he tried to rise. He had taken two bullets in the thigh and was bleeding badly.

Lennox took in the whole picture in one glance as he charged past the railing. He jerked open the back door and found himself in the printing room. There was a linotype, a small printing press, and racked boxes of type. He moved cautiously around the linotype, and saw the alley door was open.

He went out to the alley and saw it was deserted. At his feet was the gun, where Tierney had dropped it. Lennox took out his handkerchief and picked it up. He went back inside, moving like an old man.

A crowd was gathering at the front door. Lennox dispersed them, and went back to the desk. He sighed as he picked up the phone, thinking how tough it would be after all these years to be busted back into uniform. But that was a minor thing. The bitter part of it was that he, Lennox, who hated gambling like a disease, had just gambled. And lost.

Abruptly Lennox slammed the receiver back on the hook. He walked past Potok, who had fainted. Garth was crawling towards the railing, favoring his broken collar bone and biting his lip to hold back the scream. He was reaching for the typed editorial when Lennox picked it up and began reading....

Tierney stopped running as he rounded the corner and saw the Olds still parked on the side street. He slowed to a walk, breathing hard, rubbing his hurt shoulder.

It was five-thirty, dusk. He got into the car and drove toward the coast highway.

You've got twenty minutes, he told himself, maybe half an hour at the outside. Once they get a description of this car from Garth, you're incandescent. They set up their roadblocks like so many sardine nets and you're hooked. He floorboarded it, and the Olds was a pale arrow in the blue dusk,

You've got to hide out at Holly's, he decided. It's strictly no choice. You'd like to help Ann, but that's out of the question. She might be at Pineview, but there's no way of making sure. You've got to head for Newport Beach, where Holly's waiting. Quite a girl, Holly. She's in love with you, in a manner of speaking, and she wants so terribly to take care of you. And you really need taking care of right now. That shoulder feels feverish where Garth hit it, and it's started bleeding again. Your whole arm feels numb, and that means infection, doesn't it? Maybe you'll even lose the arm.

He was thinking about his left arm when the traffic lights flared crimson, and he hit the brakes, burning rubber for twenty feet. And he saw that he was only two miles south of Newport, he was going to definitely make it before the police picked him up.

Only when the signal turned green, the steering wheel seemed to move of its own volition. The Olds swerved up the inland cutoff, and he found himself driving inland, towards the Irvine Hills.

Hey now, he thought. You're losing control. You're headed in the wrong direction. You meant to keep driving straight ahead, to Newport. But now you're headed inland, and this won't do at all. He willed himself to step on the brake, to flip a U-turn and go back to the coast highway. He concentrated until the sweat burst out on his forehead. But his right foot seemed glued to the accelerator. The speedometer showed eight-five, and he was driving past alfalfa fields and intermittent stands of eucalyptus. Now he was doing ninety.

Presently he relaxed a little, and smiled. With a gesture something like a shrug, he turned on the headlights. Twenty minutes later he was driving slowly up the winding hill road, past orange groves and farmhouses. He came to a fork in the road and stopped, peering at the road sign. It said, *Santa Ana, 8 miles.*

He leaned back, feeling fatigue settle over him like a thick, dark blanket. It was nice to sit here, listening to the wind rustle in the pines, and the sharp chittering of crickets. Far below in the valley he could see the pale glimmer of lights. It made him feel nostalgic.

Then, automatically, his right hand fumbled with the ignition. He found himself cruising down the hill road, now turning off toward a lighted farmhouse. He got out of the car and stumbled toward the front porch. It was very simple, really. All you had to do was ask directions. Directions to a place named Pineview, where you were going to die.

Eight miles away, in the darkness of Holly's studio, Thad Ross groaned and stirred. He felt his temple, and saw a dozen colors of pain. He got up, grunting with effort, and turned on the studio lamp.

"Holly!" he called.

There was no answer.

He walked slowly through the apartment, turning on all the lights in each room. She was gone. He went outside, and saw that her garage was empty.

Thad rubbed his head, grimacing. He walked slowly across the dark street, got into his convertible. In that moment, Holly was forgotten. He was thinking about the Knox girl, how he had promised to see her by six, and how he had never been late for an appointment in his life. The time was six-fifteen.

Thad drove rapidly towards the coast highway.

CHAPTER 17

It was long after dark when Tierney turned off the hill road and cut the headlights. He had tried two farmhouses, and at the first place they hadn't known what he was talking about. At the second farmhouse they had told him there was some kind of rest home a mile past the Kenzie grove. But he had a hard time finding the Kenzie grove, and it was almost seven by the time he turned off the winding dirt road through the pines.

When he came in sight of the clearing, he cut the headlights, and sat studying the Spanish stucco building with the red tile roof. Two cars were parked in the gravel drive. One was Markham's black Lincoln. The other was a green convertible which he did not recognize. Tierney threw the Olds into reverse, and carefully backed down the path until he was beyond the sharp turn. He parked in a dark tangle of scrub, with the front end of the Olds eclipsing half the path.

Just for insurance, he decided. Just in case you fail. But why didn't you bring Smith's gun along? He walked down the path, wondering what subconscious quirk had made him drop the gun in the alley. When the answer came, it was a jolt.

He wanted to strangle Markham with his bare hands.

You're not being professional, he thought, as he moved silently toward the house. This job demands precision and perfect timing; you're going to get glandular, and botch it, sure as hell.

He crouched at the edge of the clearing, observing the yellow glow from the screened patio, and listening to the soft night sounds. The moon was a crooked smear of light beyond the pines, distorting his vision, foreshortening the house until it loomed like a gigantic white pillbox.

Just like Korea, he thought. You're out on patrol, and it looks too easy, only there're land mines all around you, so watch every step. Then he realized he was almost delirious from the pulsating pain in his left shoulder, and the pain was creeping slowly across his chest. He did not have much time.

Soundless as smoke, Tierney moved across the clearing.

He gimmicked Thad's convertible first. It took him less than a minute to lift the hood and disconnect the distributor wiring. Afterward he crouched in darkness, staring at the girl who sat inside the patio. She was young, blonde, and very intent on doing her fingernails. When she finally yawned and stood up, Tierney saw she was quite pregnant. She went inside, closing the french doors behind her.

Tierney exhaled softly and stood up. His right leg had gone to sleep, and he kneaded his thigh to start the blood circulating. Markham's car was parked thirty feet distant, across the gravel drive.

He frowned, hesitating. Logic told him to hurry. Hustler instinct said wait, there's a very good reason why you shouldn't walk in that gravel, why you mustn't make the slightest sound.

All right, he asked himself, what's the reason?

I can't tell you, the hustler said. Why don't you make a noise and find out?

Tierney considered it. And then it was too late, because he heard a door open on the far side of the house, and the muffled sound of voices. He heard a shrill whine, followed by a chorus of barking. Markham spoke sharply and the barking ceased.

Markham came around the corner of the house, carrying Ann in his arms. With him was a dumpy, gray-haired woman whom Tierney did not recognize. She helped him position Ann in the back seat of the Lincoln, and in the process, Ann moaned.

Tierney came quickly from behind the convertible, all planning forgotten. Louise gasped when she saw him, and fled for the patio. But Markham did not move. His expression was purely technical as Tierney came towards him, heels crunching in the gravel.

"A prowler," Markham said softly. "It looks like we've got a prowler on our hands, Louise."

The woman nodded. She turned, hurrying around to the side of the house. For Tierney it did not register. There was only Markham, who now wore a sad, remote smile.

"Last chance, Cliff. It's still not too late to reconcile differences."

Tierney just shook his head. From around in back came the rattle of a chain, the sliding rasp of a kennel door. He was five feet from Markham when the Doberman bounded lithely around the corner of the house. Markham gave a shrill whistle and feinted at Tierney. That did it, and the Doberman became a black streak of murder going for Tierney's throat.

There was the snarling, and the writhing in the gravel, and the other sounds that Markham did not wish to hear. He got into the Lincoln with a dim regret for the years of training that had been wasted on Tierney, wasted because Tierney was a rube at heart, and had allowed emotion to destroy him.

Then Markham saw what was happening in the gravel drive, and he froze behind the wheel. Instead of an animal tearing a man to shreds, he saw two animals, and the larger animal was by far the deadliest.

Quite suddenly it was over, and the larger animal lurched erect, coming for him. For the first time in twenty years, Markham felt something like fear. He punched the ignition, and the Lincoln leaped across the clearing. He was doing thirty when he hit the dirt road, and he made the sharp turn much too fast: He had just snapped on his headlights when he saw the Olds parked halfway across the road, waiting for him.

From inside the house, Louise heard the crash. The sound was a distant metallic cough. She jerked erect, listening to the sudden stillness.

She walked quickly down the linoleum corridor.

One of the doors opened and a girl in blue negligee blinked at her, sleepy and frightened. "What happened, Mrs. Rucci?"

"Dog scared off a prowler," she soothed. "Go back to sleep, honey."

"But I heard a crash—"

"Now, honey, we've got rules here. Please go back to bed."

The door closed reluctantly. Louise hurried to the end of the hall, cursing softly. She opened a door and went into the white-tiled delivery room with the bright overhead fluorescents.

The Knox girl was pale and unconscious on the delivery table. Thad Ross was working with a feverish desperation. Otto, the white-jacketed orderly, was helping him. Louise started to talk, suddenly frantic, and Ross looked at her, his face gray.

"Get out," he said, and Louise saw that the Knox girl was hemorrhaging badly. She withdrew, closing the door.

She went down the hall to the screened patio, biting her lip nervously.

In the yellow wash of patio light she could see the dead Doberman sprawled out in the gravel path.

Then she heard the far faint cry of the sirens....

Tierney moved slowly down the dirt road. It was very dark, and each tree was a gnarled shadow. When he saw the red gleam of taillights ahead, he stopped. The Lincoln had sideswiped the Olds and plunged off the road into a thicket.

"All right, Tom." He spoke with great effort. "Come on out, I can see you."

"No you can't," Markham said. "Just stand right there."

Tierney stood. His thought processes were rusty cogwheels, but he finally remembered that Markham never carried a gun.

From behind the eucalyptus, Markham was watching him intently. The moon came from behind scudding clouds and he saw that Tierney's shirt hung in tatters, and there was a black smear of blood on his face. But he looked calm, and completely dedicated.

"Come on out, Tom."

Markham hefted the pine branch thoughtfully. "Can't we talk this out?"

Tierney nodded, trying to locate the voice. "I want Ann."

"I can't let you have her. She's a fanatic."

"Like me?"

"Nothing like you, you poor damned fool. Listen, this operation's big, Cliff, bigger than the Barrel, understand? And the beauty of it is it's foolproof—"

His voice trailed off. Tierney was nodding, but he had located Tom's voice, and was moving tentatively towards the eucalyptus. Markham said in a different voice, "Cliff, we're arguing about nothing. Supposing Ann didn't exist. Would that make the difference?"

Tierney stopped as if he had struck a wall. "How do you mean?"

"Supposing Ann were no longer a factor." Markham's voice was a soft purr. "What I'm getting at is, just supposing she accidentally broke her neck when I went off the road just now. Would that change your thinking?"

The meaning of it penetrated like ice, and Tierney swallowed. His head swiveled towards the Lincoln.

"I'm sorry," Markham said gently. "But it wasn't really my fault. You could consider it an act of God, kind of—"

And he did not have to go on because Tierney was running toward the Lincoln, wrenching at the back door, completely oblivious to anything but Ann. Markham came soundlessly from behind the eucalyptus, and his club whistled through the air and landed solidly on Tierney's neck.

Tierney went down, rolling. Markham followed him, flailing with the club as Tierney hit the edge of the road and toppled into the culvert below. Markham carefully picked his way through the underbrush after him. Then he was standing at the bottom of the culvert, and Tierney was a broken shadow at his feet.

"I'm sorry, Cliff," he said, raising the club. And then he heard the sirens. "Hey, now," he said, hurt. "You didn't call the fuzz, did you?"

Tierney grunted and got to his knees. His arms swept out like meathooks, and Markham sprawled in the leaves. Tierney groped for him, but the little man was eel-strong, and fast as a cat. He swung again with the club, connecting, a solid smash to the head. But Tierney kept crawling, doggedly.

"You're a fool," Markham gasped, dancing back. "You hear those sirens? Look," he said, as Tierney groped for him. "We'll make a deal, son, I'll make you full partner, understand? It's you and me, Cliff, the way it should have been from the beginning—"

The sirens were a devil's shriek, mounting, dying, as they found the dirt road above. Markham turned to run, and a hand clamped around his ankle. He squirmed as he fell, and tried for a palm shot to the throat, but now there was pressure on his windpipe, choking off the scream. Too late, he remembered the one factor that made the difference in this fight. It came to him at the very end, in the final flash of pain before he stopped thinking forever, that in the final analysis a father is powerless against his adopted son, and that he, Markham, had acted like a rube from the very beginning.

Tierney sat in the culvert for a very long time. He heard the moan of a dying siren and saw the flicker of lights above, but they meant nothing. Finally he thought of Ann, and clawed his way up the bank. When he reached the road a flashlight beam exploded in his eyes and a voice said, "Hold it, just like that."

He stood, while the flashlight blinded him. Lennox's voice said, "Thought I heard somebody down there. Move that spotlight, Tate."

Tate swiveled the spotlight down into the culvert, and saw Markham. "You heard right," he said.

"How's the girl?" Lennox asked.

"She's alive." It was a crisp voice, authoritative. "Here, give me a hand."

Tierney saw the two squad cars blocking the dirt road. The rear door of the Lincoln was open, and two cops were taking Ann out, handling her with care.

The relief was like turning a switch. First, Tierney felt the trembling weakness in his knees. Then, without warning, he blacked out completely.

There was excruciating pain in his arm and a frosty white light that burned his eyes. Tierney grunted, and tried to burrow deeper into the darkness. But the light became unbearably cold and he came awake staring at the overhead fluorescents, his teeth chattering.

"You're sure he's okay?" It was Lennox's voice, surprisingly gentle.

"He's a hospital case," Thad Ross said stiffly. "He's lost blood, and gives every appearance of being in shock. Look at him."

Tierney managed to sit up straight. In the process he discovered his left arm was in a sling. There was a bandage on his cheek, covering the six stitches it had taken to repair the damage the Doberman had inflicted, but he did not discover that until much later.

Oddly, no one was looking at him. A bald man in the olive drab uniform of a county deputy sat in the corner, scribbling on a shorthand pad. Louise Rucci sat on the bench next to Tierney, her face sullen. Lennox was regarding Thad Ross with a baffled frown. "Now do you want to finish your statement, Doctor?"

Ross nodded tiredly, and began talking. He spoke in a dull monotone for several minutes, and Louise suddenly cracked. She jumped to her feet, screeching that he was a damned liar, that the Knox girl's death was his own damned fault, that Markham had hired her under false pretenses and she had absolutely no idea what kind of place Pineview really was. Lennox motioned wearily to the deputy, who took her outside. Thad gazed after them, his face drawn and bloodless.

"Filth," he whispered. He stared blindly at Lennox, his mouth working. "You must believe me," he said in a firm voice. "An ectopic pregnancy is extremely rare. No known method of transfusion could have kept up with the loss of blood. But I sincerely tried to save the baby—"

"Sure, sure." Lennox cleared his throat. The bald deputy came back inside, and Lennox said, "The statement."

"Of course." Thad's eyes were fixed on a distant vision. "There can be no compromise with evil."

Then he started talking about Pineview, and his connection with Markham, but his voice was fretful and rambling. When he began to speak querulously about the maternity clinic he planned to build next spring, the deputy blinked at Lennox, who sighed.

Tierney sat a bit straighter, and tried to focus on Lennox. He was still floating in a warm pool of shock, and Thad's confession did not make sense. He sat passively, hoarding his strength. In a few minutes he was going to make one final play, and he needed a clear head.

Down the hall came the sound of footsteps. A raw-boned deputy opened the door. "The ambulance is waiting, Lieutenant. They've got Ann Childs and Markham aboard. Did you want them to take the Knox girl?"

Lennox shook his head. "Better save her for the medical examiner. How long ago did you call?"

"Twenty minutes ago. We've got the Rucci woman in our car. Are you finished with these two yet?"

"Your car?" Lennox stood up truculently. "We're booking them at the Paloma Beach station—"

"Sheriff Duncan told me this is county territory. He wants to arraign them at the county seat—"

"Like hell!" Lennox jabbed a thumb at Tierney. "We've had a murder warrant out for this one all afternoon! I'm taking him back to Paloma Beach."

"Look, Lieutenant, I just take orders." The deputy flushed. "I'm not going to argue jurisdiction with you. Why not wait for Sheriff Duncan?"

Lennox glared at him and turned to Thad Ross. "All right," he said shortly. "Let's go, Doctor."

Ross stood up with a frail dignity. He went out into the hall, and the bald deputy followed him. The door closed, and Lennox and Tierney were alone.

"You," Lennox said, walking over to Tierney. He was quivering with a restrained fury. Too much had happened this last hour, and it was still hard to believe. "The only reason you've got your arm in a sling is that Ross insisted on fixing you up before he made a statement. Tell it in your own words. Start from last night, when I almost vagged you."

Tierney told it quickly, omitting the interlude at Holly's apartment, or the part about Pop Stroot. He saw Lennox's disbelief give way to anger, and change finally into thin-lipped suspicion.

"You're lucky," Lennox said narrowly. "Ann talked a little, before the ambulance came. Some of it was incoherent, but she made it clear you had no connection with this baby farm. Tell me just one thing—if Witt Smith was blackmailing Markham, how come he wrote that editorial?"

"Because I needled him into it. He's weak—"

"And you're scum," Lennox said viciously. "As far as I'm concerned, you and Markham are two of a kind. You expect me to believe your only stake in this thing was to help Ann?"

Tierney shrugged. Lennox looked at him a moment and said, "Let's go. You can make an official statement at headquarters."

Tierney stood up and the room tilted. He had to grab the desk for support.

"Come on. I'm damned if I'll turn you over to Sheriff Duncan."

"Smith killed Valdez," Tierney said desperately. "I can prove it!"

"How?"

"At nine-thirty, Smith's going to be at the Carleton freeway underpass. He expects a fifteen-grand payoff—"

Lennox made a rude noise. "Crap! Smith went down to the station and signed assault charges against you, Garth, and Potok."

"Did he tell you anything about Pineview?" Lennox blinked. Tierney saw the opening and pressed it. "Damned right he didn't! You found that editorial at his office. That was what brought you out here, not anything Smith told you."

"What if it did?"

"My point is, Smith didn't plan to publish that editorial until after he'd collected a payoff from Markham."

"It's too wild," Lennox shook his head. "Let's go."

They went down the hallway and Tierney argued weakly, all the way, until Lennox offered to clip him if he didn't shut his mouth. They passed a large dining hall where Tierney saw several pregnant girls in nightgowns and wrappers sitting around the long table, looking frightened. Two deputies were busily taking names and asking questions. They went out through the patio to the waiting prowl car, and Lennox shoved Tierney into the back seat.

"Save your breath," he said wearily. "Smith had a concussion when we took him to the station. Chances are he's in the hospital right now."

"But Smith doesn't know you raided Pineview—"

"Shut up!" roared Lennox, purpling.

"Look, call the station. See if he's still there. Right now he's on his way to the Carleton underpass, figuring on a payoff—"

"You son of a bitch." Lennox made a fist, looked at it. The cop in the front seat started the motor and Lennox said, "Hold it a minute."

He got out, slamming the door and went back through the screened patio. Tierney leaned forward and asked the cop for a cigarette. The cop said he didn't smoke. Tierney leaned back in the seat and closed his eyes. When Lennox came out five minutes later, he got into the back seat and said, "Drive, Tate."

The sedan bounced down the path and found the hill road. Lennox sat looking out at the night. He said without turning his head, "Smith left the station house twenty minutes ago. He refused to let a doctor look at him. Said he had an appointment, that he was in one hell of a hurry."

"See?" Tierney said.

"I'm still not buying it," Lennox gritted. "All right, we forget Potok and Garth. With Markham you'll maybe get off with self-defense; at the worst, manslaughter. But last night, if you found Valdez's body in your room, how come you didn't call the police?" Tierney just looked at him, and Lennox drew a long deep breath. "All right," he said. "Let's have it again. Just what have you got in mind?"

"Give me a cigarette," Tierney said, and Lennox handed him the pack. Tierney took his time lighting it, then took a deep bitter drag and started talking. At first Lennox looked disgusted. Then he started listening.

CHAPTER 18

The underpass was dark and cold. Tierney huddled deeper in the shadow of the concrete abutment, shivering. From overhead came the hiss of Saturday-night traffic along the Carleton Bridge. In front of him stretched the silver wash of dry creek bed, bounded by a parallel strip of roadway.

He stiffened as he saw the yellow glare of headlights moving slowly down the one-way lane. Then he relaxed as he saw the crimson twinkle of running lights, the black bulk of a diesel rig and trailer. The rig moved slowly past, and rumbled up the far winding turn towards the overhead freeway. Again there was only the night stillness.

It was nine twenty-five.

Tierney felt the bitter premonition of defeat. By now, DeWitt Smith certainly knew of the raid on Pineview, and he wasn't about to stick his neck into an obvious deadfall.

Wait a minute, he thought. Put yourself in Smith's shoes for a minute. All he knows is that two hired killers came after him this afternoon, and by now they're safe in the pokey. Which means in a few more minutes our Mr. Smith has a rendezvous with fifteen grand. But he's got a very real problem, picking up that money. The trick is to do it without getting himself creamed.

Tierney hunched erect, staring down the road. He saw no clump of trees to shelter a parked car, no turnoff—just the bare stretch of asphalt, like a black ribbon in the moonlight.

He's got to come down this road, Tierney thought clinically. And he's got to have some gimmick, some angle to keep from being followed. Or maybe he's got a helicopter; that might do it. He shook his head dizzily, fighting the weariness that threatened to engulf him. He glanced at his watch. Nine-thirty. He crouched, listening.

A small object described a long arc against the night sky. It sailed down from the overhead freeway, a dark bundle that landed with a soft thump in the center of the road. Almost simultaneously, there was the metronome clang of a distant freight signal. From two hundred yards down the road Tierney saw the intermittent amber blinking which heralded a passing freight.

He did not understand, not even when he heard the iron groaning of the westbound fruit express and saw the long string of cars moving toward the signal light. At the last possible second a pair of headlights flashed across the intersection, just missing the oncoming locomotive. Then the car was speeding down the road toward the underpass, and Tierney was standing erect, running across the creek bed.

Clever, he thought bitterly. Very professional of him. It's a one-way road, and that string of cars blocks off any possible pursuit. Which gives him plenty of time to stop, grab the package, then get back into his car and drive up the winding turn to get lost in the freeway traffic.

Mingled with these thoughts, he felt a sinking despair. It was fifty yards across the creek bed, and there was the steep embankment up to the road. He could never possibly make it. In that moment he hated Smith, and felt a sick rage at Lennox for not giving him a gun.

Now the car had stopped. The door slammed. A dim figure emerged and picked up the package. Tierney stopped, panting. He saw, but he simply did not believe. He saw the pink Porsche and the slim figure moving across the headlight beam, and the brilliance of red-gold hair, and he felt a growing sickness of the soul.

"*Holly!*"

It was a strangled shout, lost in the chuffing of the freight, but she heard him. There was a metallic gleam in her hand as she turned.

He saw the spurt of flame, heard the spiteful crack of the shot as sand geysered at his feet. He shouted again, and this time she recognized his voice. She stood motionless, waiting.

He floundered through dry sand and tumbleweeds, a perfect target. But Holly stood at the top of the embankment, and when he was close enough, said, "That's far enough, Cliff. Are you alone?"

He nodded, staring up at her. His breath was a whistle of pain and he could not speak. Holly looked back at the long string of cars that moved slowly past the crossing. Abruptly she giggled.

"I expected Tom to try something like this. I'm glad he sent you, darling."

He was staring at the gun in her hand. "That's my gun, isn't it, Holly? You found it in my room last night, when you killed Valdez."

"I had to kill him, Cliff."

"Why?"

Holly looked down at him, her face lovely and tremulous in the moonlight. "Last night," she murmured, "Eddie came to see me. He told me how he'd checked all the local photostat shops, how he had found one that remembered me as a customer two weeks ago." Her voice broke. "It was stupid of me to have the prints made locally. But then I've never done anything like this before. I needed the money to escape from Daddy, to go to Paris, understand? When I sculpted that bust of him three weeks ago—when he got drunk and passed out at his office—I went through his pockets and found the key to his desk. I was hoping to find something that would tie him to the Pink Barrel—"

"But you found something better," Tierney said bleakly. He was thinking of Ann.

"Yes, darling. I found something much better. When Eddie demanded the photostat originals I was terrified. When he asked me if you were involved—"

"You told him I was. Just to save your own skin."

"No, darling." She looked demure. "I only wanted to stall him. He asked me if the records were in your hotel, and I told him they were. He made me go with him, and I pretended to help search your room—"

"Until you found my gun in the dresser. It never bothered you that I'd step off for his murder."

Her laughter tinkled softly. "I was worried at first, Cliff. Then it came to me that you'd manage to get rid of the body somehow. You're very competent along those lines, darling."

She turned quickly, staring back down the roadway. The long string of cars still rumbled across the intersection.

"Please understand, Cliff." Her voice was a warm caress. "Nothing's changed between us. I'm free of Thad now; we can still go away together. Come on, darling, we haven't much time."

And she stretched out her arms, welcoming him. He looked up at her, his grin twisted. "Tom's dead," he said. "They've arrested Thad."

Holly digested it in calm silence. She looked down at the package in her arms.

"That's right," he rasped. "It's a plant. You're holding a bundle of torn newspaper clippings. You've got maybe twenty seconds before the last boxcar hits that crossing. Behind the crossing there's a squad car, waiting."

She gasped, and dropped the package. She leaped into the Porsche and the tires squealed. Tierney stood, watching the Porsche whip up the winding turn toward the overhead freeway lane. From where he stood he saw the white blaze of the squad car's headlights, heard the warning blare of horn.

Holly saw it too late, swerving across the road to intercept her. The Porsche darted frantically sideways, and hit the railing with a grinding scream of metal.

From a frozen fraction of time, the little sports car teetered on the edge of the railing. Then it toppled sideways, and crashed thirty feet to the creek bed below.

Long after the crash had died, Tierney stood rooted, watching Lennox and Tate clamber down the abutment. As in a dream, he walked past the bridge arches toward the wreckage and the two cops who waited for him.

It was almost dawn.

DeWitt Smith sat in the hospital waiting room, his hat pulled over his eyes. An hour ago he had called the station house, and they told him Tierney had not been booked, he was still in the county hospital.

So Smith waited. Sometimes he smoked, other times he dozed. He came awake suddenly, hearing the light patter of footsteps down the carpeted hallway. But it was only the night nurse, hurrying down the corridor. She smiled in at him as she passed, and shook her head.

Smith fumbled for a cigarette. He was in process of lighting it when he heard the heavy footsteps climbing the staircase. In a moment Tierney came into the waiting room and sat, wordlessly. His left arm was in a sling. His eyes were dark pits of fatigue and his face was old.

"How's Ann?" A tired whisper.

"She's pretty well banged up." Smith hesitated, carefully watching Tierney's face. "Three cracked ribs, concussion, shock. An hour ago she woke up, asking for you. Want to see her?"

Tierney shook his head. "I just wanted to—you're sure she'll be all right?"

"A week's rest and she'll be good as new. Incidentally, I ran that editorial tonight. The one about Pineview."

Smith looked like a different man. There was a new strength in his voice, a firmer set to his chin. Tierney studied him wryly. "I suppose it's a little late for apologies."

"Forget it. How come Lennox didn't book you?"

"Holly died, two hours ago." The pain was naked in Tierney's eyes. "But first she confessed to killing Valdez. They're holding Thad Ross on half a dozen charges, including malpractice and extortion."

He was silent, remembering Holly. A stormy child with wanton green eyes and hair stroked by flame. In her own warped fashion she had loved him. He stood up stiffly, extending his hand. "Do me a favor, Witt? Don't tell Ann I stopped by."

Witt ignored the outstretched hand. "Aren't you staying in Paloma Beach?"

Tierney chuckled bitterly. "I'm leaving town tomorrow night, after the request. Lennox made a deal. He's got a few minor charges he could nail me on, but he'd rather I just left town. So long."

Smith let him get as far as the hallway. Then he said, "Ann happens to be in love with you."

Tierney stood motionless. Without turning he said, "I thought you and she were—"

"There hasn't been anything between us in two years. Besides, I've just accepted a foreign correspondent's berth. I sent the cablegram at midnight. Look, you damned fool, why don't you see her?"

"I'm a hustler," Tierney murmured. "A grifter. It's all I know. A week from now I'll be dealing in Reno. Thanks anyway, Smith. So long."

And he was walking toward the outside staircase, going down the steps as Smith's voice floated after him, refusing to let him go. "Hell, I can offer you a local job, hustling. Hustling newspaper ads! Eighty a week draw against commission, and if you're worth a damn you'll make two hundred! It's not charity, understand. I really need a salesman—"

From the lower landing, Tierney smiled back at him. It was a sad, twisted smile that tried to tell him thanks, it was really a nice gesture and he understood. He kept walking, and stopped on the second landing. He knew Smith was standing at the top of the stairs, but he could not look up at him. Something thick and hard was caught in his throat, and his eyes stung.

In that moment he could see his life ahead with a bleak clarity. He saw the flash of cards over the table and heard the metallic clink of chips. He thought of all the lost years, remembering Holly's derision, at his dream of a white house and kids playing football on the front lawn.

He shivered. Then he turned rapidly, climbing the steps. Smith was grinning. "She's in the third room down."

The night nurse got up from her desk like an angry, white-crested bird. Smith stopped her, explaining how Doctor Wilcox had said it was perfectly all right. Reluctantly, the nurse went back to her desk.

Tierney opened the door gently, looking at Ann. In the dim glow from the bedside lamp her face was mottled and puffy. She looked like a stranger. But he felt a vast wave of tenderness as he took the chair and moved it close to her bedside. When he reached for her hand she stirred, turning her face to the wall.

It would be awkward, when she awoke. She would confuse his love with pity, for she was so terribly vulnerable in her pride. For now, he would tell her about his staying in Paloma Beach, about the new job. He must choose his words carefully, or she would not believe them. Later, the right words would come, and she would believe.

He sat holding her hand, smiling at the first flush of dawn outside the window.

THE END

KILLER TAKE ALL!

BY JAMES O. CAUSEY

PART ONE
Stymied

1

The first thing I noticed about the girl was her swing.

She stood at the far end of the driving range, methodically drilling brassie shots into the raw April wind. She was tall, dark-haired, with good hips that pivoted beautifully into her downswing. You see far too few women who can belt a golf ball like that. There was a haunting familiarity about her, but she was not quite near enough for me to make out her features.

I started to amble over when a voice squealed from the clubhouse, "Yoo-hoo, Tony! Sorry I'm late."

I turned with a stiff smile. It was Mrs. Metzger. She is plump, blonde, and invariably late for her weekly golf lesson. She came panting up with her caddy-cart and I almost told her how she looked in those tight red slacks. But Shattuck, Briarview's head pro, had given me strict instructions about being nice to her. The lady's husband was a club wheel. Shattuck would have ordered me to sleep with her had she offered to underwrite his next pro-amateur tournament.

Mrs. Metzger is a teaching pro's typical nightmare. *Now watch, honey.* Every time you lift your head you see a bad shot. *Don't be a woodchopper.* And she kept saying I was just the handsomest man. And such a better teacher than that gruff old bear, Shattuck.

It went on like that for the next twenty minutes, with the Metzger asking me to show her an overlapping grip far too often. She liked me to touch her. She was getting to that kittenish stage they sometimes reach after the third lesson, when they ask you what you can teach them besides golf. I had the answer for that one, but Mrs. Metzger wasn't going to like it.

I kept stealing glances at the dark-haired girl down the range. She was all business. Crisp iron shots, a man's stance. Once she paused thoughtfully to light a cigarette and I got a clear look at her profile.

Recognition came with a searing jolt. Her name was Fern Davis.

Eight months ago, Fern and I had been engaged.

Engaged, and terribly, head-over-heels in love.

Six months ago I had been on the tournament trail trying to earn honeymoon money, when Fern had married someone else. A stranger. I had found out about it when I'd come back from the winter tour, flat broke and jobless.

I stood staring numbly at Fern, and the Metzger squealed, "Look, Tony!" Her spoon shot had popped all of sixty yards in the air.

"Wonderful," I grunted. "You should break five hundred today."

"That's not funny." She dropped the honeychile accent. "You're paid to teach me, not watch other people."

"Keep your head down and you won't notice those little things."

The Metzger didn't like it. She was paying five dollars a lesson for the exclusive attention of a golf pro, Tony Pearson. She was being cheated. She glared, then abruptly turned and flounced back toward the clubhouse. Shattuck would chew me about it but at the moment I didn't care.

Fern and I stared at each other across a gulf in time. She walked toward me with that remembered mannish stride, carrying her golf bag. When she spoke it was friendly, unashamed.

"Hello, Tony."

"How's married life?" I meant to sound casual, but it came out as a snarl.

Fern studied me somberly. "You've changed, Tony."

"You get old," I said. "You get disillusioned. No explanations?"

"Would they matter?"

"No," I said. "I guess they wouldn't."

Six months of marriage hadn't hurt Fern's looks. Her soft mouth still hinted of vulnerability, those dark eyes still were as stormy as on the night she had given me back my ring. The wind came up and a few drops of rain spattered Fern's golf bag. I was trembling. I blurted something about only a fool playing in the rain.

"I like to play in the rain, remember?" Soft cool voice, a little husky. "It's a good chance to be alone, to think." She walked toward the starter house, a lonely figure in gray slacks carrying a heavy golf bag. I wondered why she wasn't playing with her husband. Maybe he didn't play.

To hell with her. Some day I'd be able to remember her without it being an open wound. I struck out for the pro shop, bracing myself for Shattuck's chewing.

Shattuck is a Briarview fixture. A great tawny man with sincere gray eyes, he is most especially sincere when selling a club member a new set of custom woods, eighty dollars a matched set. He frowned when I came in and motioned me back toward the deserted locker room.

"Tony, I'm worried about you." He made it sincere, paternal.

"Look, your Mrs. Metzger—"

"She's not important. What's important is that since you've come back from the circuit you've had a chip on each shoulder. It's not my fault you're a failure, Tony." I felt my mouth tighten but he continued. "Failure. Live with it, mister. Think it every time you look in the mirror. You're not Snead or Middlecoff. You're just a sour assistant pro who's been letting the shop go to hell. You think a club pro only teaches and plays in weekend pro-ams? He also sells clubs. He encourages new memberships. He's a personality kid and public relations man and assistant greenskeeper. Understand?"

I said I understood.

"Then smile at the customers, Tony. Be glad you're working at Briarview. So you shot a sixty-four once and tied the course record." His voice softened. "So did I. Fifteen years ago. Thought it was the beginning of something. I hit the tournament trail like you did—and failed. Took me a long time to grow out of that phase, son. Just like you're going to do. Or I'll have to fire you, Tony."

He left me alone in the locker room.

The first reaction was fury. A blazing rage, shot with nausea. I started out into the pro shop to tell Shattuck he could shove this job sideways, and just before I reached the door, caught a reflection of myself in the mirror and stopped dead.

A stranger glowered at me. A tanned bleak stranger with blond hair bleached to cotton by the sun. A brooding stranger who could drive a ball three hundred yards and three-putt from five feet. A failure, with tattered dreams of glory.

But I couldn't really blame Fern.

We had first met at a Briarview pro-am. She played a man's game of golf and her paintings had been displayed at the Laguna Art Festival. There was a wildness in her. Some of her friends were homosexual art critics. Some were smooth gangsters who had made their pile in Eastern rackets and retired to the expensive Laguna sunshine.

Fern was intense as a dark flame, insecure as quicksand. Her parents had separated when she was a child, leaving her to be raised by her uncle, a Laguna art ceramist. All things considered, he had done a good job. Fern and I clicked, right from the start. Those first three months we shared a crazy splendid kind of magic all our own. We fought, yet the fights only sweetened our reconciliations. Fern wanted a quick marriage. She wanted me to land a rich country-club berth and settle down.

But I had visions of hitting that tournament trail and bringing home a million dollars to marry Fern in style. Fern insisted on following the sun with me. I told her it was no life for a woman, living on hot dogs and beans, sleeping in flea-trap motels. We argued. It became an issue all out of proportion. Our last session had been a furious one. "*I won't wait for you, Tony. It's now or not at all, darling.*"

Stubborn female pride, I had thought. She would wait. But she didn't.

And Tony Pearson had broken his heart on the tournament trail.

That time at Pinehurst, remember? You qualified with a sixty-six. Then withdrew after a disastrous eighty-three on the second round.

Then Oakmont, a month later. It was the second day and you were right up there with Burke and Littler, tied for first place. You *had* to come in the money. It was your last chance. It takes dough to follow the circuit and you had exactly twelve dollars left in the world. Came the fourteenth, a wicked par five dogleg. You put the first drive out of bounds and the gallery murmured. You teed the second ball carefully and hooked deep into the rough. You gave the gallery a sick smile. Your nerves were shrieking piano wire, you wanted to vomit.

The rest of the round was a bad dream. Tony Pearson, another flash in the pan from Hickville. Cracked under pressure. Out of the money.

Those who can, do. Those who can't, teach.

Live with it, Pearson. Some day you'll be a big club pro like Shattuck. You'll own a percentage of the club bar and a piece of the pro shop. A distinguished graying citizen making fifteen thousand a year, beaming sincerely at well-heeled club members. And Fern will be just a painful memory.

My anger at Shattuck faded. I went out to the pro shop and helped unpack a new display of irons. Tomorrow I would interest some club member in trading in his old irons. Shattuck would like that.

At seven o'clock I dutifully swept out the shop and locked up. Outside it was dusk and the rain had died to a fine drizzle. I went over to the driving range and switched on the spotlights. For the next three hours I savagely belted out drives. It was no good; I still had that unpredictable hook which had ruined me at Oakmont. About ten o'clock the rain came down hard. I drove home to my Belmont Shore bachelor apartment and went to bed.

Next day was a humid Saturday. All morning I rang up greens fees at the pro shop and practiced being cheerful. I even sold one club member a new set of woods. In the afternoon I relieved the starter and it was four o'clock when I saw Fern. She came up to the first tee with that heavy golf bag slung over her shoulder. As always, she disdained a caddy-cart. Looking at her, I had trouble breathing.

She wore green shorts and white halter. Long, honey-tanned legs, and the halter tight over fine deep breasts. When she saw me at the starter window she paused. I got the impression of a startled uncertainty.

"Hi!" I tried to make it sound relaxed. "How'd you do yesterday?"

"Seventy-nine." There was a breathless catch in her voice as she gave me her greens ticket. I tore the ticket slowly and handed back the stub, hating myself for the way my hand shook.

"I've got a twosome at four-ten if you'd like to wait." My voice, tight, thick.

"No, thanks. I want to go around alone."

She walked nervously up to the first tee. She took three practice swings and made a point of not looking back at me. Her drive was straight and true, landing somewhere beyond the two-hundred-yard marker.

There was no affectation in her. She really wanted to be out there in her own quiet green world. It reminded me of the times we used to quarrel, how she would invariably head for the golf links. Alone. I used to kid her about potential catatonia, hurt withdrawal from the world.

I was still thinking about her when I closed the starter shack at five and went into the clubhouse. Shattuck was in foul humor.

"You sold a set of woods to a guy named Peterson this morning?" His voice was too bland.

"Sure. Proud of me?"

"You over-allowed him twenty dollars on his old woods, Tony. Why?"

He was actually angry. I mumbled something about reconditioning the old woods and Shattuck snapped, "We inventory trade-ins at two dollars a club. It's all they're worth. Will you please consult me next time you decide to give away club equipment?"

It stung. But I forced a smile and he grunted. "Stick around, I'll be back by seven."

It was five, it was five-thirty, and nobody came into the pro shop. I chain-smoked, trying to put Fern out of my mind. Trying to hate her, and failing. After a time I went back to the locker room and found Tommy. Tommy Blake is a tow-headed fourteen, very eager. He scoops practice balls off our driving range and runs odd errands and dreams of being a top pro.

"I got the locker room all swept out," Tommy said respectfully, "just like Mr. Shattuck said."

The locker linoleum sparkled. "Good job, Tommy. I'm going out for a few holes. Watch the shop, will you?"

He nodded uncertainly. Shattuck would never let Tommy run the pro shop by himself. But what the hell, I thought, I'll be back before seven. I only wanted to talk to her, to get some kind of explanation. I didn't know what the hell I wanted.

I got my clubs and headed across the first fairway, walking fast. She would be on the seventh hole by now, a long par five.

The eighth tee was deserted. I stood panting. I had run the last hundred yards. Then came the lurching fear that she wouldn't show at all, that she'd played the back nine instead.

Then I saw her through the oaks surrounding the seventh green. When she saw me she got a white trapped look.

"Fern?" I made it cheerful, the most natural thing in the world that I should suddenly appear on the eighth tee. "Mind if we finish the front nine together?"

Fern minded. She came up to the tee, lips tightly compressed. "Why, Tony?"

"Don't you think I'm entitled to some sort of explanation?" I swallowed. "Hell, I didn't even get a Dear John. I had to hitch-hike back to California, ragged and broke. Shad was decent enough to put me back on the Briarview payroll, but it was a week before I scraped up nerve to go around to your uncle's. That's when he told me you had just married some guy named Steve Locke."

"You think it was rebound, is that it?"

"I want to know if you love him," I said stubbornly.

She looked at me with a queer remoteness.

"I'll tell you what you don't want to hear, Tony." Fern spoke with carefully controlled effort. "With you it wasn't real. We fought too much over trifles. It was unstable, an adolescent love. With Stephen it was different—"

"He was there and I wasn't, huh?"

It was the wrong thing to say. She teed up her ball without another word. We drove off together and walked down the fairway.

Fern's second shot was a spoon. The ball faded into a trap just short of the green.

"Your right hand's riding a little high," I said inanely.

No answer. My hands were sweating as I came up to my ball. I took out a five iron. It was a poor shot. Sand sprayed from the same trap. Fern's smile was impersonal.

"Too much right hand," she said in a fruity voice. "Head down and follow through."

I laughed. We studied our trap lies. My ball was completely buried in the sand. I took out my wedge and exploded. The ball dropped two feet past the pin and rolled to the far apron.

Fern didn't congratulate me. She took out a seven iron, squinting man fashion into the sun. It had become a silent deadly duel, to win this hole.

Her chip shot was clean, but strong. We both needed twenty-footers for our par. I started to line up my putt and she said, "I'm away, if you don't mind."

"Go ahead." I held the pin.

She putted, playing the break high. At the last possible second the ball curved sharply downward, hesitated on the lip, and plopped in.

I studied my putt. It was slightly uphill. I putted too strongly and my ball rimmed the cup and slithered past. Just like at Pinehurst.

"You're one up," I said tightly.

"Look," she said in a choked voice, "it's no good, Tony. It was over eight months ago. Why don't you go to the clubhouse?"

"Sorry I bothered you, Mrs. Locke." I felt suddenly tired as I picked up my bag. "It sure as hell won't happen again."

I turned away and she said, "Damn you," in a fierce whisper.

That left just one thing to do. I dropped my bag and started for her. Her eyes got large and dark. Her lips kept saying "No," soundlessly as I grabbed her and then she came alive, fighting, twisting her head away, and all at once her long body spasmed against mine and she was clinging to me like a drowning woman. She was kissing me and crying.

It seemed a very long time before I let her go. Fern was wiping away tears, trying to smile. "I can't see you again. This is wrong. The only reason it happened is that three days ago I found my husband doing the same thing with another woman. And I still love him, Tony."

It left absolutely nothing to say.

We walked off the eighth green in silence.

At the ninth tee, a stranger waited for us. A tall tanned man leaning on his caddy-cart.

When Fern saw him she made the smallest possible sound and I was suddenly no longer holding her hand. She said in a flat dull voice, "Hello, Stephen."

Stephen's smile was brilliant against his dusky tan.

"You're a hard wife to find." His voice was deep and resonant. He turned a piercing blue gaze on me and I felt the impact of his personality like a sledge.

He had that indefinable charm possessed by certain movie stars, by titans of industry and top-flight salesmen. Drive. Personality plus. Every country club boasts at least one such. They are usually scratch players and throw money around like confetti and have their pick of the club wives. Invariably they own a Jag and belong to a prominent yacht club.

"Hello, Steve," I said numbly.

He nodded and didn't bother to shake hands. "Would you like to play in to the clubhouse, darling?"

"You and Tony play." Fern was bleak, withdrawn. "I'll gallery."

Stephen gleamed at me and teed up his ball. There was a smooth thrust of power in his swing. The ball took off in a flat soaring arc. About two-eighty, straight bind true.

I drove listlessly and walked down the fairway, looking straight ahead. Stephen was talking urgently to Fern.

Something about taking three days to find her, but it had to be a golf course. How what happened had been a mistake, a stupid misunderstanding.

I came up to my ball and selected a brassie. The green looked more than two hundred yards away, but the late afternoon sun can play strange tricks with distance.

Stephen had outdriven me by a good fifteen yards. He was holding a two iron and smiling patronizingly at my brassie. It rankled. I slammed the brassie back into my bag and took out a two iron. It was a poor choice. My shot landed thirty yards short of the green.

Stephen was laughing as he substituted a spoon for his two iron. The old Hagan trick. I wanted to hit him.

His ball split the pin all the way. I saw it bound on the distant green and stop dead.

As we walked down the fairway I caught sight of Shattuck standing in the doorway of the pro shop. He would be unhappy about my leaving Tommy in charge, but at the moment I didn't care. I only wanted to finish this hole and get the hell away from Mr. and Mrs. Stephen Locke.

I came up to my ball and hit a solid wedge that held the pin. When we reached the green Stephen putted almost carelessly. A ten-footer that rolled straight into the cup for an eagle three. Fern's face was pale and set as I picked up my ball, conceding.

Stephen came forward smiling, blue eyes friendly. "Thanks for the game," he said pleasantly. "Incidentally, you forgot to wipe off her lipstick."

He hit me with a short right that traveled no more than ten inches.

It was the hardest punch I've ever received in my life. When the rockets stopped flaring in my brain I was sitting helplessly on the green.

I tried to get up. My arms and legs were paralyzed. A jealous husband with a Marciano punch. I finally got to my feet and stood swaying. My entire face was numb.

They were walking side by side across the roadway to the parking lot. Once Fern looked back. Stephen helped her into a red Thunderbird and they drove away.

When I went into the pro shop Shattuck fired me.

2

"I don't care whose fault it was." Shattuck's smile was paternal, but there was a hot angry light in his eyes. We were all alone in the pro shop. "You're no good to me, Tony. Look, why don't you hit the spring circuit and starve a while? Live on hamburgs and failure until you decide a club pro's life is the best there is. Then come back to Briarview. Two weeks' severance pay okay?"

I said it was fine.

Shattuck punched the cash register and counted it out. "Luck, Tony. I mean it, boy."

"Thanks." There was no point in shaking hands. I walked outside to my ancient Ford convertible.

Driving past the stone pillars that framed the driveway I took a long last look at Briarview. My jaw throbbed.

Stephen knew how to throw a punch. I drove slowly toward Seal Beach and turned right on the coast highway.

It was one of those warm California nights with the air full of salt freshness and the Pacific dreaming under a fat orange moon. A good night to be with your girl, making plans or making love. Somewhere else in the night Stephen and Fern were reconciling. I thought about them as I drove past Naples—the new flagstone-and-glass motels on the bay front—into the soft glitter of downtown Belmont Shore.

My apartment was three blocks from the beach, a converted rear duplex with double bed and hot plate in lieu of kitchen. Mrs. Finch charged me sixty a month with a straight face and took pains to remind me that come July she could rent it for ninety. I carefully stowed my golf clubs in the closet and opened the bureau drawer. There was a virgin fifth of Haig there but I decided not to touch it. I had to focus on the plight of Tony Pearson, unemployed.

On the nightstand was my pocket board of chessmen, arrayed in a titanic end game. I scowled at them, wondering how white could possibly mate in four. Someday I was going to look up the solution.

I sat on the studio couch and rationalized. The smart thing was to find a job immediately, some swing-shift aircraft deal so I could use every waking second to perfect my game. Maybe in six months, a year, practice would pay off.

I got out my putter and some balls. For two hours I practiced putting on the threadbare rug. When I went to bed I dreamed about Fern.

Next morning I was shaving in my two-by-four bathroom when the sharp rap sounded on the door. Mrs. Finch? My rent wasn't due for two days.

"Come in," I called, and the door opened.

It was Stephen.

For a moment I just stared, lather drying on my face. He stood tall and sleekly handsome, almost filling the doorway. He wore softly tailored beige slacks and a white linen sport shirt that must have set him back forty dollars.

"Shattuck said I might find you here." He said it humbly, as if it explained everything. "May I come in?"

I nodded mutely, wiping lather from my face. His gaze darted about the room, encompassing everything in one quick sweep, me, the shabby bureau, the chessmen on the nightstand.

"You play chess I see." A warm smile. We were old chess pals. He peered at the board. "Alekhine and Marshall, isn't it? Baden-Baden, 1925? Queen to bishop's six and mate in four?"

"Yeah," I said sourly, studying the board and wondering why I hadn't thought of that rook move before. "All right, what do you want?"

"To apologize, Tony."

His smile would have made an angel weep. His blue eyes were a little ashamed. Somehow his richness made this room a little shabbier, more down at the heels. He was of the elite, the white-flannel yacht club boys, the Austin-Healy crowd. Rich tan and cultured baritone. Today he was slumming.

"So you've apologized," I growled. "So I kissed your wife, so you got me fired. Beat it."

A dreamy look came into his eyes. I tensed. He had me by twenty pounds, none of it fat, but I hoped he'd swing. Instead he chuckled and sat on the bed. His grin was rueful and charming as all hell.

"I don't blame you for being sore, Tony. Look, would you like to be head pro at Point Rafael?"

"*Huh?*"

"Starts at eight thousand a year, plus a pro shop rake-off. It's no charity, we really need a home pro." He grimaced. "Fact of the matter is, I'm in a spot. I promised my boss I'd produce a pro within twenty-four hours."

This was too wild. I sat weakly on the bed. Point Rafael was an exclusive new course not too far from Laguna. Veddy upper-crust and loaded with money. It simply didn't make sense.

"Your boss?" I said.

"The owner, Max Baird." He said it like announcing Caesar. "I'm his business manager, attorney and nursemaid. You've heard of Baird?"

"Something to do with tuna canneries, isn't he?" Then memory came and I blinked. "Didn't he get a big play in the papers two years back? F.H.A. contracting scandals, smuggling dope on his tuna boats? He's the Frank Costello of the coast, something like that?"

"The grand jury refused to indict him," Stephen said quietly. "Sure, he had greased a few officials to get loan priority, what contractor hasn't? But that dope angle was pure vomit. The tabloids smeared him because one of his friends was a high-rolling gambler who knows the Sunset Strip boys. Guilt by association."

His smile was etched with strain. It was terribly important that I believe him. But Max Baird was a name with blood on it, one of the twilight names like Frank Costello and Joe Adonis. And Fern was married to this man who worked for him.

I said, "Trying to sell me on Max Baird?"

"He's—eccentric. One of those self-made men that worships strength. Last week he fired the club pro, Loomis, because he was a short knocker. Couldn't drive a ball over two-fifty."

Tommy Loomis was a former PGA champ, and one of the finest golfers on the coast. I said slowly, "I don't get it. I'm just an assistant pro. What makes me so special?"

"You hit a long ball." Stephen was patient. "Baird likes that sort of thing. Besides, he's an avid duffer with a roundhouse hook and the disposition of an army mule. He just can't take instruction. Fern said—" He flushed. "She said you were a good teacher."

I almost grinned at him.

"You probably won't last over a month," Stephen said stiffly. "But I've got a hunch you just might work out. Well?"

It was the undertone of challenge in his voice, the arrogance. Cheap psychology, and it worked. I stood up, said, "I'll drive out to Point Rafael this afternoon. Okay?"

He looked delighted as we shook hands. He had the personality of a chameleon. One moment you got the impression of a brilliant sophistry, now it was all boyish awkwardness. "Mind filling me in on your background, Tony? Max might ask."

I didn't mind. I told him about Tony Pearson. High school and city college golf champ. How my parents were killed in an auto smashup while I was in Korea. My caddy days at Briarview, then the assistant pro job. The tournament trail and failure. I told him nothing about Fern. And, as I talked, I kept studying Stephen's elegant profile. This was the man who had taken Fern. He must have been violent and ruthless in courtship, like an attacking army. A brilliantly sincere errand-boy for a retired mobster. He had a chemotropic charm and could chill you with one sneak punch.

After he left I sat on the bed, smoking moodily, trying to plumb the fascination of Stephen Locke. Many days later I realized that evil has its own deadly *glamyr.* In the zoo, you may stare at the shimmering little piranha for a long time. At the oiled sleekness of a coral snake. Later, I developed a theory. The stalking carnivore excretes an aura which dulls the perception of its prey. Carnivores may be two-legged. You may meet them at business luncheons, cocktail parties, anywhere, brilliantly adapted to their jungles of steel and stone—or their country clubs.

After a time I went into the bathroom and finished shaving. I kept telling myself it was some sort of mad joke. Then I tried to tell myself it was the money, a chance to save a few bucks before hitting the tournaments again.

But I kept thinking of a cool determined girl with hair stroked by midnight and a haunted look in her eyes. I had to see Fern again.

If Stephen had considered that angle, possibly he wouldn't have been so quick to offer me the job.

Only one thing bothered me. Maybe he *had* considered it.

3

That afternoon I drove out Highway 101, past Newport. It was a good clear day, with the wind creaming the Pacific off Laguna as I hit the long coast stretch into Point Rafael.

Small, even for a beach town, the place consists of a new pink motel, three filling stations, and two drive-ins. A rotting pier with a *Condemned* sign on it juts two hundred yards out into the surf.

And there is the Lee Shore Hotel.

By daylight the hotel is merely stunning. The swimming pools glisten aquamarine through a forest of palms. Three stories rise into flying buttresses of stone lace. By moonlight it is a palace of champagne witchery, a maharajah's dream. Two years before the scandal sheets had blasted it as a Babylon temple of sin, catering to jaded movie stars and degenerate millionaires, a place where anything could be bought in those plush suites for the right price. Anything.

I turned left at the inland cut-off and drove back through rolling green hills a half mile before I hit the winding road to the golf course. The clubhouse was a fieldstone miniature of the Lee Shore, surrounded by palms and tropicals. I parked the Ford between a black Eldorado and a Lincoln Continental, and walked into the pro shop.

A short wizened man was leaning over the glass showcase. He had the bright feral gaze of a lizard. "Are you a member, sir?"

"I'm looking for Steve Locke." Now he would turn on that aloof smirk reserved for visiting non-members. He would tell me he didn't know any Stephen Locke. And this would all turn out to be an elaborate nasty joke.

But he beamed as if I owned the place. "Yes, *sir!* You must be Mr. Pearson. I'm Chad Lupo. Care to look around?"

I said thanks and went outside past the frosted-glass starter house. The first hole was a rolling emerald dogleg, lined with live oaks and cottonwoods. A blue lake bisected the fairway, curving back toward the huge putting green by the clubhouse. I saw Fern, all alone on the green, concentrating on a putt.

I walked over and said, "Hi."

She missed the putt by a foot and stared as if I were a man in a dream. Again I got the impression of shock, of controlled fear.

"Relax." I made it a sneer. "I only attack wives on Thursdays."

"Why did you come here, Tony?"

"Your hubby offered me a job. Monarch of Point Rafael."

It rocked her.

"Beggars can't be choosers," I said. "This job might give me a stake, if it lasts long enough."

"You won't like Baird, Tony. He's—he's vicious. You'll be his third pro this year." She touched my hand with swift urgency. "Listen, how much more of a stake do you need?"

"A grand or so. Why?"

"I'll lend you a grand, Tony." Her gaze was intense, unflinching. "It's not charity. Call it an investment in your future. You can give me your personal note and pay me back out of your first big win. Fair enough?"

I looked at her. She flushed, but kept those dark eyes steady. I said savagely, "Husband offers a job, wife offers a thousand to turn it down." She tried to turn away and I grabbed her arms. "Why are you so afraid of Stephen? And why so damned anxious to get me away from here?"

"All right." Her voice was tired. "Forget it. It's just that Stephen has—whims. Sometimes they hurt people."

"Question," I said awkwardly. "Do you really love him?"

Nothing changed in Fern's voice, or her eyes. "Yes. I love him very much, Tony. See you around."

She walked like a queen toward the clubhouse. I wondered why she was lying.

The whole thing was too pat, too wonderful. Rich husband gets itinerant pro fired. Offers him dream job on a whim. It just didn't jell. Suddenly the lush expensive links, the sunlight glitter on the blue lake, seemed ominous, unreal as a Hollywood set. I started for the first tee, wondering where the gimmick was.

A dark heavy man occupied the tee, practicing drives. He looked keenly at me. "You're Pearson?"

Everybody knew me. It was all part of the act. "I'm Pearson," I said. "You must be Mr. Baird."

"Max to you." He had a bear's handclasp. His eyes were green ice under grizzled brows. "So you're Steve's latest find. He told me you were a good teacher."

Gruffness in his voice, bordering on challenge. He looked about fifty, thick and hard. His hair was silver wire over mahogany features. Greek, possibly Sicilian. My answer sounded flip.

"Depends on my material, Mr. Baird."

His grin was humorless. "Belt one, Pearson." He handed me the driver. "Go on, belt one."

I hefted the club, fighting a slow red anger. He had more money than manners. In just one minute I was going to tell Mr. Baird where he could stick his driver and his job.

I teed up a ball and swung. It was one of the longest drives of my life. The ball hissed in a flat white trajectory just above the lake, gradually soaring, finally dropping with a good overspin bounce on the fairway. Three-thirty, at least.

"Not bad," Baird grunted. "Now watch."

He took the driver and teed up another ball. He took his time addressing it. He had a baseball grip, a spraddle-legged stance. With that vicious swing, he looked oddly out of place at plush expensive Point Rafael. I had a vision of him on a tuna boat in the blue water past Clemente. A dark angry Greek with fish scales shining on his denims, roaring at his crew to grab those albacore jigs. Max Baird, formerly Max Bardos, who had clawed his way up from bait boy to become owner of three canneries and a fleet of tuna boats. Owner of the Lee Shore and Point Rafael country club. A ruthless amoral gangster with the wistfulness of a child.

He hit the ball cleanly and it hissed away in a white streak. A hundred yards out it hooked sharply into the lake.

"I hook," Baird said bleakly. "Irons and woods. You're going to fix it, understand? *Without* changing my swing. As of now, you're hired. Seven hundred a month and what you can steal from the pro shop. If you try to change my stance or grip like Loomis did, you're fired."

I almost told him to go to hell. What checked me was the gruff overtone of pleading in his voice. I caught a glimpse of naked vulnerability, the fierce dumbness of a man too proud to beg. It went far deeper than a golf swing. He needed something money couldn't buy.

"You're asking a miracle," I said.

"So I'm willing to pay for it. Can you deliver?"

"Try that swing again."

I watched him for five minutes. His feet were planted wrong, he had far too much right hand. If he could possibly slow down his wrist action he'd have an even chance of hitting a straight ball. But Max Baird wasn't a man who changed his style.

"Well, Pearson?"

Suddenly, I wanted this job. I wanted just once in my life to have my own pro shop. I wanted the chance to be near Fern, to tear her thoughtful mask away and find out what had happened between us. But I shook my head and said, "Sorry, Mr. Baird. I can't help you unless you're willing to swing properly."

I left him on the tee, staring after me. Dark proud man built like a barrel, too stubborn to change his stance or grip. But there was one way to cure his hook. An unorthodox way, a joker's way. I kept thinking about it as I walked under the palms toward the parking lot. Finally I shrugged and turned into the pro shop. Baird might fire me later, but later wasn't important.

Lupo gave me a bland smile. "Tough, isn't he?"

"Not so tough." I selected a driver at random from a display rack and went behind the counter. "Where's the screwdriver and lead?"

The little man found them and watched expressionlessly while I took the backing plate off the clubhead.

"Weighting it, huh?"

"Got a better idea to slow down his swing?"

He gnawed at his lip. It had never occurred to him.

I really weighted that clubhead. When it was finished I checked it on the scales. It came to E-9, which is about the same as putting a half-pound weight on the end of a tennis racket.

"Good luck, baby," said Lupo as I left the clubhouse.

Baird was still on the first tee. The eagerness in his voice belied the scowl. "Forget something, Pearson?"

"Try this on for size, Max." I handed him the weighted driver. He hefted it uncertainly.

"Feels clumsy. What's the idea?"

"Hit the ball with it. Just once."

He grunted and teed up a ball. His swing was exactly the same, an inside-out roundhouse. There was only one difference. The ball creamed far out over the lake, rising, hitting the fairway two hundred and forty yards away.

Baird said something softly in Greek. He stared at the driver, then teed another ball. The result was almost the same, except that this time the ball faded slightly to the right.

"You son of a bitch," he said with emotion.

"Am I hired, Mr. Baird?"

"Max, you clever bastard, and don't forget it. Tell Max what you done."

The bastard business prickled, but I let it lie. I told him about the factors of swing versus clubhead speed and made it sound simple. "Pretty soon, Max, you'll start compensating for that weight and pushing the ball to the right. Then you'll fire me the way you did Loomis."

He chuckled and clapped my shoulder. His fingers were tool steel, digging in, hurting. I kept my grin in place.

"You're coming out to the house." It was an imperial command. "You can have the guest house next to Lupo. You'll be a resident pro. Tomorrow you hire a greenskeeper and two assistants. Next week we throw a pro-am, get some of the La Jolla snobs out here. You're going to give me class,

Tony."

He kept talking about it as we walked into the parking lot, all of his plans for Point Rafael. He waved happily at a twosome coming off the eighteenth tee, and they came over.

Even for Point Rafael they were something special. The man was bronzed and handsome, a red-gold crew cut and vital smile. The woman was a pale exquisite madonna. Her hair was soft platinum and her features had the classic purity of a medallion. She kissed Max on the cheek. "I broke ninety, darling. George was gallant in defeat."

"No spot next time," said George warmly. "She beat me four and three. Does it rate a drink?"

"Champagne at my place." Max was expansive. "Meet my new pro, Tony Pearson. He just cured my hook. Tony, this is Val, my wife. George Fair's a Newport real estate thief."

It brought me a friendly nod from George and a long look of appraisal from Valerie. Val's eyes were gentian blue, and she had that trick of looking at you as if you were the only man in the world. George didn't offer to shake hands. As far as he was concerned Max had bought himself another new toy for seven hundred dollars a month.

"We'll take my wagon," Max said. "George, you and Val can follow us out in your heap. I got to orient my new pro."

Max's wagon turned out to be the Eldorado. I mumbled something about not wanting to leave my battered Ford and Max paid absolutely no attention. "You got brains," he said, slapping my knee with those iron fingers. "We'll get along fine. Within a month you'll have me shooting par golf, Tony."

He almost made you believe it. He was much man. I began to understand the drive and enthusiasm that made him a coast legend. We drove up the steep grade, past a flagstone ranch house, then a copper-and-glass modern, screened by live oaks and poplar. Once I glanced in the rear-view mirror. George and Val were a hundred yards behind us, and George was driving a black Porsche with the top down. He had one arm around Val's shoulders and she seemed to like it. Laughing, platinum hair streaming in the wind. Max kept on talking about the club and never once glanced into the mirror. Maybe he was part Eskimo, I thought.

The house turned out to be white Colonial set in a rolling green vista of elms, with a sprinkling of guest houses between the pool and flagged tennis courts. From the shoulder of the house you could see down a long bluff path that sloped to a private cove and landing. Max pulled into the half-moon driveway behind two Jags and an Austin-Healy. "Val's friends." He sniffed at the little cars. "Newport yacht-club stinkers. She and Steve are hogs for class." His grin turned wistful. "Like I am. Did you know Steve started out as a bait boy?"

"Really?"

"Hell. He ran away from his home town when he was fourteen. First time I saw him he was a snotnose kid starving on the San Pedro wharfs. He had a kind of eagle look about him, even then. Sharp. Hungry. I gave him a job and he worked his can off for Max. Nights he read books. Law books, Shakespeare, the works. It give me an idea. I owned my first cannery by then and was beginning to stick my fingers in other pies. I needed brains, the kind of shyster brains you can trust. Lupo was all I had, and he was only muscle. So on Steve's seventeenth birthday I sent him off to Stanford to be a lawyer. He cried. You know he graduated *cum laude?* Smartest investment I ever made in my life. Now Steve gets twenty grand a year to run things for me. He worries about taxes and the monthly take at the Lee Shore while all I worry about is curing a hook so Val will play golf with me."

I slowly revised my opinion of one Stephen Locke, playboy. Max glanced back toward the graveled hill road. Val and George were taking their time about getting here.

"I want you to move into one of the guest houses," Max said. "You might as well live here like Chad and Steve."

"Baird and family," I said slowly.

"Exactly." Max missed the irony. "Listen, Tony. Two years ago I'm a big name in the headlines. They make me out to be a wheel in the syndicate. They call me doper, pimp, mobster. It makes Max wonder what he's getting out of life. So Max retires and becomes a country gentleman. He buys himself a beautiful wife and country club. Real fine. Steve says I'm spread out too thin. He says the Shore is a white elephant that's costing me a grand a day. He begs me to sell—"

He broke off, glanced back at the white graveled roadway. No black Porsche. No Val and George. It was making me nervous. "Why don't you sell, Max?"

"I've got other assets," he said bitterly. "They get sold first. If I sell the Shore, Point Rafael becomes a different kind of town. I like it the way it is. Clean. Nice people. They respect me."

I was trying to figure out what selling the Shore had to do with Max's self-respect when the Porsche whipped onto the gravel in back of us. I heard Val's throaty laughter mingling with George's. She looked flushed and bright. Max got out of the Cad and walked into the house. I followed him.

I wanted to see what was happening in the Porsche, but I did not look back. Neither did Max.

4

The party was going full blast. In one corner of the great vaulted living room at an ivory grand piano, sat Stephen, improvising. Next to him sat a willowy redhead singing a Cole Porter parody in unexpurgated French. There was a portable bar by the terrace, and couples playing darts and arguing over score. Everybody had drinks. The men showed that careless assurance that comes of enough money and enough time to spend it. The women were leggy and tanned. Even in denim shorts they looked sleekly expensive. Fern was nowhere in the room.

Stephen stopped playing when we came in. The dart game came to a gradual halt. Max said with a soft restrained violence, "Thought I told you to stay at the airport."

"His plane's late." Stephen got up quickly and handed Max a telegram. "He'll land at the Los Angeles airport sometime tonight. I left a call for him on arrival."

Max relaxed. Some of the stillness went out of the room. He grinned at the guests. "Hi, everybody. Potluck on the terrace okay?"

It seemed to be fine. Everybody nodded politely and smiled. Then they went back to their dart game. Max might have been part of the fireplace for all the attention they paid him. That redhead was eyeing Stephen with a possessive speculation.

Val and George came in. Val squeezed Max's hand perfunctorily and hurried over to the dart players. One of the men murmured something and Val threw back her head and laughed. Max watched her with a dumb hurt look.

"Tell Chad to bring me a sandwich in the den," he told Stephen. "Call me when Ramos gets here."

He walked slowly past the french windows and up the lucite staircase. I felt puzzled and a little sorry for him.

"He's got a mile-wide inferiority complex," Stephen said softly. "He thinks Val's friends laugh at him behind his back. It's one of the reasons he wants so terribly to be a sharp golfer, to belong."

I couldn't resist the thrust. "Too bad nobody ever sent him through Stanford."

Stephen winced. Then he grinned. "He likes to throw it into me about owing him my existence. Which, of course, I do. How about some food?"

Dinner turned out to be smoked turkey buffet on the outside terrace, with a white-coated Filipino mixing gibsons, and George and Val very gay over the scotch foursome tourney they were planning for next month. I smiled with my mouth and made polite noises and sat on the stone parapet munching a drumstick, and I watched the willowy redhead.

Her name turned out to be Lorraine, and she had hot black eyes that focused entirely too much on Stephen, and not enough on Paul, her stocky unsmiling husband. I saw Stephen bring her a fourth gibson, and bend over her whispering something, and take entirely too long to tell her what he was undoubtedly telling her, and I noticed how Paul began talking loudly about his new cabin cruiser and the Acapulco cruise he and Lorraine planned for June. Lorraine ignored him completely.

These were the hollow people, the Metzgers and Shattucks of Point Rafael. Their world consisted of Sunday foursomes and Catalina regattas and casual infidelity at the weekend club dance while their mates were too potted to care. Val and George Fair were entirely too much of a twosome. But she laughed loudly at Paul's banalities and kept stabbing glances at Stephen and Lorraine. She looked actually jealous.

Fern appeared on the terrace, cool and distant in a green linen dress. Stephen got up solicitously and helped her to the buffet. "How's the headache, darling?"

"Fine, Stephen." She made a point of not looking at me. Finally her eyes flicked mine and to me it was a glance alive, electric. But she had put up an intangible barrier that I intended to tear down before the evening was over.

Maybe Stephen sensed it. "How about chess, Tony? Spot you a rook."

He was calm, matter-of-fact, rather than patronizing. He was obviously a superior player. I wanted to hit him.

"Fine," I said, following Fern with my eyes as she went back through the french windows into the living room. Dusk was falling, with a damp evening breeze that promised rain. Johnny, the houseboy, brought us a stand and chessmen.

"You can have white," I said. "We'll play even."

Once, when I was seventeen, and the wizard Steiner was giving a simultaneous exhibition in Los Angeles, I held him to a draw. I was a competent player.

But I had never played anyone like Stephen Locke.

His gambit was a formless attack, without apparent purpose or shape, exploding into a brilliant middle-game.

It hinted of a mind incredibly complex, and patient. He smashed me with almost contemptuous ease.

"Again?" Stephen asked.

We played again. From inside came the soft throb of Cuban drums and I saw that Val had turned on the hi-fi and was dancing very close with

George. The dart couples were drinking too much and arguing. Fern was playing dominos with the wizened man I had met at the clubhouse.

"Chad Lupo," said Stephen, following my glance. "Lupo did big time in Folsom and came out a very fine domino player. He's Max's bodyguard, valet, and watchdog. He'd die for Max. He's hurt and puzzled that Max prefers the simple life to the rackets."

"So those headlines were right," I said. Stephen's smile was twisted.

"Past tense, Tony. Two years ago Max withdrew from certain—enterprises. He got a respectability obsession. He married a well-bred tramp named Valerie, but in his own eyes he's still a boorish Greek fisherman who embarrasses her friends. He kicked his hundred-dollar-a-night call girls out of the Lee Shore, and smashed the roulette tables. Now the Shore is costing him, but he won't give it up. It's a symbol, like the country club. He's selling the Rembrandt instead."

"The what?"

"He bought it right after the war, from a private collector. One of the big Nazi looters who needed quick cash for a trip to Argentina and the obscurity that a hundred grand could buy. Technically, the picture still belongs to the Dutch Government and Max is in illegal possession. It's a self-portrait in miniature, and priceless. I've managed to contact a South American collector who has offered three hundred thousand for it. Very hush-hush deal. His representative flew in from Venezuela today to see if it's a genuine Rembrandt. Check. Mate in three, I believe."

I studied the board. He had cracked my fianchetto like a walnut. My king was doomed. I shrugged and stood up.

"Let's go inside," Stephen said. "Smells like rain."

Inside, the sob of violins filled the living room and Val was dancing with her eyes closed. George looked smug as he held her. I looked around for Fern and felt a hollow ache when I saw she was no longer in the room. I wanted to ask her many questions, to kiss her violently until her composure was shattered in tears and reconciliation. But after all, I was of the hired help. I went over to the bar and had a double rye. It helped.

Johnny, the little Filipino, must have had supersonic eardrums. It was impossible to hear the front door chimes, but he did. He flitted past me to the hall, came back with a tall man, dark, with a pencil mustache and beautiful, liquid black eyes. Stephen said, "Mr. Ramos?"

"The same." A crisp bow. Ramos handed him a card. "You are Mr. Baird?" He spoke flawless English, with only the faintest trace of accent. His face was thin, saturnine, wary. He had come to decide whether a piece of ancient canvas was worth three hundred thousand dollars.

"Baird's upstairs," Stephen said. "This way, please." He winked at me. "How would you like to see a real live Rembrandt, Tony?"

Damn him. I had to find Fern. But I shrugged and followed them upstairs. Once I glanced back.

George and Val were no longer in the room. The french windows were open and I could see them on the terrace, a merged shadow, moving with the music. Lupo sat toying with his dominos, staring at them with an unwinking basilisk fixity.

We turned right at the top of the stairs, and went down a hundred yards of jade pile broadloom to a small oak door. Stephen knocked twice. Then twice again. The door opened and Max stood dark and squat in blue denims. He shook hands with Ramos listlessly.

"Tony's never seen an old master," Stephen said lightly. "Is it all right?"

Max gave me a quick look and shrugged. "Why not?"

It was a strange room. The first impression was one of cheap surrealism. The tattered fishing net on the knotty pine wall was out of decor with the walnut hi-fi, the comfortable morris chair. In the middle of the room was a curiously shabby poker table. The green baize was torn. A mounted bluefin stared glassily at us from beside the barred windows. Next to it was the metallic glint of brass, which on closer inspection turned out to be a knuckle-knife. I saw a dollar bill, framed.

And I saw the Rembrandt.

Indirect lighting from the ceiling bathed it in rich umber. It was Van Ryn himself, staring at us from a gold frame. The king of shadows had limned himself in a cynical mood. The eyes, heavy-lidded, half-humorous, half-bitter. The tired mouth, curved richly at the corners, with his secret smile at the world.

Max closed the door. Ramos crossed the room and stared intently at the portrait. "My den," Max told me somberly. "Over there is my first buck. That net I started with, thirty-five years ago. That bluefin cost my brother his life. I'll tell you about it sometime. The knuckle-knife I'll tell you nothing about. Sixteen years ago, playing stud with another Greek named Dandolos, I won sixty grand at this table. It gave me my start. Everything in this room has got a story."

The story of Max, I thought. Bait boy to owner of a Rembrandt. The American dream. Ramos said reverently, "*Señor,* would it be permissible to remove the canvas from its frame?"

Max nodded bleakly, and took the portrait down. He placed it carefully on the table, and Ramos bent over it like an eager doberman.

"Three hundred grand," Max said in a harsh flat voice. "I hope you know your paintings, mister."

Ramos straightened up to his full height. "Señor Baird," he said with dignity, "for three years I had the honor to represent the South American Academy of Art. After the war I was retained by the French Government as consultant to authenticate certain old masters which Goering had looted from Paris. I acknowledge one equal in my field, an Englishman named Joseph Revere."

Baird chuckled humorlessly. "Once I paid Revere five grand to tell me this was the real McCoy. If you're his equal, you're pretty good."

The Latin looked at him with a faint smile. "Six months ago, in Rio, I authenticated *The Madonna of Brugas,* by Michelangelo. A Brazilian collector was paying a half million for it. Since the war, I have had occasion to verify Renoir's *Two Sisters,* and Gauguin's *Night.* Both priceless. And presumed to have been lost during the war. Certain old masters are lost forever to the museums of the world. But collectors like yourself still gloat over them in private rooms—if they had the right price shortly after the war, and contacted the right individuals."

Ramos peered at the portrait. Slowly, and with infinite delicacy, he removed the frame backing plate. "A very valuable commodity, to be kept in one's den."

"It's a very special den," Stephen said quietly. "It's bugged like the First National Bank. Takes Max ten minutes to turn off the alarms before he can even go in."

"Right." Max grinned at Ramos. "Steve, here, is another precaution. His bedroom's next door. Only Steve and myself know the door combinations. Not even my wife knows. See those bars on the windows? They look flimsy, but touch them and you get a thousand volts. Try to bust down the door and—"

The scream came ripping up out of the night. A woman's shriek, full-throated, and iced with terror. It choked off in crescendo, and for one suspended fraction of time Max and Ramos and Stephen stared at me.

The scream belonged to Valerie Baird.

5

Stephen was out of the door and halfway down the hall before anyone else moved. Baird came abruptly to life and pounded after him, Ramos and I bringing up the rear.

Halfway down the hall, Baird and Stephen stopped dead, staring over the balustrade at the frozen tableau below.

The dart players were huddled in a silent group by the bar. Valerie stood just inside the french windows, very pale. Only George Fair was missing. Chad Lupo stood at the foot of the staircase looking sorrowful.

"Little accident, Max," he said cheerfully. "I'm throwing darts and miss the target. George's cheek got a little scratched. Isn't that right, Val?"

Val nodded woodenly. Max stared down at her, at Lupo, and suddenly he looked tired and shrunken. Out on the terrace I caught a stir of white. Johnny, the house-boy. He was bending over a huddled figure that held its face in both hands. George. Evidently Lupo had a variety of functions in the Baird household.

We went back to the den in strained silence. Ramos put on an urbane smile but his fingers shook slightly as he took out a magnifying glass and pored over the portrait. He was obviously unused to this sort of thing. Stephen stared at me. We were both wondering what Lupo had done to George's face with that dart. I made a mental note never to make a pass at Valerie.

Ramos made a small sound and put away his magnifying glass. He said, enunciating deliberately, "*Señor,* your joke is in execrable taste. Where is the Rembrandt?"

Max seemed to hunch a trifle. "I don't get you, friend."

"The Rembrandt, *señor,*" Ramos said with a sour smile. "It is not likely you would expect a man to fly five thousand miles for the express purpose of telling you the obvious—that this canvas is not even a good imitation."

For the space of three seconds, nobody breathed.

Stephen said coldly, "That painting was authenticated by Joseph Revere six years ago. What are you trying to pull?"

"Please do not take my word for it," Ramos said wearily. "Ask any local art dealer. For this, you do not need an expert."

Max's eyes were terrible. "You telling me I paid a hundred grand for a fake?"

"I'm sorry. My principal will be disappointed—"

"God damn your principal to hell," Max said, and shivered. "That dutchman, Neider. Smart Nazi bastard. A hundred grand sacrifice! I wonder how much he paid Revere."

"You can still sell the Lee Shore," Stephen said.

Almost casually, Max slapped him. "Get out," he said. "All of you. Out of here!"

We went downstairs in thick silence. Stephen told Ramos how sorry he was to have wasted his time. Ramos was frigidly polite.

"It happens more often than you might believe. Shortly after the war the market was deluged with old masters which had been ostensibly looted from Europe. Frankly, I would have been surprised had the portrait been genuine—although I did expect a better imitation."

Lupo was sitting alone at the portable bar. "The party's over," he said solemnly. "Val went to bed and Fern took a walk. Everybody else went home. Who's for dominos?"

Stephen ignored him. He was apologizing to Ramos for Max's bad manners as I walked through the french windows to the terrace.

There was a raw dampness in the air, and you could taste rain. I thought about Max, in his den, staring at a fake Rembrandt for which he had paid a hundred thousand dollars. And I thought about Fern as I walked down the flagged terrace steps.

She was out there in the windy darkness, restlessly avoiding me, yet knowing it was inevitable that I would ask her questions about the tension that filled the house of Max Baird. I found her by the swimming pool, near the guest house. She was sitting in a deck chair. Her cigarette defined a long red spiral that died with a hiss in the pool.

"You're late, Tony." Her profile was still, reflective. "I've been expecting you for an hour."

I found another deck chair and sat next to her. "I've been studying a fake Rembrandt."

"Fake?" Her sharp intake of breath.

She listened tautly as I told her about it. "Oh, God," she said, standing. "Poor Max. I've got to go inside, Tony."

"We have things to talk about," I said.

The night wind came up and we felt the first raindrops. Spring lightning flickered on the south horizon.

Fern took a long deep breath. "All right, Tony. We may as well get it over with. Let's take the Thunderbird."

We walked across the graveled drive and got into the little sports car. Rain spattered the windshield as Fern drove silently past the cottonwoods. She turned off the private road suddenly and cut the lights. I lighted cigarettes, making a ritual of it. She inhaled deeply and blew smoke at me in a long shuddering stream. When she spoke the words were stiff and badly rehearsed.

"I'm a fickle bitch, Tony. I only married Stephen to spite you. He had a good job, looks, money. You had nothing. That's what you wanted to hear. Wasn't it?"

"Thanks," I whispered. I was shaking with a dry chill anger.

I reached for her shoulders, turning her, my hands gripping her shoulders hard, and she did not cry out. She came easily into my arms and her mouth was slack against mine, her whole body yielding—and cold. She had prepared herself for this, and she was limp, uncaring. I could take her, now, and she would accept it in flaccid silence as punishment deserved. I let her go. "I'm supposed to hate you now," I said with a tearing bitterness, "and go away. Is that the idea?"

"Damn you," Fern said wearily. "All right. I met Stephen three days after you hit the tournament trail. I tried to fight him, Tony. Honestly, I tried. You've absolutely no conception of his strength. It's the way he plays chess or fights—or makes love. He's utterly invincible when he wants something." Her voice broke. She looked up, her face a pale lovely oval in the darkness. "I'm not sure, even now, what Stephen feels for me."

"What do you feel?"

"Attraction," she said softly. "And fear. He can still look at me across the room and turn me into water."

"Even when you found out Max dominated him like a puppet?"

"Steve kept telling me it was only temporary. How very soon we were going away—" She bit her lip.

"Big killing?" I wanted to hurt her. "Rome and Antibes and Paris? Was making love to Val part of his job, or did he throw that in for a bonus?"

It was a blind brutal stab, based on what she had told me at Briarview, but Fern's head went back as if I'd slapped her. Her knuckles were white against the steering wheel.

"It was a week ago," she said tonelessly. "Steve thought I was playing golf. I decided to go shopping instead and came back to the house to change my clothes. I opened the door to our bedroom and—"

"I don't want to hear about it."

"It didn't make sense at the time," she mused. "Val isn't Steve's type. But something happened tonight that makes sense. Horrible, frightful sense. I'm leaving Steve tomorrow. He doesn't know yet. But it doesn't mean I love you, Tony. I've got to have time to be free, to think clearly. It's a question of evaluating what Fern Davis is, where she's going. She's not going to make the same mistake twice. Maybe in six months or a year, I can look at you objectively. Not now. Can you understand?"

Lightning crackled in a white silent blow against the night. We sat motionless in the drumfire of rain, waiting for the snap of thunder. It reminded me of another night a year before, when Fern and I had driven down to Newport for charcoaled filets at Hugo's, and had drunk too much wine and kissed shamelessly at our table, very young and very much in love. And had driven home in the rain, very gay, until our tire had blown. Fern had insisted on helping me, and we both had laughed like fools, changing that tire in the rain.

I sat hating Stephen. I thought about his apparently formless chess attack, but with a hidden meaning behind every pawn move. With Valerie it had not been just a casual roll in the hay. I said tiredly, "Explanation completed. Let's go back."

She started to turn on the ignition, then hesitated. "You only came down here because of—me. Isn't that right, Tony? You're not going to stay?"

"Why not? Head pro at seven bills a month. It's what you wanted for me a year ago, isn't it?"

"Tony, you'll hate it!" A quiet desperation in her voice. "It's like a prison—"

"With bars of gold. We'll both have what we want, baby. You'll be alone and free, and I'll have a cushy job and bored club wives to solace me for a lost love. Maybe I'll try Val. That is, if Stephen gives her a good recommendation."

Fern's breath was a dry sob. She moved in the darkness, and one hard little fist stung me high on the cheek. I tried to grab her wrists as she twisted behind the wheel, roweling me in the ribs with an elbow, panting with angry effort as I caught her in a bear hug. She was a feline fury, impossible to hold. Golf and tennis had given her good muscles and a man's coordination. She fought with elbows, fists and butting head.

I was wedged back in the corner of the seat, trying to keep her arms imprisoned, and I remember how the blue-white lightning glare showed me her face, all wet and contorted, and how I shouted at her to stop before she got hurt. Then my voice was lost in the thunder as her long body spasmed against mine and her hands came around hard to lock behind my neck and pull my face down to hers.

And it was a fierceness, a consuming violence of passion, with all the bittersweet hunger of lost months coupling us into an aching crescendo of need. Afterward she lay crying softly, her fingertips like mothwings on my cheek. I held her very close and murmured meaningless endearments as to a frightened child.

"I love you, Tony." Tired rusty voice, vulnerable softness of her, and the faint sweet pressure of fingertips.

"I love you, Fern."

"Sparkling conversation," she said gently, raising up and turning on the dash light. "Don't look at me for a minute, please, darling. I'm such a mess."

Her torn dress and tangled dark hair made her even more poignantly desirable. But I dutifully watched the rain and lit twin cigarettes while she repaired the ravages with lipstick and comb. Then she snuggled against me with a contented sigh and for a time we smoked in silence. The rain had stopped.

"You're leaving Stephen tomorrow." It sounded too masterful, but she replied in a still small voice, "Yes, Tony."

We made plans. A quick Reno divorce, then a justice marriage. We'd follow the tournament trail as man and wife. I wanted to wait until next year's spring circuit, but Fern murmured, "No, Tony. It's something that will always be between us, something we both have to get out of our system before we start keeping house."

She was right. Tomorrow we would tell Stephen. He was very civilized, he'd understand.

Yet as we drove back to Max's I felt a gnawing worm of doubt. Fern was holding something back. Something about Stephen. I would ask her, but not then. Later, I thought. Tomorrow.

A hundred yards from the house I got out of the car and kissed Fern good night. I was walking toward the front veranda when the front door opened and Stephen came out. He stood very tall in the doorway, looking at me.

"Thought you'd gotten lost, Tony." His smile was boyish, eager. "We've worked up a fishing spree at dawn. Ever catch albacore?"

I hesitated. "What about the course?"

"Lupo can watch the clubhouse until we get back. Max has a fast boat. We'd be at San Clemente by dawn, back for breakfast before noon. What say?"

"Sounds good," I said cautiously. At least it would give me a chance to talk to him about Fern. "Tough break for Max on that painting."

"Very tough. He can't stand being suckered. I'm going down to the boat now to check on the trolling gear. See you at five, sharp."

I watched him stride along the path toward the boat landing. He was whistling. I went into the living room. Johnny, the houseboy, was emptying ashtrays and cleaning the portable bar. Lupo sat by the fireplace, absorbed in dominos and a half-empty decanter of bourbon. He looked meditative. An hour ago he had maimed a man who had kissed his boss's wife.

His wizened face studied me briefly, then went back to the dominos. "Where you been?"

"Walking in the rain. Where do I sleep tonight?"

"Second house east of the pool. You make his bed up, Johnny?"

"Yes, sar," Johnny grinned. "Fresh linen, clean guest house, you bet. Just like home."

He wheeled the bar back toward the kitchen and I told Lupo good night. "Just one minute, Tony."

I looked at him. His face was a study in stone.

"You seen Steve this last hour?"

"Just passed him as I came in. Why?"

His gaze was sleepy, toadlike. Finally he shrugged.

"It's your business, chum. Steve's been outside for the past hour. When he came back inside he was white. Said you were out in the car with his wife. He sat right there and inhaled a pint of scotch in fifteen minutes. Said he was going to kill you."

"You're kidding," I said slowly.

"I never kid," Lupo said. "Good night."

6

The guest house was nice. Birch walls, a fireplace, maple provincial furniture. Nothing but the best for Max's serfs. I set the Capehart for four-thirty, and went to bed. Sleep came slowly.

Stephen wasn't the type to bare his cuckolded frenzy in public. It didn't quite make sense. Yet Lupo had no reason for lying. Come morning I'd tell Stephen, everything open and above board ...

Five o'clock found me shivering on the boat-landing below the house. It was that gray hour between night and dawn, and the cabin cruiser was a white bird poised in the morning swell. I clambered aboard, and was fumbling in the rack for a pole when Stephen came on board. He wore denims, yacht cap; and he looked white and drawn.

"Max has a hangover, Tony. The party's off. Unless you don't mind making it a twosome."

That suited me fine. I was on the point of telling him we'd catch damned few longfins in April when he brightened and said, "Look, we'll just go out of the cove. Snag a bonita apiece and come back for breakfast on the terrace. What say?"

I hesitated. His grin was rueful. "Frankly, I got potted last night. I said some pretty rough things about you and Fern. We've got to talk it out, Tony."

All this time he was fiddling with the ignition, and abruptly the engine kicked over, racketing the dawn stillness. I shrugged. At least it would give us a chance to get things out in the open. I hoped he wouldn't get nasty.

The cruiser moved leisurely out of the cove and headed east, toward Clemente. It was a calm morning, with the water greenly translucent in the dawn, and once I saw a seven-foot sand shark, cruising lean and lethal just below the surface, and two terrified flying fish that broke water and sailed for thirty yards above the whitecaps.

"Is there anything Max can do about the painting?" I asked.

"Nothing," Stephen said bleakly. "Six years ago I pleaded with him not to buy the damned thing. But owning a Rembrandt fitted his dream of class. Naturally he couldn't insure it without answering some embarrassing questions. Now he has to sell the Lee Shore."

"Doesn't he want to?"

"The only man that will give him a decent price is a smooth gangster from Beverly Hills named Castle. Castle's smart enough to realize the one way to make the Shore pay off is to import hundred-dollar call girls, private rooms with roulette tables, the works. Only Max doesn't want his fair Point

Rafael soiled with bad gangsters. He wants to keep this part of his life shining and uncorrupt." Stephen reached into his jacket pocket and brought out a pint of bonded bourbon. "Open it, Tony? We could both stand some anti-freeze."

I took a deep slug. It was good whiskey. Stephen kept his eyes on the compass as he reached for the pint and downed almost half of it.

"Hey, you're driving, remember?"

He took another slug and grinned, showing even white teeth. "Breakfast, man. Say, why don't you set the jigs? We might pick up a few strays on our way out."

I went back to the stern and fumbled with the trolling gear. We were a half-mile out, and Point Rafael glittered like a great emerald in the dawn. Stephen began to sing *High Barbaree* in a rollicking baritone. His mood had certainly improved. I was feeling sorry for him when the engine died with a cough and he came out to the stern.

"Let's try the green feather this time," he said happily. Except for a faint flush around the cheekbones, the bourbon hadn't touched him. "Longfins are fickle as hell. Last time they wouldn't touch a spoon."

He helped me string the jigs, whistling. "Strange thing, Tony. Ten years ago I hated this. Poor little bait boy, hungry for the rich things of life. Now I'm a gentleman fisherman and love it. All because of Max."

"He treats you like a son."

Stephen's smile nickered and died. "Max is a lot like my old man, Tony. Tough and arrogant and stubborn. I grew up in a filthy little coal town in Pennsylvania. I'm half Croat and half Hunky, and you couldn't pronounce my real name. My old man and my brothers worked in the mines. They hated me. So did my mother. The blue-eyed little brother in a family of black Croats. Living proof of my mother's infidelity. My old man used to get drunk on payday night and come home and kick hell out of me. Sometimes he'd kick hell out of my mother. I used to hide under the bed with my hands over my ears, crying, while my mother got it. Then he'd come after me. He'd laugh as he dragged me out from under the bed. I remember he had big hands, a miner's hands."

He stared at me blindly. This was the real Stephen behind the brilliant mask. A terrified child, reared on pain and hate.

"In between paydays it wasn't so bad. I had school. The other kids hated my guts, but teacher loved me. Mrs. Larkin said I was a 'prodigy'. She talked to the school superintendent about giving me special instruction after hours, so that I could skip two grades. I had it all figured. I was going to leave home in two years and work my way through Penn State and become a lawyer."

His face was mottled now, and he breathed heavily as he stared at the whitecaps. But he spoke with a painful intensity.

"Just two more months and I was going to skip the ninth grade. I was so proud that day I took my report card home to the old man. All A's. And a nice letter from Mrs. Larkin saying I could skip the ninth grade if I went to summer school. I had forgotten it was payday night. My old man came home drunk and ugly. I showed him the report card and the letter. He laughed. He tore the letter up. He told me next week I was starting in the mines. Said it was time I started paying him back for my keep. I started to cry. He slapped me. He backed me against the draining board and kept slapping me with those gnarled hands. We were in the kitchen. He kept laughing and telling me I had too much education already. I kept trying to scream at him and tell him how I had to go to Penn State. He kept laughing. There was a bread knife on the drainboard. I grabbed it and stuck it in his belly. I twisted it. He looked surprised. Then he thrashed like a chicken. Blood all over the linoleum. Nobody else was home. There was sixty dollars in his pocket. I hopped a fast rattler to Pittsburgh that night. I was on the road a year before I hit California ... Panhandling, shining shoes, living as a dirty bait boy. Then I met Max. One look at him and I knew he was soft inside. Soft, because he'd always wanted a son."

I stared at him, my throat dry. Stephen's blue eyes were ineffable, his smile nailed on.

"Did you know I can read people, Tony? I can look at them and extrapolate behavior curves, like a sibyl. It's a gift, like wiggling your ears, or second sight. Five minutes after I met Max I knew he was ultimately going to put me through college. Ten minutes after I met you I knew you were going to make love to Fern. And eventually wind up in the gas chamber at San Quentin. For murdering me."

His fist was a white blur in the sunlight. I tried to dodge, and a sledgehammer hit me behind the ear. I went down hard and slammed into the railing. Stephen stood over me, hands hanging at his sides. His smile was the essence of mockery. The blue of his eyes was hot and intense. "Get up, lover. It's mate in two."

I came up fast, throwing punches blindly, conscious only of wanting to blot out that sneering handsome face. It was like fighting a ghost. He moved like a ballet dancer around the live bait tank, shooting long straight ones that hurt, that pulped my lips and closed one of my eyes, that made raw meat out of the thing that had once been my face.

He could have put me away easily. He didn't try. I missed a roundhouse hook and spun off balance, across the railing. As I careened wildly, trying to find the deck with my feet, Stephen moved in, his eyes sparkling, and hit me with three short lefts that turned the Pacific into a floating redness as the sun pinwheeled crazily and I fell sideways to the deck.

I got up, lurching against the cabin hatch. My fingers closed around something hard. A tuna gaff. As Stephen came in I set myself and swung. I missed.

"That makes it even," Stephen said dreamily. He was very calm, a surgeon operating on a favorite patient. "Try again, lover."

He was crouched, his grin anticipant as I stumbled toward him with the gaff. Then somehow the gaff was ripped from my fingers and clattered on the deck. Stephen feinted me into throwing a futile right. Too late I saw his shoulder hunch. Something clicked. The sun gushed crimson. I was on my knees, shaking my head, watching the blood drip down to make small red spots on the deck. Stephen was laughing.

"There has to be enough blood for both of us," he said. "You understand?"

Somehow, I got to my feet. My hands weighed fifty pounds. I could not get my guard up. Stephen surveyed me clinically as I reeled toward him. Just one punch. I had to hit him once before I passed out. Only he wouldn't stand still. He kept hazing into two people, two grinning Stephens. Now he was frowning. He moved in and said, "Plead manslaughter. You might get off with ten years."

A bomb exploded in my solar plexus. I was down by the side of the bait tank, huddled into a retching ball of pain. Something struck the deck next to my face. Stephen's yacht cap. All during the fight it had stayed on his head. Stephen stood poised on the railing looking down at me.

"Don't forget," he called. "Manslaughter, Tony. So long."

He dived gracefully off the stern. There was a splash. The sunlight was blinding. Then the sun went out.

The sun was high on the horizon when I came to. The cruiser was drifting free in the offshore swell. I grabbed dizzily for the stern railing and clung there until the sky and sea stopped revolving and my eyes focused.

The ocean crawled like warm green oil and there was no sign of Stephen anywhere. I stumbled past the bait tank to the wheel, and fumbled with the ignition. The engine sputtered, caught with a roar.

I brought the cruiser into the cove almost an hour later. Fern stood on the landing, waiting.

Her face was pale but there was no sign of surprise as she stared at my battered face, at the blood on the deck. It was more of a bitter resignation.

"What happened, Tony?"

I told her painfully about it. "He's crazy," I mumbled through puffed lips. It was all I could do to stand erect. "It's his way of getting even for last night. Where is he?"

"Tony, listen." Her voice was low, quick, urgent. Her grip on my shoulders was surprisingly strong. "Listen carefully, darling. Take the diagonal path up to the driveway. I'll be waiting—"

"Here comes Lupo," I said.

Her whole body went rigid. Without a word she turned and started up the diagonal path to the guest houses. Lupo came down the main steps to the landing. He looked at me, his olive face unreadable. "Where's Steve?"

"That's what I want to know. He clobbered me, then swam ashore. Seen him?"

Lupo looked sardonically at the blood on the deck, at me. "No, I haven't seen him. You stuff him in the bait tank?"

I told him about it. He nodded calmly. "Come on," he said. "Let's tell Max."

We went up the steps to the main house. Twice I stumbled and almost fell.

Max was sitting by the fireplace, talking with two men I had never seen before. One of them was a pale man with white creamy hair and mustache. The other was short, balding, nervous.

"You're sure," Max said. "No possible mistake?"

The bald man's accent was crisp clear British. "No mistake. I don't even need to fluoroscope the paint samples. It's a wretched copy, not over twenty years old." He straightened erect, frowning. "Frankly, Baird, you puzzle me. Had the Rembrandt been genuine, I would have had no choice but to report it to our West Coast office. You realize that?"

Max nodded wearily. "I had to know. Thanks, Favian. I'll send you a check."

"Fine," Favian nodded. He glanced curiously at my face as he went out. Max sat staring into the fireplace.

"Beat it, Castle," he said without looking up. "We've got no business. I'll close the Shore down before I let you get your tentacles into it."

"You can't afford to," the white-haired man said in a voice of soft music. "It's draining you, Maxie. Hang on to it and you go under. You want to be a country baron, you got to pay. And Castle's got the price."

Max cursed him listlessly. "I suppose it's just coincidence that you stopped by this morning?"

"I get hunches," Castle murmured. "It won't be so bad, Maxie. I'll keep the Shore respectable." He laughed without sound. "Think about it. Think about losing a grand a day until you finally lose your little country club. You always were a percentage player." He stood up and saw us. His pale features were finely cut. His eyes were passionless, the color of half-frozen water. "Hello, Lupo," he said.

Max didn't even glance at the man as he went out. Max was staring at me, and his face was all animal, querulous with suspicion.

"Where's Stephen?"

I told him about it. It didn't seem to register. He stared at Lupo, who said quickly, "Blood all over the boat. No scales. No fish. Somebody used a gaff." Lupo had sharp eyes. "Incidentally," he added as an afterthought, "Steve gets loaded last night. It seems Fern and Tony are having a ball out in the rain. Steve talked bad action before he went to bed."

Max sat very still, gathering himself. When he spoke, the words seemed squeezed out of him by a relentless external pressure.

"Early this morning I put through a transatlantic phone call. To a limey named Revere, an art critic who six years ago told me that my Rembrandt was genuine. Revere died six months ago. Cancer. But his partner tells me this Revere had integrity. That he was the greatest when it came to old masters. That if Revere said it was a Rembrandt, that's what it was. And that bald guy who just left," Max breathed. "He's an art expert from Lloyd's. Very reputable. He came out to the coast to appraise some movie colony art collections for insurance. He just verified the painting as pure phony."

Max got to his feet in one fluid motion.

"You come out of nowhere," he said with deadly softness. "Recommended by Steve. By coincidence that same night I discover my Rembrandt is a fake. I remember how we all get excited when Val screams. How maybe you're the last one to leave the den."

He was adding it up, and it made sense. Fatal sense, like Stephen's queen gambit.

"Know what I think?" Max said. "I think you pulled a gypsy switch last night. I think Steve suspected you, that you had a fight about it this morning on the boat. I think you killed him. I think you know right now where the real Rembrandt is. Tell it over again, mister. Tell it different."

"Hell! You heard the story. Stephen planned ..."

Lupo chopped a judo punch into my spine. A thoughtful punch. I tried to get up. Lupo kicked me carefully in the kidneys.

Max looked down at me. His dark face was patient, almost kind.

"Let me tell you something about Lupo. Sometimes he is very useful."

Lupo bent over me.

"We've got lots of time," Max said.

7

Water thundered over me in an icy cascade. I gasped, tried to rise. "Easy," Max said, setting down the water carafe. "We'll try it again, Pearson."

"He's pretty good," Lupo said. "Three times he tells it the same way. He must of rehearsed."

Max stood biting his lip, not liking it. His stoic face was heavy with indecision. "So make it four times," he said. "Start over again, Tony. From where Steve first offered you the job."

At first I had cursed them and tried to fight. But Lupo had convinced me of the futility of that. He had convinced me with his clever sadistic hands and his knowledge of nerve centers. One of my wild kicks had found his face, bringing blood. Yet he exhibited no anger. I was merely a job to be done, a pleasant job. And Lupo was a craftsman.

I told it again, omitting only the part about Val's infidelity. There was no point in shielding Val, but I had no wish to involve Fern. Once my voice faltered. Lupo prompted me. I passed out again.

When I came to, there were voices in the room. A harsh deep voice that counterpointed Max's rumble of protest.

"You can take him in later, Stilch. In a minute he'll confess—"

"I'll take him in now, Mr. Baird."

"Like hell," Max said. "I happen to be a personal friend of Jed Wells, the county sheriff. Call him. He'll tell you—"

"Jed's on vacation in Oregon." The voice held respect, a curious bleakness. "Sorry, Mr. Baird."

I stirred, got to my knees. Strong hands jerked me erect. The room whirled. I was staring into a young-old face with a flat mouth and high Indian cheekbones. Blond hair, crew-cut. He was big, about six-four. He had tremendous hands. At first glance he looked sleepy. Then you saw the eyes.

"Can you stand all right?" Dispassionate voice, a little tired.

I nodded and he let go of me. Lupo was standing to one side and a little behind Max. He looked wistful. The big deputy turned to him. "You mark him up?"

Lupo shook his head. Max said quickly, "I'll show you the boat."

"We'll bring him along," Stilch said.

"Sure," Lupo said.

They took me outside, and down the steps to the cove. Max took Stilch on board the cabin cruiser. The big deputy asked Max a great many questions. He picked up the gaff with a handkerchief, staring at me. I sat on the edge of the landing, fighting to keep from passing out. The sun burned down from an acetylene sky, and wavelets lapped gently against the pilings. A small army of fiddler crabs played hide and seek in the rocks. Lupo squatted next to me like a conspirator.

"Last chance, Tony. We can write Steve off as an accident. I can testify I saw the whole thing from the landing, that it was self-defense. All Max wants is his pitcher. Where'd you stash it?"

I said nothing. The deputy came back to the landing with Max.

"Let's go, Pearson."

I stood up. He put handcuffs on my wrists. Max was frowning. "Incidentally, Stilch, who called you?"

"Mrs. Locke. We may need a statement from her later." Stilch was deferential, now. Max Baird was a power in Point Rafael. He was money, to be treated with respect.

"When Wells gets back, tell him to call me," Max said.

"Yes, sir." Stilch took my arm, led me up the bluff steps. Max and Lupo stood motionless on the landing. We reached the highway patrol car parked in the shell drive, and Stilch opened the door.

"They work you over?" he asked conversationally.

"What do you think?"

Oddly enough, I felt no pain. I was in a suspended state of shock. Later, the pain would come.

We arrived at the county seat twenty minutes later. Stilch took me up stone stairs through a glass door, and we turned down a long asphalt tile corridor. We passed frosted glass doors, and turned into a large office bisected by a wooden railing. It had all the functional beauty of an operating room. Fluorescents overhead, gray steel filing cabinets, impersonal metal furniture. A rawboned man with flaming red hair sat at a desk in front of the railing.

"Hi, Barney," Stilch said. "Bring in the recorder, will you?"

We went back of the railing into a smaller room that said *Sheriff's Office* on the frosted panel. There were a desk, bookcase, four chairs.

First, Stilch removed my handcuffs. He sat behind the steel desk. "Turn your pockets inside out, please."

I emptied my pockets. Wallet, pocket comb, car keys, cigarettes and matches. While Stilch was studying my driver's license, the redheaded deputy came into the office wheeling a tape recorder stand. Stilch said, "Baird told me most of it. I want your version." He nipped a switch, said to the recorder, "Interrogation of Anthony J. Pearson, twelve-forty p.m., April twelfth, by Joseph Stilch. Witnessed by Bernard Krafve."

It took almost an hour. Stilch interrupted me several times. His questions were brief and pointed. I started with Briarview, Stephen's job offer, Max's violent discovery that his Rembrandt was a fake, the beating Stephen had given me some hours ago. Finally Stilch turned off the recorder and sat looking at me out of those sleepy brown eyes.

"Point of order," he said. "I'm not interested in Baird's painting, or your hypothesis as to what might have happened to it. I'm only concerned with what happened to Steve Locke. You were a quarter-mile offshore, right?"

The trap was obvious. "Closer to a mile," I said.

Stilch made a steeple of his fingertips, brooded at it. "It's too wild, Pearson. Why not plead husband-and-wife triangle? Locke invites you for a boat ride. Kicks hell out of you and you defend yourself. At the worst, manslaughter. A sharp lawyer might get you off with five to ten. In three years you'll be eligible for parole."

My face was throbbing. "Don't you see?" I whispered. "Stephen planned the whole damned thing! He made some kind of deal with Ramos. Ramos was the last one to leave the den when Val screamed. He pulled a gypsy switch—"

"Sure," Stilch said affably. "And Mrs. Baird, downstairs, screamed deliberately to bring everybody out of the den long enough for Ramos to swap paintings. Now, since Lupo prompted Val's scream, it corresponds that he's in on it too. And we mustn't leave out the chap who got hit with the dart. Ergo, Steve Locke and Mrs. Baird and Lupo and George Fair all conspired to frame you for a murder which never happened—"

The redheaded deputy snickered. Stilch lighted a cigarette and smiled at me through the blue haze of smoke. "You still don't want to change your story?"

"Turn me over to Baird," I said nastily. "He'll have a confession out of me inside an hour."

His Indian face was unreadable. "Supposing we find only your fingerprints on that gaff?"

"You'll find Stephen's too."

"Will we?"

I felt the noose tightening. "I told you how it happened!" My voice was raw, almost a whisper. "He's setting me up so Baird will think he's dead, so Baird won't try to find him!"

"Look at it our way, Pearson. You make a pass at Locke's wife. He creams you. Later, you shake hands and he offers you a job. We've got Lupo's statement that Steve threatened to kill you for taking a moonlight drive with his wife. Next morning you take him for a boat ride. You come back alone, with a yarn which no jury could possibly swallow." He leaned across the desk, big shoulders hunched. "And your gypsy switch angle is out. Know why?"

I shook my head, unable to speak.

"Because a three-hundred-year-old Rembrandt is a brittle thing. You don't roll it up your sleeve or do disappearance tricks with it. If you do, it cracks. Do I make sense?"

I thought about it. He was right. I said tightly, "Can I call a lawyer?"

Stilch said slowly, "I'm going to hold you on suspicion, pending discovery of the body. Right now it's too circumstantial to actually book you. If Locke's body turns up, a homicide charge is automatic. If it doesn't—then it's strictly up to the sheriff. He gets back Monday."

He was playing it safe, this soft-spoken giant. He didn't care whether I was guilty or not. I leaned over the desk. "Can I ask one question?"

"Go ahead."

"In spite of everything—you think I'm telling the truth. Don't you?"

A dusky flush mottled his cheekbones. He looked at the redheaded deputy. "Take him to the infirmary, Barney. Give him a private cell."

In the infirmary the white-smocked nurse burned my cuts with iodine and informed me that my nose was not broken. Barney took me to my cell. It was quiet and cool. I lay on the bottom bunk looking at the mattress overhead, thinking.

Fern had been waiting for me on the landing. She had seen my battered face, the blood on the boat. She had not seemed surprised. She had hurried off to call the county sheriff's office.

Fern painted well. Could she have faked the Rembrandt? Right now, Stephen and Ramos were disposing of the painting through underground channels. Within a few days Fern would take a long trip abroad, the grieving widow. I had a searing vision of her with Stephen on some sun-drenched beach in Rio. I could see them laughing in the expensive playgrounds of the world, in Antibes, Lisbon, Paris, safe, unhunted, secure. My right fist ached. I realized I had been pounding the steel railing of my cot. Slowly the hate drained, leaving me weak and empty.

I thought about Stephen's white smile over a chessboard. He had planned a long-range deathmate. Stephen, the superior being, enduring Max's thousand petty tyrannies, lusting after the treasure that hung on the wall of Max's den. Once in possession of the Rembrandt, Stephen had to disappear, permanently. For Max would be implacable in pursuit. Inevitably, he would find Stephen, though the search led halfway around the world.

From the first moment Stephen had met me on the golf course, I had not had a chance. He had catalogued me like some common variety of bug. My reactions were predictable, easily foreseen. He had known I would accept the job, that I would make love to Fern. He had used it as a motivation for his death.

I finally slept.

On the fourth morning I asked to see Joe Stilch. The turnkey gave me a queer look and shuffled away. Several hours later Stilch came to my cell.

"So far you're lucky. We've checked the cove and surrounding beaches. No body—so far."

"What body? He's probably in Brazil by now."

Stilch leaned against the bars. "I'm going to give you a break, Pearson." He made it confidential, man-to-man. "I'm going to take you back to the office, and we'll erase your statement. You can admit the way it really happened. Locke started it, didn't he? We found both of your fingerprints on that gaff. You wrestled for it, and—"

"Oh, go to hell."

"You're a fool." But he said it without conviction.

"Listen," I whispered, "I'm telling the truth and you know it! Give me a lie-detector test—"

"Inadmissible as legal evidence. Sorry."

"Then how about a lawyer?"

"You can talk to Jed, Monday."

"Meanwhile you just hold me on suspicion? I thought was allowed one phone call—"

"Who told you?" Stilch said, and walked away.

PART TWO
In the Rough

8

They released me on the fifth morning. It was Friday. They opened my cell door and took me past the tiered cells to the corridor that led to the sheriff's office. Stilch sat sullenly at his desk. The lawyer was a frail waspish man with a great shock of white hair. He glanced at me without interest, turned back to Stilch.

"Book him or release him," he said. "I don't care which."

Stilch looked angry and indecisive. "Can't you wait until Monday?"

"You want me to call Judge Carver?"

Stilch shrugged and handed me a brown manila envelope containing my personal effects. "Word of advice," he snapped. "Try to leave town, Pearson, and we'll rearrest you."

The little man sniffed. "Come on, Pearson."

It was like a dream. I followed him down the asphalt tile corridor and out into the bright sunlight of the parking lot. He opened the door of a gray Buick hardtop and I got in. He went around and got behind the wheel.

"My name's Martin Fitzpatrick." He didn't bother to shake hands. "Don't bother asking who retained me, because I won't tell you. Here."

He counted five hundred dollars into my lap. I stared at the money. "What's this for?"

"A plane ticket. Personally, I can recommend Waikiki. It's nice this time of year."

"I see." Understanding came slowly. "I'm supposed to run?"

"Fast and far. Where can I drop you?"

It was all happening much too fast. "My car," I said. "It's still at the Point Rafael country club."

He nodded and drove. He found the coast highway, and he hit ninety on the stretches. Within twenty minutes we were turning up the drive of the Point Rafael clubhouse. I saw my Ford sitting forlornly in the parking lot where I'd left it.

"Get out, Pearson. That does it."

"Just a minute!" I blazed. "You think I'm crazy? If I run, it means I'm automatically guilty—"

"Or if you stay." He was cold, incisive. "Frankly, no jury in the world will believe your story. But Stilch believed it. It's the only reason I was able to bluff him with a *habeas* writ. Had he actually booked you I couldn't have done a thing. You've got two days before the sheriff gets back. He'll arraign you. Max Baird happens to own him."

"Your client," I said. "He wouldn't, by any chance, be Stephen Locke?"

The little lawyer sighed. "If you wish, Pearson, I can drive you back to the county seat. Is that what you want?"

I got out of the Buick and slammed the door so hard I almost broke the window. Fitzpatrick drove off without looking at me. I walked over to my Ford. It started on the first try.

Before I drove out of the lot, I made a wide turn next to the clubhouse. A freshly painted sign out front proclaimed the new course pro was named Dan Brewer. Max hadn't wasted any time.

For five miles I drove automatically, in an access of fury. I drove east, along Highway 101. Rage slowly gave way to a cold appraisal of my chances. Someone wanted me out of jail. Max? Stephen? An impatient horn blasted me out of my reverie. I veered sharply to the right side of the highway, making room for the black Pontiac behind. As he shot by, I caught a flashing glimpse of the green Mercury trying to pass on my right.

Those three seconds were an eternity. I remember yanking the wheel hard to my left, and the squeal of the Mercury's brakes and how my Ford fishtailed, swerving to the left lane next to the highway railing with the Pacific shimmering two hundred yards below, and the sound of metal ripping as the Ford rocked on two wheels, then abruptly righted, slewing back across the highway.

I was back on the far shoulder, pulling to a slow stop. I sat sweating. Then I got out and surveyed the left side of my car. A scraped fender. Streak of white paint from the railing. Near miss, no cigar.

I got back behind the wheel, staring at the bright swirl of traffic. I was trembling. It is so easy for a man to die. A sudden horn blast on a sharp curve. A shove at a busy intersection. A push from a high window.

I started the car and drove slowly, hugging the far right lane. It would be convenient for Stephen were I to have a sudden accident.

Abruptly I made my decision. When a break came in traffic, I made a sharp U-turn and drove back toward Point Rafael. I had to see Fern, alone. I had to look into her face while she answered some questions.

I drove up the private road that led to Max's house and parked in the half-moon drive. I walked around to the front door, and stopped dead. Val and Fern were on the front patio. They sat in white wrought-iron chairs eating brunch.

Val saw me first. She stared at me, then stood up. Fern was wearing a plain black dress without ornament of any kind. She looked pale and drawn.

"You've got nerve," Val said whitely, "coming here. How come you're out of jail?"

I forced a grin. "Coming, Fern?"

Fern didn't move. She said clearly, "Coming where, Tony?"

What rocked me was the freezing hatred in her voice. Fine, dark eyes biting into me with contempt.

"Fern, for God's sake," I blurted. "I've got to talk to you—"

"I don't want to talk to you, Tony." She was a bleak lovely stranger. "Please go before I call Max."

"I'll call him." Val turned and strode into the house. I stared at Fern. Five nights ago we had made love. We had made marriage plans.

"You'd better go, Tony." Fern's eyes were brimming. "Please, before Max comes."

It was the same feeling as when Stephen had hit me in the plexus. She gave me no opening, no chord of remembered contact. I turned away with a sick realization of defeat. As I got into my Ford I saw Val come out on the porch. With her was Max.

I love you, Tony. Husky voice, vulnerable quick passion. Lies, all lies. I drove in quiet madness, all the way back to Belmont Shore.

In my apartment I shaved and showered. Then I put on a clean suit. Somewhere in the web there was one weak strand.

Ramos.

I brewed coffee, scalding and black, and smoked two cigarettes. I picked up the phone and dialed the Long Beach Art Center. They were very helpful, very informative.

His name was Juan Ramos. He was reputable and respected. He had once written a textbook on how to differentiate old masters from fraudulent copies. He was currently affiliated with an art dealer in Los Angeles.

When I found Ramos I was going to interrogate him. Chad Lupo had taught me a few things about interrogation.

I went out and got into the Ford. I drove carefully through the noonday traffic.

The building was a venerable six-story brownstone located far out on Wilshire. The lobby was dark and cool, with electric-eye elevators that opened with automation politeness. I got off on the fourth floor and walked down a hundred yards of green-carpeted corridor to a chartreuse cork door. The pastel letters said simply, *T. Wallquist.*

It was like walking into the Louvre.

Across a fantastic expanse of jade Persian carpeting a blonde receptionist sat at a Jacobean refectory desk. Indirect lighting brought out amber highlights in the mahogany paneling. Near the desk was a group of marble statuary, life-size. The walls were a riot of paintings. I recognized a lordly Reubens in a gilt frame. Van Gogh was a brilliant splash of color next to a somber Goya. I cleared my throat, disturbing the cathedral hush. The blonde gleamed up at me.

"Good afternoon. May I help you?"

"Is Juan in?" I had done an hour's research in the library and rehearsed this twice, but it still sounded awkward and forced.

"Juan?" Her smile faltered, then came back with renewed candlepower. "Oh, you mean Mr. Ramos?"

"I've been out of town all week," I said apologetically. "The other night he called about the Vermeer."

"A Vermeer," she said, brightening. She got up and went past the snow-white statuary to the west wall. She looked at least forty, but her body was a sculptor's dream. She indicated a small canvas reverently.

"*Burgher's Wife,*" she said, watching my reaction. "Of course you can't get the *life* in a reproduction, but this should give you some idea—"

"They're all reproductions," I said, staring around the room. "Representing originals for sale?"

"Of course. This particular canvas is owned by a client in Belgium. Mr. Wallquist listed it last month."

"I've got my heart set on *Delft Study.* Ramos has a line on it. He left word the owners might sacrifice it for sixty thousand. Where can I get in touch with him?"

She went back to the desk, nibbling her lip. She picked up a catalogue, leafed through it. "He hasn't listed it yet, I'm sure. Do we have your name on file?"

I gave her the name of Donald Carter, and an address in Pacific Palisades. She said thoughtfully, "Juan came back from Venezuela three weeks ago. He usually stays at the Beverly-Wilshire, but I haven't seen him all week. Until last Friday he stayed in his office, working on reproductions." She touched a stud on the desk. "Perhaps he left word with Mr. Wallquist."

Ramos had flown up *three weeks ago.* Yet Stephen had told Max that he had flown in from Venezuela that same night.

"May I help you?"

He had come soundlessly through the velvet arras in back of the desk. He had gray, quick-sliding eyes, a porcelain smile. The Ascot and the silver goatee were the last fortissimo touch.

"Oh, hello, Mr. Wallquist," the blonde said. "This is Mr. Carter. He's interested in *Delft Study.* Mr. Ramos—"

"Right this way, please," Wallquist said.

I followed him through the arras into an office that was a mauve miniature of the reception room. As he preceded me through the doorway

I saw a birch door across the hall with *J. R. Ramos* in raised, knife-edged script.

"Juan's a junior partner," the art dealer said, following my glance. "He spends most of his time abroad, inducing wealthy old families to part with their treasures. Some of the families, of course, are more old than wealthy." He smiled. "Your particular Vermeer is held by an English earl who I hardly think would let it go for sixty thousand."

I looked hurt. "Then why did he call me?"

"Possibly to interest you in something else. When was it you saw him last?"

"October," I said. It was a poor guess. Wallquist's smile congealed. Last October Juan Ramos had apparently been on some other continent.

Wallquist's gaze traveled over my fifty-dollar charcoal flannel suit, the twelve-dollar brogues. His smile became a smirk. Quite obviously I could not afford a Vermeer reproduction, let alone an original.

"Juan called me last night from San Francisco," the art dealer said blandly. "He's attending an exhibition there this weekend. He may be back in town by Tuesday. Can he call you?"

I said that would be fine. "On second thought, why don't I call him? What's his hotel?"

"The—Mark, I believe." His gray eyes were utterly opaque. "I'm not really sure. Now if you'll excuse me—"

"I understand Juan is very good at reproductions." I stood up, wanting to smash him like a fat grubworm.

"Juan's a very talented man."

At the doorway I paused. "Come to think of it, you could interest me in another painting. I might go considerably higher than sixty thousand."

"Really?"

"A Van Ryn self-portrait. Small, almost a miniature."

He moistened his lips. I was finally getting to him. "No such portrait exists. I don't recall—"

"Before the war it hung in the Prague. Currently it's owned by a private party. You'll have Ramos call me?"

He looked at me with cold hate. I grinned at him and walked out. As I passed the blonde she gave me the number-three smile, reserved for sixty-thousand-dollar customers. I wondered what she would have done had I wanted a Michelangelo.

Driving down Wilshire, I tried to classify Wallquist. A reputable apple-cheeked art dealer, with a Latin partner very good at reproductions. If you had a spare hundred grand and lusted after a certain old master, they'd be delighted to contact the owner. If his price seemed too high, maybe they'd steal it for you.

Ten minutes later I walked into the lobby of the Beverly-Wilshire. The desk clerk was a polite sallow man who called registration, and then informed me that Juan Ramos had checked out last Monday afternoon. His forwarding address was Caracas, Venezuela.

I thanked him, and walked slowly over to the phone booths. I called the Mark Hopkins Hotel in San Francisco. They had a Gonzales registered, but no Ramos. Naturally. I smashed the receiver back on the cradle and started outside.

She was waiting for me near the potted palm by the lobby entrance. A dark, full-breasted woman in a white sharkskin dress.

"My name is Consuela Ramos." Her voice was a muted bell. "You are looking for my husband?"

9

Her face was finely chiseled copper. She had attractive, black eyes. I gave her my Sunday smile. "That's right, Mrs. Ramos. Any idea where I can find him?"

She turned to the green leather couch by the palm. "Juanito," she said.

"*Sí* mama?" The boy looked up from his book. He was about seven, the male image of his mother.

"Please take a walk by the pool, Juanito. Come back in ten minutes."

The boy nodded with adult gravity. He walked through the lobby without looking back. Consuela and I sat on the couch. She said simply, "I have asked the clerk to tell me of any messages or inquiries." She hesitated, took the plunge. "You are of the *policia?*"

"No," I said, and she relaxed, visibly. "But I've got to find your husband, Mrs. Ramos. Didn't he fly back to Caracas on Monday?"

"No, *señor.* I feel he is here, in Los Angeles. Where did you see him last?"

If it was an act, it was a good one. Suddenly I liked her. And felt a touch of pity for what I had to do.

"Your husband," I told her bluntly, "may be in trouble. He could be a thief."

Consuela sat motionless. Her shining dark eyes searched mine. "What has Juan done?"

I told her briefly about Max's Rembrandt. She listened impassively. "I can tell you very little, *Señor* Pearson."

"What does Juan do for a living?"

"He paints," she said simply. "He makes—contacts for Señor Wallquist. I met Juan twelve years ago. He was very poor, very proud." Her eyes were luminous with recollection. "He had a great talent and was ashamed of it. He had the gift of mimicry. He copied the great religious masterpieces of the church, the Goyas and the Rafaels. He was a pious man, yet embittered because he could only reproduce, not create. He met Señor Wallquist four years ago, at an art exhibition in Buenos Aires. It was a great opportunity for Juan. That first year he made twenty thousand dollars. Only—he would be abroad for months at a time. Things went bad between us. Juan had a passion for the rich things of life, the gaming tables. Once, in Rio, there was a woman—"

She stared across the hotel lobby. I sensed strength in her, and a bitter pride.

"Always, Juan has come back to me. Two months ago he came home with a great desolation in his face. He paces our house like a tiger. There is a secret weight upon his soul and I am afraid. Then—a letter from *Señor* Wallquist. Juan is drunk with joy. He kisses me many times, and speaks of much money, a second honeymoon abroad. We fly to Rosarita Beach. Juan leaves me at the hotel. He has business here on the coast for a few days. Then, last week, Juan phones me. He will be delayed a few more days."

"When did he phone you?"

"Last Sunday. There is a coldness in his voice that frightens me. But I—I wait for him. Each day is a year. I say many prayers to the Virgin that he is not involved in some dishonest thing." Her fingers touched the tiny gold cross at her throat. "Yesterday, I call his hotel. They tell me he has checked out three days ago. I come at once." She looked up at me and said fiercely, "He is not a bad man, only weak. What has he done?"

Suddenly, I hated Ramos. I reached over and touched her hand. It was cold as stone. "Did you ask Wallquist about him?"

"He said Juan is in San Francisco." Her eyes held a primitive flame. "Could it be another woman?"

I thought about Val. Fern. "No," I said.

"I shall be at this hotel, *señor.*" She stood up. "When you find Juan, will you call me?"

"I'll call you, Consuela."

She walked across the lobby like some proud splendid animal. I never saw her again....

Driving back to Belmont Shore, Fitzpatrick's five hundred dollars felt uncomfortably warm in my wallet.

Flight money. I was supposed to run. Until Max Baird caught me. Or Lupo. Max was a big man, and he had the connections, the power. He would never believe that Stephen was still alive, that he had set up a Venezuelan art agent to fence the Rembrandt through underground channels.

If I stayed in town, I was dead. The county sheriff would be back Monday. Max would make a quiet phone call. And within an hour, Tony Pearson, a nobody, would be picked up on suspicion of murder.

Circumstantial, but men had died in the gas chamber for less. *Jealous lover kills husband.* The usual headlines, the quick trial. *Plead manslaughter,* Stephen had said. Damned considerate of him. A good lawyer might get me off with five to ten.

It was after four when I got back to my apartment. I was brewing fresh coffee and thinking about the weak, elusive Ramos, when the door opened. It was Joe Stilch. He came in soundlessly, closing the door behind him.

"You might at least bother to knock."

"And give you a chance to lock the door? After all, I haven't a warrant."

He no longer looked sleepy. He looked big and angry, a little tired.

"Why? You need a warrant?"

He didn't answer at first. I got out an extra cup for him and poured coffee. "Black," he said. "No sugar." He moved to the bed, sat warily. I handed him the cup, wondering what in hell he was after. He looked at the coffee and sighed. "Driving out here, I wanted to break your neck. No cop likes to be played for a fool. Then it came to me that I couldn't really blame you. You were gambling they wouldn't find the body. You had nothing to lose."

It was like a cold wind blowing through the room. My throat felt dry. "Are you trying to tell me—"

"Funny thing," he mused. "I believed you. There was a kind of pitiful integrity about your story that got me. The wilder the yarn the bigger the sucker." He sipped his coffee. The cup looked like a demitasse in his huge fist.

"Drink up, Pearson. Let's go."

"Where?" I whispered. But I already knew.

"Mrs. Baird found him three hours ago," Stilch said bleakly. "In the cove. The crabs have been at him for five days, but it's definitely Steve Locke. Both Mrs. Baird and Mrs. Locke made positive identification. The M.E. fixes the time of death some time Monday morning. The time you took him for a boat ride, give or take a few hours."

"Listen," I husked. "I didn't—"

"On your feet, Pearson." He stood up, big hands hanging loose at his sides. "Technically, I'm out of my own territory. But we'll call this one a citizen's arrest. And please resist me." He gave me an iron smile. "Just a little."

Certain decisions are made without conscious thought. Panic flames in a soundless spasm of time. *Do this and you die. Do this and you may live.*

It all happened too abruptly. Stilch standing over me like an executioner, looking eight feet tall. My right wrist moved without volition. It nicked the cup of scalding coffee squarely in Stilch's face.

He made a soft sound and clawed at his eyes. I was down, rolling, as he hit the chair where I had been. The crash shook the whole room. He came up fast for a big man, face contorted, eyes closed.

For perhaps three seconds he stood motionless in the center of the room. Then his hands came up, shoulders hunching. The hands were open, fingers stiff. He squinted and came at me.

I grabbed the coffeepot off the hot plate. It was hammered aluminum, with a nice heft. As Stilch came in I brought the coffeepot down on the right side of his head.

Hot coffee scalded us and I went momentarily blind. Stilch's right hand was a snake striking and there was a soundless explosion in my left shoulder. The entire arm went dead. I flailed wildly, and the coffeepot slashed across his temple. Stilch caved to his knees, clawing blindly at my groin. His breath made a curious whistling sound.

I brought my knee up squarely into his forehead. He toppled sideways, hands plucking at the carpet.

I stepped gingerly over him and opened the door. I was panting like a spent miler. A few minutes later I was on the coast highway, driving toward Laguna. My insides felt like whey. My left arm ached as I tried to flex my fingers. Stilch had tried for my carotid artery, where a slicing palm chop kills.

I was scared. Never in my life had I felt so alone. Within a half hour the roadblocks would tighten, the descriptions would clack out over a dozen teletypes. The net would close, inexorably. Another triangle killing. Jealous lover slays husband. They had the motive, the witnesses, and my fingerprints on the gaff. And they had the corpse.

Ramos, I figured. It had to be Ramos.

Stephen had contacted him, had arranged the switch in paintings. Stephen had planned to disappear permanently, framing me for his murder.

I could see Stephen, laughing inside as he swam to shore. Swimming to a secluded spot outside the cove where Ramos was waiting with dry clothes and a fast car. Ramos killing him instead. Planting his body in the cove. Checking out of the Beverly-Wilshire a few hours later.

Exit Ramos with three hundred thousand dollars' worth of painting which he would not now have to share with Stephen.

Stephen had finally met his chess master....

It was around five when I drove into Laguna Beach. A prowl car wailed past, and I froze behind the wheel. But they were only after a speeding Chevy. As I passed them I stared stonily ahead.

I had to ditch the Ford, and quickly. For a few days I could only hole up in some beach hotel. With luck, I might even reach an airport.

My left arm ached in dull surges of pain. In a fair fight Stilch would have broken me, no hands. No cop likes to be played for a fool and I had made a fool of Joe Stilch. When they finally found me and brought me in, I could see Stilch's sleepy smile as he walked into my cell. An hour alone with him and I would be very glad to sign a confession.

I drove aimlessly through the heart of Laguna. Ceramic shops and shining new motels. Ocean-front homes in redwood and glass. The shimmer of blue neon in the dusk, *Hidaway Bar.*

A year ago I had taken Fern to the Hidaway often. We had made lovers' plans and laughed together over gimlets.

Under stress, man can be a weak, regretful animal. I retrospected bitterly, going back to the exact point in time when I had first met Fern. And I saw myself suddenly as an adolescent. Life had always given me a second chance. Life was a scotch foursome with changing partners where a shanked iron shot did not matter, because your partner would always sink that fifty-foot putt to tie the hole.

A year ago, I had closed my eyes to Fern's insecurity, had gone to the golf wars full of fatuous confidence that she would be waiting when I returned. I had underestimated her need.

The thought hit me like a sledge. I slammed on the brakes so hard that there was an indignant horn squall from the car behind. I whipped into the Hidaway parking lot and fumbled for a cigarette.

I had gone to Max Baird's house at noon. Val had been surprised to see me. An hour later she had found Stephen's body. She had found it in the cove, where the county deputies had failed to find it for the past five days.

I thought about Fern. Tired voice, dark eyes dull with contempt. Could it have been an act for Val's benefit?

Fern had sent me away hating her. Women in love can do cruel, unpredictable things to save their men. Could Fern—?

I went into the bar and found a phone booth. Information gave me Baird's number. I dialed, my fingers slippery with sweat. If Baird answered I could hang up.

"Meester Baird's residence." It was Johnny, the house-boy.

"Is Mrs. Locke there?"

A pause. He had recognized my voice.

"Mrs. Locke not home. Sorry."

"Johnny, this is Tony. I've got to talk with Fern—"

"Sorry, she not home." He sounded unhappy, "—now."

Someone else could be near him. Baird or Lupo or Val. Somebody else could be tracing the call on an extension.

"Tell her I'm in Laguna," I said. "Fern knows the place. We used to drink gimlets there. If she's not here by six, I'm coming after her. Tell her that, Johnny."

"I hang up now," Johnny said.

I held the phone a moment, listening. I thought I heard another soft click of an extension. I couldn't be sure.

I took a long deep breath and went back to the men's room. I washed my face and combed my hair. Stilch had torn my coat sleeve and my shirt was minus two buttons. I adjusted my tie carefully, hiding the missing buttons. It seemed terribly important that nobody notice them. I went out to the bar and ordered a vodka gimlet.

It was ten after five. One gimlet later it was five-thirty. Once, this bar had held a special magic for me. The green baroque mirror over the bar, the driftwood and fishing nets on the walls, the vivid murals depicting leering pirates and their women.

But now the murals were faded, and it was just another bar where the laughter was too loud and the juke too discordant.

I had made a desperation gamble. At any moment two big state troopers would walk through the door. They would take me in, not gently. I had roughed up a cop, possibly fractured his skull.

Time to run, still time.

I ordered another gimlet.

It was five after six when Fern came into the bar. She came in quietly, walking like a queen. She was alone.

10

We sat in a dark corner booth, not talking. Fern finished her gimlet and looked levelly at me.

"Hungry, Tony?"

I nodded. She beckoned for the waitress. We ordered steak sandwiches, fries and coffee. Fern was studying my face with cool detachment.

"You've matured," she said. "The Tony Pearson of twelve months ago would have hated me for what I said this morning. It would have taken him a week of sulking before he came back. It took you only five hours."

It stung, but I deserved it. Fern added quietly, "You understand, of course, that I was afraid of Val. She's been studying me minutely all week to make sure I'm a shattered widow. I had to reject you in front of her. Otherwise you'd have stayed until Max came out. He would have killed you."

Understanding came, and shame. "Then you hired Fitzpatrick," I said. "But that morning, when I came back alone on the boat, why did you call the sheriff's office?"

"You'd rather have let Lupo continue to work on you?"

"Sorry." I looked down at the table. Fern's hand found mine. The juke was playing *Lisbon Antigua*, the way it had twelve long months ago. For just a moment we recaptured a very special mood. Then the steak sandwiches came.

We ate, hungrily. I told Fern about Wallquist's art emporium, about Ramos checking out of the Beverly-Wilshire three hours after killing Stephen.

"There's one missing factor," Fern mused. "I'm sure Val was in on it. She's leaving Max."

"He'd let her?"

"He doesn't know. This afternoon I went into Val's room to return a sweater I borrowed from her last week. I was hanging it in her closet when I saw her two bags, packed. When I went downstairs she was telling Max she had a sick headache and couldn't go to the Shore with him tonight."

The waitress brought coffee, hot and black and delicious. I lighted cigarettes. "Fern, where do you think she's going?"

"To join Ramos, possibly. Wait here a minute, Tony."

She got up and walked back toward the phone booth at the end of the bar. I sat, extrapolating. The sands were running out. We could sit here for hours making futile plans, and in the end the police would find us. In trying to help me, Fern was making herself accessory after the fact. I felt anger and self-contempt. I tossed a five on the table and started outside.

"Tony!"

Fern caught me at the door. She grabbed my arm, dark eyes snapping. "Idiot! They've got roadblocks out by now. You can't drive three blocks in your Ford without being picked up—"

"All right," I growled, as we went outside. "It was stupid to call you in the first place. Who did you phone?"

"A friend." She was smiling a secret. "First, we're going to prove your innocence to Max. He's the only one powerful enough to help us."

I made a polite noise of disbelief. Fern's Thunderbird glistened blood-red in the lights of the parking lot. She opened the door, slid behind the wheel. "Get in," she said dangerously. "Tony—"

"Oh, hell." But I got in.

She drove fast and smoothly through the south end of town. She was driving toward Point Rafael.

"First," I said caustically, "we tell Max the whole story. Then he apologizes while Lupo disembowels us—"

"Don't you *see?* If I can convince Max that Ramos forged the painting, he'll help us. He's a hard man, but he's fair. And he respects me. I think we'll find that proof in Ramos' office."

She had it all figured out. I leaned back in the seat and gave up. It was a warm night, and the moon washed the Pacific with platinum. A fine night to be off to Mexico for a six-week honeymoon.

I saw two black-and-white prowl cars parked at the comer intersection, and stopped breathing. Fern hit the green light at fifty miles an hour. Then we were on the long coast stretch, doing eighty.

"Relax," she said confidently, "they're looking for a blue Ford." She turned on the radio and there was the soft tinkle of a piano. I tried to relax, but my thoughts kept flashing back to Stephen. Parricide at fourteen. Bait boy at fifteen. Stanford graduate at twenty-one. Master chess player, lover, thief. Graduated from life at twenty-eight, *cum laude*.

A random thought struck me. I glanced sideways at my girl. Her face was pale and set, eyes fixed on the highway.

"Stephen never really loved you," I said.

"No," she said softly. "Although I did not fully realize it until a few days ago. A month after we were married he asked me to paint a replica of the Van Ryn. It was to be some kind of joke on Max. I refused. He insisted. I pointed out that Max would hardly appreciate that type of joke. He backed off. A cool smile. But from then on it was different between us." She shivered. "He was like ice. He'd hurt me in bed. Around people he was terribly polite. Very correct, with all the cruelty and hatred behind the mask. I couldn't understand. I kept loving him. I'm sorry, Tony."

"He fascinated you. The way a snake might."

"I wouldn't give him a divorce. In a way he was trapped. Max had taken a liking to me, and Stephen would never risk Max's disapproval. So it became a silent angry stalemate, my hanging on, Stephen trying to break me." There was a broken catch in her voice. "Two Sundays ago I answered the phone. A man's voice, with a faint Spanish accent. He wanted Stephen. After Stephen hung up he had that white calmness which meant he was excited inside. We had a scotch foursome at the club that day. He told me to go without him, that he had to go into town on business. I felt unaccountably furious with him. After he left the house, I stayed. I was outside by the pool when he came home an hour later. When he got out of the car he was carrying a small flat package. He looked at me and went into the house quickly."

"The fake Rembrandt," I said slowly. "He met Ramos in town and picked it up."

"Two days later I saw him making love to Val. I went away. But when he found me at Briarview, I was—glad. Can you understand, Tony?"

I said nothing. The Thunderbird rounded a high curve, and you could see the waves foaming over the rocks below, white lace and jade in the moonlight. I stared at them, full of hate and bitterness for a dead man.

"When I first saw you at Point Rafael," Fern said, "I was afraid. That night when you told me Max's Rembrandt was a forgery, I knew Stephen planned to frame you. Yet a tiny part of me still loved him. This afternoon when Val and I went down to identify the body, I cried. He looked like a tattered side of beef. Please be patient, Tony. I don't want his ghost to come between us—"

I reached out and switched off the ignition. The Thunderbird coasted on a dead motor.

"Pull over," I said harshly. We floated to a stop on the bluff shoulder. I took her in my arms. She was trembling. She tried to speak and I stopped her mouth with mine. I held her very close. After a time she sighed and burrowed her head into my chest.

"No ghosts?"

"No ghosts, Tony."

I turned on the ignition. Fern touched the starter. Her smile was tremulous and bright.

"I love you, Tony."

We drove through the night. There was no need for words. Ten minutes later we rounded the long bluff curve and came into Point Rafael.

The Lee Shore was a festival of light and color. Cads and Buicks shone in the festooned lights of the parking lot. I saw people in evening dress walking through the doorway arch. The pink marble facade was ablaze with colored spotlights, and you could hear the faint sob of violins from the swimming pools.

Fern slowed to a stop a hundred yards later. A dim figure waited in the palms.

"Hello, Midge," she said. "Get in."

He was a wizened Negro no more than five feet tall, wearing horn-rimmed glasses. I opened the door for him and Fern introduced us. "Midge Combs, Tony Pearson."

We shook hands. Midge had a seamed intelligent face, a tired smile.

"You work at the Shore?" I asked.

"I quit ten minutes ago," Midge said. His voice was husky velvet. He glanced at me quickly, at Fern. "This the boy they looking for?"

"He's the boy," Fern said. "Why did you quit, Midge?"

"Castle wanted me to play deckhand on his yacht," Midge said with soft dignity. "He lent it to some friends last week for a La Paz cruise. I refused. Next, he wanted me to wear a big turban and tight gold pants. To usher at the private shows. He said I was too small to tend bar. He prefers strapping Nubian types."

"What kind of shows?" I asked, knowing the answer.

"The penultimate, man. Fifty skins admission, and they pack those back rooms." He made a sick grimace.

Fern made a reckless U-turn beyond the parking lot, almost colliding with an oncoming Jaguar. The Jag's horn blared, then it turned into the parking lot. Two blondes got out; tall sleek showgirl types. One of them wore a pink evening dress; the other, black satin slacks. They walked across the lot, holding hands.

Castle was drawing a crowd tonight. The whisper had gone out to the well-heeled sensualists and the jaded millionaires. *The Shore's wide open again.*

If you liked your kicks frantic, if you craved sin at any price, the Shore was the place to go. Here was madness for sale, sweet and terrible.

"So Max sold the Shore to Castle," I said.

"He had to," Fern said. "Without the Rembrandt, he was strapped. The last two nights he's gone down to the Shore and come back brooding drunk. Let's change the subject. Midge, tell Tony about yourself."

Midge sighed. "A few years back I had fame. The cat burglar of Westwood. I'm quite good at opening locks. In Quentin I took up painting. I met Fern last year at the Laguna Art Festival. Poor child thinks I have talent."

"He's a genius," Fern said with that breathlessness peculiar to artists discussing each other's work. "Very advanced color sense. I keep hounding him to have a showing—"

"I'm modest," Midge said, dead pan. "Fifty years from now I'll be another Matisse. Fern got me a job tending bar at the Shore. If it hadn't been for her I'd doubtless be back in Quentin." He hesitated. "I hope you aren't carrying heat."

I said no, and he relaxed. Armed robbery would probably get him ten to life, while breaking and entering might only mean five years. I touched Fern's knee. "I like your friend."

"Man's in trouble," Midge said, "you help him. Still on that pastel kick, Fern?"

That started her off, and for the next half hour they were off in a world of their own, arguing the respective merits of oils versus water colors. We hit the Hollywood Freeway, and the Thunderbird was a silent arrow through the Friday night traffic. Then Wilshire, headed west. Behind us the Civic Center was a dazzling smear of light. Fern slowed. Those last two miles seemed like two hundred. Nobody spoke until we turned into the alley in back of a brownstone office building.

Fern got out first, staring tautly at the black Chrysler parked a dozen yards down the alley. Her fingers tightened around my wrist. "Tony, that's Castle's car!"

"What would he be doing here?"

"I don't know."

Midge murmured, "This mean a change in strategy?"

Fern shook her head, tight-lipped. We went around to the lobby entrance. The lobby was still and deserted, except for a tired janitor who glanced up briefly and went back to his squeegee and pail.

In the elevator Fern said quickly, "Tony, give Midge a hundred dollars."

Midge looked pained. "This trip's for free. Later, however, you may visit my garret to purchase a few minor masterpieces." I made a mental note to do just that.

As we left the elevator, Midge took out a pencil flashlight and large key ring. When we came to the chartreuse cork door at the end of the corridor, he examined the lock and smiled. He handed me the flashlight. I held it steady while he worked on the lock.

There was a soft snick and the door swung open. From inside came the indistinct blur of voices. Midge looked at us questioningly, putting his finger to his lips. I made motions for him to wait downstairs in the car. He nodded, and disappeared down the corridor. Fern and I went inside and softly closed the door.

The reception room was a jungle of inky shadows. Behind the Jacobean desk, the tapestries were a pale screen of light. A man's shadow appeared on the screen, as we knelt behind the Greek statuary.

"He *knows*, I tell you!" It was Wallquist's voice, bitter and defiant. "The way he grinned at me this afternoon when he asked about the Van Ryn. When the cops find him he'll spill his guts."

"And who's to believe him?" The other voice was cynical, yet soothing. "He's practically a convicted murderer. You're a respected art dealer—"

Wallquist cursed. "If only Juan weren't so damned greedy! He got me into this mess, Castle. And to you, it's amusing!"

Fern stared at me in chill realization,

"—relax," Castle was saying. "Ramos is still on the coast, Wally. The sooner he gets his end, the sooner he goes back to Venezuela. How much longer does he wait?"

"Two, three days. These things take time, Ronnie." There was a cunning note in Wallquist's voice. "If he would settle for—thirty thousand tomorrow—"

Castle's flint laughter. "I promised him fifty thousand. And I always keep my word, Wally." The scrape of a moving chair. A distorted shadow shivering behind the tapestry. "By Monday noon, then?"

"Listen, it's a Canadian client. He's got millions. But he may have difficulty in transferring funds—"

"Monday noon, Wally?"

"All right." The art dealer's voice collapsed. "Why should you care? You've got what you want."

"Naturally," Castle said coldly. "But I want to pay Ramos off, get him out of the country. Understand?"

"Obviously. Did you tell him his wife is in town?"

"I told him. He's going to let her get tired of waiting for him. Ultimately she'll give up and go back to Caracas. As far as she's concerned, he's found another girl."

I had a picture of Consuela sitting in her lonely hotel suite, waiting for a phone call that would never come.

"Juan's a cold fish," Wallquist said. "But why did he have to—"

"Stephen became greedy. You can learn from that." The tapestries parted. Castle appeared, a regal figure in blue serge. His creamy hair shone.

"One for the road?" The sound of a glass clinking.

"Not that stuff," Castle said with contempt. "And lay off it until Monday, will you?"

The tapestries closed. Castle walked past us in the dimness, so close I could almost touch him, opened the corridor door and went out.

From the inside office came a heavy sigh. Silence. Then the sound of a phone dialing. Wallquist's voice, moist, thick. "Thelma? ... Wally, honey."

A pause. "I'll be over in ten minutes, baby—what? Why not?" His voice turned harsh. "So you've got migraine again. Take an aspirin. Sure, you can sleep in tomorrow morning—on one condition." He chuckled. "*If* you wear the blue negligee. That's right baby—ten minutes."

He hung up. "Bitch," he said. I thought about the blonde receptionist with the fine body and the tired eyes. The lights flicked out as Wallquist's shadow passed us. The outside door closed.

I stood up and stretched, helping Fern to her feet. She was trembling.

"Fern, I can't feature an operator like Castle mixed up in a phony art racket."

"He's not," she whispered. "All he ever wanted was the Lee Shore. The Shore's worth a million dollars a year, if you know how to run it. Castle knows how."

I thought about the private saturnalias in back rooms, fifty dollars admission. "Then Stephen was deliberately mismanaging the Shore to put Max in the red. He must have contacted Castle originally, with his scheme to steal the Rembrandt. Purpose: to strap Max, so he'd have to sell the Shore to Castle."

"But Ramos tricked Stephen, killed him. Why didn't Castle care?"

"Why should he? Let's find Ramos' office."

We went back of the Jacobean desk through the tapestries. I turned on the hall light and tried the door to Ramos' office. It was locked. I threw a shoulder against it. On the fourth try, wood splintered and gave. We went inside and turned on the lights.

It was more of a studio than office. I saw swathed canvases, an easel. Oil reproductions hung on the cork walls. Fern examined them.

"He's good," she said. "He's very good. Open the desk, Tony."

The rosewood desk was locked. I tried to pry the drawer open with a palette knife. Finally I smashed it open with my heel.

My nerves were shrieking piano wire.

We found what we wanted, five minutes later.

It was a cracked lithograph reproduction of the Van Ryn in the bottom drawer of the desk, buried under several water colors. With the lithograph was a short article clipped from a German art magazine, *Die Kunst Fer Alle*. The date of the magazine was June, 1936. In another drawer were two preliminary charcoal sketches. Fern compared them with the lithograph carefully.

"It's all we need, darling!" Her eyes were shining as she put the sketches into a manila folder. "Max won't believe us, at first. But at least he'll question Wallquist. I've a hunch Wallquist will talk, once Lupo starts on him."

I had the same hunch. "Let's get out of here," I said.

We left, turning out the office lights. In the elevator I kissed Fern, long and hard. The elevator doors opened. As we stepped into the downstairs lobby there was a flicker of motion on my left. Then the darkness splintered apart in white pain.

I was down on the marble flooring on hands and knees, shaking the agony out of my head, trying to rise.

There were two of them. The one who stood over me was big, blond, neatly dressed. The other was lean and darkly immaculate. He had Fern backed into the corner alcove. She was holding the manila envelope in a death grip, staring at him like a snake-hypnotized bird.

"Give," he said patiently, holding out his hand.

Fern's eyes darted to mine. Her scream died stillborn as he slapped her, and took the envelope.

I lunged erect and hit him. A weak, glancing blow. The other man spun me expertly and threw his knee into my groin. I went down, retching. He stood over me, amused.

"No more heroics, please. George?"

"Right here," George said, glancing into the art envelope. He paid no attention to Fern as he took out a silver cigarette lighter and set fire to the sketches. She gave a wordless cry and flew at him. George casually backhanded her against the brass elevator gates.

I tried to push the marble flooring away from me. The blond man kicked my elbow. I fell heavily on my side. The sketches were flaming brightly in the sand-topped cuspidor. Blondie grinned down at me in gentle reproof.

"We're helping him," he told George. "He doesn't appreciate it."

"His type never does." George poked at the burning sketches.

"Typical felon," Blondie said. "No gratitude. He steals someone else's property, then tries to stop us from destroying the evidence."

I cursed him. Fern huddled in the alcove corner, crying without sound. The alcove was secluded from the main lobby, beyond eyeshot of the glass entrance doors. I realized what had happened. Castle must have spotted Fern's Thunderbird in the outside alley.

"That does it," George said, poking at the embers. "I trust you've done your duty as a public citizen."

"Quite," Blondie said with comic righteousness. "I've already called the police."

"Let's go," George said, glancing at his watch. Side by side, they walked across the lobby, not looking back.

The entire thing had taken less than ninety seconds. Ninety seconds of deft violence by two men who resembled young corporation executives, and who did their jobs with expensive deadly precision. Two sleek hoods who had not even bothered to kill me because I was already cold meat for the gas chamber.

I was choking with a wild sick rage as Fern helped me wobble to my feet. My entire body felt like mush.

"Hurry," she whispered through tears. "Please hurry, darling."

As we turned into the alley we saw the Chrysler purring down Wilshire. Castle sat in the back seat, looking almost bored. To him I was a minor organism, a gnat with its wings smashed, left to die. A potential threat that had been disposed of, nothing more.

When she saw the Thunderbird, Fern made a small broken sound. The air had been let out of two tires. Midge slumped motionless over the wheel, blood on his forehead. His breathing was thick, stertorous.

Then we heard it. The distant scream of a siren.

George and Blondie had timed it with loving care.

Midge stirred, moaned.

"Help me, Tony!" Fern's voice was a frantic sob as we slid Midge from behind the wheel. He stood erect, rubber-legged, shaking his head and wincing.

"Man skulled me," he grunted. "For why?"

"Later!" I grabbed his arm. "Can you walk, Midge?"

He couldn't. Half-dragging, half-carrying him, we made it to the street. Down the block I spotted a cruising cab. It moved toward us with agonizing slowness. The siren was a devil's shriek that died as the prowl car careened into the far alley entrance. The red spotlights impaled Fern's Thunderbird as we ran to meet the cab.

11

"Where to?" The cabbie gave us a sharp glance to make sure we weren't drunk. All three of us were panting in the back seat.

"Western and Santa Monica." I blurted the first intersection that popped into my head. He shifted into second. As we passed the office building I saw the prowl car parked in the alley mouth. One cop was examining the Thunderbird and the other was cautiously entering the lobby. For a little time I was free. Not for long.

Two hours ago, I had beaten a law officer unconscious. The story would hit the big metropolitan dailies by morning. *Fleeing Killer Breaks Arrest.* An hour, six hours, a day from now, someone would frown at me in quick recognition. They would walk to the nearest phone. And, within minutes, a hard-faced plainclothesman would come up behind me and say, "Let's go."

And I would go. All the way to that cyanide chamber at Quentin.

Midge fingered his scalp, wincing. "Just for nothing," he said plaintively. "Just because. Two men walk by the car. They look at me. Then—*wham!*"

"Castle likes to make sure," Fern whispered. "Let me look at that scalp, Midge."

The little Negro had an egg-sized lump, but there was no evidence of concussion. I told Midge what had happened. I spoke in guarded whispers, staring at the cabbie up front. Midge clucked sadly. "All my fault, children. It was very unprofessional of me to wait there."

Fern's hand found mine. "We shouldn't keep the cab too long, Tony."

I knew what she meant. We had left a warm trail. Within an hour the police would check out the trip tickets of all cabs operating along Wilshire. They could trace us easily. Already, the driver was eyeing us in the rear-view mirror.

"You need a car," Midge said softly.

"Brilliant," I grunted. "You can excrete one, maybe?"

"Maybe." He leaned forward and gave the cabbie a Sunset Strip address. Fern looked at me with a beaten hope.

"Last chance coming up, darling."

"Val?"

She nodded. Val was leaving Max, sometime tonight. Possibly she had grown tired of him. More possibly she had a rendezvous with someone else.

Ramos? Castle?

Ten minutes later we were shooting past the glittering supper clubs on the strip. Midge said suddenly. "Next corner," and the cab pulled over to the curb. I paid the driver and we got out. He gave us a long look before he drove away.

The place was a hundred yards back from the boulevard. For the strip, it was drab, unpretentious. A curved brick walk, and dwarf pines festooned with Chinese lanterns. There was a blank white cement wall with a single Chinese hieroglyphic on it in blue neon.

"Friend works here," Midge said, leading us through the red lacquered doors.

The dining room was the ultimate in oriental decor. The tables were ebony, scarlet and gold. We passed a long onyx bar with exquisitely carved stone buddhas flanking the fireplace. The headwaiter was a stooped Chinese with a fixed smile and eyes like wounds.

"Reservations, sir?"

"Friends of Charlie Wong," Midge said. "Tell him it's Midge."

The headwaiter bowed. We waited at the bar while the bartender polished glasses in the discreet gloom and pointedly ignored us. In less than fifty seconds the head-waiter returned and beckoned. We followed him around the bar and down a long red-carpeted hall into a small sitting room with gold dragons limned on black drapes. The headwaiter vanished and Midge said, "Sit a while. It could be five minutes or an hour."

We sat. A faint surf of sound came from the dragon drapes. I got up and peered through. The adjoining room was a haze of cigarette smoke. Six men sat around a table, playing fan-tan. Midge clucked disapprovingly. I sat, fidgeting.

"They play no limit," Midge murmured. "Charlie owns a third interest in this place. He's the main attraction for that back room. Professionals come from as far as Frisco to see if they can beat him."

"Do they ever?"

"Sometimes," Midge said, as a giant walked through the drapes.

At first glance he looked like a living buddha. The almond eyes were almost buried in rolls of yellow fat. He had a face like the full moon, and not a single hair on his massive skull. He weighed at least three hundred pounds. The gold earring was the final touch.

"Charlie," Midge said, standing. They shook hands. The giant regarded us briefly and turned back to Midge.

"Long time," he said. "Expected you a year ago." His voice was thin, astonishingly reedlike for so huge a frame.

"I'm proud," Midge said. "Bite the bullet and such jive."

"But now you're here." Wong's eyes swept Fern, myself.

"My friends wish a car," Midge said simply. "It will clear up an old obligation."

Wong's frown was a massive thing. "Your semantics are poor tonight, little man. I do believe you said obligation."

"Your hearing is flawless as your memory is poor." Midge stood like a frail bitter pygmy. "For your information, Charles, the hounds sweated me for days. I had but to name a name, and my five years in Quentin would have been reduced to one."

Unexpectedly, Wong smiled. "And you desire payment for keeping your white plume unsmirched? This is your pride, chappie?" Black man and yellow man, speaking their strange and terrible hyperbole. Yellow man regarding Fern as though she did not exist. I had the feeling Midge was bargaining for our lives. "I must make a phone call," Wong said heavily. "I take it your friend is hot."

"Exceptionally. His name is Tony Pearson. The girl is not involved."

Wong nodded curtly and left the room. "Amazing man," Midge told us. "Twenty years ago he took his master's degree in sociology at the Sorbonne. Five years ago he was a prominent fence for the syndicate. Today he is restaurateur and gambler."

The headwaiter came in with three drinks on a tray. Mine was a plum-colored brandy that tasted a thousand proof. Whatever Charlie Wong was, he had manners. I felt gratitude toward Midge, and faint wonder. He lived by an iron code of ethics. Part of that code meant helping a friend, regardless of danger or praise. He could have squeezed the fat gambler for a job, for money. But he had sacrificed his pride to help me get ahead, because my girl, I supposed, had once done him a favor.

I reached into my pocket and touched Fern's five hundred dollars. As I moved past Midge to set my empty glass on the try, I bumped into him. His drink splashed on the carpet. I was apologizing and picking up his glass, when Wong came back into the room. I had managed to slip two hundred-dollar bills into Midge's coat pocket.

Wong stood looking at me out of his tiny pig eyes. "Your friend is a walking sacrifice, Midge. He has offended certain ones in high places. May I suggest you disassociate yourself from him at once?"

"Where's the car?" Midge asked.

Wong closed his eyes as if in pain. "You are a quixotic fool. If the hounds do not find him by morning it becomes a job for the organization. Castle has offered five thousand dollars for him. A half hour ago he eluded the hounds on Wilshire. May I suggest—"

"The car, you fat hustler," Midge was implacable. "Before I obscenity on your honor."

Wong shrugged a gigantic shrug and tossed me a car key. "Parked two blocks down," he said. "A black fifty-four Pontiac." His chuckle was surf-breaking. "The car, friend, is hot as you are. Does it matter?"

I told him it did not matter. Midge accompanied us to the outside corridor. "Good luck, children. I'm staying. I plan to break Wong's game for him." We shook hands. I felt the rustle of bills and stared down at the money. "I told you once," Midge said quietly, "buy one of my toy canvasses some time. So long."

"Thanks, Midge." Fern kissed the little man's cheek. As we went outside he smiled after us like a small benign Uncle Remus.

We walked through the carnival glow of the strip holding hands, not talking. As I opened the Pontiac's door for Fern I felt a cold certainty that we were being observed.

Wong had the indefinable taint of the illicit about him. Hustlers can be a charming breed, but most of them would sell their sisters for the right price.

And Castle had offered five thousand for me.

I got behind the wheel and turned on the ignition. The Pontiac slid easily away from the curb. No one stared after us, there was no sudden blare of police sirens. I turned off on a dark side street and doubled back toward the civic center.

"It's eight-fifteen," Fern said tautly. "Johnny goes off duty at nine."

"You think Val's already flown?"

She shook her head. "Not this early. We've got a good hour."

An hour wasn't enough. I found the freeway, but the Friday night traffic was thick. It was after nine by the time we hit Newport.

"Fern, what kind of woman is Val?"

"Pure bitch," she said with soft venom. "An ex-model who married money when she was twenty, and got a divorce six months later. Her second marriage lasted almost a year. Max is her third. She makes a game of infidelity, but Max doesn't notice—or pretends not to."

I tried to picture Val as the scheming type. It was no use. Beautiful, pampered, with a female steak of viciousness. But not a calculating cold planner. Val and Ramos together simply did not jell.

Lupo? The little man had seemed fiercely loyal to Max. But it could have been simple jealousy that had maimed George Fair with that dart. Although Lupo was hardly Val's type.

It was nine-forty when we hit Point Rafael and turned up the winding hill road. I parked in the dark cottonwoods two hundred yards from the house. Fern gave a small sob of relief when she saw the Buick station wagon parked in the drive.

"She's still here," she breathed. "I'm going in, Tony. I'll try to stampede her. I'll tell her I've just come back from the Shore and that Max is drunk and ugly. That he's been hinting about Val and Stephen, asking me questions. Then I shall yawn theatrically and hit the hay. You'll follow her?"

"Right," I said huskily, pulling her into my arms. "Kiss for luck."

It became a long savage farewell kiss that left us both shaken. "Call me in an hour, Tony—no matter what. Promise?"

"Promise."

Fern touched my cheek with a wordless gesture, then hurried across the drive into the house. She disappeared in the veranda shadows and I felt very much alone.

Five, ten minutes. I lighted a cigarette. The poplars stood out like silver sentinels in the moonlight, and the landscape was a Goya canvas, dreamlike and unreal.

Twenty minutes later a dark figure emerged from the side door, carrying an overnight bag. Val. Before getting into the Buick she glanced back at the house. The Buick's headlights flared and its tires chewed gravel. She came up the winding road at forty miles an hour, and I counted to a slow ten before following her.

I kept the Pontiac's lights off all the way down to the coast highway. Val had turned south, towards La Jolla. For the next ten miles I stayed a quarter-mile behind, cruising at seventy. All this time I had a strange preoccupation over my last chess game with Stephen.

I remembered a knight sacrifice he had made. An apparently premature move which concealed a deadly rook mask. I had ignored the knight, and Stephen had announced mate in three.

I thought about Val finding Stephen's body in the cove five days after his death. Stephen making love to her a few days before he was murdered. I thought about Consuela Ramos' dark proud beauty. "*Juan has always come back to me, señor.*"

It was like a floodlight being suddenly turned on inside my head. Stephen's long-range planning, his deal with Castle. His obvious seduction of Val. Ramos arranging with Wallquist to fence the Rembrandt through underground channels. All the jigsaw fragments twinkled into place at once. I felt contempt for Val, and pity.

Like myself, she was a sacrifice pawn. Right now, I had suddenly realized, she was keeping a rendezvous with sudden death. Her own.

Ahead, the Buick slowed as we drove through Dana Point. I kept the Pontiac at thirty. On my right, the beach houses were thinning. Abruptly the Buick turned off on the cliff shoulder. Its headlights winked out. I drove a few hundred yards farther and pulled over to the edge of the highway. I made myself light a cigarette and wait two minutes before making a U-turn. I drove back and parked behind Val's Buick. The car was deserted. At the edge of the beach cliff was a picket fence, with a rickety stairway leading a hundred yards down to the sand. The nearest house was four blocks north, perched high on a bluff promontory.

A full moon played hide-and-seek among black, scudding clouds. Far south, you could see distant bonfires nickering on the strand. College kids, probably, waiting for the first grunion run of the season.

Nestled in the cliff hollow below, I saw the beach house. One of the windows was a yellow square of light. The moon went behind a cloud, and I started gingerly down the steps in darkness. Halfway down I heard voices and froze.

The night wind tasted of salt and there was only the distant boom of surf. I descended slowly. As I reached the bottom step the flashlight glare exploded in my face. Val's giggle was a hot knife in the stillness.

"The pose is fine, Tony. Hold it, please."

A man's voice. Light, amused. I had guessed right, but it was small consolation now. I stared blindly into the flashlight beam.

"Hello, Stephen," I said.

12

"Walk slowly, old man." Stephen shifted the flashlight to let me see the gun. "Toward the cottage, if you don't mind."

I walked toward the looming bulk of the beach cottage, hating myself, wondering how long it had taken Val to spot me tailing her. As if reading my mind, Stephen said patronizingly, "She wasn't sure until you doubled back and parked behind the Buick. Right, Val?"

"That's right, darling," she said.

Val opened the cottage door for me and I went in. The living room was a soft blend of pastel furniture and green tropicals, with one entire wall done in pale limestone. Stephen motioned Val to the pink chesterfield.

"Nice place," I said.

"Belongs to Max," Stephen said. "Fern and I honeymooned here, six months ago. Sit down."

I sat. There was a subtle difference in him. His eyes were calm and dead. In repose his lean face was utterly devoid of expression, and it came to me that evil can be a functional thing. Stephen would kill me without passion or thought, because I was an obstacle not worthy of survival. In that moment I tasted hatred like a thick bile in my throat.

"That mustache," I said, looking at the embryo smudge above his lip. "Did you reinforce it with grease paint last Monday, when you checked out of the Beverly-Wilshire as Ramos?"

"Black crayon," Stephen smiled. "Very effective. For your information,

I *am* Ramos. Since last Sunday, when you killed me."

The .32 in his fist came up, steadied on my chest. Val rose to her feet, suddenly pale. "You promised," she whispered. "We were only going to tie him up. Please, darling—"

"He's going to kill us both," I snapped. "Use your head. You're just excess baggage from here on out. All he ever needed you for was to find Ramos' body after the crabs had made it unrecognizable. By Monday night he gets a fifty-grand payoff from Castle, and probably a dummied passport. As Ramos, he flits. I suppose he told you to leave a farewell note for Max?"

"Y-yes. I—"

"The cops find us both dead, here in the beach cottage. Both of us half naked, whiskey splashed around. A drunken lovers' quarrel, with the gun still in my hand—"

Almost casually, Stephen chopped the gun across my temple. Pain flamed in a scarlet explosion behind my eyes. I touched my cheek and felt warm stickiness. Stephen glanced at Val in tender mockery. "Do you believe him, darling?"

She shook her bright head wordlessly, staring at him. But in that moment, she knew. It was in Stephen's flat smile, the way he eyed her with remote pitying contempt. I had a feeling he would savor Val's last moments on earth. He would watch her face as he pulled the trigger.

"Complex," I said admiringly. "But clever."

I tried to touch his weakness, his vanity. Anything to stall him, to wipe that execution smile off his face. I spoke as an inferior chess player to a master. And I edged imperceptibly forward in my chair, my thigh muscles tensing, trying not to look at the gun.

Stephen frowned. "Complex? How?"

I moistened my lips. "Your planning was so long range. Was it Castle's idea for you to run the Shore into the red?"

"Mine," he said dryly. "It was the obvious way to pressure Max into selling the Rembrandt. Castle was delighted. All he wanted was the Lee Shore. He contacted Ramos through Wallquist, but Juan turned out to have certain—scruples."

"That's what I mean. Too complex. Too dangerous, even if it worked."

"Not at all. We simply got him into a big game. One of Castle's back rooms. Let him win at first." Stephen chuckled in recollection. "Then we clobbered him. Thirty thousand dollars. Poor frantic Latin. When we finally offered him a chance to get off the hook he painted that reproduction like an inspired man."

Val's breathing was harsh in the silence. Her gentian eyes did not waver from the muzzle of the .32.

"Then Val's scream that night was coincidence," I said. "You had already switched paintings a few days before."

"Certainly. My original plan was to disappear, making it look like an accident. But when I met you at Briarview—"

"You decided to give Max a real corpse instead! Ramos was ideal, wasn't he? It meant a bigger split all round, besides framing me for your death. Last Sunday night you followed Ramos outside and killed him. You stripped the body and mutilated it before planting it under the landing—"

"No!" Val's voice was a thin wail. "Darling, you said Tony killed him! That you needed me, you were in danger—"

Her voice trailed off. Stephen gave her a bored glance. I said, "He planned to wait a few days longer before telling you to find the body, Val. But I got out of jail too soon."

"Not too soon," Stephen shrugged. "Both Val and Fern identified the body as mine."

"Wrong," I said. "Fern recognized it. But she played dumb. Who do you think told me to follow Val?"

His nostrils flared. The .32 was rock-steady, pointed at my navel. "Go on," he said softly.

"Fern's waiting in my car on top of the cliff. If she hears a shot she goes for the cops. Stalemate, chum."

Stephen glanced questioningly at Val. She sat on the pink chesterfield, biting her fist. "I'm not—sure," she said miserably. "I thought Fern acted funny. I didn't actually see her go to bed. She could have joined him outside, after I left."

Stephen weighed it. It was a bluff he couldn't afford to call. "Val," he said gently. She looked up at him, and for the first time I saw his magic with women. His charm lighted up the entire room. His smile was a benediction, the essence of need. "I need you, darling," he said.

"Yes," Val said. "Yes."

"Stand up, Tony." The gun gestured. I stood, slowly.

"Now turn around." I turned. Then the quick swish of his shoes on the carpet. I braced myself, trying to gauge the second of impact, to roll with the blow. I didn't, quite. He almost caved in my skull.

When I came to, there were voices. The carpeting was soft and warm against my cheek. I wanted to burrow into it drowsily, to sleep for a very long time.

"Certainly he lied." Stephen's voice, vibrant, reassuring. "Tony's a psychopathic liar and murderer. You should feel sorry for him."

"I believe you," Val whispered. The sound of a kiss. My insides squirmed. He had bound her to him with chains of passion to make her believe black was white, he was that good. "I brought a gun in my handbag," Val said proudly. "Just in case. See?"

Stephen chuckled. "You call that a gun?" Another kiss. "Darling, he's dangerous. If he moves, shoot him. I'll be right back."

The kitchen door closed. Silence. I opened my eyes and saw the sheen of Val's nylons.

I turned over on my back. She almost shot me. As I tried to get up, Val gave a startled gasp and raised the gun. It was a tiny pearl-handled boudoir special, a .22. "Don't you move," she breathed.

"You're a fool," I said. "He doesn't need you any more, understand? As soon as he comes back we both get it—"

"Be still!" Her face was chalk white, she was fighting hysteria. "I don't want to listen. You couldn't possibly understand. Stephen loves me."

"For your information, he still loves Fern." I managed a brutal grin. "Think about it a while."

It was a crude lie, but the only thing that might shatter the wall of emotion in which Stephen had enclosed her. In that fractional second her gun wavered, and I came up fast from the floor and slapped it out of her hand. "It's not loaded," Val said. She looked at me with a tired smile, and unexpectedly burst into tears. I retrieved the .22 and checked the magazine. Empty. It was typical of Val.

Stephen would be at the top of the cliff by now, moving like a shadow in the darkness. I gave him thirty seconds to inspect the empty Pontiac and decide I had lied about Fern, another fifty seconds to descend the bluff steps four at a time. I grabbed Val's arm. "Come on!" To my surprise she did come, listlessly.

Outside, we headed south, toward the bonfires a half-mile down the beach. Tidal sand sucked at our shoes. We hugged the base of the cliff, moving slowly through inky shadows. It was a temptation to ambush Stephen when he returned to the cottage. But his gun was loaded. Val's wasn't. And it would have been childish to risk her life in the balance.

Val paused, panting. "I'm tired, Tony."

I shushed her. "Listen!"

The sharp slam of the cottage door. Stillness. I peered back at the cottage and saw nothing. Two hundred yards away, Stephen was coming after us in silence. Val and I were two errant pawns. Very unsporting of us. I pressed Val back into a deep niche between the rocks. Her body tensed, then relaxed against mine. Her breath was warm in my ear. "He's not bad, really. Don't hurt him. Promise me you won't hurt him—"

"Quiet!" I wanted to hit her.

The moon came out from under tattered clouds. Fifty yards of salt-white sand separated us from the ocean. Here the beach was a narrow crescent bounded by cliff and dunes, gradually widening as it stretched south. We were utterly alone. Stephen could take his time. No one would hear the shots.

I bent down and groped for a handful of rock shards. Val drew a quick convulsive breath and I squeezed her arm for silence. I threw the rocks back toward the cottage, aiming at the curve of cliff wall. They struck with a faint clatter.

We saw Stephen.

He had been waiting behind a grassy dune. Now he stood motionless, thirty yards away. The moonlight etched him with a terrible distinctness. Two-legged carnivore with a white smile. The .32 glinted in his fist as he moved to another dune.

"Oh, God," Val's nails dug into my wrist. "Look at his face!"

Stephen stood in a balanced crouch, studying the cliff minutely. Abruptly he vanished behind a rise of sand. At first, I didn't get it.

Then I stared south and felt a sick realization. Ahead, the boulders curved diagonally outward toward the surf, forming a wide angle against the sand. To go that way meant target exposure. We were boxed in.

Val stirred against me in the darkness. "Tony?" A ragged whisper.

"Hush!"

"I'm a fool, Tony." Her face was a dim oval, raising to mine. "He's going to kill us both, like you said."

"It's a standoff, Val." I put an arm around her shoulder. "He thinks your gun is loaded. He'll be cautious—for a while."

"And then?"

I said nothing. We listened to the crash of the surf. The tide was coming in. Unexpectedly, Val's body moved against mine.

"Tony?"

"Stop it," I said.

She made a sound that was half giggle, half sob. She kept on with what she was doing, and the thunder in my blood drowned out the waves. I groped for her hands, pinned them.

"Please." Her breath was a soft furnace against my ear. "Yes. I'm crazy. But you don't know what it's like. Stephen knows. He's rotten, but he understands. He—"

I clamped a hand over her mouth. She bit me. I swore.

"Please," she said.

"Haven't you ever been to a doctor?"

"Many times. They talk about basal insecurity and father fixation and usually wind up making a pass at me." Her bright head tossed restlessly. "Sometimes they complete the pass. Max suspects, but doesn't know. Still, Max doesn't need me. He doesn't need anybody. Poor Max."

"Poor Max," I said bitterly. "So you helped Stephen rob him blind. Didn't you know he killed Ramos?"

"No," she whimpered. "Stephen called me Tuesday, the day after he disappeared. He told me you were tied in with Castle's syndicate, that you had killed Ramos by mistake. That his life was in danger, he needed my help ... Tony, you're not going out there!"

"No choice." I patted her hand. "No matter what happens, stay hidden."

I hit the sand flat on my belly, crawling toward the high dunes.

Five years ago it had been like this. Five years ago, in Korea, squinting through the dawn of Punchbowl Ridge and waiting for the impact of a sniper's bullet. Crawling through sand, with your belly muscles knotted in anticipation of sudden death.

Nothing stirred on the dunes. The beach grass was motionless. I crawled face down, moving from one shadowed depression to another, praying for the moon to stay behind the clouds another five minutes. In my right hand was Val's useless gun.

He could be a hundred yards down the beach by now. He could be watching me from the other side of the dune. Far to my right, the beach flats were churning in phosphorescent needle splashes. A school of grunion, spawning in the shallows. I huddled behind a tiny dune, looking back at the cliff. It was a gigantic wall of shadow. Then I saw Val and almost cursed aloud.

She had emerged from the depression. She was standing silhouetted clearly in the moonlight, staring at me like a pale frightened doll. Much later I wondered if she had some wild idea of diverting Stephen's attention, or possibly pleading with him. I never found out.

He came up over the dune directly in front of me, ten feet away. His face was polished bone in the moonlight. He did not look quite human as, hardly pausing to aim, he fired twice.

My shout was lost in the roar of his gun. From five feet, I hurled Val's automatic squarely into his face. He lurched sideways. The .32 slammed again and sand kicked up inches from my face. I hit him low and hard, knees driving, and we rolled down the slope in a thrashing tangle of arms and legs.

I couldn't hold him. He moved with a writhing steel strength that flung me clear as we hit the wet beach flats. Then we stood facing each other a yard apart, panting. The .32 glittered in the sand ten feet away. He ignored it. He came at me, lips peeled back over his teeth, fists driving like pistons. I tried for his groin and he took my knee easily on the outside of his thigh and knocked me down with a whistling left hook that almost tore my head off.

I was down on my back. Stephen leaped. I rolled, desperately, as he came down stiff-legged where my face had been. It was an utterly unequal fight. Take a ninety-pound collie, a brave, determined beast. Pit him against a forty-pound lynx. The lynx invariably tears the collie to shreds. And Stephen weighed a lot more than forty pounds.

I managed to roll to my feet, gasping, my whole body shaking. Stephen came in, measuring me for a right that would have broken my jaw. But I was holding a fistful of damp sand. I threw it in his face. As he clawed for his eyes I grabbed his shirt, slumping forward, and butted him in the face. I felt the crackle of breaking cartilage, and Stephen made an animal sound in his throat. I brought my right elbow down like a hammer into the side of his neck. He quivered, stumbling toward me. I dodged back from his hands, and scooped up the .32. Stephen hesitated, his face a devil's mask of blood. I fired from eight feet.

And missed.

He had moved with incredible speed, veering sideways behind a dune.

Killing lust clotted my vision. It was a madness, an obsession, to destroy this man who had stolen my woman, had beaten me, had framed me for murder. I ran after him, and he was a darting, fleeing shadow that vanished down the south slope of beach. I fired after him again, futilely.

My breath came in great racking sobs. I ran after him, and stumbled, falling to my knees. The impact brought back sanity. I got up slowly, and went to find Val.

She was lying in the sand, eyes closed. The front of her dress was soaked with blood that looked like black ink in the moonlight. I cradled her in my arms and started toward the bluff steps.

13

Halfway up the cliff steps I sat down, fighting to keep from passing out. In my arms Val moaned softly and stirred. "Tony?" A burbling sigh.

"Take it easy," I said. "I'll get you to a doctor."

"I'm—sorry, Tony." Her eyelids fluttered, closed.

It gave me strength to reach the top of the steps. I got her into the front seat of the Pontiac and slid behind the wheel. When I pressed the starter, nothing happened.

I got out and lifted the hood. In the darkness it was impossible to see what he had done. It could have been the timing rotor, the distributor, or a disconnected battery. I didn't know. All I knew was that somebody was swearing in a cracked, hopeless monotone. Me.

Val was dying. I had to get her to a hospital. Later, I realized Stephen had counted on that. He had fled realizing that Val was my only living witness. With her dead, the police would never believe me. Another murder charge, open and shut.

I looked at Val's Buick, and started back down the cliff steps. Fatigue was a twisting scalpel in my side. The moon was a great silver floodlight, bathing the still peacefulness of sand and sea. I tried to imagine Stephen lurking in the nearby shadows. But there was only the slap of the waves as I walked into the cottage. Val's handbag was lying on the pink leather chesterfield. In it were the ignition keys to the Buick.

It took me a gasping, staggering eternity to climb those steps a second time. But I finally fell into the Buick, fumbled with the ignition. The engine kicked over with a purr. Why hadn't Stephen disabled it, also? No time, maybe. Maybe he expected to make his own getaway in it. I didn't know. I sat, drawing long shuddering breaths of utter exhaustion before I went back and lifted Val out of the Pontiac, as gently as I could. She was heavy, flaccid. As I lifted her into the Buick she coughed weakly, spitting blood.

I drove into Dana Point at eighty miles an hour. The dash clock said almost eleven-thirty when I found an all-night diner and consulted its phone book. There was an emergency clinic a mile north, just off the coast highway.

The clinic turned out to be a sprawling Spanish stucco with a dim light in the foyer. I kept punching the door buzzer viciously, and it seemed like a very long time before the male nurse opened the stained glass door and stared at us.

We were something to stare at. I looked like a tramp, with my clothes torn and sandy, my battered face. Val looked like a pale beautiful corpse in my arms.

"Later!" I snapped as the nurse started to ask questions. "She's hemorrhaging badly. She's got two bullets in her. Is there a doctor?"

He nodded calmly and helped me get her down the hall to a sickroom. He was a blond stocky man with big hands surprisingly gentle as he stretched Val out on the emergency table.

"Go back to the desk and fill out an admittance form," he said crisply. "I'll call Doctor Slattery. He'll be here in five minutes."

"How—is she?"

"Bad. She needs plasma." His frown was coldly suspicious. "How did it happen?"

"Tell you when the doctor gets here." I went back down the hall to the reception desk. I was filling out the admittance form when I saw the newspaper lying on the desk. A late night final.

I picked it up and turned to the front page. The story was on page one. *Slayer Resists Arrest, Flees.* Reading the story I felt a weird sense of unreality. Only a few hours ago, and it was already in the newspapers. On the fourth page was a photograph of my face. A photo that had been taken three years before when I had won a local tournament. Stilch had probably found it in my room. The picture made me look very young, fatuous. The story said nothing about my hitting Officer Stilch with a coffeepot. Only that the police expected an arrest before morning.

In a few minutes the nurse came down the hall. Without looking at me he sat down at the desk, rubbing his temples.

"It's been almost ten minutes," I said harshly. "Where's the doctor?"

"He's coming."

He looked at me with tired gray eyes and lighted a cigarette. "But there's no hurry now. Pity you couldn't get here sooner."

"You mean she's—"

"She died while I was administering plasma."

Suddenly, all I could think of was Max. I had a vision of his big ugly face distorted in grief. Lament for an unfaithful wife. His rage would be a killing thing—If Max discovered Fern had been with me tonight ...

"I called the police," the nurse said. "You'd better stick around— *hey, come back here—*"

Once again, I ran. Out to the foyer and through the stained glass door. I had to warn Fern, and quickly. I had to get her away from the house of Max Baird. I was outside, in the Buick, hitting the starter, when I heard the growing shriek of sirens. They were very close. On the coast highway, I wouldn't have a chance.

I jumped out of the Buick and ran back to the foyer. The nurse tried to bar my way. He set himself and swung clumsily. I straight-armed him. He was shouting as I ran down the hall. Those sirens were a soft moan outside, and there was the metallic slam of car doors. The nurse was in the foyer doorway, shouting incoherently. I dodged into one of the wards and closed the door behind me.

Lying on the hospital cot was an old man, sleeping. In the dimness, his face had a faint bluish pallor. I stepped gingerly past him to the washroom and stood rigid against the marble basin. From this angle I could not be seen from the doorway. My breathing was a harsh rasp in the silence.

Heavy footsteps sounded down the corridor. The deep authoritative voice of the law. The shrill explanations of the male nurse. The voices faded.

The bathroom window was about two feet square, slightly above my head. I grabbed the sill with my fingertips and hoisted myself up to eye level. From almost directly under the window I heard the thrashing of shrubbery. Voices:

"You say he ran out the back door?"

"Yes, sir. I tried to stop him and he slugged me." The male nurse's voice. "He must be out there."

"If he is, we'll find him." A gruff voice, edged with caution. "You say he had a gun?"

"I'm not sure. The girl was shot twice."

"But you can definitely identify him as Pearson."

"Yes, sir. He looked just like his picture in the newspaper. He even signed the admittance statement as Pearson."

"Cold son-of-a-bitch," the officer said. "You'd better go inside. We'll need a statement."

Silence. Distant door slam. By craning my neck I managed to peer outside. Below was a dimly lighted garden with a small Spanish courtyard. In the center of the courtyard was a stone fountain. The surrounding brick walls were lined with thick tropicals and shrubbery. I saw three indistinct figures with flashlights and drawn guns, methodically probing the bushes.

"Funny thing, him showing in Dana Point. We got a flash earlier that he'd been spotted in Los Angeles. With Mrs. Locke."

"So he's crazy. You can't figure them. Did you call Stilch?"

"Yes, sir. He should be here any minute."

"This bird must have an obsession for women. First he kills Locke over his wife, then kills Mrs. Baird. Is Headquarters contacting Baird?"

"I believe so. Captain, I'm afraid he's not out here."

More thrashing of brush. "Strange," the captain said. "Delahanty's covering the outside area. You think he could be hiding in the clinic?"

"It's possible, sir. He damned well isn't down here."

A heavy grunt. "Come on."

I had perhaps three minutes. They would cover the clinic room by room. The footsteps died away and there was the slam of the back door. I loosed the screen catch. I pushed the screen outward and it gave on its hinges. I hoisted myself through the window, head and shoulders. I was some six feet above a bank of acanthus. I wriggled through the window and fell, landing heavily on my back and shoulders. The screen had swung back to position. After a while I shifted delicately. I moved to a thicker area of shrubbery in the corner of the courtyard. Above me was a lighted window. I heard muffled voices. They became suddenly clear. I was huddling under the reception-room window.

"Pearson's on foot?" Stilch's voice, calm and cold. He hadn't wasted any time getting here.

"That's right," the captain said. "We've got three squad cars blocking the south edge of the highway and two cars combing the immediate area. A mouse couldn't get through. How did Baird take it?"

"Hard. He's on his way here now to make identification. You've got the M.E.'s report?"

"Death at approximately eleven-thirty, confirmed by the nurse's statement. One bullet in the left side, the other near the lower right ventricle. But why should he bother to bring her to the clinic?"

"Probably a passion killing. Afterward he was scared. He figured maybe she had a chance to live if he got her here in time. Most of that type feel a superficial remorse—after it's too late."

"I'd like to get my hands on that bastard," the captain said thoughtfully. "Just for two minutes. I'd make him forget all about women. What's your theory with regard to Mrs. Locke?"

"The old triangle story. He was reported with her earlier tonight. He apparently had a later tryst with Mrs. Baird. I can't figure why. Did you pick up Mrs. Locke for questioning?"

"She disappeared from Baird's house earlier tonight. We've got her description on teletype. You figure her for accessory?"

"Probably. I've a hunch we'll find them together."

"I sure feel sorry for Mr. Baird," the captain said. A pause. "Baird's a pretty big man in Point Rafael, isn't he?"

Sharply: "How do you mean?"

"He owns the Lee Shore. Understand it's quite a place." A smirk in the captain's voice. "Of course, I've never been there. Out of my territory."

There was frost in Stilch's tone. "You'd have to talk to Jed Wells about that. I'm only his deputy."

The voices drifted beyond earshot. I huddled in the dank tropicals, listening to the small night sounds. I was beyond hope, beyond planning. Fern had vanished. And if the police didn't shoot me on sight, my predestined end was that little room with the bad smell at San Quentin.

I tried to sleep. It was no good. My teeth kept chattering.

It was four in the morning. The clinic was dark and quiet. The press members had come and gone. But there would still be patrol cars cruising the nearby darkness. I was a fish in a net.

With Val dead, Stephen had nothing to fear. Right now, he was contacting Castle. He needed money, a plane, a fast boat. By this time tomorrow, Stephen would be in Acapulco or somewhere.

A random thought jerked me erect. Castle didn't actually *need* Stephen any more. And the lean, white-haired gangster was utterly amoral. His obvious payoff for Stephen would be a moonlight swim with concrete water wings.

Ergo, Stephen had some kind of hold over Castle. Wallquist? I didn't know. But it gave me an idea.

I flexed aching muscles, and moved. The courtyard was dark and still. The garden gate was unlocked. I opened it cautiously and peered outside. There was a highway patrol car still parked in front of the clinic. Nobody was in it.

Five minutes later I was walking rapidly down the palm-lined road towards the coast highway. Morning fog was rolling in from the Pacific, a thick gray curtain that could mean the difference between life and death. Once a cruising prowl passed and I flattened myself against a palm.

Fifteen minutes later I reached the coast highway. On the southeast corner the neon sign of a Serve-Yourself gas station shone redly in the mist. I went around in back, to the men's room. The attendant sat in his lighted glass cubicle. He glanced up, yawning, then went back to his paper.

First, I stripped. I was blood and sand from head to foot. I used paper towels to dry myself, rubbing until the skin tingled. The face that stared out of the bathroom mirror looked incredibly tired. But rest was not what I wanted.

I replaced Stephen's .32 carefully inside my shirt, under the waistband. There was one cartridge left in the chamber.

I was going to find Wallquist.

Outside the washroom I found the phone booth, near the grease rack. I dialed an all-night cab agency and gave them the station's address. They promised to have a cab there within five minutes.

The attendant was no longer in his office cubicle. He was out by the pumps, wiping a customer's windshield. I walked boldly toward the corner. I was standing there, seconds later, when the red spotlights hit me and there was the sharp whipcrack of a voice:

"Don't move, Pearson! Hands behind your head."

The prowl car had stopped abreast on the highway. Now it swerved into the station and two officers got out.

They approached me with professional caution, guns drawn. One of them was tall, with a tanned hawk face. He handcuffed me, and found Stephen's gun.

The station attendant came over. He had a slack, bucktoothed grin.

"Thought you'd never get here." He eyed me in fascination. "Is there any kind of reward?"

"We'll let you know," hawk-face said. "Appreciate your calling."

The cop saw the look on my face and added: "We've alerted every place in the surrounding area, mister. He called us while you were in the can."

I said nothing. They shoved me into the back seat of the squad car. We drove north, toward the county seat. In the east you could see the gray sickness of dawn.

14

I was officially booked on suspicion of murder, photographed and fingerprinted. They took me down the asphalt tile corridor to a room adjacent to Stilch's office. It was a small room with three barred windows, four chairs, a large oak table. They left me alone with a big sunburned deputy. I asked for a cigarette and the deputy handed me a pack, and matches. My body was one vast throbbing ache. But oddly enough I did not feel the need for sleep. Not yet. That would come later, under the glare of bright lights and the stabbing questions.

A wide, hard-faced man came in and sat at the table. He looked about forty; rimless glasses and thinning sandy hair. His voice was a courtroom bell.

"My name's Golightly. Assistant county prosecutor. Would you care to dictate a confession?"

"Am I entitled to a lawyer?"

A contemptuous frown. "You figure on pleading temporary insanity, something like that?"

"Not at all. Stephen Locke killed Valerie, and I can prove it! Bring in the recorder and I'll make a detailed statement."

Blood darkened his forehead. "You'll get a sanity hearing within two hours after you make such a statement. If our psychiatrists declare you sane we'll ask for—and get—an automatic death penalty. You killed Locke six days ago! We're giving you a chance to level—"

"There's a black fifty-four Pontiac hardtop a mile south of Dana Point. You'll find Locke's fingerprints on the hood where he put them earlier tonight."

The sunburned deputy stirred in his chair. Golightly sat motionless, looking at the table. Finally he said with repressed fury, "Bring in the recorder, Tom."

They let me tell it in my own words. I said nothing about Midge or Charlie Wong. I confessed to stealing the Pontiac from a lot on Sunset Strip. Once, Golightly interrupted me. He called in another deputy and had me give him the location of the Pontiac. He let me tell the rest of my story without interruption. When I finished he turned off the recorder and leaned forward. His questions came like blows from a tack-hammer.

"First, Deputy Stilch came to your apartment. You attacked him. Why?"

"I was scared. Free, I could clear myself—"

"And when you found these—ah—charcoal sketches in Ramos' office, you thought you had partial proof of your innocence. Right?"

"Yes. That's right."

"Then why didn't you call the police from Ramos' office?"

The question came like a whip, and left me with my mouth open, fumbling for words. I finally muttered something about giving the sketches to Max first, and Golightly grunted. His pale eyes were relentless on mine.

"You say two men attacked you and burned the sketches. You and Mrs. Locke fled in a cab, correct?"

I just nodded.

"And where did you steal this Pontiac?"

"In the parking lot of The Players." The Players was a night club two blocks from Charlie Wong's.

"Then you drove back to Point Rafael. You let off Mrs. Locke at Baird's house. You followed Mrs. Baird to a beach house south of Dana Point. There, Stephen Locke tried to kill both of you. Valerie Baird was fatally wounded. Again, Pearson, why didn't you notify the police?"

The question was asked with a theatrical weariness. In Golightly's eyes was a growing disgust.

"Because I wanted to get her to a doctor," I said.

"Very laudable. Where is Mrs. Locke now?"

I just blinked. He leaned across the table and said savagely, "Baird arrived home a little after midnight. He found a Dear John note from his wife. Fern Locke was nowhere in the house. Her bed gave no evidence of occupancy. Where is she, Pearson?"

"How the hell should I know?" The implication hit me, and I stood up, shaking. So did the deputy. "Listen," I whispered, "I happen to be in love with her. Wherever she is, she's safe—"

"Is she, Pearson?"

I sat, limply. Fern had waited at Baird's house for my call. An hour later she had gone to some undesignated rendezvous by herself. Wallquist? The Lee Shore?

The door opened and a deputy motioned. Golightly left the room. He was gone almost ten minutes. I lit a cigarette. My fingers kept twitching from fatigue. My eyelids weighed a ton. The deputy sat watching me like a cat. Golightly returned with a faint smile.

"Getting back to that Pontiac you stole. It fascinates me. How come the lot attendant didn't stop you?"

I hesitated. "He was at the side door helping some lush into his Cadillac. He never noticed until we drove out of the lot past him."

"I see. Let's review the beach cottage incident. You left the side door unlocked, right?"

"That's right."

"And the Pontiac you left at the top of the bluff with an inoperative motor." He was relaxed, almost benign. "Do you recall leaving the ignition keys in the car?"

"I think so. Yes."

"You must have. They weren't among your personal effects." Suddenly he shifted attack. "Quite a devil with the ladies, aren't you, Pearson?"

"How do you mean?"

"Look at you. Six-one, blond hair, big handsome golf pro. I'll bet you could have just about any girl you wanted."

What got me was his patronizing smile. He was talking as to a small child.

"Quite a feat, keeping two women on the string at the same time, isn't it?"

I saw where he was leading, and how it would look to a jury. "Wrong route," I said. "I never even met Valerie Baird until last Sunday night."

"You can prove that, of course." Bland deadly voice, eyes like blue ice.

"You know damned well I can't prove it! What are you trying to build?"

"Simply that there was no black Pontiac. Deputy Carstairs just called in from Dana Point. He checked the beach cottage you describe and found the doors locked. There was no sign of disorder, no Pontiac parked at the top of the bluff."

"Stephen doubled back," I breathed. "He locked the cottage. He ungimmicked the car and drove it away."

"Right after Carstairs phoned in his report, I called The Players. Did you know they're closed down this week? Remodeling. Try again, Pearson." He wasn't bluffing. It was in his eyes, his smile.

"Then it was King's," I said. "Or some other place. I don't remember."

"Damned right you don't! Because you never followed Valerie Baird anywhere. It was all prearranged for her to pick you up, wasn't it? Only Fern suspected. You tried to shake her and she became violently jealous. You had a fight with her. Perhaps you killed her. When Valerie found out she became afraid of you. She saw you for what you really are—an oversexed psycho, subject to killing rages when crossed. She backed out of her promise to run off with you. So you cracked, completely. You killed her with two shots from that .32 you were carrying when we picked you up."

I wiped sweat from my eyes. "Then afterward, why did I take her to the hospital?"

He shrugged. "Fear. Remorse. After she died you became panicky, and tried to run. Where's Fern Locke?"

"I don't know!"

"Look at me. You killed her, didn't you?"

I was getting groggy. "I want a lawyer."

"No lawyer in the world would touch your case with a ten-foot pole. Why'd you kill Valerie Baird?"

"Locke. It was Stephen Locke."

"Locke's dead. Dead. Like you're going to be if you don't come clean. Valerie left the house at approximately ten o'clock. Where did she pick you up?"

"It was Stephen."

"Was it Los Angeles? Laguna?"

"It was the beach house. Baird's beach house."

"You were with Fern at the time. The police found her car abandoned in an alley in Los Angeles about eight o'clock last night. They found blood on the steering wheel. It was Fern's, wasn't it?"

"No. It was Midge's—"

"Who's Midge?"

"Nobody. I don't know whose blood it was."

"Fern threatened to turn you over to the police. She was jealous. Is that why you killed her?"

"It was Baird's beach house."

"Is that where you hid Fern's body?"

"Fern's alive. I don't know where she is."

"Val became afraid of you, didn't she? She changed her mind. You felt furious, betrayed. So you shot her."

"It was the Rembrandt. Stephen and Ramos—"

"That Rembrandt angle is pure hogwash, and you know it! We've got the gun you killed Valerie with. We've got method, motive, opportunity. I'm not making any kind of deal, Pearson. You might get off with life if you tell a straight story. No promises. Pearson, look at me!"

His words rattled at me like hail, without meaning. His face looked fuzzed, out of focus. Now his palm came down on the table like a gunshot, and I jumped.

"I want a lawyer," I mumbled.

His questions were spikes, nailing the lid down on my coffin. It went on and on, and after a time I could see yellow sunlight coming into the room. I was retching with fatigue when the questions finally stopped and they took me to my cell. I did not remember whether or not I had confessed. I did not care.

My cell was small and clean. Steel casement windows, a cot, a sink, a toilet. I lay on my bunk with the echo of Golightly's questions still going on in my brain like a mad metronome. The turnkey came down the corridor with breakfast on a tin tray. Oatmeal and black coffee. The coffee was weak and had tiny spots of oil floating on top of it, but it was the most delicious coffee I have ever drunk in my life. I broke my last cigarette in two, and smoked one of the halves. Then I slept.

They woke me late in the afternoon. Two strange deputies took me back to that little room with the oak table. It was just like the morning, only worse. Golightly ridiculed me. He did not shout or swear. He kept probing the weak points in my story with his soft courtroom deftness, and twice he made me contradict myself about the times I had followed Valerie. Finally he brought in the recorder.

"Last chance, Pearson. I sincerely believe none of the killings were premeditated. Tell it again in your own words, what really happened. Locke's death was an accident, wasn't it? After that you became panicky—"

I cursed him. His smile turned glacial. "Have it your way. Just answer one question."

"Go ahead."

"Based on the testimony you've given so far, do you honestly believe even a jury of your own relatives would take less than thirty seconds to convict you?"

I thought about it. "I guess not."

"But it's the truth so you're stuck with it, right?" He was a tower of righteous contempt. I just nodded.

"You figure the wilder the story the more chance you'll have of a hung jury. It's poor strategy, boy. Tomorrow morning you're going up against two specialists. You'll receive comprehensive written and oral sanity tests. The results of those tests, plus your recorded statement, will send you to the gas chamber."

"All right," I said wearily. "Now can I have a lawyer?"

The door opened and Stilch came in. He looked tired. "Come on back to your cell, Pearson."

Golightly gave him a queer frown, but said nothing. Another deputy took me back to my cell. Fifteen minutes later Stilch came along the corridor. The turnkey unlocked the cell door and let him in.

"Cigarette?" He extended a pack.

"Thanks," I said.

I inhaled greedily. The big deputy leaned against the bars, his smile quizzical. He had a small white bandage on the crown of his head.

"You swing a pretty mean coffeepot, dad."

"I'm sorry," I said, and I was. "I was scared."

"You lied to Golightly about that black Pontiac," Stilch said gently. "Want to tell me about it, off the record?"

"A friend helped me. The friend has a record and isn't involved in any of this. The same friend helped me sneak into Wallquist's office. I wouldn't tell you where he is now, even if I knew."

"I see," Stilch nodded. "Do you know what I did yesterday evening, after you crowned me?"

"What?"

"First, I called the county seat and had them put out a general fugitive alert on you. Then I had four stitches taken in my scalp. It hurt like hell."

His face got that stony Indian look. "Next, I did something no self-respecting cop would do. I asked the M.E. to go over Steve Locke's corpse with a fine tooth comb. Know what he found?"

I shook my head, not daring to hope. Stilch said, "A portion of the right thumb was still intact, enough for a print. Last night I had it checked with Sacramento. We got the call back ten minutes ago. This particular corpse has a different thumb print than shows on Locke's driver's license. Ergo, it's not Steve Locke."

When it sank in, I almost choked with relief. "You mean I'm free?"

His smile was brutal. "Hardly. Ballistic tests show Valerie Baird was killed with two bullets from the same gun the arresting officers found in your shirt—"

"Stephen's hiding out within fifteen miles of here! He's probably in one of Castle's back rooms at the Shore. Castle will probably sneak him out of the state by tonight. For God's sake—"

"Take it easy. I believe you."

"You do?" I blinked. This was a switch. "Then how about questioning Wallquist? You could pull Castle in, sweat him—"

"And he'd be out in fifteen minutes," Stilch grunted. "We've got nothing to hold him on. What I should do is wait for Jed to get back Monday, let him worry about the whole mess."

"By then Stephen will be out of the country! And Fern—"

I choked off as I realized where Fern was, where she had to be. Last night I had kissed her goodbye. She had looked at me with a shaken intensity. *Call me back in an hour, Tony. Please.*

Stilch read it in my face. "You know where she is?"

"At the Shore," I said. "She must have gone there last night when I didn't call her back. Castle's got her."

"Tough."

I was on my feet, yelling at him. "You callous bastard, you know I'm innocent! You can't sit by and let them kill her—"

The back of his hand felt like sheet iron. The slap came without warning, knocking me down.

"Four stitches," Stilch said with a tearing bitterness. "You stupid bastards who think you're clever enough to break ordinances—withholding evidence, resisting arrest. Who think a cop is some kind of fumbling parasite on the civic payroll. If you hadn't fought me last night Valerie Baird would be alive right now. We could have questioned her. She might have told us where Locke was hiding. I'm sorry, Pearson. You're a day late and a dollar short."

The cell door clanged behind him. After a time I got up. I sat listlessly on the bunk.

Ten minutes later Stilch returned to my cell. The turnkey opened the door and he said, "Come on." I did not ask questions. We went down the corridor to his office. He shut the door and sat down. His jaw muscles were knotted and his eyes held a hard wet shine.

"I'm just an ordinary cop," he said softly. "That's why I'll never be county sheriff. Baird backed Jed in the last election because he can handle him. Nobody handles me. Understand?"

"I understand."

"Officially, I've no right to go after Castle, to raid him. The Shore is Jed's business. He's paid to look the other way. Two weeks after I shut them down they'd be wide open again. And inside of a month Jed would find some excuse to lift my badge. You've got just one chance to clear yourself, Tony. If it fails—you stand trial for Val's murder, and I'm an ex-cop."

He went over it, step by step. His plan was excellent. It had only one flaw.

If it failed, I wouldn't have to worry about the gas chamber. They don't execute corpses.

15

First, Stilch had me repeat descriptions of the two men who had slugged me outside of Wallquist's office. He left the room and returned with a handful of mug shots. I leafed through them. One of the photographs looked familiar. "Blondie," I said.

Stilch nodded. "His name's Donlevy. Two years in Quentin on a narcotics rap. Arrested a few times on morals violations, once for assault. He works for Castle. Let's go."

Within the next fifteen minutes Stilch cut red tape with amazing efficiency. I was officially released in his custody for the purpose of securing additional evidence. Outside, it was blue dusk and the stars were coming out.

"Seven o'clock," Stilch said. "You've got two hours. Where's your car?"

"At the Hidaway, in Laguna. Would it be better if I took a cab?"

"Your car's better." He hesitated, looking at my clothes. "You've got time for a shave and shower at my place, if you wish."

It brought a sudden lump to my throat. As we drove toward Stilch's Newport apartment, I decided this unpredictable giant was one of the nicest guys I had ever met.

It was seven-thirty when I stepped out of Stilch's shower. I shaved, and found a clothes brush in his towel closet. It helped little. My suit was still a mess. I found Stilch in the kitchenette, brooding at the phone.

"I just called Baird," he said. "He doesn't like any part of it. He thinks you killed Valerie. But he'll go along."

I felt sympathy for Max. A big tough Greek with the heart of a child. He would accept Val's death with a surface fatalism but his inner anguish would be unspeakable. I was glad, in that moment, that I was not Stephen Locke.

Our next stop was Laguna. Stilch dropped me off at the Hidaway. Miraculously, my Ford was still parked in the back lot. Nobody had bothered to steal it. "You get ten minutes' start," Stilch said bleakly. "Then I call headquarters, tell them you escaped from my custody. The Highway Patrol might shoot you on sight. Feel like backing out?"

"No."

He grinned. We shook hands and he drove away.

I walked across the street and got into the Ford. I drove slowly down the coast highway and passed two drive-ins before I found one that looked busy enough. Dinner was a beef sandwich, soggy fries, black coffee. I ate like a starved wolf. The carhop hardly glanced at me as I paid the check. It was twenty minutes after eight.

Driving toward Point Rafael, I tried to analyze the tension gripping my insides. It had been like this during the big tournaments—the avid hush of the gallery as you concentrated on a delicate approach shot. But now there was something added. A sense of destiny, a hard core of anger. It might be interesting to take such a mental attitude into a golf tourney some time—if I lived.

At nine o'clock I pulled into the parking lot of the Lee Shore. Mauve spotlights bathed the facade in shifting colors as I walked boldly toward the doorway arch. The doorman was a gigantic Negro—Gargantua in silver pants and vest. He looked impassively at my seedy flannels, but did not try to stop me.

The lobby was a plush cathedral of marble pillars and sea-green carpeting. Giant tropicals exploded from flagstone planters and you could see the outside pools through a wall of glass. Your first impression was of sedate, carefully tailored splendor.

Then you heard the laughter from the bar. You saw the faces in the lobby, male and female, the glazed anticipation. Ahead of me, a woman in cerise slacks and gilt sandals was walking into the bar. She had brightly hennaed hair and looked at least seventy years old. I followed her.

The bar was a murk of red light and cigarette smoke. The erotic sob of invisible violins counterpointed hushed giggles from the booths. It was like a hall of mirrors, the garish light distorting expressions, accenting the slyness, the moist smiles, the shamed hunger.

The bartender drifted over, soundless as smoke. He looked like the doorman's twin brother.

"Pernod," I said.

He gave me a half-moon grin and moved down the bar. That order had just branded me as one of the boys. I belonged. The woman on the adjacent stool stirred, looked at me. She was the hennaed crone I had seen in the lobby.

"Are you from Paris?"

"Not lately," I said.

"I knew it." She leaned breathlessly over. "I lived there for twenty years. Spotting continental types gets to be a hobby. Is this your first time?"

I hesitated. She flashed a withered, intimate smile. "Try the amethyst room if it's your first time. You'll feel so *cleansed* afterward, know what I mean?"

The bartender brought my Pernod. As I paid him there was a furtive burst of titters from one of the booths. I did not turn my head.

"Poor things," said the hennaed grandmother, looking. "Sick people with money. Dykes and queens, groping for expression. You're different, I can tell." She glanced at her watch and slid off the stool. "I'm going upstairs, dear. The amethyst room, don't forget."

I promised not to forget. She left the bar raptly. Four other couples were also leaving. I watched them cross the lobby to a private elevator near the reception desk. All on their way to cloud seven. I felt soiled, ashamed of being a member of the human race.

Then I saw Blondie.

He came into the bar wearing a midnight-blue jacket and white slacks. He sat two stools away. The bartender poured him a cup of coffee.

"Hi, Donlevy," I said.

He looked over and spilled his coffee. Carefully, he set the cup down. His eyes were bemused.

"Where's Castle?"

"Upstairs. In the Cinnabar Room." He said it almost diffidently. For him the situation must have been without precedent. I should have been safely behind cell bars, not sitting here in this bar, calmly sipping a Pernod.

"I'm supposed to see him." I stood up, decisively. "It's about the Rembrandt. He'll understand."

"Fine." Blondie moistened his lips. "Sure."

We went out of the bar together. He seemed dazed, but grateful to me for taking the decision out of his hands. We went into an ivory elevator with blue leather lining. On the way up neither of us spoke. Then his face changed and he snapped, "Hands over your head."

I stood meekly while he patted my clothes for weapons. "You won't find it," I said, dead pan. "It's a midget cobalt bomb concealed behind my left wisdom tooth."

"Wise," he spat. "Cute."

The elevator door opened. We walked down a hall of rose-colored carpeting, past picture windows framing the Pacific. In front of us a green leather door opened and a fat man in tuxedo came out. His face was pearled with sweat. He stared blindly at us, retching. Blondie ignored him.

Two doors down we went into a small dark alcove. Two quietly dressed men looked at me without recognition. "Identification, sir?"

"He's with it," Blondie said nervously. "Castle wants him."

"Right now?"

Blondie's thought processes were tortuously clear. Whatever Castle wanted could certainly wait until this particular floor show was over. While he was deciding, I shoved hard on the swinging gilt door on my right. They grabbed at me, too late.

I was in the Cinnabar Room.

The first confused thought was that I had blundered into a ballet recital chamber. About fifty people sat in tiered seat rows, looking at the brilliantly lighted stage dais. Five girls in crimson leotards pirouetted to the raw throb of drums. Unnoticed, I sank into the back row of seats.

Castle sat four rows down, regal in dinner jacket, intent on the dancers. A few seats away, I recognized a fading movie queen who had gone through four husbands and was still big box office. Near her sat a once-famous bandleader who had dropped out of sight a few years back after some unsavory publicity resulting from morals charges. Sick people with money.

The drumbeats quickened. The stage lights turned dusky purple. I stared at the dais. Five flawless bodies, moving in primitive abandon.

Their leotards were painted on.

Once, I had been to a stag show. In the middle of it I had left with sick revulsion. But what was happening onstage made stag shows seem stilted and Victorian.

Two men came onstage. They wore loincloths and were muscled like Hercules. They advanced with tantalizing slowness, silhouetted in gigantic shadow against the drapes. Their movements were stylized as a Japanese frieze. The music sank to a raw demanding whisper. The lancers were completely preoccupied. It did not seem as if they could possibly be doing what they were obviously doing. Yet their movements were perfectly synchronized to the music. Choreography by Dante.

It was beyond paganism, beyond black mass. The stage was a nexus in time drawing you back three thousand years to the wild fertility rites of

Carthage in the temple of Tanit. One of the dancers raised her head. Her scream blended with the harsh dissonance of brass.

Simultaneously, someone nudged my elbow. I turned, as in a dream. Castle sat next to me.

I stood up. Castle motioned me toward the door. Once, I looked back. A woman in the audience was crying out incoherently. She was stumbling toward the dais, ripping off her clothes.

We were outside, in the alcove. "Move," Castle said. He held a gun steady, a short-barreled .38. We walked along the corridor. Those dancers curled in a slow pinwheel like slime in my brain. I wanted badly to vomit. At the end of the corridor we turned down a short flight of steps to an oak door. Castle opened it, and we went in.

It was a large room with parquet flooring and fireplace. French windows framed the dark slope of beach. Fern sat in a white womb chair by the fireplace. Across from her, on a leather chesterfield by the french windows, sat Stephen.

16

The room was choked with a harsh dry tension. My first emotion was wild relief. They had not harmed Fern. Not yet.

"I'm sorry, Tony." She looked up at me with a tragic smile. "When you didn't call me last night, I became panicky—"

"And came snooping here to see if I was safe," Stephen grinned. "Obviously, she still loves me. We're married, remember?"

One of Stephen's cheeks was darkly swollen, and his broken nose was bound with adhesive, yet he sat cool and deadly amused. Castle beckoned with the .38. "Sit down, Tony."

I sat on the chesterfield opposite Fern.

"How did you get out of jail?" Castle asked.

"Bail," I said. I had rehearsed this twice with Stilch. "Valerie talked before she died. There's a fugitive warrant out for Stephen right now."

It had all the potential of a hand grenade.

Stephen sat motionless. Castle rocked easily on the balls of his feet, studying Stephen like a lean, white-haired cat. "So you had it all wrapped up," he murmured. "No loose ends—"

"He's lying!" Stephen's eyes flicked mine in chill appraisal. "I've played chess with him, and he's lying."

"We'll see. Here."

Castle tossed Stephen the gun. I tensed on the chesterfield, and relaxed. Stephen was too fast. "Soon enough." He tasted the words. "Very soon, now, Tony."

From the adjoining room came the sound of a phone dialing. Castle's curt voice. I glanced at my watch. Nine thirty-five. I had to stall, desperately, for all possible time. But time was running out. Stephen leaned back with a faint smile.

"An interesting gambit," he said. "But it's over, Tony. Your mistake was letting Fern help you. Because, deep down inside, she still happens to be in love with me. See? She's blushing."

Fern gazed at him steadily, her lips tremulous. She was fighting to keep from going to pieces and I wondered, with a pang, how strong his basic attraction still was. Stephen read my face and chuckled.

"You're right, our love life was a cold war. Yet if I died right now, she'd grieve, terribly. Right, darling?"

Killing him had become a necessity elemental as breathing. I moved delicately on the chesterfield, gauging the split seconds that would mean grappling for the gun, or writhing on the parquet with my guts torn out by .38 slugs.

"Don't, Tony," Fern whispered. My chance was gone.

Castle came back into the room. He stared at me with sardonic perplexity. "You fool," he said. "Just what did you hope to gain?"

I said nothing. Castle turned to Stephen. "Val died without talking. Pearson escaped an hour ago. They're combing the entire county for him."

"Well," Stephen's smile turned dreamy. "Stand up, Tony."

I saw it in his eyes. He had never been able to break Fern's spirit while they were married, but now he was going to break her completely and forever. By killing me.

"Stephen," Fern said.

"Yes?" The gun steadied on my chest. He did not look at her.

"I'll go with you," Fern said in a carefully controlled voice. "Like you wanted me to. I swear it, darling. He can't hurt you—"

"But it's necessary," Stephen said seriously. "Don't you see how necessary it is?"

He was no longer quite sane. The pressure of hiding had finally cracked his brilliant instability. Castle saw it, and stopped smiling. He said, "Wait. Not here."

"Why not here?"

"Because it stinks. His being here stinks. Alive or dead, I don't want him near the Shore. Supposing you leave tonight—"

"I told you earlier, I'm staying. I leave Monday night, after we've settled up."

"You're being glandular again," Castle said coldly. "Wallquist doesn't collect until Monday. Ask them, they were both eavesdropping."

"He's right," Fern said. "It's a Canadian client. He's paying four hundred thousand for the Van Ryn."

I wanted to kiss her. Stephen sat with a curious rigidity. "*Four* hundred—"

"Don't be a fool!" Castle took two furious steps toward Fern. "Isn't it obvious? She's playing cute."

Stephen frowned at Fern, reading her. "It's true," I said. "He's holding out on you. Why not call Wallquist, ask him?"

Almost, it worked. For a moment the .38 wavered, and I saw uncertainty in Stephen's eyes. Then Castle laughed with shriveling contempt. "Go ahead, call Wallquist. You're dead, remember?"

Stephen sighed. "Ronnie, if this is a holdout—"

"It's not, but I'll still up the ante, you suspicious clown. I'll make your share a hundred thousand—provided you stay on my yacht until Monday night. The Shore's too risky."

It was like a clash of wills between father and son. Stephen, with a jungle wariness, examined Castle's soft lethal logic.

"I was planning a Catalina cruise this weekend," Castle said patiently. "The yacht's anchored two miles out. My cabin cruiser's at the landing on the other side of the jetty. You can run the cruiser out to the yacht, and dispose of these two on the way. A year from now, the police will still be looking for them."

Fern stirred, her dark eyes fixed on Castle. Her smile was the prelude to hysteria.

"You're wrong!" I fought to keep my voice hard. "When both of us vanish, Stilch starts wondering. So does Max. They pull Wallquist in, start grilling him. He'll crack like a walnut—"

"Jed Wells comes back from vacation tomorrow," Castle breathed. "A smart sheriff, Jed. Too smart to interrogate innocent bystanders."

It was cut and dried. Wells would smother any sideline investigation. Ultimately it would be one of those cases that gather dust in the sheriff's unsolved file.

"Not bad." Stephen stood up, handed the gun to Castle. I had no chance to jump him. "Only one exception, Ronnie. Fern goes on board the yacht with me. We can have a brief, second honeymoon. Objections?"

Castle seemed oddly relieved. "As long as she doesn't talk."

"She won't." Stephen stood over me, hands loose at his sides. "Just so Tony doesn't prove troublesome beyond the breakwater—"

His palm whipped at my throat. A quick, killing blow, but I was already in motion, rolling backward across the chesterfield.

As I hit the floor Stephen kicked me in the temple. A glancing blow, but it turned my muscles to water. Fern screamed. Stephen's heel drove down to crush my windpipe, and Castle shouted, "*Listen!*"

We heard it. Distant, frightened shouts. The muffled pounding of many feet. "A raid," Castle said incredulously. "How—"

The door flew open. Blondie stared glassily at us. His face had been battered almost beyond recognition. Someone shoved from behind and he staggered and fell. Stilch came into the room. Behind him were Max and Lupo.

For one incredible second no one moved. Max stared at Castle, at Stephen. His dark face was expressionless, cast in stone.

Then the room exploded in a crescendo of movement and sound.

Max roared incoherently and charged at Stephen. Castle shot from ten feet and Max went down like an eyelid. Stephen was a blur, moving diagonally across the room as Lupo went after him. Stephen's fist struck; it seemed a tapping backhanded blow. But Lupo went sideways like a thrown stone. Glass shattered as Stephen knifed through the french doors. Stilch was on his knees behind the overturned chesterfield, shooting methodically at Castle. The shots blended into a drumfire of continuous sound. Castle collapsed in a writhing coil on the parquet.

I was on my feet, running across the room. Fern divined my intention and got in my way. I pushed her aside and went through the french doors, slashing my hands on the glass shards. I sprawled on my knees on hardpacked beach sand. Fifty yards down the strand Stephen was running fleetly toward the stone jetty.

I got up and pounded after him. Then someone tripped me from behind and I sprawled on my face. It was Fern. She was sobbing, her face bright with tears in the moonlight, and she was trying to tell me something. I struck at her savagely, turning after Stephen, and damned if she didn't trip me again.

I got up. She had her arms around me, her damned lying arms around me, and I tore them away. Did she love him that much? I was sobbing, deep in my throat. It had taken this to bring it out, the thing I had feared. I had known it was inside her, and Stephen had known it, known that he had left his bright corrosion forever on her soul, and years from now he would think about it and he would laugh, remembering.

I shoved Fern so hard she fell, and I ran down the beach after Stephen. He had too good a start. I reached the jetty in time to hear the cough of the cruiser's motor as it moved away from the landing. I hurdled the jetty, splashing knee-deep in water, and I was too late.

The launch was fifty yards beyond the surf, gathering speed. Stephen waved me a mocking goodbye from the helm.

It was all over.

I felt drained, empty. On the other side of the jetty my legs gave out and

I sat down on the sand.

I sat there for what seemed a very long time, watching the confusion in the Shore parking lot. Protesting figures in evening dress were being herded into paddy wagons. I counted four squad cars. Stilch was making a clean sweep. I thought about the headlines and wondered if they would indict Jed Wells when he came back Monday, or if he would simply resign because of ill health, the way they do.

Two figures came down the beach. Fern and Stilch. "We won," Stilch said somberly. "Finding Stephen justified the raid. An hour ago they picked up Consuela Ramos and brought her down from Los Angeles. She definitely identified her husband's body."

I said that was fine.

"Castle's dead," Stilch continued. "He talked before he died. A sketchy confession, but we had Max and Lupo for witnesses. Max got a superficial scalp wound."

Fern's eyes were pleading, but I would not look at her. "He got away," I said tiredly. "In Castle's launch. He'll head for Newport harbor, somewhere down the coast. They'll never catch him."

Stilch winked at Fern. He seemed remarkably unconcerned. "Pearson, you're a fool."

Looking at Fern, I agreed.

"For a while we were afraid Donlevy wouldn't tell us where you were," Stilch said. "Lupo worked on him. He came around very quickly. Lupo, incidentally, has a broken collar bone."

Fern knelt in the sand. Her voice was a clear whisper. "Remember when Midge mentioned Castle had rented his yacht to some friends for a La Paz cruise last week? Remember, Tony?"

I looked at her without understanding. Stilch lighted a cigarette. "Castle never had the slightest intention of splitting with Steve," he said. "Yet he couldn't risk any violence at the Shore. Fern suspected it when he lied about his yacht being offshore."

His words were meaningless. But Fern looked so lovely and pitiful that I put my arms around her. She gave a choked sob. "Forget it," I said tiredly. "You were married to him. You couldn't help it."

"It's not what you think, Tony—"

"Sure." I patted her head. "Of course not."

We started back down the beach. I said, "We might at least notify the coast guard."

"Forget it." Stilch squinted out to sea. Both he and Fern seemed tensed, waiting for something. "Castle told us something else before he died. There's no honor among thieves."

Then it came.

It came in an orange sheet of flame illuminating the entire ocean a half-mile out. The explosion followed seconds later, a giant cough. Scattered red sparks glowed distantly, then winked out.

"No point in bothering the coast guard," Stilch said cheerfully. "Come on, let's go down to the county seat."

It was two in the morning. We were drinking coffee in Stilch's office at the county seat. Max, Fern, myself. Max sat chewing a dead cigar, a bandage around his forehead. He had seemed utterly withdrawn from the entire proceedings, the recorded statements, the flash of newspaper cameras, the questions. Stilch came in, calm and tired.

"Downtown Los Angeles just called in. They've had Wallquist in the station house for the past two hours. When they threatened to throw a murder accessory charge at him, he confessed. They'll probably charge him with grand theft. We're contacting the Canadian authorities first thing in the morning to recover the Rembrandt."

Max said, "So where does that leave me?"

Stilch shrugged. "Ultimately, the Dutch government gets their Rembrandt back. It's out of my hands. You might even catch a fine for illegal possession."

Suddenly Max seemed shriveled, old. In the end they had all turned on him. Adopted son, faithless wife, treacherous business partner.

"I've lost the Shore." Max was speaking to himself, not to us. "The Rembrandt. Val's gone. Stephen's gone. I've still got me a big house, a country club. I've got Lupo." He shivered. "I'm sorry, Tony."

"Forget it."

Max sat stiffly erect. "I want to make it up to you. Yesterday I fired my new pro. He tried to change my stance."

Fern's finger tightened in mine.

"I'll give you a five-year contract," Max said huskily. "A piece of the club. What say?"

Big, lonely, vulnerable Greek, pleading for something I could never give him. Fern looked at me, her eyes soft. A year ago we had fought about this. I had wanted the tournament gamble, she had craved security. I loved her. It was no choice.

"Thanks," I said, trying to smile. "Thanks, Max ..."

"We're sorry," Fern interrupted gently, "but let us take a rain check on it, Max. First, Tony and I are following the sun for awhile."

It was like gold, and I stared at her, afraid to believe it, and her smile was all the reassurance I needed.

"The Phoenix Open starts next week," Fern said shyly. "It still gives us time for a honeymoon."

Max was saying something else, something about staking me to the summer circuit if I'd sign with him. But I wasn't listening.

I was kissing my girl.

THE END

FRENZY

BY JAMES O. CAUSEY

For Rosemary

1

For a moment I sat fighting for breath, watching Robin cross the dance floor with that lilting pelvic swing that made you want to cry.

Then, shivering, I downed my drink. It tasted like water. The bartender hovered over me, nervously.

"Please, Norm. It's after eight."

"Shut up," I said, staring across the quiet splendor of the Arbor Room. Robin was mounting the band dais. She stood sheathed in black satin smiling at the patrons—the way she had smiled at me just now. Her voice still shuddered inside me like music, aching and sweet: *"He knows, darling. I think he's going to kill you."*

The quartet hit a grinding blue note like thunder. Robin began to sing.

She had a kind of magic. It was in the way her voice crept through the air like a mood, like a dream; the way people slowly set down their drinks to listen. She began moving her hips, trying to dance, and the black satin gown impeded her like a halter. She frowned as the drumbeats faded to a whisper, then smiled savagely as she ripped the satin from hem to waist. Her legs flashed free while the drums beat in your brain and the audience screamed.

"Nice, Norm?"

Ingrahm sat next to me, smiling. He was a frail man with eyes like wounds and a beautiful silver toupee.

"Too nice for me, is that it?" I asked bitterly.

"You mustn't drink on duty." His voice was velvet. "It's an off night, the customers want action."

Ingrahm never got excited, never raised his voice. He was soft-spoken, as befitted an emperor. His empire included the Aladdin Club. It included Robin. And me. I sat crucifying him with my eyes, feeling the hatred bubble inside me like lava. He said, "You've been indiscreet, but we'll talk about it later. Go find a table."

It was the way he said it, that remote smile. I went.

I walked numbly past the bar through the swinging glass doors and across the parking lot to the casino. It was almost nine and about half of the thirty tables were occupied. The house girls threaded their efficient way among the tables, collecting chips for the next half-hour of play. Garth Anders, the casino chief, was marking game openings on the blackboard. He smiled hello. Garth was a small blond man, nervous and quick. He had worn that same friendly smile last week when he fired a cashier for being fifty cents short in her night's tally.

I selected a lowball table, five-dollar limit, ten after the draw. A house girl sold me chips. From the adjoining table Angelo Ventresca nodded, his pock-marked face impassive. As Ingrahm's number-one errand boy, Angelo rarely shilled.

Angelo was a very special type. I had met men like him at Santa Anita, Las Vegas and Del Mar. Wherever the money flows easily, you see men like Angelo. They are invariably big men, but they move with the lithe grace of a featherweight. It's as if nature was experimenting with the survival possibilities of Neanderthals in a jungle of concrete and steel. A nimbus of violence hovers about them. Their eyes usually give them away. Angelo's eyes were dark and as hard as obsidian; he had the unwinking gaze of a carnivore.

For a time I played in a kind of sick fury, wondering how Ingrahm had found out about Robin. Last night Ingrahm had been out of town. Robin's last show was at midnight. Afterward, she had gone straight home, and I'd phoned her ten minutes later. I'd gone to her apartment at one-thirty and crept out at dawn. No one had seen me enter or leave.

How had he found out?

It didn't matter. What mattered now was that I would be punished. Ingrahm was not the kind of man who relished being cuckolded—at women or at cards.

Two years ago I had stalked into the Aladdin shabby and dirty, with the grime of a boxcar on my jeans and six dollars in my pocket. It took the house boys until closing time that night to find out that their new customer was methodically thumbnailing the aces on each clean deck. By then I was five hundred dollars richer. When I left, Angelo chastised me severely in an alley. Ingrahm subsequently offered me a job.

Gardena is a strange town. An obscure loophole in the California statutes permits draw poker and lowball, while banning stud, blackjack, and other variations. In this town, poker is big business—a respectable big business that builds schools and libraries to placate the reformers.

Even the house shills are honest. We spot the grifters, the pros who work in teams, and politely show them to the door. Normally we gravitate to the games that are dying of anemia and do our job there with accomplished artistry. Whether it's a tired aircraft worker or a shrill, bargain-hunting housewife, we can, with a glance or a smile, prod raw nerves to a shrieking frenzy of getting even, hands clutching at the cards, while smiling blondes come by every half-hour to bleed the victim for a quarter.

The Aladdin closed at four in the morning. I cashed in my chips, looking around for Angelo and Garth. They were gone.

Suddenly I was afraid.

My duplex was five blocks from the club, on a quiet side street. I pulled the convertible into my driveway, hurried up the steps, fumbled with my door keys—and stood frozen, listening to the rustle from the opposite side of the porch.

I turned and saw them. My guts turned to ice.

They stood in the darkness, smoking. Angelo and Garth. The ape and the scorpion.

"This is a lady killer," Angelo said. "This is a pretty boy."

"Nothing personal." Garth's smile was almost friendly as he moved forward.

"Look," I whispered. "Let's not be kids—"

Angelo chopped a big paw into my groin and I doubled over, trying to scream.

They did a quick professional job. Groin, ribs and kidneys. It was over in two minutes. They left me retching on the porch steps, tasting blood.

In my circle there are various types of beatings. This was not the kind that left you with ruined kidneys and a broken soul. This was the casual cruelty a Pomeranian would receive for defiling the carpet. Tomorrow I would go to the club as usual. Ingrahm would nod politely and that would be that. Except that I would not speak to Robin again, ever.

I lay there hurting, sick with hate, and then there was the scrape of footsteps on the graveled walk.

"Up, Norm."

The voice was distant, amused. The hands under my armpits were gentle. I staggered to my feet. He was a stocky little man with sad blue eyes and a pouting mouth. His name was Art Mallory. He was a cop.

"Nice job," he said admiringly.

"Why didn't you do something?" My ribs felt broken. I could hardly breathe.

"They didn't need any help."

"You gumshoe bastard."

As I opened the front door, Mallory's pout grew into a smirk. "*I* told them what you were up to last night. An anonymous phone call this afternoon. Nothing personal." He chuckled.

I turned the lights on and fell across the gray leather couch. I cursed him weakly as he crossed to the sideboard and calmly poured himself Haig on the rocks. He had enough decency to hand me the bottle.

"Why? Why?" I kept repeating.

"So you'd be bitter. So you'd set him up."

I almost dropped the bottle. Mallory's blue gaze was sleepy, toadlike.

"Ostensibly, Norm Sands, you're a shill. He pays you one-fifty a week to keep the customers interested. Rather high for a shill. So sometimes you run errands for him. Two weeks ago, for instance. You and Angelo went fishing off Point Fermin. You contacted a live bait boat near the breakwater."

I spilled Scotch on the shaggy green carpeting.

A harsh voice began to make gobbling sounds, and Mallory said, "Don't make me vomit. I don't want a two-bit grifter. I want Ingrahm. Do we deal?"

I said yes.

"I'm just a local cop," Mallory mused. "You make a pinch on a poker-palace employee, you got to have the nuts. Or you're through. I'm too old to pound a beat, Norm." He said it patiently, as if to an idiot child. "You understand? Within the week you're setting him up. With two kilos of horse." He had left me back at the far turn. I blinked and he wearily explained. "Heroin. Coming in from La Paz, usually by boat. First a trickle of marijuana, now Heroin. The FBI is working with the Mexican authorities on this one. And we've promised to tie it up nice and quiet. Because the reform crowd is beating the election drums this year. All they need is a dope scandal in connection with a club owner to blow the lid off the garbage can. We nail Ingrahm, he'll tell us his backers. The syndicate gentlemen who got him the Aladdin franchise. You're going to finger him, Norm."

"Two kilos." I was stunned.

"Just the beginning. Three days ago they caught a distributor in La Paz. He talked. The syndicate is using Ingrahm for their front man on the coast. He's scared, wants to pull out. They won't let him."

"They wouldn't send *me* for—"

"You make all his pickups. Besides," he said nastily, "you'd think it was tea. For San Pedro High School kids. Well?"

I promised to play ball. Mallory said fine.

He paused for a moment, then went on. His knuckles gripping the glass were polished bone. "My next-door neighbor. Name of Johansen. Nice guy. We picked up his daughter the other night at a reefer pad. She's sixteen. She's two months pregnant and can't remember who the father is."

His hand blurred. Ice cubes slashed into my face.

"I've got a daughter myself, Norm. See you."

He walked out. I sat watching the ice cubes ruin my carpeting.

I got up and slowly washed Mallory's glass, putting it back into the sideboard. I walked into the bedroom. The face that stared at me from the bureau mirror was a furtive face, with haunted eyes, an ashamed grin. My unfinished letter was there in the portable typewriter on the bureau. I gazed abstractedly at it.

Dear Matt—

Twelve years and I've written twice. I'm sorry, little brother. Still going steady with Laurie? How's little old Mason Flats? I'm doing fine, by the way. Own a half-interest in a night spot, just the beginning. This Gardena's the town I've been looking for. Right next to Hollywood—bright lights and easy money ...

I was trying to finish the letter when panic hit me. It came in a surge of adrenalin-stabbed nerves and stammered obscenities as I tore the letter up and flung it into the wastebasket, threw open the bureau drawers and started packing.

It was dawn. By sundown I could be in another state, in Las Vegas. I could be packed and ready when the bank opened at ten. Hell, I had five hours!

I made myself walk calmly into the kitchen. I brewed coffee, drank it scalding and black, and tried to add up the percentages.

Item: Ingrahm was through, regardless. With or without my help, they would get him.

Item: Mallory had me cold. And you can't run far with only six hundred dollars in your bank account.

Item: I wanted Robin.

My ribs throbbed horribly and that was what finally decided me. In his own way, Mallory was a very smart man.

2

I got up late that afternoon and could not eat a thing. I drew a hot bath and lay in the tub for an hour with my eyes closed, retrospecting dully.

How does a man become a two-bit grifter?

To begin with, he gets orphaned at five, when his parents are killed in an automobile crash. No self-pity, Norman Sands. Some orphans grow up to become bank presidents.

And don't blame it on Aunt Ruby. Aunt Ruby tried. She tried with her raw, red laundress hands, and sometimes she tried with tears.

We lived in a five-room frame house on Orange Street, and there was the insurance, and Aunt Ruby took in washing, and so we got by. I was a dark child, moody like my old man, Aunt Ruby said. Matt was a year younger, big and blond, with a shy smile. People liked Matt. He was an honor student, and the best basketball player in Mason Flats High.

Aunt Ruby had an obsession that Matt should be a lawyer. The summer after Pearl Harbor I got an evening job setting pins in Hermann's bowling alley. Some of the money I made helped put Matt through a summer extension course so that he was able to skip the ninth grade. Aunt Ruby was ecstatic the night Matt told her he had been elected president of the freshman class. "Isn't it wonderful, Norm?" she'd asked me.

I just grinned. A fixed grin. It got so that later the grin would not come off, even when I wanted to cry.

That year I didn't give much of a damn about school, and got lousy grades. The fierce protectiveness I used to feel for Matt had now vanished. Matt didn't *need* me anymore. He was now shooting for a scholarship. I was shooting pool in Hermann's back room. I felt restless, moody. I ran with a fast tough crowd that picked gang fights with the Mexican kids. I began to get a reputation for wildness. After a while people started calling me "that other Sands kid," which made it worse.

When I was in the eleventh grade I fell in love with Laurie Flagg.

Laurie was lovely, a madonna. She had hair the color of a leaping flame, and she was as exquisite as a porcelain figurine. I used to dream about her, breathless sixteen-year-old dreams, full of stardust and glory.

Laurie was Hal Karse's steady. Big handsome Hal whose father owned an insurance agency. Hal who drove a sharp convertible, peeled and decked, with Carson top and chrome headers. All the girls were crazy about Hal.

Once Hal had been with me on a gang fight in the Mexican quarter. Kid stuff, slingshots and rocks. But Hal had used a broken beer bottle and scarred one Mexican boy for life.

Suddenly Laurie stopped going with Hal. They weren't speaking any more. I would see Hal at Hermann's on Saturday night, brooding over a snooker table. The junior prom was coming up, and now it was Laurie and Matt. You saw them together everywhere; at lunch period, and after school. The whole class talked about it. I felt envious, and yet glad for Matt. Hal walked alone, proud and bitter.

You read in the papers about teen-age violence, about rat-packs and brutal, senseless killings. But sometimes you forget how it really was—the volcanic jealousy of adolescence, the killing fury that can erupt on the school grounds or in an alley after gym period.

On prom day Hal picked a fight with Matt. Matt kicked hell out of him.

All afternoon I worried about it. I knew Hal. But when I tried to warn Matt after school, he shrugged.

That night I was setting pins at Hermann's, and thinking wistfully about Laurie, when Hal came in with Claude Younger and Tommy Larkin. Claude weighed two hundred pounds and was the best tackle in Mason Flats High. Tommy had been expelled the month before.

They came in flushed and excited, their eyes feverishly bright, their laughter too loud. They had been drinking. Once, between the thunder of the pins, I heard them mention Matt's name. That was when they saw me and their laughter turned furtive.

Something cold came over me. I slipped quietly out the back way.

When I got home the house was dark and still. Aunt Ruby was snoring in her bedroom. I went into our room. Matt lay on the bed, his shoulders shaking.

"How come you're not at the prom?" I turned the light on.

"Go away."

He was a mess. Smashed lips, black eye, and his new blue suit in bloody tatters. He had scrimped to buy that suit. His body kept twitching in quiet agony.

"Hal?" I asked, whispering.

He nodded. I turned the light off.

All the way back to Hermann's I could feel that grin freezing my jaw muscles.

I found Hal's convertible parked in front of Flagg's bar and grill, near an alley just down from Hermann's. The chrome glistened against the black lacquer finish. Hal was very proud of that car.

I really did a job on it.

First, I started on the upholstery with my pocketknife. Working quietly in the darkness, I ruined the dash panel and slashed the padded top to shreds. I poured dirt in the crankcase. In the alley I found a brick and came back to smash the windshield. Then I looked up and saw them.

Claude and Tommy had me hemmed in from the alley. Hal stood in the street, staring at his car, at the thing which had once been his car. He made a sobbing sound, then came at me in a bull's rush.

They hit me together, all three of them. Claude got me by the neck and wrestled me across the walk toward the alley. Hal got hold of my hair and pulled my head back. His fist drove into my face three times and the white street light gushed bloody red. I kept trying to free my right hand from Tommy's grasp, to use that brick.

I bit Tommy's wrist and he grunted, and for a moment my left hand was free to claw at Claude's eyes. His grasp slackened and I twisted, my back arched like a cat's, my face in the gutter.

Then my right hand came free. That brick swung like a flail. It hit Claude alongside the head and he dropped. Hal let go of me and scuttled sideways like a crab, begging. The brick caught him right between the eyes.

I stood up, panting. Tommy screamed and fled down the alley. I started after him, but somebody had me by the arm. Men were boiling out of Flagg's bar. Somebody was shaking Claude. He sat up whimpering, rubbing his head. Jonas Flagg was bending over Hal. He stared up at me and said quietly, "He's dead, son."

Dead.

The word hit me like a grenade. I felt nausea and a blinding panic. The man holding me stretched his head for a look and I kicked him in the kneecap. He swore, then I was around him and down the alley.

Six blocks later I had shaken them. Darting down the dark streets and through the alleys, shaking with terror. By now they would be at home, waiting for me. The cops would be there, and Aunt Ruby would be crying. It was eleven o'clock. At eleven-thirty the freight made a junction whistle stop.

When that freight pulled out of Mason Flats at eleven-thirty, I was huddled in a forward gondola, shivering. A killer at sixteen, running away in the night.

You learn fast at sixteen. It doesn't take you long to learn about degenerates, about filth, about hunger. You learn about sadistic brakemen, fond of crippling hobos. You learn survival.

At eighteen you are hustling in a west Los Angeles poolroom. At twenty you graduate to floating crap games. You have good reflexes and a natural talent for cheating at cards.

You celebrate your twenty-first birthday by having an eardrum punctured to avoid the peacetime draft. You hang around the tracks in season—Del Mar, Hollypark, Santa Anita. Grifting. A dollar here, a dollar there. Your friends are con men, pimps, thieves.

When you are twenty-five, you drift to Vegas. You get a job dealing blackjack at one of those fantastic luxury hotels. You see how the other half lives, the sleek, richly-tanned men with their women and their good clothes and their Lincolns, down from La Jolla for the weekend. You get so the envy is a knife twisting in your guts.

At twenty-five you're a pilot fish, a scavenger. And you want desperately to become a killer shark.

So one night you decide to score. You plant a ringer at your table and deal him six thousand dollars' worth of blackjacks.

And the house finds out.

And the fingers of your right hand never heal quite straight again.

After that you are reconciled to being a grifter. You shill for Ingrahm, and finally graduate to picking up parcels of Heroin for him.

There are women. Bored, sex-starved housewives who hang around the casino looking for excitement. Some of them are good for a Catalina weekend.

Then one night, you see Robin Page. She is lovely. She reminds you of Laurie. You want her terribly, and this is dangerous. She belongs to Ingrahm. But you don't give a damn.

I stepped out of the bathtub, inspecting the welts along my ribs and kidneys. There was a sour taste in my mouth. Someday I would learn that a pilot fish cannot afford to want anything too badly.

An hour later I went down to the Aladdin. I was drinking coffee in the casino lounge when Ingrahm called me into his office. He asked me how I felt. I said lousy.

"An object lesson," he said dryly. "Stay away from her. Incidentally, I may need you Monday night." Monday was my night off.

"At the Casino?"

"Curious?" He looked at me out of his pale eyes. For the first time I saw him as a shrivelling scarecrow, pitifully vulnerable where his sex life was concerned, worried about his toupee, and about his forced role as distributor for the stuff that dreams are made of.

I said no.

"Perhaps," Ingrahm said, "you're wondering why I didn't fire you?"

He wanted me to look contrite, interested. I did.

"You're a very functional tool, Norm. A tool gets broken, you fix it. You're fixed. Aren't you, Norm?"

I said yes.

He made me crawl for a few more minutes and finally dismissed me. Someday I was going to yank that toupee off his scalp, blow my nose on it, then grin at him.

It was a bad night at the table. I lost too many players. At eleven I went into the lounge for coffee and saw Angelo. "About last night—" he began.

"Nothing personal," I said.

"Good." He looked at me with respect.

"What's with Monday night? A coast run?"

He shrugged and I didn't press it.

As I went back to a table I felt suddenly exhilarated, hopped up. All my life I had scrambled frantically for that quick kill, that one big break. All my life I had failed. But part of getting a break is knowing one when you see one.

I found a seat at a five-and-ten table. It was a tense, quiet affair with only four players. When my deal came, I shuffled the cards a little longer than necessary. After the player on my right cut, my fingers covered the deck for a fraction of a second before I commenced dealing. When I picked up my hand, I held three aces.

Five and ten draw goes fast, and by midnight it had become one of those no-holds-barred games with side bets on high spade and cashing chips over the table instead of calling the house girls for more ammunition. By one o'clock I had salted over five hundred dollars.

That was when I left the game for a while. Casually I went outside, walked across the parking lot to the alley entrance to the Arbor Room, entered and strode on down the hallway and into Robin's dressing room. She whirled from the dressing table.

"Norm, are you crazy?"

"I had to see you."

"Darling, he's taking me home in five minutes. Please—"

I kissed her. She was stiff in my arms for a moment, then all at once her long body relaxed and she began to cry.

"Oh my poor darling, I've been so scared, so miserable. He hurt me. Did he tell you?"

I phrased the lie carefully. "He's going to destroy you by degrees. Little by little. He bragged about it last night."

"Oh God."

"It's good-bye, honey. I'm leaving for Vegas Monday night. He doesn't know."

She stood motionless, the idea seeping in. I added, gently, "With a few thousand of his. He'll never miss it. I've got connections in Vegas. The manager of the Flamingo wants me for his new casino boss. It's a break, baby. I'll miss you."

Slowly she pushed me at arm's length. Her eyes got large and dark. It was a moment of revelation, of sickness. She was not quite thirty. Her magic was fading. She had never landed that spot at Ciro's, or the Paramount contract that Ingrahm had promised. In a little while she would be just another singer working for scale in a second-rate night spot and sleeping with the owner, as required.

"Norm," she said faintly. "Darling. Please take me with you. I love you."

I kissed her. I played it straight. I told her they were begging for talent like hers in Vegas, that she would take them by storm. I could see it clearly as an end game in chess, our gradual drifting apart as passion died, as, ultimately, we each came to grips with the incredible selfishness of the other. But now I wanted her.

We planned our departure carefully. Young lovers fleeing in the night. Robin's eyes were wet and shining. She kept telling me how much she loved me.

I went back to the casino and played until closing time. By then I was twelve hundred dollars ahead. I managed to salt most of it and only cashed two hundred in chips at the cashier's window.

I remember whistling as I pulled into my driveway at four-thirty in the morning, and how the whistle died when I saw Mallory sitting on my porch steps like some bland but deadly Buddha.

"For God's sake, suppose somebody sees you?"

"Nervous?" he said sardonically. Without sound he asked the question.

"Nothing definite," I answered. "Not yet."

"Sure?"

"On my mother's grave."

"You never had a mother, Norm." He tossed his cigarette butt at my shoes and got up, yawning. "See you tomorrow night."

I stared after him. I was shaking.

3

Sunday was a big day at the Aladdin. I went in at noon and chose a five-and-ten lowball table. I did not leave that game for twelve straight hours, not even to go to the bathroom. By midnight I had won almost two thousand dollars.

My prime pigeon was a gaunt, tanned man in rumpled tweeds with a diamond stickpin in his tie. After I had hooked him for a hundred, he played in a broken sort of frenzy, staring viciously at my mounting stack of blues. Once I cashed a check for him and that was fine because the hardest part was not in winning but in converting those blues into cash, keeping my stack from growing too large. Our house girls had sharp eyes.

Shortly after midnight I saw Garth, marking game openings on the blackboard. He was signaling at me. I took a slow, deep breath and excused myself, heading for the men's room. A moment later Garth came in.

"Tomorrow night," he said. "A coast run. You and me."

"My car?"

I made it sound casual, unconcerned, though I was feeling the perspiration between my fingers.

"You're not sore about last night?"

"No hard feelings," I shrugged. "You step out of line, you get clipped. Say, I think there's a ringer at my table. That tweedy character playing oil baron. I'm going to take him."

"None of that," he said sternly. "If he's pulling cute stuff, ask him to leave. If he's on the square, he's entitled to the courtesy of the house. You've been here long enough to know that."

Garth was astonishingly moral at times.

By closing time I had won almost three thousand dollars. Driving home I felt strong, ruthless, invincible. I kept trying to recall that line from Shakespeare about a tide in the affairs of man.

Mallory knocked on the door fifteen minutes after I got home. I let him in and mixed him a drink. "Tomorrow night," I said. "We'll probably leave from the casino. I'll be driving a gray Olds convertible."

"That's not enough. Where—"

"I haven't the faintest idea, sorry. You'll have to tail us from the club. Catch Garth *flagrante delicto*."

"We catch both of you," he said. "You're going to turn state's evidence."

"Not a chance," I snapped. He blinked. "Listen, the minute that happens I'm a dead man, and you know it. In or out of jail, they'll get me. Once you catch Garth in the act, he'll sing like a nightingale. But *I* flit. If you don't like it, you can haul me in right now. Well?"

His teeth bared in a mirthless smile, a fat man's grin. "I tried to tell them," he said softly. "I pleaded with the commissioner. But the poor cautious slob wanted to make sure. Play it safe, make a deal." Mallory sighed. "You don't know how lucky you are, mister. If we'd only had a little more information ..."

The hate in his eyes shook me. It was the frozen bitterness of an honest cop who has to deal with filth, and despises himself for it.

"Don't lose the Olds," I said.

Garth and I left the Aladdin at nine-thirty on Monday night. I drove, and they turned on all the green lights for us until Highway 101. A light fog was rolling in from the Pacific and I kept squinting into the rearview mirror.

"Jumpy?" he asked.

"I'm paid to be."

His tight smile.

We were halfway to Balboa beach when he said, "Pull over. We're being tailed."

We waited while cars hissed by in the fog. I couldn't breathe. It was like dying. "My mistake," Garth said, and I swore at him.

The place was two miles east of Balboa, a deserted stretch of beach cliff with an ancient boat landing in the cove below. We sat chain-smoking for an hour, and a soft rain began to fall.

Finally Garth cut the lights on and off, twice. He took a flashlight from the glove compartment, said sweetly, "Watch the highway, baby," and got out of the car.

The yellow arc of his flashlight receded slowly down the cliff path. Once the light winked out and there were only the breakers clawing the landing in a silver-crested roar of foam. Then, above the slap of the waves and the drumming of the rain on the canvas top, I heard the throb of the motor launch.

I cut on my parking lamps and eased the Olds in reverse back to the highway cutoff. Two squad cars were there, parked on the apron of the cutoff, glistening in the rain. A spotlight blinded me. I made frantic gestures and the spotlight vanished. The door of the lead car opened and Mallory jumped out. He hurried toward the Olds and I pointed down to the cliff path. He nodded, beckoning me past. His pale face was filled with contempt.

At the highway junction I stopped for a traffic signal and peered back through the dark curtain of rain. One squad car had reached the cliff. Dim figures were emerging. A spotlight flared. I shoved the accelerator down to the floorboard, and the tires sang.

I was doing sixty before I shifted into high. As I hit the dark stretch into Balboa, the faint rattle of gunfire echoed in the wind.

It took me an hour to drive back to Gardena. I drove quickly on the long highway reaches and slowly through the beach towns. I felt as if my brain had become an efficient analogue computer clicking out each move with cold precision.

It was midnight when I wheeled into my duplex driveway. Seven minutes later I had both suitcases in the luggage trunk. At twelve-thirty I coasted to a stop in front of Robin's apartment, scanning the dark streets for Ingrahm's blue Cadillac. No danger. He would still be at the Aladdin, biting his fingernails and waiting. I sat for a moment, reviewing my assets. The Olds. Four thousand dollars in my wallet. Robin.

I was whistling as I went upstairs and knocked on Robin's door.

She opened the door and said, "Come in, darling." I took one look at her face and turned to run.

Angelo leaped out from behind her and hit me alongside the temple, and the hall carpet careened up into my face.

He dragged me inside and shut the door. I weighed a hundred and eighty, but he handled me as if I were a child. From the sofa Ingrahm said, "Where's Garth?"

Robin was sitting next to him, trying to smile. "Please," she said. "They just got here, darling. I didn't—"

Ingrahm gave her a weary glance and she stopped talking.

"He's at the club." My mouth felt dry. "I dropped him off at the club."

Angelo cradled the phone in one huge fist. He dialed. I took a deep breath to scream and Angelo broke my nose with a kick that did not travel over ten inches.

For a moment there was only blackness, shot with yellow spears of pain. From a far distance I heard violins soaring and it came to me that Ingrahm had turned on the radio. Angelo was talking quietly into the phone. Now he was hanging up. He was talking to Ingrahm.

"Cops," he said, and there was a curious dullness in his voice that made me want to vomit. "At the casino. They got warrants for us."

He bent over me. "Where's Garth?" he said.

Robin was hunched forward on the sofa, biting her fist and crying.

"Don't blame her." Ingrahm looked old, tired. "One of the house girls reported you two hours ago. We examined the decks you used this afternoon."

Angelo took my wallet. He tossed it to Ingrahm who opened it and sat for a moment, very still. Then he went over to the radio. The sound of violins filled the room.

Angelo started in on me.

Angelo was a craftsman and a specialist in his field. He probably knew more about the location of certain nerve centers than most doctors. It took him about ten minutes to break me, and I told him about Mallory, about everything.

Ingrahm was talking to Robin. He talked in a low, patient voice about staying in Mexico until things could be straightened out. He was very calm. He gave her money and talked about plane tickets. She kept biting her fist and nodding. When they took me outside, she did not look at me.

They herded me downstairs to the Olds. The rain had started again and my teeth were chattering. Angelo shoved me into the rear seat and gave my car keys to Ingrahm.

Ingrahm talked as he drove. He said there was not much time. He said I reminded him of a tomcat he used to have before it was castrated. He did not sound angry, only tired and defeated.

I took a slow, grinding breath and sat up straight. Angelo turned quickly and I mumbled, "Cigarette?" He handed me the pack and a book of matches.

We were passing a switch yard on the edge of town. There was the iron groaning of the freights and the junction lights twinkling crimson as Ingrahm slowed down at the crossing.

I stuck a cigarette in my mouth and fumbled with the matches, holding the heads together. As they flared, I ground that bright little inferno into Angelo's eyes.

He shrieked and clawed at his face. I dived across the front seat, pulling at the door handle as Ingrahm fought the wheel and struck at me; then the door flew open and I was rolling down the embankment.

For a moment I lay in the darkness, tasting track cinders. Abruptly, the blind, yellow eye of the locomotive limned me. I lurched upright and stumbled on along the ties. Twenty feet above, the Olds had stopped. Ingrahm was carefully picking his way down the embankment. Something gleamed in his hand. The freight was picking up speed, roaring. I ran to meet it.

Ingrahm fired three times. He had a bad target and the freight's glare blinded him. I jumped across the track just before the locomotive ground past, pistons snarling. I had maybe thirty seconds. On the opposite side of the track Ingrahm was waiting.

A gondola came by and I grabbed the iron ladder and held on. I climbed with my eyes closed.

Two gondolas back there was an empty refrigerator car with the door half-open. I squeezed inside and found two hobos who swore with hostile relief when they discovered I was not a brakeman.

"Pally," one said, "that door wants to be closed."

"So close it." I was done, finished. If Ingrahm had appeared at that moment, I could not have moved.

One of them lit a match and stared at my face. "My God," he said.

"An accident, pally?" the other asked.

"Argument with a brakie," I mumbled.

You could feel them melt. I belonged.

4

Those next few months I really hit rock bottom.

At night, shivering in a hobo jungle or cattle car, I would dream about getting a stake and heading for Vegas. Only it was February, March, and the California winters are warm, and panhandling was so easy. You had gotten the purple heart in Korea, and it was a loan, buddy, just a loan.

The muscatel helped, too. It helped me forget that I was a piece of decayed flotsam gradually drifting down the sewer. A grifter's prime asset is nerve, and Angelo had broken mine. Then one night they arrested me for vagrancy in San Bernardino—ten days. I had time to take a long merciless look at the beaten wino that had been Norman Sands.

A castrated tomcat! I went quietly mad and bloodied my knuckles against the cell bars. But there was a way to get that stake. The idea scared me, and I tried to forget it. But somehow, after that, I kept drifting down, closer to the flax farms deep in the border southland.

They found me in May, in a rear gondola where I'd tried to hide, and the hard-luck-veteran stuff didn't go. When my feet quit stinging from hitting the dirt and my throat was raw from calling them all the sons-of-bitches I could think of, I looked around. It was the outskirts of one of those jerkwater towns near the border. Sunlight glittered on tin-roofed shacks. Down the tracks, Mexican kids were playing follow-the-leader. Somehow the scene was ominously familiar, part of a half-remembered dream.

Then I saw the sign. It came at me like a fist.

MASON FLATS
Pop. 9,318

I stumbled along the ties. As I passed the Mexican kids, they stopped laughing and stared at me. I walked faster, feeling a dull sickness inside, shivering. A murderer always returns to the scene of his crime.

On my left, sun-baked flats shimmered in the noon haze. On my right, there were tired cornfields and straggling little truck farms. A half-mile down the tracks, I saw the rig.

It was about fifty feet high, on the cleared edge of a cornfield. The rotary engine throbbed deeply to the whine of the cable drum. Two drillers in tin hats were arguing by the silver storage tank.

My chuckle had a harsh, flat sound. Ever since I could remember, small outfits had drilled wildcats here, small outfits with oil fever that invariably hit salt water and sand.

A few hundred yards later, I cut across a weed-grown lot and walked down the lane of clapboard shacks that was Orange Street. In twelve years the houses had grown older, poorer. A dying street in an aging town. I turned up an alley.

Center Street. Old man Hermann was mopping the sidewalk in front of his bowling alley. He looked yellow and old, his cheeks mottled with liver spots. He peered sharply at me as I passed and suddenly I felt naked, as if everyone on the street was staring at me.

Once I would have died rather than let Matt see me ragged and dirty, with my shoes falling apart. But that stake was becoming an obsession.

I passed the alley where I had killed Hal. There was Flagg's bar and grill. Next to it was a two-by-four stucco office with a sign in the window: *Matthew Sands, Licensed Real Estate Broker.*

Matt had wanted to be a lawyer so badly.

I took a deep breath and walked into the bar.

Darkness after the sunlight. The warm, quiet smell of sawdust and stale beer. The bar was deserted except for a big blond man who was polishing the bar and whistling. He gave me a little-boy frown.

"Draw one," I said.

He hadn't changed much in twelve years. He still had those football shoulders and puzzled blue eyes. As he scraped the foam off the glass, he paused, looking at my shoes.

"One dime, mister."

"I'd think it would be on the house."

"All right now, that'll be ten cents."

His mouth got hard and I chuckled. "Okay, Matt. But *I'd* sure buy a long-lost brother a drink if—"

"Norm," he burst out. Beer foamed on the counter, "Norm! I'll be utterly *damned*." He reached across the bar and almost broke my shoulders in a bear grip.

"Ouch, you big bastard, don't spill my beer."

"Beer, hell," he said, reaching for the bonded sour mash. "How come you didn't write, let somebody know?"

And it was good, sitting there drinking with him, the way it had been fourteen years ago when we had both had our first drink out behind the garage and gotten sick together. Matt talked about it. He talked about how Aunt Ruby had died; about his two years in Korea; about quitting law school when Laurie's father had a stroke, and running the bar for her; about his real estate business and how he and Laurie were finally getting married next month. It was good until he stopped talking and began to stare at my clothes, at my three-day-old beard. But there was no pity in his eyes. If there had been, as much as I needed a stake, I would have turned around and walked out of his life forever. But his look held only bewilderment.

"What in hell happened to you?"

"Business reverses," I said wryly. "Look, I need three hundred bucks. If you haven't got it, I need two hundred. You'll get it back next month, promise."

"If that's all you want," he said, hurt. "I was hoping you'd hole up here awhile, put on twenty pounds."

"Hal. Remember?"

Matt grinned. "Six stitches and a concussion. You couldn't kill Hal with an ax."

It took a moment for his words to sink in. When they did, there was only a queer numbness. I wondered why I did not feel a vast and heady relief. Later, it came to me. You live with a leaden weight on your soul for twelve years, and when the weight is finally lifted, it leaves an indelible scar. I was scarred for life.

"How about some breakfast, Norm?"

He looked at me, wistful and full of hope. He had it all figured out. I would stay, maybe go into real estate with him, help him tend this fourteen-stool bar. I would be best man at his wedding and some day marry a nice home-town girl and have kids and play bridge with him on Saturday nights while our wives gossiped across the table.

"Some ham and eggs and you'll be a new man." Matt started through the swinging doors of the kitchen. "Oh, Laurie." He almost knocked her down.

"It's Norm," Matt said proudly. "He's staying awhile."

I stared at her and couldn't speak.

Her hair was still the color of flame. Her fine gray eyes slanted imperceptibly at the corners and her lips were full and rich. Under the black turtle-neck sweater her breasts leaped at you, and even through the blue jeans you could see the outline of those long lovely legs. There was nothing in her face, absolutely nothing.

"Fix him some ham and," Matt beamed. "I've got to tend bar."

I followed Laurie back into the kitchen. I felt weak, giddy.

"Over easy all right?" She broke eggs onto the grill, not looking up.

"Fine." I swallowed. "How come you two aren't hitched yet?"

"We've been engaged for six years," Laurie said evenly. "First it was Matt's finishing college. Then the postwar draft. Then Korea. Then college again. Then Papa's stroke—the operation cost three thousand dollars. Then Papa died. Money," she said with an infinite bitterness.

"Lovely word."

"Then," she said, "it was Norm."

We stared at each other. For one fleeting instant I saw in her face something that was like a throbbing volcanic fury, a wild thing at bay. Then it was gone. She brought the eggs over, her face expressionless. The coffee cup rattled in the saucer as she set it down.

"In case you want a bath," she said coolly, "Matt's room is upstairs. First door on your right."

She went into the bar and I stared at the eggs. Two days since I'd had a decent meal and now I couldn't eat. The food choked me. The coffee was acid.

I found Matt's room upstairs, a cramped cubicle with an old army cot and dresser. In the bathroom I discovered a razor, and I kept chuckling as I shaved, crazy giggles of pure delight as I lathered under the steaming shower. In Matt's dresser I found a pair of clean denims and a white shirt. His shoes were a loose fit.

Coming downstairs, I heard them arguing in the kitchen. "But honey, he'll be a natural in real estate. Norm's a hustler, a go-getter. We'll be partners—"

"Partners!" Her searing contempt made me wince. "We're getting married next month, remember? Then we're selling the bar and moving away from this rotten town like you promised."

"But Sam Peabody called this morning, about the wildcat. They're in showings, black sand at twenty-six hundred! Sam gave me a net listing on the adjoining acre last month. When the well comes in—"

"It won't come in," she said wearily. "Like your big apartment deal last month that fell through on escrow. Like all your pitiful golden schemes that evaporate. For once in your life stop dreaming!"

"Please, honey—"

I started whistling loudly, and came into the kitchen. Laurie looked knives at me and went out to the bar.

"I'll be moving on this afternoon," I blurted out. "Thanks for the clothes."

"Aw, stick around awhile," he said miserably. "Just for this afternoon." He brightened. "You can help me tend bar."

"Why not?" I had blundered into a place where I wasn't wanted, but it didn't really matter. I wasn't staying.

For the next hour, I helped Laurie strew fresh sawdust on the floor. Once she looked at me with a faint smile. "Clothes fit all right?"

"Fine." I wanted to slap her.

A few customers drifted in and I helped Matt serve them. For a Sunday afternoon, business was slow. Laurie went about her duties with a tight-lipped precision, not speaking to either of us. Two men started a game of shuffleboard and Matt told them enthusiastically about Sam Peabody's wildcat, about how Mason Flats was going to be a boom town. It was a good time to sneak out the back door and hop a fast rattler to Bakersfield.

That was when the fat man with the briefcase came in and ordered Scotch and water. I served him, trying not to stare. He was something to stare at.

At first glance you got the impression of a circus freak. The face was a pasty white with full red lips twisted into a perpetual smile. It was a face to pity, to laugh at. Until you saw the eyes. He wore a rumpled gray tropical worsted that bulged over massive shoulders, and he was not fat at all.

"Seventy cents, sir," I said, and he chuckled, moving down the bar toward Matt at the cash register. I started around the bar, fast, and Matt grabbed my arm. His smile was a corroded grimace. "Hello, Mr. Lombard."

"Tom Bullock was here last night," the big man said gently. "With some county officials."

"We appreciated the business." Matt's grin shook.

"He spent forty bucks."

"It was thirty-three-fifty," Matt said stiffly.

"Tom said forty." The fixed clown smile.

Matt slowly took two tens out of the cash register. He handed them over and Lombard said, "The yokels with him spent twenty-eight bucks. Fifty percent comes to fourteen."

A tiny muscle leaped in Matt's jaw. He gave Lombard three fives. The big man handed him a dollar and looked at me with cold amusement. "Who's the punk?"

"His brother," I said, not liking it. "What's the pitch?"

"Better tell him the facts of life, Matt. Incidentally, your Scotch stinks." Deliberately, he upended his glass. Ice cubes danced on the bar, whiskey splashed on my shirt.

Rage exploded inside me, molten and seething. I grabbed him by the coat lapels, yanking him halfway across the bar. "You small-town hick bastard," I said. My right fist speared him flush in the mouth. He went backwards, arms flailing, and sat down with a spine-jarring thud.

Nobody moved. The men playing shuffleboard stared. And Matt was whispering, "God, Norm, please," and was vaulting over the bar, helping Lombard to his feet, babbling, "I'm awfully sorry. He didn't know."

Lombard pushed him away. He straightened his tie, not looking at me. Then he walked through the swinging doors and Matt said thickly, "Did you have to do that?"

"Who in hell *is* he?"

"His name's Pete Lombard. He used to be a sadistic vice-squad cop. Now he's Murdoch's hatchet man. Murdoch publishes the *Clarion*—he owns this town, stock and barrel. Tom Bullock happens to be chief of police. He brings in business, he gets a cut."

I was amazed. "That goes on here? In this jerkwater town?"

Laurie came in from the kitchen and slammed down a jar of pickles on the bar. "Tell him about our fair city," she said viciously. "Tell him about the red lights on the edge of town, the basement crap games, the graft!" Her lower lip was trembling. "And how they'll shut us down now because your plague of a brother stepped on the wrong toes."

She bit her lip as some customers came in. I watched her serve them beer and mumbled, "You mean that might revoke Laurie's license?"

Matt nodded tiredly. "They'd say we served beer to minors, that we were running a fag joint, anything. One of the city council cousins wants this spot. He offered Laurie two thousand for it last month; she turned him down."

One of the shuffleboard players ordered a hamburger and Laurie brought it out from the kitchen. Now she was talking with him. They were both coming over. Laurie's smile was bright.

"Norm, you're staying awhile, aren't you?"

"Well—"

"It's flax season at the mill and they're taking on temporary help. Norm, meet Hal Karse."

The tall man stared at me. Slowly his hand went to the scar on his forehead. "I'll be damned," he said.

"I know you're too big a man to bear old grudges," she said. "Norm's our guest. He's looking for work."

"I'm just a foreman," Hal said woodenly.

"You drag weight with the super." She touched his hand. "Please, Hal."

He couldn't take his eyes off me.

"You can come around to the grain elevator, six in the morning," Hal mumbled. "If you want."

"You're such a dear," Laurie twinkled.

Hal went back to the shuffleboard and finished his beer. When he left, Matt said, "Gee, that's swell."

"You might at least say thanks," Laurie said.

"Thanks," I said.

5

That night I slept in Matt's room. He was very cheerful about the future. Soon Mason Flats would be a big town. We would prosper together in real estate. Next month I would be best man at his wedding. I finally fell asleep and dreamt about Laurie.

Next morning I went down to the mill at dawn. Hal put me to work bucking hundred-pound sacks of grain onto a conveyor belt. The yard was like an anthill, incoming trucks dumping flax down the scale chutes, Mexicans everywhere, men dragging bags of grain into the storage sheds through a haze of flax dust. A buck-forty an hour. Those Mexicans loved it. Most of them were wetbacks, tramp fruit pickers down from Imperial in the off season, and this was a soft political job, this was wealth.

Hal rotated the other men's jobs, stacking empty bags, shoveling flax into the hoppers, but I stayed behind the conveyor lifting sacks waist-high, an eternity of hundred-pound sacks. Every ten minutes Hal would walk by and say, "Keep them moving."

I mopped sweat from my eyes and sneezed from the flax dust. I thought about Laurie, wanting to kill her. But what the hell had I expected, sucking around where I wasn't wanted, trying to mooch a handout they couldn't afford? I felt very tired.

Nine o'clock and spell time. Men lounged against the loading ramp, lighting cigarettes. I slumped, dead tired.

Hal came over to me, hands on hips. "Spell time only for permanent help. Buck those sacks."

I got up slowly.

"Don't you like your job?"

I tugged at the last sack. It weighed ten tons. Abruptly, my knees gave way and I sprawled across the sacks with the world going round in a fiery pinwheel of sunlight and sweat and dust.

"I guess you're not used to work," Hal said sadly. "Better go get your time."

It was a quarter to ten when I walked into the bar. Laurie was all alone in the kitchen. She looked at me, very pale. "What happened?"

"Hal paid me off for that brick. I just stopped to say goodbye."

Her bright head bent wearily. "I'm sorry. It seemed like a good idea at the time. Today is like one of those old silent flickers; you know, the tragedy scene where everything goes smash. Our liquor license is being revoked. Selling liquor to minors, they say. I called city hall and they just laughed at me." She made a grimace. "Big-businessman Matt is next door, getting blotto. It seems he just lost another million."

"How come?"

"He's not a businessman." Her eyes were brimming. "But he won't admit it; he keeps trying. He was too proud to get married before the justice, he wanted us to go first class, a big white wedding. All his life he's tried to be like you, the big man, the sharpshooter. What's funny?"

"Nothing's funny."

"Good-bye," she said.

"Good-bye, Laurie."

I walked slowly out to the street. Through Matt's office window I could see him slumped over the desk with a bottle. I opened the door.

"What gives?"

He stared up vacantly. There was shiny sweat on his face and his eyes were glazed blue marble. He said, with a terrible effort, "The well just came in. A half-hour ago. Looks like three hundred barrels a day."

"I don't get it! You've got a listing on the adjacent acre—"

"Had," he corrected owlishly. "It was an open listing; I never insisted on an exclusive. Last night one of Murdoch's sharpies talked Peabody into an oil lease. Peabody just called me." He giggled. "I've still got a listing on the lot, exclusive of mineral and petroleum rights. Matt Sands, the big-time operator!"

I looked at him, feeling sorry and ashamed and trying to think of some way to say good-bye. Then I felt that old fierce protectiveness welling up inside me.

You spend twelve long years living by your wits, and you acquire a very specialized education. Any grifter has a good memory, and mine was excellent. It was almost a conditioned reflex, my brain growing as keen as winter starlight, as I was evaluating, remembering a man called Pop Toren.

At least, "Pop Toren" was the name he went by. I had spent a very profitable summer with Pop six years ago at Santa Anita. Pop was a white-haired old gentleman who looked like a saint and happened to be one of the best bunco artists in the business. During the second Huntington Beach boom, he made two million dollars. Pop had taken me under his wing that summer, had taught me certain things.

I said to Matt quietly, "Who knows about the well?"

Drunk as he was, something in my voice made him look up. "Nobody yet." He hiccoughed. "By noon it'll be all over town. Why?"

"What time does the hall of records open?"

"Ten o'clock. Who gives a damn? Hey, come back with that bottle!"

Ten seconds later I was next door, behind the bar. My hands were shaking as I poured certain things into a highball glass. It was a brutal way to sober him up, but there wasn't much time. I ran back into the office and handed Matt the highball glass.

"Where's the bottle?" he protested.

"Drink this first. It's good. Real good."

He drank it and promptly vomited. Messy but quick. It took me five more minutes to get him back to the bar kitchen and start pouring black coffee into him. Laurie watched us with listless contempt.

"It won't help," she said. "He'll just get drunk again."

"No he won't. Where's your car?"

Matt was white and twitching, but at least he was sober. "Laurie?" he said helplessly, and she gave him her car keys. I grabbed him by the arm. "Now come on!" I yelled at him.

Her car, an eight-year-old convertible, was parked two doors down. Before we started I made Matt bring along his checkbook and some standard lease forms from the office. He didn't get it. Driving the four blocks to City Hall, I tried to explain, but he kept saying pitifully, "Honest to God, Norm, I've only got ninety bucks in my bank account."

It was one minute past ten when we walked into the Title Records Office. The clerk yawned at us while we pored over the townsite map, then he took an agonizingly long five minutes to thumb through the property-records ledgers. All the time we were jotting down landowners' names and addresses I was scared that somebody else would walk through that door. But nobody did, and it took only ten minutes to find the names I wanted—the names that owned the ten nearest land parcels adjoining the Peabody wildcat.

I had parked the convertible around the side of the building. As we got in, I saw two men hurrying anxiously up the hall steps. One of them carried a briefcase. It was Pete Lombard.

Five minutes later I brought the convertible to a grinding stop on Orange Street. We started for one of those ancient frame houses with a parched front lawn and dirty paint peeling off the front door. I rang the bell. Inside, a baby squalled fitfully. The door opened. The woman wore a faded blue wrapper, and her cowlike eyes were dull with resentment. "We don't want any, mister. You woke the kid."

"We're from Consolidated Oil. Are you Mrs. Cashin?"

She stared dumbly. Her lips parted. Suddenly she wheeled and fled back through the house. "Ma. The well come in!" I took Matt firmly by the arm and steered him into the parlor. The furniture was a dusty, faded velour, the rug was threadbare. A *God Bless Our Home* needlepoint hung over the mantel. From the depths of the house the baby's squalls rose to a shrill crescendo, and stopped. It had either died or gotten its bottle.

Mrs. Cashin and daughter finally came into the parlor.

"Here they are, Ma," the daughter said reverently. "They're from Consolidated Oil. Isn't that what you said, Mister?"

"That's correct." I beamed at Mrs. Cashin. She was one of those shriveled grandmother types with sharp black eyes—the kind that love to ask questions. I had to gamble on the windfall approach and pray that she didn't ask for our credentials.

I cleared my throat. "Mrs. Cashin, you own the half-acre parcel north of Peabody's, right?"

"That's right," she said, and I relaxed. Her voice was quavering and eager. This was going to be easy. "Is it a big well?" she asked.

"Thirty barrels a day," I shrugged. For a moment I thought she was going to cry.

"However, Mrs. Cashin, our company has authorized a dozen leases on property within a half-mile radius of the well. Yours happens to be the last lease. You'll get standard landowner's royalty, naturally."

Mother and daughter looked at each other and smiled.

It went off perfectly. I filled in two lease forms granting Mrs. Cashin one-eighth landowner's interest and giving Norman Sands, agent, exclusive mineral and petroleum rights. Mrs. Cashin read the lease twice, pursing her lips. She finally started to sign when the daughter said nervously, "Ma, don't you think we ought to wait for—"

"Of course," I interrupted smoothly, "you'll get a thousand-dollar advance against royalties. Give me the checkbook, Matt."

He handed it over. He was lost, a man in a dream.

I wrote Mrs. Cashin a check for one thousand dollars, and hesitated. She eyed the check hungrily.

"Our chief geologist says your parcel doesn't lie along the fault line," I said carelessly. "Apex and Standard Oil think we're crazy, but Consolidated likes to gamble. Of course, if you'd rather wait for another company to contact you ..."

She signed. I had her daughter sign as witness. They were both smiling at that check as I pushed Matt out the door.

"You idiot!" Matt blazed. "I don't *have* a thousand dollars in the bank."

"I signed the check, little brother."

He kept shaking his head. I wanted to explain, but we had nine more places to hit and our path would very shortly intersect that of Pete Lombard and friend. When that happened, we were finished.

But I took a few minutes, anyway, and talked patiently and earnestly until Matt got it. His face was rapt with something akin to adoration. Then he frowned. "But supposing you can't redeem those checks today?"

"Then I go to jail. Where in hell is Larkspur Street?"

It was on the west end of town and we wasted ten precious minutes finding the address. Wasted, because this particular landowner was not at home. I kept punching his doorbell and swearing. Then I had a chilling thought.

Suppose Mrs. Cashin scurried right down to the bank and deposited that check. But she wouldn't. It was human nature to gloat, to flaunt that check in front of the neighbors. I seemed to hear Pop Toren's voice, mild and soothing. *"It's the oldest swindle in the world, son. But if they're got oil fever, it always works."*

Two hours later we were shaking hands with a hayseed named John Tolliver, congratulating him on his lease. Out of eight landowners, we had managed to sign three people to leases. Two of the eight hadn't been at home and the other three had already heard about the well and wanted to consult their lawyers before doing anything rash. I had written three rubber checks for one thousand dollars apiece.

As we started to drive away from Tolliver's house, a black Packard sedan ground to a stop in the driveway. Lombard jumped out, followed by a hawk-featured little man. They hurried up the porch steps and rang the bell.

Presently the front door opened. Lombard and friend expostulated with Tolliver while I lit a cigarette and blew smoke rings, Now Lombard was shouting. The front door closed in his face. He turned, saw us.

"Hi," I waved cheerfully. "Gobbling up leases today, gentlemen?"

Lombard started down the walk fast, and the little man grabbed his arm and whispered something. Lombard nodded. They came up the walk.

"You didn't waste much time," the little man said, trying to smile.

"You got to skim off the cream afore the flies come," I said in a nasal twang. "Mister Murdoch's going to be right unhappy, isn't he?"

It jolted them. Matt got out the duplicate leases and showed them to Lombard. He grunted. "Pretty rough, huh, Ted?"

"But legal," Matt said.

Ted squinted at the leases. He looked at me, at the battered convertible. "I see you paid through the nose for these." His smile turned dreamy.

"Might you be interested in selling?"

"You catch on quick," Matt said, overplaying it.

"Did you pay cash for these, friend? Or issue the good old bouncing check?"

I managed to look blank, but Matt flinched. Ted pounced like a cat.

"It's an oldie, friend. Nice try, though. You'll probably get off with eighteen months."

"I don't know what you're talking about," Matt said, white. I could have killed him.

"Like hell you don't," Lombard said, getting it. He grinned. "Tell you what, fellows. You sign these leases over to us and we'll see those checks you wrote are honored. Otherwise—"

They were fast. Fast and rough. But I still had one final hole card. "The checks happen to be good," I said softly, "but we still want to sell. Directly to Murdoch."

They hated the sound of that name. Their glances crossed. "He'll flay you," Ted said.

"Possibly. But when he finds out how you boys botched this little caper, I wouldn't give much for your chances either."

"You're bluffing."

"Can you afford to call?"

They couldn't. They withdrew and argued for a while in angry whispers. Then they came back and started haggling.

It was almost closing time when we walked into the bank. Matt kept staring at that check as I endorsed it and handed it to the teller. The check was for five thousand dollars, made out to one Norman Sands.

"Two thousand in clear profit," Matt breathed. "Not bad for four hours' work."

I wanted to hit him, but what was the use? "If you hadn't given it away, it would have been ten times that," I said. "Hey, look."

It was Mrs. Cashin, standing in line at the cashier's window. Matt licked his lips. "Pretty close."

"Life is a gamble, little brother."

Driving back to the bar, Matt kept chattering happily. Within a week there would be five thousand hungry strangers standing on each other's shoulders for breathing space in Mason Flats. The boom was here, and we were getting in on the ground floor. We were both going to be filthy rich. When he finally ran down, I broke it to him as gently as possible.

"One grand apiece," I said. "Fifty-fifty. It's enough for you and Laurie to move away, to get married on. Tonight I'm leaving for Vegas."

"Gosh, I thought we were going to be partners and—"

"Listen," I said brutally, "and try to understand. You've got no talent. You'll never have it, not if you live to be ninety. I can't afford to stay here and wet-nurse you the rest of your life. Get an honest job somewhere, you'll be happier."

I coasted to a stop in front of the bar. Matt sat forlorn, crushed, looking at his hands. After a long moment he said quietly, "At least come on in, have a drink. Say good-bye to Laurie."

I didn't want to see Laurie again. But I followed him into the bar and had a drink while Matt told her about the whole deal. As he talked, Laurie's eyes got that strange primitive intensity again. She stared at me, and now the intensity was stronger, almost frightening.

"Congratulations," she said. "Are you still leaving?"

It was the way she said it, the taut smile, her breasts thrusting defiantly against the black sweater. My mouth felt dry. All right, I thought, you tried to fight it. At least you tried.

"No," I said. Matt looked up, eagerly.

"Damn, that's swell!" He was radiant. "Tomorrow we'll open up a decent office downtown. Oil securities, acreage! Look, I may not be the smartest guy in the world, but I can learn. You'll see."

Laurie's eyes still held mine, but fading, slowly being replaced by fear.

"Sure," I said. "You'll learn."

6

Our office was on Main, across the street from the Clarion building. At first Matt howled about the two-hundred-monthly rental. Six weeks later he spent a thousand dollars on carpeting and a flagstone planter framing the front window.

We ran splashy ads in the *Clarion*: *Sands Realty. Land. Oil. Leases. Securities. Come in, you lucky ground floor speculators. Get rich!*

They came. Some of them were Matt's friends, Laurie's friends. A queer frenzy attacks people during an oil boom, a mad compulsion to draw out their life savings and give them to the first broker who promises a fifty-percent return. I promised a hundred percent. We had a map on our office wall where I pointed out gusher sites to prospective investors. In those first two months the population of Mason Flats tripled. A city of tents and trailers mushroomed on the edge of the flats. Everywhere the drillers—drunk, their jeans spattered with oil—were spending. Giving their money to the girls in the back room, to the smiling cold-eyed boys in the basement keno parlors.

That first month we grossed three thousand dollars.

Laurie used to stop by our office daily. She loved to catch Matt in the middle of closing a deal and beg him to take her to lunch. They would usually be gone half the afternoon. When they returned, Laurie would be wearing that cool, possessive smile, and the needle she seemed to have for me would be out and ready.

"How're the parasites doing today?"

"Very funny," I would say inanely, wanting to penetrate that brittle smile, to hurt her. By now our antagonism was a naked sword. Matt never noticed. He had a virginal innocence about such things.

After the first two months, Matt began to get squeamish about our prosperity.

"Fifteen hundred, kid," I'd point out to him. "A good day's take, what?"

He had a white pinched look. "I feel like a skunk, Norm. All my friends went into that Cormont lease. The sure-fire gusher, remember?"

I remembered. The Cormont development had come in salt water and sand. "All investments are gambles, little brother."

"Laurie wants me to quit. She says these securities aren't worth a plugged nickel. That it's the same as stealing."

I stared at him. His eyes slid away from mine. "You want to quit, Matt?"

"No."

Matt was finally learning. Matt, with his new twisted smile. He drank too much. He drank far too much the night Laurie gave him back her ring.

"Forget about her, kid. Let's go to Amy's. She's got some new girls, a blonde six feet tall. Real fine, just like a stepladder. Come on."

"Go away."

"You goddamn jellyfish! You promised her you'd quit working with me and she still wouldn't say yes, no, or go to hell. She's not worth it. Give me that bottle and come on!"

He came.

The following night I was working late, setting up our weekend ads, when Laurie stomped into the office and put her hands flat on the desk and her face six inches from mine and said, "Where is he?"

I reached into the sandalwood box on my desk and took out a dollar Havana. I lit it, taking plenty of time. I flicked imaginary lint from the sleeve of my two-hundred-dollar imported Oxford flannel, all the while smiling at her and savoring it. Laurie's breasts rose tremulously with her breathing.

Then I picked up the phone and dialed. "Amy?" I said. "Norm. Matt sober yet? Fine. He'll probably make a two-day party of it. That's right," I said, looking at Laurie. "He likes redheads. Soften him up with redheads and send me the bill."

I hung up. Laurie sat unsteadily, her eyes never leaving my face. She had lovely legs. "I deserved that," she whispered.

"You got it."

"All right." She was listless. "So we're even now. Let him go, Norm. Please."

"Listen," I said patiently. "Within a few months we'll be out of business." Hope flared in her eyes, then slowly died as I went on talking.

"In the first place," I said, "the boom's leveling off. People are getting smart, demanding solid leases. It's not *my* fault your friends won't talk to you anymore because they were dumb enough to make some bad investments. But if it'll make you feel better, I've got an option on a proven quarter-acre. We're drilling. When the well comes in, I'll pay your friends back, dollar for dollar. Fair enough?"

"No!" she wasn't buying it, any of it. "Do you know what you're doing to Matt?"

"I'm making him rich, that's what I'm doing to him. And you're glad."

"Glad?"

I stood up. My tongue felt thick, swollen. "Because now you don't have to feel sorry for him anymore. He's found something bigger, and it galls you." I came around the desk toward her. "You never did love him and were ashamed to admit it."

"I—"

"It's me," I said, "isn't it?"

She stared up at me. She was trembling, visibly. Her gray eyes were wide and frightened. I was standing near the wall switch. I felt hollow, all cold inside. I reached out and turned the lights off.

"Norm—"

I took her by the shoulders. She stood up easily, her face a pale blur in the darkness. I could hear her breathing. I reached out and she melted into my arms.

For just one moment it was all right. Her lips were hot and wet and she made a small moaning sound. Then, suddenly, she was crying. She tore free, and her hand slashed across my mouth.

"Damn you," she sobbed wildly. "Damn you, Norm." The office door slammed behind her. I touched my lip, tasting blood.

The following month our business got a little dirtier, a little more shabby around the edges. We made money. It had become an obsession, to forget about Laurie and make money.

I was no longer a pilot fish; I had finally grown my dorsal fins.

One day Pete Lombard came to our office and invited us to join the civic realtor's league. A thousand-dollar membership fee plus five percent of our gross take. "Tell Murdoch," I said, "that we're not pimps or bookies. We don't have to play ball with the county sheriff and local Johns. Tell him that, clown."

"Don't call me that," he said in a low voice. "Someday you'll slip. Punks like you always slip. Clem says I can have you then. You're going to cry, mister."

I stared at his pink smile, remembering the stories I'd heard—how in his vice-squad days he'd loved to make arrests; how one girl had died of internal hemorrhages shortly after he'd booked her.

"Sure," I said tightly, wanting to smash him like a fat grubworm. "I'll bet you're a big man with the whores. Especially when they're handcuffed and you've got a blackjack. Beat it, clown."

"Someday," he said, and went out.

"They'll wait," Matt said, shaken. "One slip, that's all it takes."

"Relax. These two-bit grifters give me a pain."

The following weekend the *Clarion* refused to accept our advertising. It should have worried me. The Sands Brothers had managed to acquire a rather smelly reputation, and business was falling off badly. The bubble was starting to burst. But I didn't give a damn because we were finally drilling our own wildcat, on the south end of the flats.

We had twenty grand by now, in a joint checking account, but Matt seemed strangely reluctant to touch it.

"Keep it for a nest egg," he said. "Give the bank their six percent; you never know when you'll need cash."

Good old cautious Matt. I played along, blind, unaware of the gathering storm.

"We're getting sued," Matt announced one day.

"Huh?"

"Craven. The northwest development that petered out last month. He claims misrepresentation. Wants his money back."

"Tough luck."

"He's suing next week."

I yawned.

"I saw Laurie yesterday," Matt said.

"Oh?" I said carefully.

"She's working at City Hall. Records clerk." Something in his voice made me look up.

"Still carrying the torch?"

"No."

But there was a time fuse smoldering in him, and two nights later the bomb went off. It took a white-haired widow with bright eyes and a trusting smile.

"You're sure it's quite safe, Mr. Sands?"

"Solid as the mint, Mrs. Gride," I reassured her. "You're a lucky little lady."

Matt sat quietly watching me take her money. When she left he said,

"Very smooth."

"Four hundred bucks."

"The bank called today." His face was wooden. "Their interest was due yesterday."

"So they'll get their interest." I felt very cheerful. "I went out to the well this afternoon. They're in showings finally, good old black sand! Just two more weeks and we'll be sitting on top of the world."

Matt worked very hard that night.

"Hey, those are marks we've already had. Forget them."

"I need this list." He was stubborn-drunk. "I got to have this list."

It happened next day. Matt drew out every penny in our joint account, and vanished. I didn't see him for three whole days. I almost went crazy.

Saturday afternoon he came in and threw a briefcase on my desk.

"Where in hell have you been?"

"Here's your securities back. Your gilt-edged toilet-paper securities."

I just stared.

"I bought it back." There was a holy glare in his eyes. "Every bit I could find. Only the money ran out. Here's a list. We still owe these people."

"My noble little brother," I said.

Then I was on my feet, moving around the desk. "You crazy Galahad, you dumb son of a bitch," I said. I hit him in the mouth. He stood there, blood trickling down his chin; then he turned and walked out. The following Monday he got a job bucking tongs on a pipeline. Fourteen bucks a day.

A few nights after that I saw him walking along Center Street, holding hands with Laurie. They were smiling. I walked into the nearest bar and got quietly drunk.

Six weeks later I was flat broke. Everything had been so beautifully timed! The same day the bank clamped down for their interest, crybaby Craven filed suit. The *Clarion* splashed the suit all over the front page.

That morning I sat staring, numbly, at the paper, at Murdoch's acid editorial. *"Unscrupulous bunco artists posing as decent realtors ... butter-tongued parasites who prey ..."*

After a time I threw the paper in the wastebasket and went back to the washroom. I stared at my gray face in the mirror, then took a tranquillizer. Better. Much better. I went back and glared at the phone, waiting for the bank to call. If only they hadn't read the morning paper. If they extended the loan just one more week, I'd be stinking rich. *Why didn't they call?*

It finally rang. I was shaking so hard I could hardly pick up the receiver.

"Yes, Mr. Cromwell," I said. "No, Mr. Cromwell. Oh now listen, you can't do that. There's a lake of oil just another hundred feet down. Look, if it was that yellow rag's smear story this morning—I'm suing of course—you're crazy," I screamed, my voice raw. "Just another week! I'll give you half-interest! Make you rich as Midas. You got to leave that equipment alone—"

I was mouthing things into a dead wire. I threw the phone at the wall and slumped behind the desk, shivering.

In six months I had come full circle. From rags to riches to bankruptcy.

I sat staring at the unpaid bills on my desk, frantically trying to think of some loophole, some angle. There didn't seem to be any. I was dropping the unpaid bills in the wastebasket when the phone rang again. It was Harker, about the rent. I hung up on him and went outside.

Halfway across the street, I stopped. He was a gray, tired little man lounging on the corner, and he had Finance Company written all over him. I kept walking until I hit the street corner, then doubled back up an alley and jumped into my Cadillac.

I drove fast, down Orange Street, toward the edge of the flats. Out there was my well, the Sands Number One, with no men to run it, no money left to pay for the pipe I'd borrowed or the back salary of the drilling crew. The crew was all right. They'd wait another few days. Another three days and it would be a thousand-barrel-a-day well. The bank wouldn't strip the equipment for at least a week. Pipe. I had to have pipe.

I drove across the tracks to the cluster of long galvanized sheds that marked the beginning of the derrick jungle. I went from place to place, sweating and feverish, trying to make them understand about the pipe. Just one week and I'd pay. They laughed. I kept at it all that long, hot, horrible afternoon, but it was no good.

And then finally, through the choking dust, I saw my rig looming up, deserted.

I got out of my car and climbed up onto the derrick platform. I gazed at the next well across the way—its bailer working, its bit smashing through solid rock a thousand feet down, and I wanted to scream. I saw Matt on the other platform. He was bailing, one foot on the sand wheel drum, that sand line shimmering past his sweating face. Suddenly, I wanted that bailer to snag, the cable to cut him in half.

Down by the sump there was a liquid flurry of motion. Oil splashed blackly as two Mexicans writhed in the sump. The four men, who had pushed them in, stood on the bank laughing. The Mexicans stumbled waist-deep through oil and clawed painfully up the bank. A squat brown man in a leather jacket started after them, three big toughs trailing at his heels. The two Mexicans retreated.

"We'll be back, *amigo*," one said calmly.

"Any time," leather jacket said, hands on hips.

I walked across to the sump. Leather jacket came up, stocky and smiling. "Friends of yours?"

"I work for Murdoch," I said coldly.

He stood motionless as I mounted the platform. Matt gave me one wary glance and bent back to his sand line. "Watch it, that's the line super down there—"

"Those greasers," I said. "What was their pitch?"

"You wouldn't be interested," he said bitterly. "They've got some stupid idea that Mexican roustabouts should make more than six bucks a day. Beat it."

"Sure," I said, and leaped to the ground. I ran over to the Cadillac.

Two minutes later I caught up with the two lean fanatics, who were plodding wearily along the highway. "Need a lift, fellows?"

"We'll manage, *gracias*."

"Look, I saw what happened back there and it's a damned shame. Get in, it's four miles to town."

The nearest one scratched his long, broken nose reflectively. "We'd mess up your car, *amigo*."

The fools wouldn't get in so I just cruised along next to them, talking, and presently I felt the old familiar excitement take hold. This was perfect! A hundred yards later they had talked their hearts out. I told them I'd just remembered an appointment, and off I flew in a cloud of dust. They gaped after me. It takes all kinds.

Driving back to town in the blue dusk, I kept thinking about it, smoothing the rough edges. It was one hell of a gamble, but I had absolutely nothing to lose. I parked the car in an alley six blocks away from the office.

The little gray man still dozed in front of the office, sullen because of the waiting. He stuck the repossession notice in my face. "Whereas," he droned, "by default of monthly payments—"

"Thanks, pop. Good night."

He scowled uncertainly. "Where's the car?"

"Loaned it to a friend."

I started to shut the door and he put his foot against the jamb.

"You got a warrant, pop?"

I shut the door in his face and went over to the desk. I wrote until midnight, then plugged in the hot plate and heated a can of beans.

I wrote and rewrote until four in the morning. It was good stuff, but not strong enough. It had to scare them, grab them by the throats. It needed names, incidents.

Next day I did field work. I went from derrick to derrick, cautiously avoiding those I had visited the previous afternoon, telling everybody that I was a reporter from the *Clarion*. Alter a couple of hours they got wise and I saw the line super hurrying after me with two roughnecks. I made it to the car just in time.

I pawned my watch that afternoon and went over to the American Legion auditorium. They wanted seventy-five bucks for the hall Saturday night. I started to walk out and they called me back. We dickered and finally they came down to forty for Friday.

Next I went to a printer's shop. When I showed him what I wanted, his eyes popped and he said fifteen bucks instead of five. I didn't haggle, but it left me with exactly eighteen dollars and seven cents, all the money I had in the world.

Now I needed help. I needed help for the filthiest swindle a man ever pulled on his friends.

So I sat down and called Matt.

Then I called Laurie.

7

"I don't get it, I just don't get it."

"Like I told you, I've changed."

Matt kneaded his big hands painfully, looked at Laurie. "What do you think, honey?"

She looked thoughtfully at the yellow handbills on my desk. "So the wolf grows fleece. Why, Norm?"

"What's in it for me, is that it?"

She picked up one of the posters and began reading: *"Dear Mr. Murdoch and Associates:—We, who mine your black gold, we who toil—"* Her wry smile came on again. "... *Why are we discriminated against? Because we are Mexicans? Because our skin is brown? ... The vampire of starvation wages, hazardously rotten working equipment*— But that's not quite true, Norm."

"So I want a crowd."

"But what will you—"

"A coat of tar and feathers, that's all I'll get out of it. Murdoch ruined me with his slimy editorial and I'm going to hurt him back, right where it'll hurt the most—his big hairy pocketbook!"

My voice broke off as I stared out the office window. My Caddy was rolling grandly down Main Street. So Mr. Finance Company had finally found it.

"I could have gotten out of town with a whole skin," I said bitterly. "I had to play it dumb. Help the little guy. I asked you here because you two are the only decent people in this town with enough guts to help me. If you don't want in, say so."

Laurie's smile was suddenly breathtaking. "All right, Norm. Your motives are dangerous. But the thing in itself is good."

Matt picked up a batch of handbills, grinning. "She'll hand them out on street corners and I'll cover every rig on the flats. You'll get your crowd."

I said that was fine, and they went out holding hands. Looking after them I felt suddenly sick, unclean. Then I had a horrible thought. Suppose Murdoch ignored the whole thing? Would he? Could he afford to?

Next morning I found the eviction notice on the office door. I laughed, picking up my handbills. Either way it wouldn't matter.

All morning I nailed those handbills on fences and telephone poles. That afternoon I canvassed the Mexican quarter. I found a dozen starving wetbacks who were delighted at the prospect of earning a dollar each to play shill. At first they thought I was *muy loco*, but finally they got it. It was a mere matter of listening to a speech tonight, and clapping the hands.

It was dusk when I knocked on Matt's apartment door. He was just finishing supper. "Laurie's meeting us down there in twenty minutes," he said eagerly. "Had supper yet?"

"Sure." I was starving. "Let's go down to the hall."

When we got there we found a few Mexicans milling about uncertainly in front of the closed doors, and a small reception committee standing on the auditorium steps. Pete Lombard and a cop.

"The party's off, boys," Lombard said gently. "Nice try."

"What's the idea?"

"Give me the injunction, Dave." Lombard took the paper from the cop's hand and purred, "Whereas your use of this hall for inflammatory and libelous speeches is a public nuisance—"

"Public nuisance my fanny," Matt snapped. "You can't keep us out."

The cop drifted forward, one hand on his nightstick. He was a big cop, with a serious, round Irish face. I licked my lips and stared past him at that auditorium door. Behind that door lay money. Money and power. Only I would never get past that door. Murdoch was a thorough man.

"You can't do this!" Matt was shoving Lombard to one side.

"It's a free country—"

The cop's nightstick blurred. Matt crumpled on the steps.

"Inciting a riot," Lombard said. "Better take them in, Dave."

They jerked Matt roughly erect and started down the steps. That was when Laurie pushed her way through the gathering crowd and confronted them.

"Where's his gun?" she whispered. Her cheeks were flaming. "Who did he kill?"

"Libelous speeches," the cop said awkwardly. "The law—"

"Damn the law!" The Mexicans watched, quiet brown faces in the dusk. "A man has a speech to make," she cried. "This country isn't free if a man can't speak, can't raise his voice when he sees something evil. They can't shut our mouths with clubs. I'm going in!" Laurie started up the steps. "Hit me!" she shouted at the cop. He stood frozen. "No—I'm a woman. People are watching. Well, there's going to be a speech. And people are going to listen."

She walked, tall and proud, through that door. I followed her. Nobody stopped me. I felt weak, dizzy. The footsteps behind me were many drums beating.

"... Murdoch's got you and *you* by the throat! Sure, he pays the drillers decent wages. He has to. But you boys are Mexicans. Cheap greaser labor! You're being exploited and you're too gutless to do anything about it. Ugly word, gutless ..."

The swimming sea of brown faces. Laurie, sitting in the front row with Matt, pale and rapt. Lombard leaning against a pillar, looking amused. "... pay you what they want, dole out accident compensation when they feel like it. Jose Garcia—yes, *you*—remember your brother Pedro? Sure! We all remember Pedro. I went to school with Pedro. A rusty crown block falls on him, and they call it carelessness! And you there, Juan Mendez—how does it feel to get caught in a sand line backlash and lose an arm? How does it feel when you think about the accident compensation you're not getting, the money that's your rightful due? Look at him, men—but don't pity him. Pity yourselves!"

The applause rocked the rafters. Those shills had been a good investment. Lombard was gone now. I could not see him anywhere. I held up my arms for silence.

"They tried to stop this speech because they're afraid. But you boys are going to organize. We're going to lick Murdoch. We're going to make him install decent working equipment, pay accident compensation, and a fair day's wages!"

The shills started again and the applause rolled. That was the end. Suddenly I was afraid. These boys wanted more than a ten-minute speech. They wanted organization, action.

Thank God, here they came.

They drifted casually through the side doors—big men, quiet and purposeful. Lombard walked down the aisle toward the stage. I could have fallen on my knees with relief.

"You communist son of a bitch!" Lombard yelled.

Heads swiveled, stared.

"Get off the platform, you stinking red!"

"Listen to me, boys," I roared.

Boos and catcalls drowned me out. Then a sudden spurt of movement, hecklers shoving people, overturning chairs. A tomato splashed on the stage curtain behind me. Matt, white-faced, bulled his way toward the thrower. Another tomato came, this one right at me.

A many-throated snarl. The eruption. I leaped into it.

Faces bobbed in front of me, red and angry. I had my back to the stage dais, a chair in my hand. I splintered the chair over heads—it didn't matter which heads. I saw Lombard a few feet away using a leather sap with grinning deliberation.

A careening truck smashed into my face and I went down. Someone was kicking my ribs in. I tried to cry out, and then there was only a spangled darkness.

"He's all right. Norm!"

I sat up, wincing. The empty hall was a shambles. Laurie was bending over me. She had a black eye. I tried to grin at her. "What time is it?" I croaked.

"Ten o'clock." Matt's face was a tear-stained mask. "Those bastards."

"No cops?"

"They didn't need cops. Come on, we'll get you to a door."

"Murdoch. I got a date with Murdoch. Let go."

Laurie was biting back tears. "Oh, Matt, look at his face. Go get a doctor, please. Hurry. I'll take him home."

Then, somehow, Matt was gone and Laurie had my arm, was helping me toward the door. Nausea spun blackly in my stomach as we went out into the night. Now Laurie was helping me into a car, her little convertible.

"I'll drive," I said. She handed me the ignition keys.

We sat for a moment in darkness. I was aware of the warm pressure of her thigh against mine. She did not pull away. I stared at her, at the tremulous rise and fall of her breasts, and a thousand jigsaw pieces spun slowly into place. Her petty bitchery, her eagerness to find a cause, her desire to save Matt, to save me. She was one of those women who search desperately for a vision greater than themselves, and right now I was that vision.

I lit a cigarette. I had to see Murdoch. And fast! He had made a tactical blunder, and now it was my move. But it was all gold, this thing I had found, and Murdoch could wait. As I snubbed the cigarette out, Laurie's lips were wide, moistly parted. Twin spots of color glowed in her cheeks.

I kissed her. She did not fight. Her fingertips were moth-wings on my face and her lips were hot and avid. We kept kissing and her breath came wildly in my ear. She was panting something about Matt going for the doctor, and she had to take me home. I laughed.

I flipped on the ignition and drove fast down Main, past the rail junction and the galvanized shacks of Supply Row, and now the speedometer quivered at eighty as we raced past the derrick jungle. My hands were frozen on the steering wheel.

I turned off the road, skidding to a stop in a darkened eucalyptus grove. Laurie shook as I took her in my arms.

"Oh, my darling," she whispered. "When I saw you up on that platform, I really knew. I love you, Norm."

I ran one hand under her dress and she stiffened, her face buried in my shoulder. "Please," she said. "Not this way, Norm. I'm all yours, but please—"

My hands kept moving, and she said faintly, "All right. Whatever you want, dearest."

There was a proud humility in the way she took off her sweater. She was trying not to cry. And it would always be this way between us—anything for Norm, our whole life together.

She looked at me, waiting, and a part of me slowly shriveled and died.

"What is it?"

"Put the sweater back on." My voice sounded strange.

I flipped the ignition and gunned the motor. Driving back to town, I didn't say a word. She sat very close to me, murmuring, "Please tell me, Norm. I've failed you, haven't I?"

"Shut up."

She was still.

I turned on Main, and parked in front of the Clarion building. Murdoch would still be in the pressroom writing a vitriolic editorial about the local commie element.

I opened the car door. "Good-bye, Laurie."

"Norm."

"Listen." I took a deep breath and shivered. "I want you to stay away from me. I'm strong poison, do you understand? I slime everything I touch."

"It's not your fault, darling. The union—"

"There won't be any union," I said through my teeth. "Get that through your thick head. It was a gimmick, a crowbar to use on Murdoch, get it?"

My words were steel barbs sinking in, hurting. "Marry Matt," I said. "Marry him soon. And if you happen to see me on the street, turn around and run like hell."

She sat white and stricken. I got out of the car and slammed the door. I walked across the street without looking back.

8

The downstairs lobby was deserted except for a colored janitor who goggled as I passed. My face was a devil's mask of dried blood.

I climbed the marble stairs, my ribs aching. On the third floor I limped down the corridor toward the lighted office marked "Clem Murdoch, Publisher." I stood with my hand on the doorknob, frantically trying to remember my pitch, the way I'd rehearsed it a dozen times.

The hell with it, I thought, and threw the door open.

The talk and the laughter died.

A cone of smoky light hung over the green poker table. Cards and chips stopped rustling. The faces that turned in my direction were blank and hard. Lombard languidly got up from the table and started toward me. He was smiling.

"Peter." The thin, sharp voice came from beyond the cone of light.

Lombard stood motionless as I walked past him and around the poker table. Murdoch sat there, silver-haired and stiffly erect. His eyes held mine. They were frosty blue, derisive.

"You play poker, son?"

"I want to talk to you," I blurted. I fumbled for a cigarette.

Big men sat around that table, the powers of Mason Flats. Fat Sam Kramer, head of the city council. Fat Sam with his soft woman's body, who got a take from those basement crap parlors, a percentage on civic-construction bids. Sam looked at me coldly, then at Murdoch.

Little Tom Bullock, the best chief of police that money could buy, sat next to Kramer. Bullock the middleman, who kept both the county sheriff and the city council darlings happy with rake-offs from the perfumed brothels on Orange Street.

Bernard Kroll, toying bitterly with his stack of blues. Kroll's construction company was a large thorn in the city council's side. His consistently low paving-contract bids made the construction grafters uneasy. Ultimately, Kroll's honesty would destroy him.

Next to Kroll sat the most beautiful woman I had ever seen. She was blonde and sleek and her smile was catlike. Our glances locked. Her name was Shannon Quinn. I had seen her once at a country-club dance with Murdoch. Rumor had it that she was a thousand-dollar whore Murdoch had imported from Las Vegas.

With an effort I ripped my gaze away from her and looked back at Murdoch. He chuckled and glanced sharply at Kroll. "Like I said, a man who doesn't fold when he's beaten is a plain damn fool. Bernard?"

I was being ignored. Everyone was suddenly looking at Kroll. I got the impression of a silent duel being fought by two titans. Kroll hesitated, his face impassive. He flicked a blue chip across the felt.

Murdoch grinned and shoved a small stack of blues forward. "And five hundred," he said.

Kroll stared at the pot, Indian-faced.

"Look at him." Murdoch's voice hung softly in the haze. "He knows I'm bluffing, but he's afraid. A three-thousand-dollar pot, and he's afraid to risk five bills." He tapped his cards on the green felt. "Tell you what, Bernard. Call me, and I'll add this—and this—" He added ten blues to the pot, then another ten. "Four thousand, five. Bernard?"

Kroll's face knotted with concentration. His eyes darted from the pot to his own scant stack of blues. He squinted at his hands, then at Murdoch's face, and finally tossed his cards into the discard heap.

Murdoch's laughter was like ice crackling. He spread his hand, face up. A soft sigh rippled around the table.

"Just two jacks," Murdoch drawled. "Openers." His voice became very gentle. "Could you have beaten them, Kroll?"

Kroll's smile was bloodless as he reached for the whisky. But it was the girl's face that held me. Her lower lip was full and richly curved with mockery as she refilled Kroll's glass.

"Excuse me, gentlemen." Murdoch got up stiffly. "Take my chair, Peter."

Lombard came forward and Murdoch walked toward the door in back marked "Private." I followed him. My cigarette tasted as bitter as lye.

Some office. A naked light bulb dangled glaringly from the ceiling. A rickety roll-top desk stood by the window, with a great brass cuspidor beside it.

"Don't look so shocked, Norman," Murdoch grunted. "Only the rich can afford to sacrifice show for comfort." He sat in the old leather throne behind the desk. "Sit down."

We measured each other.

His weathered face had a thousand wrinkles. The thin lips were those of a fanatic. The flint jaw properly belonged to a Caesar, a Bonaparte. He was a ruler of men, and power was his obsession. And now he was waiting for me to make my pitch before he laughed in my face and turned me over to Lombard.

I took a deep breath and plunged.

"A yellow handbill," I rasped. "Mexicans unite, one man making a two-bit speech. And right away you get scared, call out the riot squad, rotten tomatoes, clubs. Shall I tell you why you're scared? Because you're a figurehead, someone for the town to hate—"

"Knock it off," he snapped. "The Mexicans don't *care*. They're wetbacks, they drift like sand. They're paid scale for roustabout labor and you know it. Lombard offered you a chance to join the fold."

"For peanuts!"

"So now you eat hulls."

"Wrong again."

"Lay it on the line, Sands. You've got something to sell."

"Only that I can hurt you."

"You could annoy me." He made a fly-swatting motion. "Nuisance value only."

"How much is nuisance value worth?"

"Ah," he said sardonically, "so you want to work for me?"

"For *us*. I want you to appoint me Municipal Landowners Agent."

He began laughing. Shrill, spasmodic gasps. I kept talking, outlining my idea.

"The city of Mason Flats owns a hundred-odd acres of tax-delinquent titles—vacated eminent-domain stuff which it farms out to major oil companies. I propose that you, the city council, establish a staff to represent the city as an active corporation, said staff's entire duties to consist of running down oil acreage, buying it in the city's name, sandwich leasing when direct buying is impractical—"

"And you'll be chief agent in this little setup, eh?" He looked thoughtful. "Obviously the city might benefit from this with the proper staff. However...."

"What's in it for Murdoch, huh?"

"Precisely."

"The plums. I could ferret out enough producing acreage to keep the city treasurer happy, and then the hundred-barrel-a-day stuff—"

"Well," he said slowly, "well, well."

He sat, toying with the idea, weighing it. Then he smiled wolfishly. "It's a good idea, Norman. Brilliant. Now I'll tell you what I'm going to do. First, I'll give you twenty-four hours to get out of town. Then I'll have Peter Lombard appointed Municipal Landowners Agent. Thank you for the idea, Norman. Good night."

He waited. I didn't move.

"I'll want ten thousand a year," I said deliberately, "and bonuses. Plus the right to pick my own staff. I'll go see Sam Kramer tomorrow morning."

His eyes bored into me, a cold, joyous light flickering in them. "If I'd had a son ..." His hungry grin flashed on. "Suppose you stay a while, son, and we'll talk about it."

I stayed, and we talked about it.

I found Matt next afternoon, in the derrick jungle. He stood stiff and intent at the humming sand line as I mounted his derrick platform. At first he'd be furious and hurt, but he'd listen to reason. We needed each other; that was the important thing.

The men at the cable drum ignored me. Matt looked up, and his eyes were alive and scared. "The bailer snagged an hour ago ... I can't leave the line. Look, I can loan you a few bucks to stay out of town until this thing blows over."

"You haven't talked to Laurie?"

He shook his head painfully. "She called me late last night. Said she was sick. What happened?" Then he stared past me, to my parked Cadillac. "You got your car back. How come?"

"Murdoch and I made a little deal. We're in!"

His eyes were rapt. "You mean he came through? He'll pay a decent scale to the Mexicans?"

"That's dead. Forget it."

I started explaining about the new job. As I talked, his face grew slack. He stared at me dully.

"Ten grand a year, and bonuses! Don't you get it?"

"I get it," he said. "A lot of guys got their cans beat off last night so you could get a foot in the door." He turned back to the sand line.

"Matt," I said.

"Take your goddamn hands off me."

The two roughnecks watched us. I was getting sore. I grabbed Matt by the shoulder. "Listen, stupid—"

The blow came out of nowhere. It caught me flush on the mouth.

I spun sideways on the oil-slimed planking and landed hard against a joist. Matt stood over me, pale and shaking. "Now beat it," he said thickly. "Stay away from me or I'll kill you. And stay away from Laurie."

I got up, slowly: I feinted, and Matt drove his right fist into my belly. I went down, retching. When I finally got up, Matt's swing was wild. I palmed him hard in the throat. As he slipped, I drove a knee into his groin and he slumped with a moan.

I fell on top of him, beating his head against the platform railing. He managed to wriggle sideways and deliver a short chopping right to the temple that broke my hold. Then he had me in a bear hug over the railing, and I felt my spine give. He came up with his hand and drove that balled fist right into my face. He was sobbing brokenly.

Suddenly he stepped back. I clung to the railing. He was trying to say something.

I stumbled forward and threw my left fist at his chin. He skidded, went down. I aimed a kick at his face.

He scrabbled sideways, painfully, and his ankle folded. I lurched after him and the platform reeled beneath my feet. Someone was shouting, *"Bailer's snagged. For Christ's sake, duck!"*

I stared drunkenly at the sand line. It hung slack, quivering.

Then it backed. It hissed angrily out of the shaft and began to unravel, coil upon coil—twenty feet, thirty, fifty. It was alive. It writhed in hissing coils over the derrick platform, knocking me down.

For one moment I blanked out. When I opened my eyes I was flat on my back, staring at blue chunks of sky through loops of cable, the black cross-beams of the rig. The cable moved. I moved with it, a fly caught in a web of steel.

I clawed madly at the web, and suddenly I was free. The two roughnecks were fumbling with the cable drum, trying to reverse it. Matt was enmeshed in a dozen loops of cable. His face was white. The cable tightened slowly about him as the sand line slithered back into the hole.

I stumbled over to the drum, yelling at the roughnecks to put the cable into forward. I pointed at Matt, and they stared. They got it.

I ran over to Matt's side and tore at him. He had two lengths of cable knotted around his waist and over his shoulder. His lips moved. He was praying.

The cable drum moaned.

From above, the sand line began to drop, slackening ever so slowly. I stumbled blindly about the platform groping for the cable cutters. One of the roughnecks still fought the drum; the other tugged uselessly at Matt's shoulders. I fumbled for the cutters, and all the time my eyes were fixed on that cable sliding like a long, oiled snake into the shaft. I could almost see it before it happened—Matt being dragged, screaming, across the platform, the cable fouling at the shaft in a tangle of flesh and steel.

Finally, I found those cutters. I floundered to Matt's side. My hands kept slipping in the oil. I cut through the first two strands.

There was twenty feet of cable left on the platform, then ten, five. The driller wrapped his hands around that steel rope, trying to keep a half-ton bailer from sinking deeper into the earth. Suddenly he shrieked and stared at his maimed hands, at the flesh which had sloughed away as easily as butter.

There was one strand of cable left. As I ground the cutters into that strand, the cable thrummed taut. Matt slid six feet away. I followed him, but he was being jerked away, faster, toward the mouth of the shaft. I closed my eyes, waiting for his scream as he was torn in half.

Silence. I looked up, numb.

Matt lay still. There was no more cable on the platform. That last strand had parted.

We finally got Matt free. His grin was crooked as he grabbed my shoulder for support. "You sprained my ankle, you bastard."

The two roughnecks helped me get him to the car. It was a miracle; they couldn't believe it. "You *both* all right?"

"We're fine," I told them. "Go fish for that bailer."

We drove silently through the derricks. My whole body was one tired ache. My face felt bathed in flame. Matt was smiling ridiculously through puffed lips. "You still want me to work for you?"

"We need each other," I said.

"Supposing I pull another double cross?"

I thought about it. "I'll take that chance."

"Fair enough," he said in a strange voice. "Partners."

9

"But the geologists said—"

"Damn the geologists! I'm telling you the region's all hard-rock shale! Even if there was oil, they couldn't get through with a diamond bit. Look, Mr. Davis, the city needs this new school. We'd hoped to find a few public-spirited citizens who didn't have oil fever, who'd sell their land for a fair price."

"Well, I don't know."

He chewed his little mustache and wiped his horn-rimmed glasses and squinted nervously at me from behind the hotel desk. Every few minutes a roomer would come down the rickety stairs and he would peer sharply at them to see if they were taking any luggage with them.

"Two thousand dollars." I made it sound like two million. "Well?"

His smile was an awful thing to see. "Well, Mr. Sands, I hate to tell you this, but a Fargo Oil scout approached me three days ago. They want to drill. I'm to get standard landowner's interest."

I thumped on the desk and told him the Fargo people were crazy (the bastards), and he was apologetic and frightened, but that's the way it was. Neither of us mentioned the 500-barrel well a thousand yards north of his two acres or how the field had been moving southeast the last few months.

"The city has authorized me to go to twenty-five hundred," I said. "Last offer."

"I think I ought to wait."

"You can't afford to."

His eyes got round and scared. I crossed the lobby and stood at the window, staring through the gilt "Davis Hotel" sign at my Cadillac across the street. I lit a cigarette—our prearranged signal. Matt got out of the car.

"Pretty old hotel," I said. "You know the city condemned Schultz's Boardinghouse last week. Terrible eyesore. Fire hazard."

Davis' mouth opened, but no words came. Matt entered, looking big and cruel in his new blue gabardine. "Mr. Davis," I said, "my brother Matt. Matt's with the Public Health and Sanitation Department. You won't mind showing him around."

"Just a routine inspection," Matt said. He frowned darkly at the front door. "This your only exit?"

"Yes, we—"

"Let's look at your fire escapes." Matt started up the stairs, and then paused as he looked back at Davis. "What's the matter?"

"There ... aren't any," Davis whispered.

Matt looked at me and shook his head. "Let's inspect the second floor."

I watched them go upstairs. Davis was talking a blue streak now, telling Matt what a fine, sound building it was.

I blew smoke rings and waited.

They came downstairs in a few minutes. Davis' face was gray. Matt was writing things down in a notebook.

"Seen enough?" I asked.

Matt nodded sadly. "Nothing personal, Mr. Davis, but the city's making a public-safety drive and ..." His shrug was pure eloquence.

"Sorry, Mr. Davis," I said. We started for the door.

"Wait." A pale ghost of a voice. We turned. "Please," he said, "if you ..."

"The city always plays square with public-spirited citizens, Mr. Davis. You know that." I whipped out the quitclaim and inked in the figures. "Sign here."

"But this says a thousand!" He was strangling. "You said—"

"Property goes up, it comes down. You're a public-spirited citizen, Mr. Davis!"

He almost died. But he signed.

Driving back to City Hall, Matt was bleak and withdrawn. It worried me. We had pulled some pretty rough ones in the last two months but the Davis deal was one of the rawest. I was trying to jolly him out of it when we passed the Center Hotel and I saw Pete Lombard walking down the steps, carrying his inevitable briefcase.

Inside that hotel was silken sin. And money. A steady stream of money from the mill hands, the oil boomers.

"You know how much that fat slob collects each week?" I snarled. "Ten thousand, easy. Six cathouses, a dozen poker joints going full blast, night and day." I was choking with rage. "I created a new con for these crumbs.

We've made them a cool fifty grand in leases so far, and what do we get? A lousy five hundred a month—with *promised* bonuses."

"You're getting a bonus tonight," Matt said quietly.

"Huh?" My rage evaporated. "Why didn't you tell me?"

"It's a conditional bonus." He smiled faintly as I pulled into the City Hall parking lot. "Come on upstairs and I'll tell you about it."

The office was a twenty-by-thirty glass and chrome layout on the second floor. Our two secretaries became very busy as we walked in. I told one of them to trace title on Mr. Davis' two acres, then walked further back to our private office.

Matt was already on the phone. "Yes *sir.* Tonight, Mr. Murdoch. I'll tell him." He hung up. "You're to finish sewing up the Larkspur Street options today. He wants them tonight."

"But there's no oil—"

"The City Planning Commission authorized the new civic center site this morning," he said patiently. "You want I should draw you a picture?"

I whistled softly. "A thousand feet of frontage, including two intersection corners!"

"He mentioned a fat bonus. And you'll be promoted to helping Lombard with the collections."

"That's *bad?*"

Matt shrugged, and that shrug should have been an alarm bell, but I was on fire with the idea that I was finally being taken into the fold. For two months I'd followed orders, kept my mouth shut, taken their crap, and made money for them. They thought they were big-time operators with their bookie rake-offs, their pitiful garbage-hauling contract payoffs, their slot-machine graft. They'd never even heard of the numbers racket, had no idea of the thousand-a-day take a dozen good gage pushers could bring. They lived small and they thought small. Once in the fold, I'd show them! My mouth watered thinking about it.

I got out the Larkspur file and stopped dead. Matt was cleaning out his desk.

"What the hell?" I stood staring at him.

"I forgot to tell you," he said blandly, "I asked for a transfer this week. To the City Auditor's Department. They okayed the transfer this morning."

"Are you crazy? That job only pays four bills a month!"

He went right on emptying out drawers, a stubborn set to his mouth. I watched him, trying to figure it out. Then it came in a blinding flash of clarity.

"The City Auditor's Department," I said softly. "Access to all the civic expenditures, the construction bids. Well, well. So you've had an ulterior motive all the time. Young Galahad, playing the spy. You poor chump, do you really think you can get anything on them?"

Matt's lips were pressed tightly. He made a neat stack of his belongings on the desk blotter.

"Don't get me wrong," I said. "I want to smash Murdoch, too. But for different reasons. Lots of luck, kid. You'll need it."

Matt ignored my outstretched hand. "Just stay out of my way, Norm. As far as I'm concerned you're worse than Murdoch. You've got a greater capacity for evil. If you try to stop me, I'll kill you."

I sat looking at this stranger that had once been my brother, and I felt a warm empathy, and also sorrow. But the die had been cast thirteen rotten years ago. Neither of us would ever change.

"Good hunting," I said, and his nostrils flared. "Relax, I won't spread it around."

The door closed behind him. I sat there, feeling tired and alone.

It was a hectic afternoon. I sifted titles, made confirming phone calls, and nearly drove my stenographers crazy. At four o'clock there was only one Larkspur lot that was open. It belonged to a man named Hermann.

Old man Hermann who had given me a pin-setting job fourteen years ago, when I needed a job terribly.

At four in the afternoon the bowling alley was almost deserted. Grandma Hermann sat at the cash register, benevolently watching the two teen-agers who were bowling duckpins. The boy was tanned and handsome, with a crew cut. The girl was laughing as she made a spare, a pretty girl with long, slim legs. I watched them with a nostalgic ache, remembering, and Mrs. Hermann said, "You want to bowl, *ja?*"

"Where's Mr. Hermann?"

She motioned toward the hallway, and I walked slowly past her into the back room.

He was all alone, at the snooker table concentrating on an impossible bank shot.

"*Dummkopf*," he said sadly, muffing it, and then he looked up, recognized me. His face burst into a wrinkled grin. "Norman! He finally comes to see the old man. I hear you are a big operator these days, Norman."

"Just small potatoes." My smile felt nailed on. "Incidentally, I've got a check in my pocket already made out to you. A check for three thousand dollars."

I went right into my spiel, but it was strained and awkward and the words tumbled out like lead. As I talked, Hermann's smile slowly congealed, the scorn in his eyes was a naked thing. Who did I think I was kidding?

"They told me," Hermann said, looking at the snooker table. "One hears stories. I did not believe them. You were a good boy once, Norman. A little wild, perhaps, but a good boy. What happened to you?"

I said desperately, "The city had planned a park—"

"Indeed? A park made of oil wells! *Mein Gott*, how stupid I must look. Get out."

"Now take it easy," I whispered. "Any geologist will tell you there's no oil—"

Deliberately, he turned his back on me and racked up his cue. Something snapped. I grabbed him by the shoulder. "Listen, you goddamn old idiot—"

"Please." He was coughing violently. I let go. He stumbled over to the water cooler, strangling, and popped a capsule into his mouth. His Adam's apple worked convulsively as he gulped the water.

"My heart," he said with as much dignity as he could muster. "The doctors say I must never get excited. You excite me, Norman."

"If you're holding out for—"

"Good day, Norman."

I walked slowly back to City Hall in the gathering dusk. My one big chance, and I had failed. Failed like an amateur. Now take Angelo Ventresca. *He* wouldn't have failed. Angelo would have found a lever, a gimmick.

But I wasn't Angelo. I was a hunger-crazed rat in a crystal cage, drooling at the food just beyond the bars. When Murdoch discovered the missing option he would smile gently and place the food a little closer, but still out of reach. Murdoch knew how to punish a man.

As I climbed the City Hall steps I passed Matt and Laurie. They were just leaving. Matt nodded to me stiffly. Laurie's smile held a touch of pity.

I went up to my office, pricking myself with failure, feeling consumed by a nagging hatred for Murdoch, and there was a pint of Old Overholt in the lower drawer of my desk. It took me four hours to kill that pint.

At eleven o'clock I stood in the foyer of Murdoch's home taking in the quiet splendor of his living room. That room was the index to Murdoch's personality; it was meant to make you feel dwarfed and insignificant, and it did. An eight-foot-wide stone fireplace, fronted by a magnificent tiger-skin rug; overhead an immense vaulted ceiling; in the corner standing sentry, a gleaming suit of armor with a spiked mace. The spiked mace would have been an anomaly in any living room but Murdoch's.

Kropke, the butler, ushered me in with his usual funereal smile.

"Clem's expecting me." I started across the acre of jade oriental carpeting.

Kropke said with icy satisfaction, "He's in the game room, sir. You may wait by the fireplace."

"Big game, I suppose?" I wanted to hit him.

"Quite. Might I fetch you a drink?"

I said yes and went over to the gray leather couch in front of the fireplace.

"Likes to keep people waiting, doesn't he?" The voice was throaty, sensual. I blinked down at her. She was half-lying on the couch in a crumpled swirl of emerald silk, white frothy ermine and golden hair.

"If it's business, walk right in." Her cat smile. "The devil's playing for souls tonight."

"He's got mine."

"So you're Norm Sands," she said softly. "Clem's new hatchet man."

"And you're Shannon Quinn."

We appraised each other.

Her body was voluptuous, breathtaking. Her face was a study in concavities. Her high cheekbones and enormous, wide-slanting eyes produced an effect unreal, almost surrealistic. Yet when she smiled, the aquiline features grew radiant. Kropke came into the room silently, with my Old Fashioned. Without looking at him, she took the drink from the tray and drank half of it slowly. Her penetrating green eyes made me feel suddenly naked.

I moistened my lips. "How about your soul?"

"You don't miss what you never had," she said remotely. "Clem tells me I'm the essence of amorality. He says I'm the female counterpart of Norman Sands."

It rocked me. Behind that lazy smile I got the impression of a cold alertness, a hunger. Mantis, I thought, male and female. I said uneasily, "Who's he playing poker with?"

"Bernard Kroll." Her voice was calm, matter-of-fact. "They've been in there for five hours. It's interesting to watch Clem find a man's weakness and break him. Sometimes he uses women, sometimes money. The end's always the same."

"Supposing Kroll wins?"

Her laughed was warm music. "You're priceless!"

"No I'm not."

It was like watching two different women. A moment ago she had been sleek and deadly as a feral thing. Now her face held a little-girl wistfulness, forlorn and defeated.

"It's a rotten game," she murmured. "Kroll's in love with me. Clem wanted to make sure." Her green gaze was vibrant, searching. "I wonder," she breathed, and she was talking to herself, not to me. Suddenly she leaned her blonde head on my shoulder and gazed into the fireplace.

I was beginning to feel that pint. I looked down at her taut silken breasts and my pulse was hammering.

Most women, like Laurie, identify sex with an acute emotional need. But there is another, rarer type of woman. The type that often die violently at the hands of a lover. These women are elemental; they use sex as a deft and terrible weapon, the way Shannon was using it now.

She stirred against me with a contented sigh, and this was madness.

I tried to tell myself that we were both a little drunk, that she was Murdoch's property and we were in his living room. It didn't matter. She wanted me to have her—here, now, on that tigerskin rug by the fireplace, and I had as much choice about it as a drowning lemming.

I kissed her. Her lips were moist and plush. Her long body moved scaldingly against mine, her breath roaring in my ears. Then she moved away, delicately. She was standing with her back to the fireplace, her eyes bright with triumph.

"Come here," I said thickly.

"You can't afford me, darling."

I lit a cigarette with trembling fingers. "You bitch," I said.

"You'll be able to afford me some day. Eventually, darling."

I heard voices in the hallway. Murdoch's metallic laughter, then Kroll's voice, an agonized, croaking thing. Shannon stood, cool and regal, her hair soft gold on her shoulders. She was watching Murdoch.

Kroll's face was shiny with sweat. His eyes were wild. "Please," he said, "we can work something out."

"Kropke," called Murdoch, "bring Mr. Kroll a drink. Something strong. Now you're being reasonable, Bernard. Of course we'll work something out. I'm going to make you a rich man, Bernard."

Kroll slumped wretchedly on the couch. Murdoch came forward smiling. His face was the color of old ivory. He had just won another soul.

"Sorry to keep you two waiting." His hard gaze softened as he looked at Shannon. Then he saw the cocktail glass lying on the rug. Nothing changed in his voice or his eyes.

"Bernard's finally joining the grafters at the public trough. Tomorrow he's accepting a juicy paving contract, right, Bernard?"

Kroll nodded dully. There would be a joker in this paving contract. A fatal, concealed joker that could destroy him any time Murdoch wished.

"The options, Norman?" Murdoch was waiting and I took them from my coat pocket and handed them over. As he riffled through them, I held my breath. After a moment he paused and looked at me. "Hermann?"

"He wouldn't go," I said. "He—"

"You poor, inept hustler." He sighed. "See this, Norman?"

He showed me a check for ten thousand dollars. It was made out to Norman Sands. "I hate to be disappointed," Murdoch said. "Don't you?"

As in a dream I watched him cross to the fireplace and toss the check into the flames.

Shannon threw back her head and laughed. It was shrill, piercing laughter with a thousand needles in it. Murdoch was saying, "Good night, Norman."

I seemed to float across the jade carpeting. And then I was at the door. Shannon's laughter followed me out.

The night was cold and I shivered as I got into my car. I gunned the motor and the tires whined as I whipped around the corner. I drove fast. It was a quarter past twelve when I jumped out of the Cad and ran up the sidewalk to Hermann's door. The place was closed. Inside, I could see Hermann limping across the alleys, turning off the lights. I pounded on the glass door, panting. I pounded again and he came up, querulous, then angry, and shaking his gray head as he turned away. The glass was rattling as I hammered on the door.

He turned, his anger growing, and opened the door. "*Lieber Gott*, must I call the police?"

"Listen," I gasped, shoving my way inside. "You've got to play ball. There's no oil on your stinking half acre. It's the new civic center site—"

"Get out," he said, and I blurted, "we can make it four thousand," and he shrieked, "Get out. Are you crazy? *Get out of my place!*" And his eyes were round and popping, he was pushing me with his frail old hands, his face contorted. "*Gott*," he wheezed in a horrified, strangled voice, and he was beating at my face, foam on his lips. "My capsules," he said through the foam. "I can't breathe—"

He lay at my feet. I stared numbly at Mrs. Hermann who was standing, almost in a stupor, by the cash register. She moved forward. "*Liebchen*," she said, bending over him.

She touched him and looked up at me. "You knew his heart was bad," she said without expression. Her face was gray and her voice was a part of the grayness. "You killed him."

Then she began to scream.

10

The coroner cleared his throat and said, "Please, Mrs. Hermann, did you actually see Mr. Sands kill your husband?"

I sat in front of the coroner's jury, wooden-faced, remembering Murdoch's quiet venom ... *"You dumb son of a bitch, what were you trying to prove?"* And later ... *"Don't worry about it. They'll say death through accidental causes, and it'll cost like hell."*

I kept remembering how I had tried to explain it to Murdoch, and his dry, knowing chuckle. How I had tried to explain it to Matt, frantically, and Matt's saying, "Sure, Norm, sure. I understand." And Matt's wretched smile as he backed away from me. It was like that over and over again, and the tired voice of the coroner in the hot afternoon.

When they finally announced death through accidental causes, Mrs. Hermann made a thin, whimpering sound. Then she came over and spat in my face.

I walked slowly toward City Hall. The biting desert wind blew in from the Flats, acrid and scorching, and the late afternoon sun was the color of blood. When I got to the hall, I found them moving desks on the second floor. A gnarled old janitor was methodically scraping my name off the frosted glass door.

"Hey, pop, this is the Municipal Landowners office. *My* office."

"Was," he said.

I stormed inside. Laurie was there, with two other stenographers from the Tax and License Bureau across the hall. They were gutting my files, cleaning out the office.

"What the hell gives?"

They stared at me. Laurie's voice was mocking. "Didn't they tell you? There is no more Municipal Landowners Agency."

I stood, shocked, and the other girls bustled out with armfuls of file folders. "Look," I whispered, "it's a mistake. If Kramer wanted us to move to bigger offices, he should have told us." That was it. I laughed, and my laughter had a harsh sound. "I told Kramer last week we were cramped for space —here, I'll help you with that drawer."

"Touch me," she said evenly, "and I'll kill you."

I chuckled. "Still sore about that night?"

"Grateful," she said somberly. "But Hermann's death was deliberate, wasn't it? Why didn't you just use a knife?"

Rage boiled up in me like lava. I started around the desk award her, and Lombard's voice purred from the doorway, "Aren't you in the wrong building, chum?"

Lombard's smile was vicious. "The little lady told you, but you're real slow. You finally fell out of bed, and your name's off the door."

Laurie went out discreetly. Lombard and I were alone. I reached feverishly for the phone. Kramer was not in his office; he was gone for the day. I called the mayor and His Honor was out, indefinitely. I called the *Clarion* and Murdoch was not there.

"I'll see you around," Lombard said sweetly, showing me the leather sap. "Maybe tonight. Clem won't mind. Think about it," he said as I stumbled past him and outside.

Driving out to Murdoch's house, I kept trying to relax, to think calmly. When I got there his arbored driveway was jammed with the familiar

Packards and Buicks. I climbed he flagstone steps and banged on the front door.

It opened. Kropke sneered politely. "Mr. Murdoch's in conference—"

I put my hand in his face and shoved. I strode past him, across the immense living room, and jerked the library doors open.

They were there, all of them, the king rats in the civic corruption. They sat quietly around the long mahogany table, their faces still. Tom Bullock, Mayor Cliff Harkness, fat Sam Kramer, Matt, Murdoch at the head of the table, Kroll, the others.

"I'm sorry, sir," Kropke said excitedly at my elbow, "he burst right in—"

"Quite all right," Murdoch soothed. "Shut the door, please. Sit down, Norman."

I slid into the chair opposite Matt. He didn't even look at me.

I didn't get it. Everyone ignored me, all eyes riveted on that little man with the white hair and the soft voice. The room was choked with tension. Murdoch was speaking.

"Any idea who wrote that letter, Martin?"

Martin Rand was the county sheriff. His hatchet face was dark with worry. "I only saw it once, Clem. When the county attorney called me in yesterday and started firing questions about local graft. That letter was plumb nasty. It gave names, rake-offs, amounts ..."

"It could have been any one of us." Judge Miller's frightened words hung in the stillness.

"But *why?*" Mayor Harkness' pink cheeks were moist. "Clem, what kind of game are you playing?"

"Trying to find who wrote that letter," Murdoch said blandly. "It was so beautifully timed. Five weeks before election. An eager cub of a crusading district attorney who smells blood and is out to get some. The question is, whose blood shall we give him? There's going to be a grand jury inquest, gentlemen. Before the primary. There'll be a stench to high heaven and a great many red faces. We need a sacrificial lamb. Any volunteers?"

Silence. Murdoch gazed from face to rigid face.

"Goddammit, Clem!" Kramer exploded. "Who're *you* to pick a scapegoat? You're in this thing too, ten times as deep."

The sullen murmur of rebellion was swelling around the table. Angry voices. Murdoch lifted a hand and the room was still. He spoke with a terrible softness.

"Pigs at the public trough. Pigs with dirty muzzles that squeal when the ax falls. You'll find no gravy spots on my vest, Sam. But let's inspect yours—your Oregon ranch with the blooded horses, that five-bedroom home with the swimming pool—"

Kramer muttered something about shrewd investments and Murdoch's laughter was like a branding iron. "The houses and lots, Sam? Whorehouses and lots of money, you mean! I've preached caution, but you wouldn't listen, none of you. But you'll listen now, by God. Shall we review *your* honorable record of public service, Mister Mayor?"

"Please," Harkness said, swallowing. "Just tell us, Clem—who is it going to be?"

There was a roaring in my ears as I stared at Matt. He sat, chain-smoking, and his eyes held a tiny, triumphant flame. It flooded over me with a sharp, tingling pain—Matt's eternal preoccupation with the vice payoffs, the construction bids. My Sir Galahad-Benedict Arnold-bastard of a little brother.

I stared at him and his face was a study in stone. But his eyes said, *"So you know?"*

My eyes answered his. *"You think one stinking letter can smash them? You're a fool."*

His eyes insisted. *"We've just begun. Laurie's helping me. Sewer cleaners, that's us."* And, without sound or motion, he laughed.

"I'll blackmail you," I told him in silence. *"I'll use this. For me."*

"And so," Murdoch said thoughtfully, "we need someone dispensable to the organization. Someone like you, Bernard. I'm afraid you're elected."

A relieved sigh rippled around the room.

Kroll's eyes popped. "No you don't," he whispered. "You can't do it." He was glaring wildly around the table. "You can't make it stick. I've only been in this rotten mess for ten days. How can a man—"

"You accepted a city paving contract," Murdoch said icily, "subject to certain rigid specifications. A half-block of paving is already laid. Shall we examine the construction, Bernard? The hundred parts of sand to one part of cement?"

Kroll's face was yellow and old. "I'll tell them about the rest of you," he said brokenly. "I won't play patsy."

"Yes you will," Murdoch said. "Meeting's adjourned, gentlemen. Bernard, you and Norman stay. Incidentally, Tom, you'd best close down a few houses. Just for the time being." He frowned. "And break a few sergeants while you're at it. Clean up the force and all that sort of thing."

Bullock said briskly that he certainly would see to it, and they filed hastily out with much shuffling of feet and backward glances. The three of us sat alone.

"It's no good," Kroll whispered. "It's not fair. You can go to hell."

"I thought you were smart," Murdoch said with contempt. "An eighteen-month stretch for fifty thousand dollars. Look, he's astonished. He didn't know the organization takes care of its own. Fifty thousand dollars," he repeated, tasting the sound. Kroll shook his head wearily. "Deposited to your account before you leave." His words were honey and velvet. "And when you get out, Shannon will be waiting."

Kroll's mouth opened, tortured.

"She loves you," Murdoch went on, gently. "She'd run away with you now, but how far would you get? You're broke, Bernard. A girl like Shannon needs nice things, things money can buy. If you're smart you can give her those things. She's in the next room. Go to her, Bernard."

Kroll's eyes were glazed. He stared at the library door as it slowly opened.

Shannon stood there. Her hair was soft gold on her shoulders and her smile was as old as sin.

Kroll stood up, moving like a drunken man. The door closed behind them.

"Poor bastard," Murdoch yawned. "You shouldn't have come, Norman. They'll wonder why you weren't picked."

My mouth was dry. "Why wasn't I?"

"I have plans for you. After the election. Meanwhile you'll scrounge around in the gutter for pennies until I see fit to put you back on the payroll. You need disciplining." His blue stare was hypnotic.

"You're crazy!" I said. "My name isn't Kroll. I'm blowing this stinking town, right now. I've got a stake—"

"Two thousand dollars in the bank and a five-thousand-dollar car. That's a stake?"

"It's enough, you old bastard." I stood up. "So long."

He let me get to the door.

"Norman," he said tenderly.

I turned. He was toying with a deck of cards.

"Ten of my chips to one of yours, Norman. And you deal."

"You're joking!"

"No, just confident."

"And you'll let *me* deal?"

"Sit down."

I broke out the cards, peering suspiciously at the backs and corners. It was a fresh, clean deck. I took a deep breath. *All right, you cocky old idiot. You asked for it.*

"Straight draw," I said. "Joker barred."

"First," he said, amused, "give me a bill of sale for your Cad. I'll write you a check for five thousand."

I scribbled a bill of sale and tossed my car keys on the table. I bought fifty blue chips, grinning a little inside. Ten to one!

"Deal," he said.

My first hand was a pair of tens, an ace and two sixes. Murdoch passed, and I bet three blues. Murdoch carefully counted out fifty chips from his huge stack, then thirty more. "Raise you three," he said.

"Sandbagging?"

"You mind?"

"Raise *you* five more."

He called, chuckling. He drew three cards. I stood pat. "Your bet," I said tautly.

He pushed fifty blues into the pot, calmly. "You don't have it, Norman. You stood pat on two pair."

I raised him five, my face a careful mask. My insides were cold. He might have threes and my only chance was to make him run.

He called, and I laid down my two pair. I was sweating. There was over seventeen thousand dollars in the pot.

"No good," Murdoch said sadly, spreading his hand. He had three deuces. "You mustn't bluff a poor old man, Norman."

We played for six straight hours. And it was not a man I was playing, but a machine, inexorable, flawless. I waited with a sick, furious patience because I had, not one, but four aces in the hole. It had taken me five painstaking hours to thumbnail the corners imperceptibly—with an artist's skill, just enough to make the cards mine any time I wished. Eventually, he would have to take his eyes from the deck. And I waited, playing very tight, and I kept losing.

It was two o'clock in the morning. I was writing a check for my last two thousand and buying more blue chips when Shannon came in with a twisted smile.

"He got drunk," she said. "And he cried. But he'll go." She walked, unsteadily, to the sideboard and splashed Scotch into a glass. "For fifty thousand he'll go. And for me."

"Are you really going to wait for him?" My question sounded foolish, even as I asked it.

She came over and stretched out in the Morris chair at Murdoch's elbow, her green eyes infinitely wanton.

"She goes to the highest bidder," Murdoch said. "But she hates losers, Norman. Right, my dear?"

"That's right," Shannon answered listlessly.

"Deal, Norman."

I began playing with a blind, reckless fury. I drew to inside straights. I held kickers and connected. And I won the next four hands.

Murdoch's mouth was grim.

I had eight thousand dollars in front of me!

Shannon got up and crossed to the sideboard, her hips rolling like water, and for a fraction of an instant his gaze followed her. And in that instant my fingers moved with a flashing volition of their own—and the deck was ready.

I slid the deck in front of him. There was a lump in my throat. He cut, casually.

I dealt, picked up my hand. Four aces and a queen.

Murdoch passed. I gingerly bet two blues, praying. *Don't let him pass, God, please. Just give him a pair. Let him catch, just this once. Make him stay.*

He stayed. He drew one card. I drew one card.

I bet three blues and he hesitated while I slowly died inside.

"Raise," he said finally, "sixty of mine, six of yours."

My frown was worried, convincing. I called and raised ten more. And Murdoch raised again. My heart was pounding like a kettledrum. I pushed my entire stack of blues forward. "All of it," I said.

Murdoch's eyes closed. He had a trapped, pained look, but he was hooked, he had to call, and triumph was soaring through my veins like wine.

Shannon stood by the sideboard, smiling and voluptuous. Her green eyes were saying, *"My price is high."*

And my eyes said, *"I'll meet it. Blue-mink and diamonds. You're going away with me. Tonight."*

And her eyes answered, *"Anywhere, darling. Any time."*

Murdoch was shoving his chips forward in a slow agony. I was already on the road to Acapulco, Shannon warm and sleek beside me in the Cadillac. We were lying on the white sand at Acapulco and the sun was pure gold on her bare skin and her kisses were deep and full of promise. And we were having dinner on the terrace by the hotel pool and you could see the dazzling strand all the way down to the blue water, with the waves crashing silver and white lace. We were having champagne in our suite and Shannon was taking off her clothes with a lazy abandon, her eyes on mine as she pulled her gown over her head, letting it fall in a shimmering puddle around her feet

"You're called," Murdoch said.

I looked at him stupidly.

"And raised one last hundred," he said.

"I'm tapped."

"That's a nice watch."

I was laughing as I took off the watch and dropped it in the pot, laughing as I spread my four aces and began raking in that mountain of blues, over eighty thousand dollars. Murdoch's grimace was wry as he spread his hand.

"I have a straight flush, Norman."

The three, four, five, six, seven of hearts.

I sat, numb. He gathered up the pot, put my car keys in his pocket. Someone was laughing. It was Shannon. She brought me a double shot of rye. I spilled half of it trying to get it to my lips.

"You're not bad, Norman," Murdoch said thoughtfully. "Not bad for an amateur. Incidentally, I ran an El Centro gambling house before the war." He gathered up the deck, the cards passing through his fingers like water. "Come back in six months, Norman. Good night."

Shannon showed me to the front door.

"Look," I breathed. "I've got to see you. How about tomorrow?"

"All right." Her expression was searching, intent. "But it's business, darling, not pleasure. Tomorrow afternoon, five sharp." She gave me her address. "Know something? It was my idea for him to break you. I wanted you to be hungry, sweet. I've got plans for you." Her lips formed a kiss as the door closed in my face.

For a moment I stared at the door, shaking in a sick reaction. I had given up trying to understand her, this bitch with the golden body. I was staring down the flagstone steps when I saw the black Packard parked across the street. Lombard's Packard.

He had waited a long time. A big man with a grotesque white face and a sadistic smile. I was finally broke and friendless. He was going to have fun.

I was edging around the corner of the house when Lombard saw me and got out of the car. Leisurely, he started across the street, toward me. He was swinging that leather sap in his right fist.

I jumped over Murdoch's back wall, tearing my clothes and crashing through the shrubbery. I ran like hell.

11

Shannon lived in a Spanish stucco duplex on Olive Street. It was almost six o'clock when I mounted the red brick steps that evening. The door swung open before I knocked.

"You're late," Shannon said coldly.

She wore a green satin negligee, cut very low. "So those wonderful things are real, after all," I said, looking.

"Sit down, I'll get you a drink."

The quiet richness of the apartment took my breath away. It was decorated in soft green and silver. The drapes were gray velvet. A single yellow rose flared from a ruby vase on the ivory baby grand.

Shannon noticed my admiring appraisal. "Yes, darling," she said, walking into the kitchen. "The wages of sin are high."

I stood looking after her, a queer tightness in my stomach. Then I followed her into the kitchen. She was pouring Martinis, her back to me. I put both hands on her shoulders and turned her around.

She stood passive, lips gleaming wetly, a tiny flame of mockery in her green eyes. I brought my mouth down on hers and her body came alive. Her fingers were deft lightning against my shirt; then her palms were roving and electric against my bare chest. She laughed softly into my mouth. "Business, darling, remember?"

She pushed me away. "You should have been here at five." She handed me the Martini. "Clem's coming in twenty minutes."

I gulped the Martini, hating her. Shannon leaned against the kitchen table and watched. "Norm, what do you know about me?"

"That you're a very expensive whore," I said brutally. "That you hate men. Is there anything else that's important?"

She could flinch, and that, at least, was something. Then she smiled faintly. "But you want me."

I said nothing.

"Once upon a time I was nineteen." Her voice was somber. "Nice, middle-class family, nice-girl nineteen. I was a freshman at USC when I married Rudy. He was a gambler, a hustler. In some ways you're very much like him, darling."

She finished her Martini and stared moodily at the empty glass. "We moved to Vegas." Her voice was soft with memory. "Those first wonderful months when Rudy's luck was hot. He was going to take me to Paris when he made his next big killing. Then his luck went sour. He ... died."

"How?"

"None of your business. The important thing was, I didn't care after that—do you understand? For three years nothing mattered. You were right about my hating men." She shivered. "You want to know how I lived those three years?"

I didn't want to think about it. "When did you meet Murdoch?" I asked.

"Six months ago. He made it sound like a straight business proposition, me and Kroll. At first I didn't care. That was before I found out what Murdoch really was." She leaned forward, tautly. "Tell me what Lombard does."

"He makes the collections."

"From where?"

"All the places," I said slowly. "The Acey Deucey, the Golden Wheel, the bars and the cribs. Why?"

"And the basement crap games," she prodded. "Percentage?"

"Five, ten percent." What was she getting at?

"Don't forget the bookies," she continued. "He's on the move always, making the rounds. But not this week. The county attorney's here. The town's clean—for the moment. Tell me what happens when they leave."

"Let's play twenty questions," I said. "You tell me."

"All the places open up again, full blast. And Lombard makes the rounds for twenty percent, a double collection. It's Kroll's incarceration fee."

I shrugged, and she went on talking. Then my glass shattered on the linoleum floor as I stared at her in dazed horror. Because what she had in mind was insanity, death. "You're joking," I whispered.

But she was deadly serious. And she wanted such a little thing. All I had to do was hijack Lombard's big collection, seventy thousand dollars. That was all.

"You're out of your mind!" I seized her wrists. She looked away from me. "Look, baby, give me six months. They'll stick me back on the payroll. You want us both to get killed? Is that what you want?"

Her eyes focused tiredly. "A small-time grifter," she said. "I thought you were a man. Clem's coming soon. Get out of here."

I shook her. "Goddammit, *listen!* I'm going to take this town away from him, do you hear? But it takes time."

"While I wait," she said with searing bitterness, "while I let that scaly old bastard touch me, make love to me—"

"Shut up!"

"He's got skin like a lizard." She grimaced. "Dry and old. His touch makes my flesh crawl. He's got a whip in his bedroom, a silk whip. He used it on me again last night. Look."

She did something with her shoulders, and green satin whispered to the floor.

She was like the goddess Ashtoreth rising from the waves: the classic thighs, the proud, creamy shoulders, the splendid full breasts thrusting defiantly as she turned.

Then I saw them. The angry welts, scarlet and purple around her hips.

"Put that thing back on." My throat constricted.

"Look at me, Norm."

"You're crazy. *Crazy!*"

"Come here."

"Get away from me."

"In two weeks," she said huskily, "the big take." Her arms stole about my neck. "You're going to do it."

"That's murder." I was shaking. "Look, in six months—"

"Then come back in six months," she said softly. "Think of me at night, darling. Every time I kiss him, I'll be thinking of you."

I slapped her and she fell back against the kitchen sink, eyes flaring. Her right hand scrabbled across the tile. "You son of a bitch," she said, her voice a serpent's hiss. She lunged at me, holding the butcher knife low.

I pivoted, grabbing her right wrist with my right hand as I turned outwards and spun. She flew past me and slammed up against the stove, sobbing and clawing for the knife that had fallen. I kicked it away from her.

"Get out," she said in a mangled fury. "Go root for pennies, you gutless wonder. Get out!" she screamed. "The back way."

I went out into the purple twilight. As the back door slammed, I could hear her sobbing.

I don't know how long I walked the dark streets. Somewhere else in the night, a sadist with a leather sap was looking for me. Somewhere else, a bitter-eyed man named Kroll was facing eighteen months in prison for the vibrant loveliness that was Shannon Quinn.

Somewhere else, Matt was patiently gathering evidence to write the district attorney another anonymous letter about civic corruption. I thought about Matt for a long time before I walked toward City Hall.

At ten-thirty, the second floor of the building was like a tomb. The dark rows of desks were sarcophagi, hushed and brooding. I found Matt in the Municipal Utility Records section scribbling under a desk lamp with intense concentration. At the sound of my footsteps, he froze. Then his right hand blurred. I stared at the gun.

"Who's there?" he croaked.

"Put it down, Galahad." I walked into the light, and he slowly lowered the gun.

Matt's mouth worked. "You almost died just now, Norm."

I wanted to laugh, but didn't dare. His fingers kept inching toward the gun. He had found something big; it was in his quivering smile, his shaking fingers.

"You won't find anything," I grunted with elaborate unconcern. "What kind of dummies do you think they are?" He relaxed, warily. "I need two hundred bucks," I said. "And I need a job."

"What's wrong with the rigs?" He thought about it. "Oh, I forgot, you're too good to get oil on your hands. All right, Norm, the owner of the Acey Deucey owes me a favor. Wait till I call you."

I said fine and he gave me a hundred. "This is quits," he said. "You never saw me tonight."

"Sure, whatever you say. Good hunting."

I walked out, half-expecting a bullet in the back. My own brother. It made me chuckle, thinking of him up there nights, punishing himself, grimly excavating the skeletons. The nicest part of it was, he was working for me and didn't know it. Later he would wish he had used the gun.

The next ten days were hell. I paced my apartment and waited for Matt's call. I drank a lot, and thought about Shannon. A tight, raw stillness hung over Mason Flats. The town was clean. The county attorney's boys—big, soft-spoken men—were here. They probed and found a ten-cent stud game in back of Bud Tolliver's poolroom and a Mexican madam with three girls in a tarpaper shack on Orange Street. They were satisfied. Finally they left.

Matt phoned me on the tenth day. The town was alive again. I went down to the Acey Deucey and shook hands with Frenchy LeJohn the owner, and he treated me with hostile politeness until I showed him what I could do with a deck of cards. Then he thawed and said ninety a week, instead of sixty. It didn't matter. What mattered was not thinking, being an automaton from seven at night until five in the morning. I needed to keep my nose clean. I had big plans and they didn't include playing the fool for any woman. So I was a good dealer and tried not to think about Shannon. On the fourth night she came in.

Like a queen she strode past the onyx bar and the green roulette tables. Kroll was with her. I kept dealing, blindly, as they came over to my table and sat down. "Let's make it a good night, darling," she said to Kroll. "A night to remember."

I dealt. They both lost. They kept losing and after a time Kroll went over to the bar, wearily. Shannon sat alone, opposite me. "His trial comes up next week," she murmured. "Let him win, just a little."

The cards felt moist and sticky. "It's no good," I said. "I won't do it. Stay away from me."

She said softly, "Clem told me to be very nice to him tonight."

"You slut."

"Lombard starts collections in two nights," she said.

My relief man finally came. I told Frenchy I was sick and he gave me the evening off. On the way home I bought a fifth of rye. It didn't help.

She came back the next night, alone. She played roulette and won and came over to my table after a time and played dollar chips. When the other players drifted away, she said, soft and urgently, "Tomorrow night ... the big collection. They'll start here, at the center of town. You can wait for them at Amy's Roadhouse, on the Flats. Slade stays in the car guarding the loot while Lombard goes in for the individual collections. You can take Slade first, darling."

I dealt, silently, not looking at her.

The next night she came again, with Kroll. They sat at the bar. Once I heard her laughter, high and silvery, and I shivered. She wore a red chiffon evening gown and her back and shoulders were tanned a creamy gold.

Now they were passing my table. Kroll said hello to me and asked how things were. I said fine. They went to the roulette layout and for the next two hours my table was filled. Then the cards ran cold and my players drifted away, one by one. I sat alone, praying for my relief.

Shannon came over. "Deal," she said.

I dealt and she leaned forward, giving me an excellent view of her breasts.

"After Kroll's conviction, Clem's taking me to Acapulco for awhile."

"That's nice," I said, and it came out like a snarl.

"Two glorious weeks. And it could be you, sweet. It's still not too late; Lombard won't hit Amy's for an hour." Kroll joined us. "It's late, honey. Shall we?"

"Certainly, darling." She beamed up at him as his hands rested on her shoulders possessively. His wrinkled brown hands.

My relief man finally came.

I watched Shannon and Kroll cash in their chips. My stomach was churning uncontrollably. I turned, threading my way through the crap tables, and got to the side door just in time.

It was dark outside, and still. I vomited quietly on the flagstone terrace.

12

"But *mon ami*, you were off last night."

"So I got the flu. I'm sick."

We were in Frenchy's office. Now he leaned forward, nostrils twitching and round eyes narrowed. "You have been drinking."

"So?"

He spread his hands. "*Mon Dieu*, you know the rules. One cannot risk drunken croupiers, dealers—"

"Damn your rules! I'm fired, is that it?"

He looked miserable. "Rules are rules."

It was perfect. It had been necessary to waste precious moments at the bar, but it would have looked dangerously coincidental to quit the next day. Being fired was ideal.

And I still had thirty minutes to walk over to Orange Street, to hurry past the squalid shacks and garbage-choked alleys, past the dark rail junction and out to the main highway, toward the roadhouse.

Amy's place was an institution in Mason Flats. It stood just outside city limits and had survived brief morality purges and county reforms ever since I could remember. Amy bought new Fords for half the police force each Christmas.

I moved quietly through the parked cars in back, searching the front driveway with the terrible fear that I was too late. Then I saw it, the black Packard sedan parked arrogantly by the entrance. Slade, a plainclothesman on the vice squad, sat at the wheel, chain-smoking. On the front seat next to him was a briefcase containing almost seventy thousand dollars.

I found a rubbish barrel filled with empty whisky bottles. I grabbed one and ran around to the front driveway, then weaved toward the Packard with my head down, muttering in guttural Spanish.

"*No tengo dinero por las muchachas. Es muy triste.*"

Slade sniggered. "That's real tough, Pedro. Why don't you ask her for credit?"

Drunkenly, I staggered sideways, off balance, weaving in closer to the car.

"Scram, Pedro." Slade's voice was like a curt whiplash. "Go home and sleep it off."

"*Quiere beber?*" I giggled, thrusting the bottle at him. I held the bottle tightly.

"Beat it," he said; then his face paled in startled recognition. His right hand darted to his shoulder holster as I hit him just behind the ear. He sagged against the horn and the sound blared through the night. I was swearing prayerful little obscenities as I got him off that horn and down on the floor and eased myself behind the wheel. I was groping for his shoulder holster when Lombard's footsteps sounded on the graveled walk.

I slouched behind the wheel, Slade's hat tipped over my eyes. Icy perspiration crawled down my spine. The footsteps came closer, paused; then the back door opened and the rear seat creaked heavily.

"Wake up, stupid," Lombard wheezed. "Let's roll."

I drove down the driveway to the main road, my brain spinning like a broken flywheel. If only he'd waited another ten seconds! I wondered how long it would take to reach down and grab Slade's gun.

"She damn near died," Lombard said happily, "but she came through. They'll kiss us tonight, baby. Guess how much the take was!"

I grunted, and nothing changed in Lombard's voice; he kept on chatting away. Unaccountably, though, my hair began to bristle. I stole a glance in the rearview mirror. There was a dark blur of movement.

My reflexes saved me. The blow glanced off the left side of my head and the universe filled with colored fire.

The blows rained on my head and shoulders like hail as I ducked down in the seat and jammed the accelerator to the floor. We were doing sixty, seventy, and cold metal jammed into the back of my neck and Lombard shouted, "Slow down!"

"Go to hell!"

Stalemate.

We roared through the night at eighty miles an hour as the wind screamed past the windows and Lombard was swearing, "You son of a bitch, you dumb idiot bastard." He tried to shove the gun through my spine. "I'll count five. So help me, I'll count five and that's it. One, two, three ..."

He meant it. He was crazed beyond fear. He would blow my head off and taken his chances. We were still on the main highway parallel to town, and the derrick jungle was thinning.

"Four," Lombard said, and I slammed on the brakes, skidding all over the highway. I yanked the wheel hard to the left as we spun and the Packard screamed like a frightened horse.

We jumped the road.

I slammed across the seat against the right door. There was the tearing of metal and smashing of glass as I clawed at the handle, and then abruptly, the door pitched open and I was hurtling through cold night air and the world snuffed out in glass and darkness.

I lay on my back looking at stars. They were thin and peaceful and a tattered fragment of moon gave enough light to see the Packard ten yards away, silent.

I tried to move, on one knee. Agony thundered along my right side. At least one rib was broken and I could not see out of my right eye. I touched my face and my fingers came away wet and sticky.

I crawled toward the Packard, my breath a dry sob. Lombard was in the back seat. Waiting for his target to come to him.

Something moved. The right rear door creaked and opened. Something flopped heavily to the ground. There was a groan. I got to my feet and floundered forward, pain like a hot knife in my side, toward the limp bulk on the ground—a wheezing thing that stared up at me through a mask of blood, cursing through broken teeth.

I kicked Lombard as hard as I could. He kept cursing in a dull monotone as I kicked him in the head again and again. Finally the cursing stopped.

It took me ten minutes to drag him, somehow, back to the Packard. I finally got him in the back seat, pushing him like a bag of flour, and fell on top of him, retching, while bells jangled in my brain.

Lombard's briefcase was in back. I hefted it, and peered over into the front seat. Slade was still there, crumpled up on the floorboards. Then I crawled out and went around to inspect the front of the car. The grille was a shambles, as was the right fender where it had sideswiped the base of the derrick.

The derrick was an old one, deserted, and the storage tank was thick with rust. This was the south corner of the flats where a few ill-starred wildcats had been drilled six months ago, and quickly abandoned.

There was a sump in back of the rig frosted with dust and sand. A fine, big sump.

It took half an hour to adjust the idling screw on the Packard's carburetor, working in darkness and searing my fingers on the hot motor. The horrible part of it was Lombard's coming alive again, his bubbling moans from the back seat.

But I got it set at fast idle finally, got behind the wheel and kicked her over. The car lurched along the dirt road around the derrick, and I threw myself out as it kept going.

The car was like a sinking cruiser. There was one frantic moment when it hesitated, half over the brink, the hood buried in stagnant oil. That was when the rear door flew open and I saw Lombard trying to claw his way out as the Packard slid grandly over the edge.

It was a good, deep sump. But I waited, kneeling, my teeth bared like an animal's—waited with a sick, hideous certainty for Lombard to rise bubbling and wheezing out of that slime, to come and get me. But there was nothing. The wind was a soft dirge.

Five miles back to town and that briefcase weighed a ton. I shambled along the highway, pain molten in my side.

The stars were dead and cold as I reeled down Olive Street. A false dawn silvered the sky as I hammered on Shannon's door.

She wore that green satin negligee and she looked tousled with sleep, and lovely. Her face drained white with shock as I grinned at her and stepped inside. The oil-slimed briefcase dropped to the carpet and she knelt, clutching it, fumbling with the clasps.

"Norm," she said, and she was crying, laughing and crying. "My darling," she said, and it was a benediction. "You did it, lover! Was it bad, darling? Was it terribly bad? It's over now, sweet, isn't it? All over. Sit down, I'll get you a drink."

I stumbled toward the bathroom, nerves singing with fatigue, and tore off my clothes as I went. They were a mess. Blood on my coat, blood on my shirt, great rents in my trousers.

I was busy swabbing the cuts on my swollen face with iodine and cursing when Shannon came in. She handed me a tumbler half-filled with whisky, and a lighted cigarette. Then turned the shower up full and closed the bathroom door gently behind her.

The whisky was good, the hot shower was good, and a steamy lassitude crept through me like warm fog as my shrieking nerves became still. Then the cold water, the icy shock of coming alive again.

I toweled myself vigorously and combed my hair. I'd have the ribs taped tomorrow. The face in the mirror was bruised and incredibly tired, but it was my face again, not a thing from a delirium. I knotted the towel around my waist and opened the bathroom door.

The living room was dark and still. I padded along the hall and she was in the bedroom.

The empty briefcase lay on the rug.

Money was scattered on the floor, on the yellow bedspread. More money than I had ever seen. Twenties, tens, fifties, crumpled in green profusion. Shannon knelt in the center of the bed, running her hands through the bills, sifting them over her breasts, crooning softly, eyes closed.

Then she opened her eyes and smiled. "Come here," she said. Her body was alabaster and ivory. She swept one leg along the coverlet and money cascaded through the air.

"Come here," she said, and her breasts were full, amazingly sculptured, perfect. "Be neat, darling," she whispered. "Hang the towel on the doorknob. Hurry, lover. Please hurry."

I threw the towel on the floor.

I did not hurry.

13

Shannon's clock radio woke me at nine. "Wake up, darling. Breakfast."

She wore a filmy pink housecoat that contrasted wonderfully with her golden hair and made her look about fourteen years old. I sat drinking coffee, listening to her talk animatedly about Paris, and trying to analyze the drowning sensation that hit me every time I looked at her.

This wasn't love. Love is something warm and human, like the feeling I still had for Laurie. This was a stark compulsion, chemotropic. For her I had killed two men.

Shannon was scrambling around the rug on hands and knees, picking up money. I tried to feel contempt for her, and couldn't. I tried to feel guilt, shame. There was nothing. Slade and Lombard were two-dimensional memories, unreal.

"Norm." There was something in Shannon's voice that made me spill my coffee. "Help me find the rest of it."

We hunted for fifteen minutes. We tore the bed apart and looked inside the empty briefcase. Then, for the third time we counted it. We stared at each other with a hard, mutual suspicion.

"Eight thousand dollars," she said. "Where's the rest of it, darling?"

I shook my head helplessly. "That's it."

"You're a liar."

"Dammit, there was only the briefcase—" My mouth hung open, foolishly. Fool, fool! Not to have remembered that Slade also had a briefcase on the front seat, not to have realized that Lombard's satchel contained only the last payoff, from Amy's.

"It's still in the sump." I felt sick. "Probably fifty grand, at least."

I told her about it as she lay across the bed smoking, her green eyes half-shut. "You could go back, Norm."

"Not for a million! Even if I could find the right place."

"Eight stinking thousand," she said.

"It would go a long way in Mexico. We could live like kings—"

"For a year." She laughed without sound. "Eighteen months, maybe. Then?"

The phone on the night table rang. She picked it up listlessly. "Hello? ... Yes, Bernard. Of course, honey. Tonight? ... Fine." I made frantic motions, and she smiled at me wretchedly. "See you at seven, lover," she said, and then hung up.

"You goddamned tramp," I said, "we're going away, remember?"

"*You're* going away." She threw the money on the bed. "Take it all. You've earned it."

"Listen, we can skip to Mexico! Cuernavaca, maybe."

"I can just see us," she said dully. "Six good months. Then I go back to shaking my hips in a night club. Some cheap Mexican dive where they sit, fat and greasy, and throw pesos at you. But you'll have big deals cooking, oh, yes! *Step right up, amigos, guess which shell the little pea is under! For two dollars extra you can sleep with my wife.*"

I grabbed her roughly, and kissed her. She was limp, uncaring. Her lips were cold. I thought about Kroll pawing her, making love to her, and I wanted to scream.

"Stop it, Norm." Her eyes were wet. "For what it's worth, I love you. But it's no good, darling, not the way we like to live."

She was right. That eight thousand might just as well have been eight cents.

For the next few weeks, until his trial was over, she would be Bernard Kroll's consigned property. After he was safely in prison, she would revert to Murdoch. He could afford her; I couldn't. I thought about these things as I got dressed. I thought about Matt.

"You'd better burn that briefcase," I said, picking up a handful of twenties. "I'll take these for expenses. Hide the rest of it. The council boys will figure Lombard and Slade got greedy."

"Try to understand, Norm."

"I've got something in mind," I said, kissing her. "I'll phone you this afternoon."

The first thing I did was go home and shave and put on a clean suit. The second thing was to go downtown to a doctor and get my ribs taped. Then I walked fast, seven blocks over to North Street, to Matt's flat.

He had found something big at City Hall, and he'd had two full weeks to work on it. By now it would be ripe and rotting. It would not be in his desk at City Hall, but in his apartment, carefully hidden. I went around to the empty alley, pried his window screen loose, and eased myself inside.

One hour later I stood scowling at the shambles—the gutted mattress, the bureau drawers lying on the floor. It *had* to be here. I looked again through the bookcase. I riffled through Plato, Shakespeare, the Bible. There was nothing.

Then I had an idea.

Fifteen minutes later I found Matt in the Tax Records section at City Hall. I caught his eye and he came slowly over, past the clattering typewriters and busy file clerks.

"You got a minute?"

He nodded, frowning. We walked down the hall to the lavatory. It was deserted; I looked in the booths to make sure.

"It's good-bye." I extended my hand. "I'm leaving town."

He took my hand warily. "How come?"

"I got fired last night. There's nothing left in this crummy town for me. It's just that ... well, you've been damned decent and I wanted to warn you."

"Warn me?" His chin jutted forward. He reminded me of a great blond bear hearing a hunter crashing through the thicket.

"I was over at the *Clarion* this morning," I told him. "Murdoch didn't have a job open. But before I went in his office, I did a little keyhole listening. What kind of filth have you been into?" His jaw muscles clenched and I added hastily, "It's none of my business ... but I heard Mayor Harkness and Tom Bullock talking. About you. They're scared green. Certain records are missing from the Utility Records file."

I held my breath. He had been in the utilities section that night. If I'd guessed wrong, he'd laugh in my face now and walk out.

I hadn't guessed wrong.

"What else did you hear?" Matt moistened his lips.

"When you leave this building, you'll have a plainclothesman on your tail. One of Tom Bullock's Gestapo." I shrugged. "Like I said, it's your business. So long."

Now he'd snap at the bait. He would tell me where the records were hidden, tell me to take them to the county attorney, quick. But he simply clapped me on the shoulder and said thanks, and not to take any wooden nickels, and walked out.

I swore.

Two minutes later I sauntered by Tax Records. Matt was at a corner desk. He picked up the phone and spoke guardedly, eyes darting. I waved at him as I went by outside.

He hadn't dialed. He'd asked the operator for an extension. That meant somebody in the building. It had to be Laurie.

I hurried down the steps of the building, cursing myself for not having thought of it before. I cut left down an alley, running, and the pain in my side crescendoed into agony. I slowed to a walk, sick and dizzy. Thank God she lived just five blocks away.

I got to the alley corner in time to see Laurie's little convertible come to a quick stop across the street, in front of her apartment. I watched her hurry up the stairs to the second landing. I counted to ten, slowly, giving her time to unlock the door and go inside; then I trotted across the street and took those steps three at a time.

My timing was perfect. She was just coming out of her apartment when I got to the top of the landing. She saw me and froze, one hand still on the doorknob. In her other hand there was a large manila envelope.

"Going somewhere?" I asked cheerfully. Laurie's face was white. "Let's postpone that little trip to the county seat, shall we?" I pushed her inside and slammed the door.

"Get out," she said.

"Give," I ordered, balling my right fist. It never occurred to her to scream. She stared at me like a snake-hypnotized bird as she slowly backed away. For just one instant her eyes flicked to the window, and then I moved in and struck.

She crumpled, and I caught the folder before it reached the floor. I leafed through it and caught my breath. This was big. Far bigger than I had dared hope.

Laurie shuddered, slowly got to her feet, then flung herself upon me like a wildcat—scratching, clawing, raking my face with her nails. I slapped her halfway across the room.

"Sorry," I said. "But we took our chances, didn't we? We tilt at windmills and break our little lance."

I found some nylons in her bureau and tied her tightly and efficiently with them as she crucified me with her eyes.

"You're rotten," she said. "I never knew a man could be so rotten."

"You've got to work at it," I said. "*Where're the copies?*"

Her surprised contempt was genuine.

"Just wanted to make sure." I tied her ankles and gagged her. "If you work at it, you'll be free in six hours."

I walked out of her flat with the manila envelope, whistling.

It was two-thirty when I left the photostat shop. Five minutes later I was at the bank, renting a safe-deposit box for the originals. Ten minutes after that I was walking through the City Hall lobby. Matt gave me a frightened look as I passed by Tax Records. I winked at him.

The mayor's office was on the second floor. His secretary was frigidly polite. "Sorry, but His Honor is in conference all afternoon and—"

"They're in conference about me," I smiled, thinking about Murdoch squirming, trying to explain Lombard's disappearance to a raging bunch of councilmen. "Matter of fact they're waiting for me right now."

I walked into the mayor's private office.

The big four sat there: Murdoch, Mayor Harkness, Bullock and Kramer. They glared at me as I walked to hizzoner's desk and threw down the stack of photostats with a crash.

"Read them and weep, gentlemen."

"Throw him out," Bullock said. Kramer got up and started toward me. Murdoch merely looked irritated.

"Holy God," Harkness said. It was a prayer.

Kramer hesitated. The mayor's face was ashen. He leafed through the photostats, his lips moving, and Murdoch craned his neck to look. So did Bullock and Kramer.

They read and they looked at me, then at each other. Then they read again.

Murdoch's face was bloodless. "I underestimated you, Norman."

"Where did you get these?" Kramer whispered.

"What's wrong with everybody?" Bullock demanded. He was only the chief of police; this espionage stuff was beyond him. "So there's pictures of a torn-up road, pages of figures. So?"

"So the figures are double-entry water-utilities audits," I said. "And there are obviously several thousand dollars in discrepancies. And the dates on the accounts payable sheet just *happen* to coincide with the dates of bank deposits made by one Sam Kramer." I coughed, delicately. "They've been holding out on you, Tom. That photo of torn paving is ground under repair right now, the current low bid for a new water main down Center Street. The specs, you'll notice, call for three-foot depth instead of eight inches. The low bid was taken by Hogarth Construction, of which Harkness happens to own—"

"Shut up!" The veins in Harkness' forehead were red streaks.

Bullock turned on Kramer like an enraged animal. "You greedy, conniving louse, it's all your fault! You got us into this! You'll step off alone!"

"I didn't!" Kramer was a terrified pig, squealing in the vise. "If you hadn't run the houses so wide open—"

"You maggots," Murdoch said wearily. "You poor, blind, greedy maggots. Bleed them white, Norman. I want to hear them howl."

"Wrong," I said. "Nobody loses a penny."

"Then what *do* you want?" Mayor Harkness demanded.

"Ten percent. Of everything."

"But that's all there is!" Kramer gasped. "Besides, Lombard and Slade have skipped."

I shrugged. "What about Kroll's fifty thousand?"

"We've got to raise it out of our own pockets," Bullock spat. "Damn Lombard!"

"Wait a moment." Murdoch's eyes were frosty blue marbles, searching and suspicious. "How did you know last night's collection was to go to Kroll?"

My grin felt frozen. "Guessed. Incidentally, if you've got any ideas about killing me, the originals of these photostats are in the possession of a very dear friend who lives at the county seat. Once a week I mail a registered letter. Should I fail to mail that letter, the county attorney will see these originals. Immediately."

They glared with baffled hatred, and Murdoch said sharply, "I've played poker with him and I can tell he's lying. In the first place he hasn't any friends, and in the second place it's a bluff."

I smiled at them. "It's not," I said. "But even if it was, you can't afford to call, can you?"

Bullock shook his head listlessly. "What's with this ten percent?"

"Simple. We up the total take to twenty percent. I get half, you get half."

That started it off. They beat their breasts and howled. They said the houses couldn't stand the strain. I shrugged. They pointed out that I was killing the goose that laid the golden eggs. I inquired if they would rather reduce their end of it to five percent, and they subsided, muttering. Murdoch said my greed would destroy me, and I beamed at him. I picked up the phone and dialed.

"Hello," I said, looking at Murdoch. "Shannon? It's Norm, honey ... Everything's fine. Get rid of Kroll early." Murdoch's eyes were blind, shocked. "... Damn right it's a celebration! I'll explain tonight."

I hung up and clapped Murdoch on the shoulder. "Like you said, Clem, she goes to the highest bidder."

He didn't answer. They were studies in dejection, all of them. Murdoch stared at me, suddenly old and tired.

"Tom," I said, "we'd better hold my brother incommunicado for a few days. The minute he finds I stole these he'll run straight to the district attorney."

Bullock's little mustache bristled. "You mean he—"

"He's got ideals," I said. "Book him on an open charge. Tomorrow I'll see him, talk some sense into him."

Bullock grabbed the phone and growled into it. It was five o'clock, quitting time for all the public servants. Matt would be leaving City Hall any minute.

I went to the window, savoring the evening breeze, looking down at the glowing web of neon lights on Center Street. Then I saw Matt hurrying down the steps, glancing nervously at the two plainclothesmen behind him.

Matt walked fast. The plainclothesmen followed him. Matt began to run.

They caught him at the corner. I closed my eyes.

After a moment I turned around and said, "Break out the bottle, mayor. We'll have a celebration drink." There was a sour bile-taste in my mouth. "I've got plans for this town. Big plans."

14

That first hour was the best. That golden hour in Harkness' office—the feeling of power sweeping through me like a hot wind as I told them the way it was going to be. They were sheep—Kramer, Harkness, Bullock—sheep that listened raptly, and smiled and poured more whisky. Only Murdoch sat bleak and withdrawn, the deposed emperor.

"You boys are behind the times," I told Bullock. "Mason Flats is fifty thousand, and growing! Read the paper. There's talk in Sacramento of running the new state highway through here. Did I say three more cribs? I meant five! And it's just the beginning. Did you ever hear of the numbers racket?"

They had, vaguely. I outlined it for them—the pennies, the volume, the way every corner cigar store was a potential source of revenue. How there would be just so many brokers, and we could allocate territories, and the thing would spread like wildfire. Then I brought up the dope angle, and Harkness got up, sweating. "He'll ruin us all," he bleated. "Count me out. He's insane! I'll resign quietly."

I slammed him back into his chair so hard his teeth rattled. "You goddamn hick," I choked furiously. "You stupid small-town mouse! Vice is big business. Nobody resigns. Everybody plays ball or everybody gets smeared. You all step off together."

I told them what a dozen reliable pushers could do; how there was a loss at first when you had to give it away in order to hook your joy-popper. "After you get him up to three caps a day, *then* soak him."

Kramer leaned forward, his dark eyes gleaming. "You can set this up, all by yourself?"

"All by myself." They sighed and relaxed. "And all you'll have to do," I added, "is spend the take."

Bullock pointed out that a large proportion of wetbacks rolled their own already, and I pointed out that tea was nothing, very little profit and too much risk. Kramer said, fascinated, "Where did you pick this stuff up?"

Something stirred in Murdoch's expression. He got up stiffly, congratulated me upon my vision, and wished us all good night.

They begged me to outline it again. I did. I told them this small-time penny ante crap was over, that Mason Flats was on the map and the melon was juicy enough for everybody. We were drinking a toast to that when the phone rang. Bullock answered.

"Hello," he said. "What?" His eyes slid away from mine. "Keep him there. I'll call you later." He hung up sheepishly. "The boys got a mite rough with your brother. They took him to the hospital with a broken collar bone."

My fine mood went to hell. I said slowly, "Keep him in a private ward, under sedation. I'll have a talk with him in the morning."

Bullock said fine. We arranged another meeting for tomorrow afternoon. I was in.

I walked the six blocks to Laurie's flat in a tired daze, trying to think of some way to keep Matt quiet without killing him.

I could frame him.

Chronologically, part of those water utilities shortages matched the time Matt had spent as assistant city auditor. The debit for this month was roughly three thousand dollars. Why not bank the equivalent sum in Matt's name and bring the ledger entry dates forward to coincide? Circumstantial, but it would be damning. I walked faster—and stopped dead in front of Laurie's apartment. The upstairs lights were on and Murdoch was slowly descending the steps.

"Rather unchivalrous to keep her trussed up all afternoon, Norman." His smile was cold venom. "We had a very interesting chat about you."

"Stop plotting," I said. "You can still play God with the city council. All I want is my share. Within a month—"

"You won't live that long, Norman. Good night."

He walked briskly down the block and I stared after him a moment before I hurried upstairs. The front door was unlocked. I opened it. Laurie looked bleakly at me from the sofa.

"What did he want, Laurie?"

"Where's Matt?" she asked.

"He's in the hospital," I said, watching her face whiten, "and he'll get killed unless you keep your mouth shut." I told her what would happen unless she played along, and she lit a cigarette with shaking fingers. But she did not cry. I admired her for that.

"What did Murdoch want?"

"Information," she said with weary contempt. "Your past background. I told him you were some sort of grifter in Los Angeles. Strictly small-time gutter stuff."

My chuckle sounded forced and weak. Murdoch was grasping at straws. Laurie gazed at her cigarette. "My fault," she said softly. "Matt got into this cesspool because of me." She looked at me, her eyes wet. "Did you know that? That I used him? Not because I wanted to clean up the town. Because I wanted to hurt you. God, the nights I've stared at the ceiling, hating you." She laughed harshly.

"Look, I'll make it up to you. If it's money—"

"Please go away," she said.

I arrived at Shannon's apartment a little after ten. She was ecstatic over the magnum of champagne and we had quite a party. But I was worried about Murdoch. And I kept remembering Laurie's stricken face and a strange jealousy toward Matt tore at me. Shannon noticed it.

"Darling, you're not very ... wanton, tonight."

"I'm tired."

"Poor darling, I'm a demanding bitch. There. And there. Better?"

"Fine."

"I love you," she said.

We finally slept. My dreams were vague and horrible.

"Norm."

I sat up, bathed in cold sweat. Shannon was sitting tensely at the foot of the bed. She handed me a lighted cigarette. "You kept yelling," she breathed. "You kept yelling for a girl named Laurie."

I chuckled uneasily. "Go back to sleep."

But when I finally dozed off she was still sitting there like a sleek, jealous cat.

Next morning I went down to the hospital. Matt's room was on the second floor. The plainclothesman at the door nodded politely and let me inside.

"Hi, soldier."

Matt was propped up in bed, very pale, with one arm and shoulder in a cast. "Thought you were leaving town."

"They wanted me to talk some sense into your fat head. They want to make a deal."

"What kind of deal?" He was watching me with a strange, distant smile.

"Money," I said cautiously. "Five thousand, maybe. You and Laurie could go away, make a fresh start—"

"You fingered me, Norm, didn't you?" There was no anger in his voice, no scorn, only weariness.

"All right," I said. "But it was for your own good. Listen, if you don't play along, they'll smash you. They'll deposit money in your bank account, a deposit to match those utilities shortages. Listen—"

"No deal," he said, leaning back on the pillow and closing his eyes. "Get out, Norm."

Two hours later I walked into the bank and deposited three thousand dollars in Matt's account. I kept telling myself it was strictly a precaution, that Matt would change his mind. But I knew he wouldn't. Then I thought about Shannon and felt a little better.

That afternoon I met with Kramer and Bullock at City Hall. They had thought things over. They were worried, skeptical that I could deliver.

I pounded on the desk and said they were frightened old women, that I'd handle the delivery end in my own way. "And don't worry about Matt," I told Kramer, showing him the deposit slip in Matt's name. "We've got a mortal lock on him."

Kramer looked at me with respect. "Very sharp. When are you going after the first batch of ... ah ... merchandise?"

"You mean Heroin?" I enjoyed watching him flinch. "Tonight." Then I asked how Murdoch was taking it.

"He left town last night." Bullock was nervous. "Any idea why?"

I had, but it was ridiculous. Still, it wouldn't hurt to have an ally. When Kramer went back to his own office, I said to Bullock, "I've got a feeling Harkness is going to resign soon. He's weak, afraid. Have you thought about the mayoralty, Tom?"

"You know Clem," he said, trying to conceal his longing. "He thinks I'm just a cop. Kramer's next in line."

"Maybe not," I said, watching the idea sink into him and take hold. "Clem can be handled. You and I could make a pretty good thing of this town, Tom. Think about it."

He would lie awake nights thinking about it, I knew. And without realizing it, he would be a little more respectful toward me, unconsciously associate me with survival. That was important. I told him not to worry about Murdoch and to phone me at the Caesar Hotel in Tijuana if anything happened in the next few days.

Later in the afternoon I bought a Lincoln convertible. It was black and low, with beautiful snow-white trim. It was a surprise for Shannon. I phoned her and said, "Pack your things, angel. Tell that damned Kroll you're going upstate for a week to visit a sick aunt. We're going south of the border."

Those first three days in Tijuana. The sleepy-faced street peddlers following us like harpies. Everywhere the seething undercurrent of greed, the brown hands clutching for the *tourista*, for his Yankee dollars. Shannon, drunk in our hotel suite at dawn, alone and weeping. Weeping because I prowled the midnight streets, the flyblown bars, alone. I was looking for a man called El Gordito. Angelo Ventresca had once told me about El Gordito. "Anything for a price," Angelo had said. "Women, horse, anything."

It was like that for three days—the hundred tiny bribes, the impassive brown faces, the negative shake of heads. I felt baffled, furious. I was handling this like some punk amateur. Ultimately, I would ask the wrong bartender and wind up in some fetid Mexican jail.

We tried Caliente on the fourth day. Shannon loved Caliente with its dog races and cockfights and horse races at which you always lost. She would swear and tear up her tickets as the horses passed the home stretch in golden thunder. We lost a thousand dollars in two days. We drank too much, made too much love in the tropical nights. I discovered a wild insecurity in Shannon. She was stiflingly possessive. She had a habit of kissing me awake at dawn and asking me if I really loved her. She dulled the edges of my perception, almost making me forget why I had come to Mexico.

Then on the sixth day, I found Rita.

We were at a Rosarita Beach hotel. Shannon drowsed next to me on the salt-white sand, glistening with sun-tan oil. "You're like a caged leopard," she complained. "Lie down, and tell Shannon about Paris."

This Paris thing was an obsession with her. I knotted my white terrycloth robe with savage jerks, wanting to stuff sand into her mouth.

"I'm going into the bar. I've got to think."

I walked past the coca palms by the pool, past the bronzed, laughing volleyball players, and into the hotel bar. Big dealer Sands! I thought about the wild promises I'd made to Kramer and Bullock, and I wanted to vomit. If I came back to town empty-handed, they would investigate, find out about the safe-deposit box, learn that I had bluffed about having a friend in the county attorney's office. When that happened, they would stamp me out like an annoying cockroach. I sat at the bar and shivered. Then I looked up and saw her.

She sat alone by the terrace window overlooking the ocean, fondling her Daiquiri. Her body was ripe and full, the arrogant badge of her profession. Her eyes were hot and black, roving. They met mine. She smiled, moistened her lips nervously.

She was obviously a hustler, but that part of it didn't matter. What mattered was that long-sleeved cocktail dress she was wearing in this heat, and the tiny pin-point pupils of her eyes.

I went over to her table, trying to grin. "Waiting for somebody?"

"Not now." A slow professional smile.

She was high all right, but not on liquor. She had it, the big habit. It was in her too shrill laughter, and in those eyes with the contracted pupils, eyes that had dark circles under them.

"The name is Rita," she said softly.

Her room was on the second floor. She shut the door, smiling vacantly, and swayed toward me. "Honey, you won't mind giving me my present now? It's just that—"

I laid a twenty-dollar bill on the dresser. "Take it off," I said. "Just the dress."

Her smile faltered. "Just the dress, honey?"

I grabbed her by the wrist and flung her, sprawling, on the bed. I held her like that, my fingers clenched in her hair, and her eyes were wild with fear.

"You didn't say it was going to be like that," she whispered. "The house dick's my friend—goddammit you're tearing my *sleeve*—"

I slowly brought her bare left arm around. We both stared at the blotchy forearm, at the tiny red kisses of the hypodermic.

"Where did you get it?" I asked her.

"None of your damned business!" She tried to bite me. I held her spread-eagled on the bed, grinning down into her panicky face.

"Don't say vitamins or cold shots or morphine," I said. "Not with that arm, baby. Or those eyes. You had a lift not one hour ago. How many caps you shooting a day—five, six? Look, I just want to make a buy. A big buy."

A choking spasm went through her. All at once she went limp. "Is that all? Just a buy? You're not a Fed?"

"This is Mexico," I reminded her, getting up. I went over to the dresser and placed another twenty on top of the first one. "Well?"

"Why didn't you just ask me?" she said sullenly, massaging her wrist. "I hate rough stuff."

"You were high. You would have laughed in my face. It takes shock. Two to one you need another fix, right now."

Her nod was very tired.

After a time, she began talking.

15

When I left Rita's room I was whistling. I went downstairs. Shannon was no longer on the beach. I looked around the pool and in the bar, and finally stopped whistling. I went upstairs to our suite.

She was still in her white satin bikini, sitting cross-legged on the bed. As I came in and closed the door, she gave me a bright twisted smile.

"You weren't gone long," she said. "How was she, darling?"

At first glance she didn't look drunk. Then I saw the empty pint on the rug, the pint that had been full this morning. There were tearstains on her cheeks, and then her right hand slid beneath the pillow and came up holding a tiny automatic.

"I saw you go upstairs with that slut." Shannon's voice was flat, utterly drained of emotion. "You lied to me, darling."

I couldn't speak. The gun was a pitiful toy, a .22 caliber pearl-handled boudoir special, but at five feet quite capable of perforating my skull. This was crazy!

"Jealousy's all right in its place," I tried to smile, feeling my lips twitch, "but this was business. I never touched her."

"Get into the bathroom." She got off the bed, swaying on her feet.

I started around the bed, trying to explain, talking very fast, and she said, "In the bathroom. Hurry."

The gun prodded my spine. I wheeled. My right elbow caught her flush on the temple.

For just one agonizing moment she teetered blindly backwards, the gun swinging up at my face; then she slumped to the rug. I was breathing hard as I recovered the gun. I wanted to break her neck, but mingled with my rage was a queer, excited pride that she could be so jealous over me. I picked her up gently and laid her on the bed. Her eyelids fluttered, opened. She turned her head away and burst into tears.

I let her cry it out on my shoulder. She cried for ten full minutes. After a time she said in a small, tortured voice, "It was four years ago, in Vegas. Rudy and I had been married a few months. I loved him terribly. He had Irish-blue eyes and a sad smile and the gentle white hands of a gambler. He used to talk about making his big killing, how we'd go to Paris ..."

Her voice broke and she turned her head away. Then she went on, rapidly.

"Sol owned half the club. Fat Solly with his golden smile and the way he had of looking at you that made you want to take a bath. Rudy played with Sol, day and night. Sol kept beating him, rubbing it in. Then Rudy got a theory about gambling, something about the psychological factors involved in winning, about guilt complexes—how Sol wanted me, but was basically a very moral man. Rudy figured it all out and finally laid it on the line. He wanted me to sleep with Sol—"

"Stop it!"

"I would have died for him," she said simply. "The theory worked. Rudy won thirty thousand from Sol that next night, playing head-to-head stud. He told me I was wonderful, that he loved me." She shivered. "Only he didn't touch me for a week after that. It scared me. Then he ran off with a cigarette girl named Lorraine."

"Look, I don't want to hear about it."

"He came back in three months. Sad-eyed and smiling and broke. Lorraine had picked him clean. He said he still loved me, that we could pick up again where we left off. We got drunk that night. Rudy kept talking about Paris. I was crying when I drove the car into the motel garage and left the motor idling, with him in the front seat, out cold. Carbon monoxide," she breathed in a dry, terrible whisper. "I killed him." She began to laugh, almost hysterically.

Then I started talking quietly, telling her how much I loved her. After a time the haunted, mad look went out of her eyes. She nestled close to me with a little sigh and I stroked her the way you would a frightened kitten.

"I'll steal for you," she said breathlessly. "I'll kill for you, anything—provided there's no other woman, ever. You think I'm crazy?"

"No," I said, holding her close, tenderly. "You're not crazy."

We sat like that for a very long time. Finally Shannon squeezed my hand and said, "Tell me about Paris, darling."

That afternoon we checked in at the Caesar, in Tijuana. After dinner we went down to the Casa Del Luz. The Casa was on the west end of Tijuana, strictly for the *turistas*. We sat near the dance floor, drinking Old Fashioneds. I looked around.

"A smooth Indian face," Rita had said. "A midnight-blue suit and pomaded hair."

He sat in a shadowed corner booth, a handsome copper-faced Mexican. Occasionally someone would pause at his table and there would be a brief, furtive exchange.

Casually, I got up and strolled over to his table. "*Buenos días*." I accented it nasally. "Business good?"

Those dark liquid eyes raked me. "I do not believe I have had the pleasure, *señor*."

"But you know a man called Morales. You can direct me."

His smile was infinitesimal, a mere twitch of his upper lip. I reached into my pocket and dropped a twenty on the table. He looked bored. I added two more twenties and the boredom vanished.

"You have, of course, references?"

"I'm a friend of Rita's. I want to make a buy." He didn't even blink. "If it helps, I'm also a friend of Angelo Ventresca's."

He smiled then. His brown grasping fingers moved and the money vanished. He scribbled something on a card and handed it to me. "Take this to the Jai-Alai Palace. The runner in the chartreuse beret."

At the Jai-Alai Palace Shannon and I watched the runners in their colored berets scurrying down the aisles, taking bets as they quoted the changing odds in a metallic chant. The one with the chartreuse beret bobbed past the seats, hesitating, then turning in my direction as I raised my hand.

"Quiere?"

He was frigidly polite. I handed him the card and he squinted at it. He gave me a flashing smile. "You are a friend of Señor Ventresca's?"

I nodded and he tossed his beret to another runner, smoothing back his oily blue-black hair. "*Ándale*," he said happily, staring down the aisle.

"See you at the hotel," I told Shannon, kissing her. "Don't wait up."

I followed my guide past the bar to the rear of the building, and outside. We walked down a dark, cobbled alley and stopped about fifty yards from the street. It was very dark and still. My guide turned, a tall indistinct figure.

Steel glimmered. He came at me.

He moved with the gliding crouch of a ballet dancer, holding the blade down low, and I stepped backwards until the cold, wet wall of the building slammed into my back.

"Hold on," I gasped. "I only wanted—"

"El Gordito is dead. You wished to see him? *Bien!*"

I stumbled sideways as be came in, grabbing at his wrist as I fell. For a moment his hand came free and pain slashed in a scarlet blaze across my ribs. We wrestled in frantic silence for that knife. He was strong, with a writhing steel strength that battered my head against the cobblestones again and again. My grip on his wrist was slipping. Suddenly I let go.

He fell sideways, off balance, and I slugged him. As he slumped, I brought my palm in a sweeping arc against his throat. He gagged and collapsed.

I got to my feet, fighting nausea. He lay face-down in the alley, retching. I picked up the knife and panted, "What the hell's the matter with you?"

"Kill me," he said dully, "get it over with."

"Explain, you *hijo de una perra*."

"El Gordito was my friend." He rubbed his throat. "Señor Ventresca killed him, nine months ago. An argument over prices, deliveries."

I began talking quickly with a rage that was as convincing as it was real, and he finally breathed, "You are an enemy of Ventresca's? You come only for merchandise?"

"Brilliant," I snapped. "So who do I deal with now?"

"I know a dealer. One Señor Morales. But there is a price." He peered at me.

"I've got it," I said.

We went to see Señor Morales.

It was dawn when I got back to the Caesar. I was tired and aching, but there were two full pounds of Grade A merchandise in the trunk of the Lincoln. Señor Morales had come through.

We were having breakfast in bed that afternoon when the bellboy brought the telegram to our suite. It was a telegram from Tom Bullock.

It took me five minutes to digest that telegram. Five long minutes, feeling the dull sickness of defeat, wanting to scream. Shannon saw the expression on my face. "Darling, what is it?"

"Murdoch," I said, crumpling the telegram. "He's back in town. He brought some strangers with him. Pack your bags."

It was seventy miles from Tijuana to Mason Flats. I made it in exactly fifty-nine minutes. There was one bad moment at the border when the guard asked what we were bringing back, but Shannon laughed and showed him the cheap silver bracelet and I said we were honeymooners, and he winked lewdly and waved us on. They never stopped you on a Sunday afternoon.

All the way back I drove in a quiet madness, hating Murdoch and praying that Bullock had been mistaken.

When we finally hit Mason Flats, I drove down Center Street and parked in front of the Golden Wheel Hotel. I told Shannon to call Bullock immediately and tell him where I was. Then I walked through the lobby and around back to the game room.

Bullock hadn't been mistaken.

Three men sat in a corner booth drinking. One was smoking a cigar and talking quietly, his gorilla shoulders hunched forward. He looked up and saw me. He stopped talking.

I walked past the roulette tables, my eyes steady on his vulpine face. Around his eyes and across the bridge of his nose there were faint purplish pockmarks—scars I had given him from burning matches almost a year ago.

"Hello, Angelo," I said.

16

"Well, well," Angelo said. "Long time no see."

"You look prosperous," I remarked.

"You got to keep up a front." He smiled. "Sit down."

I looked at this soft-spoken Neanderthal and at his two storm troopers. They sat enjoying it, waiting for the farce to end. Waiting for the signal that preceded execution.

I pulled over a chair from an empty table and sat carefully, watching everyone's hands. "How's Paul?"

"Ingrahm?" His old sorrowful grimace. "He had an accident six months ago. Very sad. Fell off his yacht near Catalina. Drunk and couldn't swim. It was just as well; the grand jury was reaching for him."

"And he sort of willed things to you," I said.

"Sort of."

"So what brings you to this tank town?"

"Santa Claus," he answered. "A little Santa Claus that drives a Buick instead of a sleigh. A Santa that comes along when business is very slow—in fact, because of grand jury investigations and police shake-ups, there is no business at all. And this little old Santa Claus tells us about a boom town, full of cribs and crap layouts. A town that's wide open, where all the cops live in glass houses." His fingers strayed to the bridge of his nose, caressing those tiny purple scars. He smiled with his lower lip. "A town where you can meet old pals."

"Look," I said, fighting to keep my voice level. "Murdoch's using you. The old squeeze play. We can make a deal. I'm setting up numbers territories next week, bringing in more girls. You need me." My voice sounded shrill. "I know where all the skeletons are buried. If anything happens to me, this town gets turned upside down—"

"Murdoch says we deal strictly with him. Besides, you don't deal with corpses."

His two henchmen slid out of the booth. They were well trained.

"Let's go for a nice moonlight drive," Angelo said. "We'll talk about it."

"You're a fool!"

"Let's go," he said.

We walked slowly toward the lobby, his two troopers flanking me, keeping perfect step. We walked past the crowded crap tables, and no one noticed, nobody turned to stare. We went through the red velvet drapes into the lobby.

Tom Bullock stood at the lobby entrance. He was flanked by three big competent-looking plainclothesmen. I almost shouted with relief.

"Going somewhere?" Bullock asked cheerfully. He winked at me, smugly.

"Gentlemen," I said. "Meet the chief of police."

Nobody moved. Bullock took efficient charge. "Book them," he directed. "Vagrancy, concealed weapons." He jerked a thumb at Angelo. "What about him?"

"He's merely an innocent bystander," I grinned. "Thanks, Tom. See you in the morning."

Angelo watched his boys being herded into the prowl car outside. A look of grudging respect came into his eyes.

"Let's go upstairs," I suggested, "and finish that little talk."

Angelo's suite was a plushy expanse of gray frieze, frosted glass, and indirect lighting. He poured himself a drink, and offered me one.

"No thanks," I declined. "Tell me why I didn't have you sent with your boys."

His grin was tight and cold. "You wanted to impress me. This way you hope we'll make a deal."

"We'll deal."

"Maybe. You got something Murdoch didn't tell us about. You got the chief of police."

"And the mayor," I said. "And half the city council."

It jolted him. He thought about it, darkly. "Okay, so you got the connections. What have I got?"

"The muscle, the technical know-how to set up this town on a paying basis."

Angelo was suddenly clinical, all business as he got out pencil and paper. "What's the present weekly take?"

"About fifteen grand. That includes ten percent from the girls, the crap games, the bookies."

Angelo scribbled. "You push much horse here?"

"Just started. I've got two pounds, ready to cut." Angelo was delighted. He pointed out his connections with the eastern syndicate, and I said fine. He said a ten percent rake-off was charity and it should be at least forty percent. I said swell. He said finally, "One organization, is that the idea? No competition."

"Partners," I said. "You and me."

He stuck out his great hairy paw and I shook it. "Bygones be bygones," he said.

His smile was as phony as a three-dollar bill. He'd play along, sure. He'd learn all the angles, who to grease and how much, and in two or three months he would no longer need me. Then I would quietly drop out of sight. I would go for a midnight swim in the Pacific with concrete water wings.

We were smiling at each other when the door opened. A girl came into the suite, loaded down with parcels. She had richly sullen lips and shimmering blue-black hair. She said, "Honey, help me with—"

She saw me and dropped one of the parcels. "Hi, Robin," I said.

"Do much shopping, baby?" Angelo helped her solicitously with the parcels. "Norm, meet my wife. Honey, Norm's my new partner."

"Charmed." I gave her my most disarming leer. "But we've met, remember?"

A dull flush started at Robin's throat, worked slowly up to the roots of her hair. Abruptly, she turned and followed Angelo into the bedroom. The door closed. There were low voices, angry voices, and after a time Angelo came out of the bedroom frowning. "She's upset," he said. "Been on a shopping spree all day. New town. Poor kid doesn't know a soul."

"So you inherited her too," I said.

"Is that some kind of crack?"

"Forget it. Look, one thing we keep straight. You'll be in on the gambling, the dope, the girls. But don't get any ideas about liquor licenses, building permits, or county graft. That's handled upstairs."

"You're the boss." Angelo was humble. He said it would be a very smooth-running organization ... no friction ... his boys were no cheap punks; they were strictly big-time.

After a while Robin came out of the bedroom and nervously mixed us fresh highballs. I sipped mine, tasting for cyanide, noting the soft reverence in Angelo's eyes as he looked at her. He really loved her. To him she was a symbol of richness and wonder. She had belonged to Ingrahm; therefore she was class. And I had slept with that woman, defiled her. I revised my three-month life expectancy to one month.

We finally said goodnight and I promised to have his boys released in the morning.

An hour later I sat in Shannon's apartment drinking coffee and explaining the new set-up. "You're a fool," she said tiredly. "They'll kill you."

"Not for awhile."

"Please." Her green eyes were brimming. "Let's run, *now*. We can be in Ensenada by morning. We've got two thousand left. It's a start."

I smiled, slowly shaking my head.

"Don't mock me, Norm. Please."

I spoke very patiently, as if to a child. "Next week," I said, "my end will be at least eight thousand. The following week almost double that. Rule out the numbers take and the dope end—it takes time to build up a trade. But the girls will kick in fifty percent, the bookies twenty-five. Sure they'll scream, and a lot of tramps will leave town. So Angelo's importing a string of girls in the morning. Right after election," I said, kissing her, "we liquidate Angelo. He does all the spadework; I cash in. It's perfect!"

She was tearfully unconvinced. I reassured her.

The telephone rang an hour after we went to bed. Shannon answered it sleepily. "Hello ... Yes, darling. I just got back this evening." Her voice turned wary. "Of course I love you. See you tomorrow, love."

"Kroll," she said, hanging up. "He's out on bail. Next week he gets sentenced." She looked forlorn. "I feel sorry for him."

"Be nice to him," I said. "Just for a week. He could upset the whole applecart."

We both lay awake, thinking about it.

The next two days were hectic. Angelo and his boys moved in a deadly pattern. They set up territories and introduced themselves to sundry bookies and madams who complained bitterly about the increased payoffs. Certain cigar and liquor store merchants could not appreciate the honor of being numbers brokers. They took convincing. Some of them took broken heads.

Tom Bullock was afraid.

"You greedy idiot," he snarled, "all day long that phone's been jangling off the hook—complaints, threats of recall petitions! The council's scared to death. We didn't bargain for an army of hoodlums, possible gang wars. I ought to clean house, throw them all behind bars ..."

"Later," I told him. "Play it cool, Tom. Wait a couple of weeks, until after the city primaries."

"Then what?"

"Then we smash Angelo behind bars. Right now he's working for us and doesn't know it."

He looked doubtful. "Just don't let him get out of line, that's all."

That afternoon I went to the hospital to see how Matt was convalescing. The tired plainclothesman was standing in front of Matt's room, arguing with two well-dressed angry men. I recognized them immediately. John Porter and Sid Oleson, two staunch pillars of righteousness in Mason Flats. They were candidates for mayor and chief councilman on the opposing ticket.

"Any trouble?" I inquired blandly.

Porter turned on me, his jowls quivering with rage. "This is the fourth time this week we've called. The doctors inform us that Matt Sands has nothing more than superficial bruises and a broken collar bone."

"He's under sedation," I said. "You can't see him."

Porter's lip curled. "Doped so he can't talk?"

"Talk about what?"

"We think you know. We'll be back tonight. And he'd better be able to receive visitors!"

I drove out to Murdoch's house in a white-hot fury. Murdoch greeted me with distant urbanity.

"You're really quite remarkable, Norman. By all rights you should be dead by now."

"If there's one thing I hate," I said nastily, "it's a poor loser."

"But I haven't lost. Not yet."

"Like hell you haven't! You really thought you were cute, importing Angelo. Well we've made a deal, understand? We're partners."

"Temporary partners," he shrugged. "As soon as he learns the ropes, he'll kill you."

"You called Porter, didn't you? You'd tear this whole town apart just to get me. You've got a goddamned stupid obsession, and some day, sooner or later, it's going to destroy you."

He looked at me with cold disdain. "You killed Lombard, didn't you?"

"Did I?"

"You're playing out of your league, you poor little hustler. You've got perhaps a week to live, Norman. Think about it."

I thought about it the rest of that afternoon. I had to have time. Time to bleed the town white before the shimmering bubble burst. Time to think of a way to destroy Murdoch.

At five o'clock I met with Kramer and Bullock at City Hall. We arranged to have Matt transferred to Happyview, a private sanitarium on the edge of town.

"We're balancing his utilities ledger at the close of the month," Kramer said, watching me narrowly. "We'll indict him then. Depositing that three thousand to his account was clever."

"Your own brother," Bullock said. "You're a bit of a bastard, Sands."

"Us bastards got to stick together."

About six hours later I walked slowly across town from Angelo's hotel. We had spent the entire evening adding up tomorrow's collection percentages. Already the numbers game was catching on and Angelo's pushers were starting to build up a trade. The vice and gambling would become a golden torrent all knitting into an organization that needed only one strong man at the helm. Me. The vision grew, coalescing into a hard, bright pattern of power. There was only one flaw. Matt. I was worrying about Matt as that great black sedan whispered around the corner and veered toward the curb. Angelo's sedan.

I dropped to the pavement as flame thundered from the rear window. I fell rolling through waves of sounds as ricochets danced along the splintering concrete. I found the gutter and hugged it, face down.

The sedan was gone.

I got to my feet. My clothes were torn. I brushed at them mechanically. Down the block, lights were yellowing the dark windows. Doors opened. People stared from front porches.

I began to run.

"Shut up. And *stop* packing."

"You're not going to stay?" Shannon breathed incredulously. "Are you mad? He's hunting you, right now!"

"Quiet. Let me think."

I paced the floor of Shannon's bedroom. Oddly, there was no panic, only a cold appraisal of my chances. I had underestimated Angelo's confidence, and now I was paying.

Angelo needed me now like a hole in the head. Bullock and Kramer were sheep; they'd go along with him. And next time Angelo would not miss. Next time was tomorrow, or as soon as he found me.

But Angelo had a weak spot.

Angelo had Robin.

"Stop crying," I said impatiently. "Look, angel, I need your help. Robin and Angelo don't know you from Eve. Listen ..."

17

It was the waiting, the sick waiting in Shannon's apartment at dawn. By the time she returned my nerves were violin strings, taut and shrieking.

"What happened? Did you meet her?"

"She likes me," Shannon said tonelessly, pulling off her slip. "I found her at the blackjack table. Angelo makes her sit in the casino while he goes out and guts the town."

"Did he leave one of his gorillas with her?"

"Always, love." Shannon climbed into bed, yawning. "She's so pitifully bored, so lonely. I told her I was a rich widow. We're having lunch this afternoon, then a spot of shopping."

"Good, good. She'll be alone?"

"She's never alone. Angelo has her guarded like a rare jewel. Incidentally, she's afraid of you."

I chuckled. Shannon's gaze was greenly enigmatic. "You slept with her once, didn't you?"

"Hell no!" I said, startled. "Whatever gave you that idea?"

Her smile had frost on it. "Don't lie to me about that, ever."
"Look, honey—"
"Don't, please. I'm tired."

Shannon left the apartment at noon. I kept pacing. My throat was raw from too many cigarettes. Once the phone rang and I seized it and a man's voice quavered, "Shannon honey? Hello?"

I hung up, grinding my teeth. That damned Kroll! Why didn't he leave her alone? The phone rang again. It kept ringing. I cursed Kroll in a cracked, thin voice.

It was two o'clock in the afternoon. I drank some more coffee. Angelo was collecting today, making the rounds—brothel and clip joint—collecting the fruits of my conniving, smug in the certainty that I had fled town. He would pay Bullock off later, explaining that I was out of town on business and telling him not to worry, that everything was running smoothly.

It was three o'clock, three-fifteen. The phone rang at three-thirty.

"Impatient, darling?" Shannon said.

"Where—"

"The Parisienne Chapeau shop on East Center. They've got some lovely creations, sweet. I bought a gold cashmere beret."

"Is she with you? Is she listening?"

"Certainly, lover."

"Oh. The watchdog there?"

"That's right."

"Give me ten minutes," I said, "At exactly three-forty you walk out of that shop with her. Exactly three-forty, you got that? You know what to do?"

"Of course, darling," Shannon said, hanging up.

East Center Street. Shimmering heat waves on the deserted asphalt, all the little shops and corner taverns huddled in the hot stillness like patient old prostitutes waiting for the Friday night bedlam. I spotted the watchdog under the awning in front of the Parisienne—a tall man with an impassive brown face. He chewed gum methodically and his sleepy eyes raked me as I pulled the Lincoln over to the curb and got out. It was exactly three-forty.

I started past him, walking briskly. Then I wheeled. I threw my knee hard into his groin.

He bent double with an agonized hiss, clawing at my knees. I brought both fists down on the back of his neck and he crumpled to the sidewalk, out cold.

Someone screamed. It was Robin. She stood at the shop entrance, Shannon right behind her. I took two steps forward and grabbed her arm. She fought. Shannon helped me drag her into the Lincoln.

Across the street a man came out of the drugstore, gaping. From the rear of the hat shop came women's voices, frightened and shrill.

I was doing sixty by the time we reached the corner.

Robin was a clawing fury. Shannon kept trying to pinion her arms, but before we reached the main drag my face was bleeding from a dozen scratches. I finally pulled over to the side of the road and grabbed her wrists. "If you'll just take it easy," I said, "you won't get hurt. We're keeping you on ice until I can talk some sense into that wop husband of yours."

But I couldn't reach her. She sat rigid with terror, like a frightened animal.

"Get in back," I told Shannon. "She'll behave."

Shannon got into the back seat. I drove slowly down the main highway, telling Robin cheerfully what would happen to her if she didn't cooperate. Robin sat very still, my words hitting her like stones.

Later, I realized that I'd overplayed it. Robin knew the rules of Angelo's dark world, the inexorable penalty for betrayal. All she could think of was that she had fingered me to Ingrahm a year ago, and now she was going to be forced to pay.

I slowed down as we hit the coast intersection. A green Ford shot past us and turned right at the inland cutoff ahead. Robin watched that Ford with a tight, fixed look. Suddenly she wrenched at the door handle. I reached over for her as she jumped.

For a frozen instant Robin was suspended against the afternoon sun, her yellow dress flaring against her thighs. Then she was gone.

I was out and around the Lincoln almost before the squeal of brakes had died. The Ford had stopped two hundred yards down the cutoff. A man's head poked out, staring back at us. Robin lay in a limp huddle on the concrete, her eyes closed. I carried her back to the Lincoln, swearing softly as that Ford started backing up the road toward us. "Take her," I panted to Shannon. "Hurry!"

I cut left, away from the Ford, squinting hard into the rearview mirror. I tried to shove my right foot through the floorboards, and kept it like that until the Ford became a dwindling green dot, and finally vanished.

"You scared her silly," Shannon said raggedly from the back seat. "I'd have jumped myself. Where are we going?"

"Amy's. She'll keep her there for awhile. Lucky I was going slow—"

"Oh my God."

I swiveled around, stared.

Shannon sat in one corner of the seat, her face chalky. Robin sat beside her like a great rag doll with her dark head lolling sideways at an impossible angle. She was dead.

"Please keep driving," Shannon whispered.

I drove, feeling the perspiration turn to ice on my forehead. "I know a place." My voice had a harsh gravel sound. "In back of an old abandoned wildcat. She'll have good company. We'll have to drive around until dark. Stop crying."

Later we watched the oil form over Robin's head.

Eight o'clock. We drove slowly along Center Street. The neons were flashing spurts of bloody light. It was Friday night—a big night for the oil tramps, the boomers with cash in their jeans, burning to throw it away on whisky or the inevitable rouged smile. As we passed the Golden Wheel, Shannon's nails dug into my wrist. We'd been spotted.

It was Shep Spinelli, one of Angelo's lieutenants. He stood in front of the hotel, his pale rodent face incredulous as he stared at the Lincoln. He turned and dashed into the lobby.

"It's too late," Shannon moaned. "We could have been in Bakersfield by now."

I parked two blocks down, near a drugstore. "Come on, angel."

She got out, smiling desperately. "You're going to phone Bullock, of course?"

We went into the drugstore. The phone booth was occupied. Shannon went into a frenzy of impatience as I made a careful purchase at the notions counter.

"Come on." I took her arm.

"But she's hanging up. Aren't you—"

"We're going to see Angelo."

"Oh, God."

She was fighting hysteria as we walked toward the hotel. "You bought a pair of cheap earrings. Why?"

I opened the box and threw the earrings in the gutter. I carefully placed the box in my coat pocket. "A bluff," I said. "For Angelo's benefit. Now smile! Look brazen, honey. That's better."

Her laughter was something out of Dante.

We went through the swinging glass doors. Two big, quietly dressed men exchanged leisurely glances as we crossed the lobby. They followed us into the elevator. On the way up, nobody spoke. This was the ultimate, the most cosmic bluff of all. Fifteen minutes from now I would either have several thousand dollars in my pocket, or be a dead man. Shannon's nails dug into my palm. But her smile was fixed, bright.

I hammered on the door of Angelo's suite. It swung open. "Hello, Angelo," I said.

The two men followed us into the suite, but they were shadows. The other men in the room were also shadows, dark nonentities beside the primal fury that rose from the sofa and stalked toward me.

I tossed a small, black pasteboard box at Angelo's feet. A soft sigh rippled around the room. "Before you kill me, open it," I said.

Angelo stopped, blindly. He stared at me across a gulf in time, and his incandescent rage slowly faded, replaced by an ancient fear.

"Where is she?" he said thickly.

"Open it."

Angelo's fingers shook as he picked up the box. He was afraid to open it. In the old days he had been a button for the Mafia. They had a lovable trick of presenting a small box to an enemy after the snatch—a box containing the finger of a loved one. Angelo's breath came in spasms as he opened the box. Then he stared at me.

"That's right." My knees felt like jelly, but my voice was cold, dispassionate. "It's empty. But unless we make a long-distance phone call in ten minutes, you get another box in the morning mail. A box with a few of her teeth in it. Or maybe an ear—"

His roar was an apelike bellow. The blow slammed into my temple and the universe exploded in a glory of crimson suns. Shannon screamed.

"You heard him," Angelo said. "You got ten minutes. Don't let him pass out."

One of them flipped me upright; another held my arms. I tried to grin. "Maybe it'll be a bonus in the morning mail, Angelo. Maybe two fingers."

A fist rammed into my mouth.

"*Stop it*," Angelo cried hoarsely. He reached down and grabbed me by the lapels. "You son of a bitch, is she all right? Is she?"

"At the moment," I said.

His arms dropped to his sides. "All right," he said. "Your deck, your deal."

"That was a bonehead stunt last night," I told him. "You've sure got some amateurs working for you. How much was yesterday's take?"

"Nine grand."

"Yesterday morning we estimated fourteen."

"All right," he said too quickly. "Fourteen."

"My half," I said, and he blinked. "That's all I want—my fourteen thousand. I'll pay the city council boys out of that, per our agreement. In two weeks, after the city elections, you get Robin back safe and sound. Well?"

"Just two weeks?" Angelo said heavily. His face was all animal cunning. "You say she's safe. Just to make sure, we'll keep this tramp as security. You got objections?"

Shannon looked at me with a trapped horror. "Go right ahead," I shrugged. "Incidentally, you've got four minutes. Where's the money?"

Exactly ten minutes later I was helping Shannon into the Lincoln. "You drive." I leaned back in the front seat and closed my eyes. I had never felt so tired.

Shannon drove in a tense, angry silence. "*Would* you have left me there?"

"Don't be silly. If Angelo thought I gave half a damn about you, it might have been different."

Shannon drove quietly across town. My head was throbbing. My thoughts were gray as ashes. We were living on borrowed time. Angelo would watch us night and day, and it would not take him any two weeks to discover that Robin was sleeping at the bottom of a sump.

I had fourteen thousand dollars in my pocket. I had Shannon. The smart thing to do was *run*.

But I wasn't going to run. I still held a few high cards in this game and I was going to play them out to the finish.

We turned left on Olive Street. I caught a brief glimpse of a car parked in front of Shannon's duplex before she hissed, "Get down! It's Kroll."

I slid down in the front seat, out of sight. Shannon wheeled into the driveway and got out of the Lincoln quickly. There was the sound of her heels tapping up the walk and Kroll's car door slamming.

Kroll's voice was tired. "Where'd you get the new car?"

Shannon's laughter was high and silvery. "It's that Norm Sands. He wants to sell it to me. Says he's broke, needs money. You know Norm."

"You're pretty good friends with him, aren't you?"

"Darling, you're jealous! How sweet—"

"I've been waiting for two hours," he said brokenly. "We had a date at seven, remember?"

The sound of a kiss. And Shannon's small, tragic voice. "I'm terribly sorry, Bernard, but I thought it was tomorrow night. I've been shopping, sweet." The sound of another kiss. My insides squirmed.

I stole a glance through the vent window, and they were on the front porch. Kroll was holding her very close.

"... such a tearing headache," Shannon was saying forlornly. "Please forgive me. Not tonight."

"I get sentenced Tuesday. Four more days."

Shannon turned on the tears. She was very good. Kroll held her close, pleading. "Please, honey, marry me now. Tomorrow morning. Look, Clem's banking the fifty thousand Monday. You can live decent while I'm away."

"Let me sleep on it. Please, darling."

Kroll kissed her awkwardly. She said good night.

For almost a full minute he stood on the porch, staring at the closed door, his shoulders sagging. Then he went slowly back to his car and drove away. I counted to ten before I uncramped myself from under the dash panel and went inside.

Shannon was in the kitchen making coffee. She was drunk on the giddy reaction of relief. "Fourteen thousand dollars, and of course you'll keep the city council's share. I'll start packing."

I lighted a cigarette, wondering how to tell her. She was prattling on about Paris—how cheap it was to live in the south of France, how we'd get along. She was a firecracker of emotion, ready to go off. Abruptly I lit the fuse.

"We're staying," I said. "Kramer and Bullock get their full share. I need them."

The coffee hissed on the stove, unnoticed. Shannon shook her bright head in disbelief. Then she came over and put her hands on my shoulders.

"Listen, darling." She was fighting for control, enunciating very carefully. "If you stay in Mason Flats, you're going to die. I don't *care* about the damned money."

"I care about the money."

"No." Her voice was lifeless. "You just hate to lose." The simple truth.

"You're my female counterpart, remember? We like nice things. With money we're champagne's bright children, all glitter and stardust. Without it we stink. In two years we'd be broke in some fleabag hotel, hating each other like trapped animals." I put my arms around her, nuzzling her hair. "I won't let that happen to us. I've got this town in my fist and I'm going to squeeze it dry—"

Shannon tore away from me, almost running. She threw open the bedroom door and there were sounds of drawers opening, suitcases being thrown on the bed.

I went into the bedroom. She was packing, furiously. She tore an armful of gowns off their hangers and crammed them into the trunk, not looking at me.

"Aren't you taking that black lace chemise? I liked it."

"Go away," she sobbed. "Go to Angelo and commit suicide!"

I stood watching her without saying a word, and after a while she stopped packing. She stood slumped over the suitcase like a tired old woman.

"How much money will it take?" She was listless, resigned. "How long before we pull stakes and run?"

"A couple of weeks," I said. "Maybe three. By then we'll have forty thousand. It's enough."

She took a long shuddering breath and walked past me into the living room. There was the click of the phone dial repeated four times. A pause. Then her voice, cool and husky. "Bernard, darling? I'm so glad you went straight home ..."

It came over me in a white-hot spasm and I charged into the living room, shouting soundlessly, "Please, please." Her smile cut me like a sharp knife.

"Yes, darling," she was saying with that terrible smile. "I'm sure. We can be married tomorrow morning. A quick Mexico honeymoon. Of course I'm sure, dearest ..."

She finally hung up, and I yelled, "You're not going through with it! I won't let you."

"Monday afternoon," she said evenly, "they deposit his fifty thousand. I can talk him into a joint bank account easily. Tuesday morning he goes up for sentence. That afternoon I withdraw it all. We can leave Tuesday night."

"No!" I was shaking. "You want to make a pimp out of me, is that what you want?"

"No choice. You can't stay, and you won't run." She came into my arms. There was an edge of cruelty, tinged with self-contempt, in her voice. "You were right about us. We both want the good things in life. The Riviera sunshine, champagne at the St. Moritz. It's the only way."

"I won't let you go through with it."

"You can't stop me."

She had a ruthless strength that I never would have suspected. I pleaded for an hour. She wouldn't listen. Finally, she looked at me with compassion and said, "I'm going to do it. Please don't talk anymore."

18

The Justice was a pink little man with a nervous smile. Shannon looked like a pale death angel as he twittered through the service. Kramer, Murdoch, and I stood solemnly as if at a funeral. Afterwards, I congratulated Kroll and kissed the bride. Her cheeks were wet.

"What's wrong, honey?" Kroll was startled.

"It's just that she's so happy," Murdoch said. "Congratulations, Bernard. We'll see you Monday."

Kroll looked proud and happy as we went outside to the glittering Buick Kramer had loaned them for the honeymoon. "Why don't we drive down to Tijuana, honey?" He squeezed Shannon's hand and she shivered. "Only two days and nights, and we've got lots of honeymooning to do."

"Try the Caesar," I said, wanting to hurt her. "They've a nice bridal suite."

It brought a last anguished look from her as the Buick purred off into the noon haze.

"What a well-fed sacrificial lamb," Kramer wheezed. "I'll buy the drinks."

We sat in the dim coolness of the Acey Deucey bar. Kramer waxed eloquent over bourbon ... yesterday's take had been far more than he had dreamed, he owed me a debt of gratitude for the present setup, this way there was more for everybody. Murdoch sat bloodless and glacial over his brandy. "Incidentally, Norman, what's this trouble with Angelo?"

"No trouble," I said.

"God, no," Kramer murmured. "Not two weeks before election. You promised to keep him in line."

"How about Matt?" Murdoch probed. "He's still under wraps?"

Kramer nodded with a worried frown. "But Porter and Oleson have been stirring up trouble. They've gotten quite a following in the young voter's league and the civic union. There's been talk. Yesterday Porter asked me pointblank where Matt was being kept. I had to play indignant, mad. I don't like it, any of it!"

I flicked a knowing glance at Murdoch. He smiled faintly. Kramer's eyes darted to Murdoch. "You wouldn't sell us out, would you, Clem?"

"He's too smart for that," I said.

The polite surface phrases, and underneath, the roiling crosscurrents of fear. Murdoch would have no compunction about throwing the entire city council to the wolves—if he could get me in the process. Kramer sensed this, and his smile crumbled at the edges.

I bought Murdoch another brandy, wondering how to kill him. He had something lethal in mind, I knew. Something that would happen soon. His sardonic smile reminded me of the night when he had savaged me with a straight flush.

Later that afternoon I wandered down to the Golden Wheel. I sat in the game room drinking, trying not to think about Kroll and Shannon and Matt.

I had picked the wrong place to relax. The chant of the croupiers, the rustle of cards and chips evoked too many memories. Memories of a soft, deadly voice saying, *"You're out of your league, you poor little grifter."* And another voice, cold with contempt. *"Your own brother. You're quite a bastard, Sands."*

I drank to that.

All afternoon I bar hopped, trying to lose myself in alcohol. It was no good. Fear walked with me. Fear of a brooding Neanderthal whose wife I had killed. Fear of an icy little man whose mistress I had stolen.

By midnight I was blind drunk. Drunk enough, I figured, to go home and be able to sleep without having nightmares.

I was wrong.

Next day—Sunday—was worse. I prowled the Center Street honky-tonks, drinking, shooting craps, trying to relax. All the bartenders and the croupiers wore polite hating smiles. I smiled back, not enjoying it. I was one of the City Hall bastards responsible for the increased collections. A parasite of parasites. A big man.

I was in the Acey Deucey, trying to make a twenty-dollar pass, when I saw Angelo. He stood alone at the bar, drinking. I walked over to him. "I'll buy."

"I'm particular who I drink with." Angelo's eyes were mean, bloodshot. "How's Robin?"

"Fine."

He was very drunk. "So help me Jesus, if you've touched one hair of her head—"

"Relax, we're gentle people."

"We?"

"I told you once I owned the police force. You had to find out the hard way."

The enormity of it stunned him. "So you had help on that snatch." He knotted one hairy fist and stared at it. "Copper help."

I let him swallow the lie. "Murdoch doesn't control everything," I said. "You were getting too big for your britches; you had to be brought in line. No point in fighting it. Let's be friends."

"Just so she's all right." His gnarled grin. "Like you say, we need each other."

We smiled into each other's eyes, reading death there.

Could I stall him for two more days? By this time Tuesday Shannon and I would be driving off into the sunset with Kroll's fifty thousand. That's a nice picture, I thought. *Focus on it, Sands. Forget about Robin in that sump. Forget about Matt's being framed.* Poor, ox-headed, crusading Matt, playing jungle rules with a boy scout knife.

I played at that crap table for two hours. I lost six hundred dollars. Anything for some excitement, anything to forget about Matt. I finally tossed the dice on the table and walked outside.

I parked the Lincoln in front of Laurie's apartment and sat there for ten minutes, trying to figure the odds and calling myself a fool, before I finally climbed the steps and rang the bell.

Laurie opened the door. "Come in," she said. Tired voice, pale lovely face, copper hair, gray eyes cold with contempt as she stared at me.

I walked past her, silently, toward the telephone on the table. If I hesitated now, I wouldn't go through with it. It was a quixotic bonehead stunt, a sucker play, but I picked up the phone and dialed Bullock's home number.

When he answered I said, "Tom, I'm worried about Matt. It might be smarter to make a deal."

"He's a goddamn fanatic," snorted Bullock. "I went over to the sanitarium yesterday, tried to reason with him. The sonuvabitch spit in my face!"

"Listen to me, Tom," I told him, "you don't know how to handle him. Call Happyview right now. Tell them you're sending a visitor over tonight. I'm going to scare him into playing ball."

"Why bother, Norm? We've got him dead to rights on that three thousand utilities shortage—"

"Call Happyview," I said.

"All right," he grumbled. "But it's a waste of time."

I hung up and Laurie said quietly, "Matt won't bargain with you."

"He won't have to. You got a gun?"

"A what?"

"A rod, a heater, an iron. Matt's going to escape." Hope flared in her eyes, then faded. "So they can kill him?"

"Listen," I said, feeling a little desperate, "if he doesn't escape, they'll either kill him or frame him. Understand? You're going to drive out to Happyview tonight. They'll admit you to Matt's isolation ward. Carry the gun in your handbag. Give it to him. He can leave it under his pillow until Tuesday night."

"Why Tuesday night?"

"I'm leaving town then. For good."

She gave me a long searching glance, then turned and went into the bedroom. I leaned back on the sofa and gazed around the little apartment. It was a cozy place ... warm, lived in. The pink drapes, the Matisse reproductions on the wall, the walnut hi-fi that Matt had bought her for her birthday.

I could be living in this apartment now.

I could have had Laurie.

And I had traded her for a high-priced slut, an amoral, jealous wanton. No, that wasn't quite fair, I thought. In her own fashion, Shannon loved me and had her own peculiar moral code. She was proving it right now.

"Here," Laurie said, coming out of the bedroom. "It belonged to Papa. There aren't any shells for it. It's just as well."

It was a .32 automatic, slightly rusty. It would do. I hefted it. "Put it in your handbag. When you walk into Happyview tell them Tom Bullock sent you down to talk to their special patient. And remember, Matt doesn't escape until Tuesday night. You'll make him promise?"

She nodded. There was a breathless intensity about her as she followed me to the door. It was in her trembling smile, the color in her cheeks. Looking down at her, I felt the old familiar urgency ripping at my senses.

"Good night, Norm." It was a whisper.

"Good-bye, Laurie." I went out. The door closed.

Driving home, I had the feeling that I had played the fool. But when I finally went to bed, there were no more nightmares.

Monday morning I got up early and started packing. Kroll and Shannon were due back this afternoon. Kroll's time expired tonight. Tomorrow he would report to the county seat for sentencing. By noon tomorrow Shannon and I would be fleeing south.

The nice part of it was that I still held that manila envelope. That envelope meant power. In two weeks, just before the primaries, certain city officials would receive photostats in the mail. I chuckled, thinking about their frantic last-minute scurrying to raise the loot necessary to keep them out of jail.

Shortly after noon I finished packing and went out to eat. I had a steak at a downtown chop house, then drove slowly toward the bank. Now was the ideal time to withdraw that manila envelope from my safe deposit box and have a dozen photostats made of the contents.

I was being tailed.

I whipped right on Center, squinting into the rearview mirror. A tan Mercury followed. It stayed a discreet hundred yards behind, keeping smooth pace with the green lights, following me as I cut left on Orange toward the outgoing artery.

Angelo? Murdoch? The key to that safe deposit box suddenly felt warm in my pocket. I floorboarded the accelerator, and the Lincoln snarled.

Exactly five minutes later and eight miles out of town, I pulled over to the side of the highway, swearing. I got out and walked back down the road to where the Mercury waited.

"What in hell's the idea?"

He was sad-eyed and wizened, a dark little man who showed me the gun just in case I should get ideas. His name was Froggy Martin, and he was Angelo's right-hand errand boy. "Angelo says I should play cocklebur," he said gently. "He wants to keep tabs on you."

"What for? I'm not going any place."

"Angelo talks with Murdoch an hour ago. Murdoch says come Tuesday you may get itchy feet and blow away in the night like an Arab. Angelo is a very cautious man."

So Murdoch had guessed. The back of my neck felt cold.

"Yesterday I beg Angelo to let us work on you. Half an hour, I tell him, and you will be happy to tell us where Robin is. Angelo says no. He says he would not like to receive Robin's finger by parcel post." He had soft, smiling brown eyes.

I was staring at the Mercury's tail pipes. "I was doing a hundred and fifteen back there. Just what have you got under that hood?"

Froggy chuckled and began expounding on the virtues of a three-quarter race cam with milled heads and duals. I walked back to the Lincoln, shaking. Froggy followed me all the way back to town.

Ten minutes before three. The bank closed at three. I began to sweat. The Mercury was almost a block behind.

I circled the block and cut right on Main, then swerved into the alley behind the bank. I opened the door and hit the ground running.

I was in the bank for perhaps five minutes. When I got back to the alley, I was carrying a certain manila folder in my coat. It felt like ten tons of nitro with a slow fuse.

And there was that damned Mercury sitting insolently in back of my Lincoln. Froggy was puffing on a cigarette.

"You sonuvabitch," I said.

"I used to be a private eye." Froggy's smile was sad, apologetic.

Whoever made up that rule about not hitting someone with a lighted cigarette in his mouth is crazy. It works fine. Froggy's head snapped one way and the cigarette another. I left him slumped over the steering wheel with the cigarette burning holes in the Mercury's upholstery.

I drove across town fast and parked on Olive, four doors up from Shannon's duplex. The maroon Buick sat in Shannon's driveway. The honeymooners were home.

For an hour I chain-smoked, watching the street for a tan Mercury.

This complicated things. The smart thing to do was run now, and join Shannon later this week in Vegas. Murdoch was goading Angelo to a killing rage. The ice was paper-thin, and cracking.

It was almost dusk before Kroll hurried out of the house and got into the Buick. After he was gone I finished my cigarette before I walked down the street to Shannon's place.

"Oh darling, darling, I thought you'd never come."

"How was he?" I said, feeling the bitterness well up inside me like acid.

"Don't be rotten, darling." She clung to me tightly, lips searching. She looked drawn and tired.

I disengaged her gently. "We got troubles. Hide this thing—under the bathtub, in the attic, but hide it good!"

She took the manila envelope without a word and went into the kitchen.

Time to run. There was still time.

Shannon came in from the kitchen, and kissed me. "In the top of the refrigerator." Her eyes danced. "In the freezer, underneath three frozen cutlets. Nobody ever looks in freezer compartments. Kiss me."

"I've got some bad news—"

"Let it wait. He'll be gone hours." She bit her lip. "Only ..."

"Only what?"

"I was in the bathroom," she said slowly, "when the phone rang. It was Murdoch. When Bernard hung up, he gave me a real strange look and said he'd be gone for two hours. You don't think—"

"I think I'm getting out of here, right now."

"Hold me tightly, Norm. Darling, I'm scared."

I held her close, stroking her blonde hair, feeling the thin edge of panic, and that was when the front door opened. Kroll stood there.

Nobody moved. Seconds stretched into tortured aeons and still nobody moved. Kroll's eyes were shocked, vacant.

"I wouldn't believe him," he said. "He told me and I wouldn't believe him. Just a fool," he said vaguely. "No fool like an old fool."

"You've got it wrong." I walked toward him, smiling desperately. "I was just wishing her a friendly—"

"Don't come near me." His Adam's apple moved. "Clem told me about you, all about you. You keep away from me." He stumbled out.

The doorway was empty. I ran out to the porch. Shannon had me by the arm; she was pleading. The Buick leapt away from the curb and down the street, the taillights winking around the corner.

"Norm, you're breaking my wrist!"

I let go. We stared at each other numbly.

"Pour me a drink," I said to her.

You plan, you scheme, you lie awake nights, and you kill. You dream of a mountain of gold, and at last the mountain becomes a shining reality. Then one slip, just one. The gold vanishes like mist in the sun. I became aware of Shannon's voice, angry and strident.

"... *do* something! You can't just sit slopping up liquor—"

"Let me think."

The pattern was murderously clear. First Kroll would get drunk. Crazy, killing drunk. He would slobber on Murdoch's shoulder. Murdoch would be very sympathetic. He would advise Kroll to spill his guts in court tomorrow, expose the whole rotten mess. That'd be very fine. Ten days before election. I could see Bullock and Kramer—half the city council—streaming all points west. I could see Angelo's face when Murdoch told him Bullock was no longer protecting me. Lovely.

"Get dressed," I told Shannon. "We're making a social call. You still got that gun?"

She had it. I checked the safety and slid it into my coat pocket. "Ever use this for anything besides killing flies?"

She inspected the long seams of her nylons critically. "Not yet."

"That day in Mexico. Would you have *really* used it?"

The sudden chill, waiting for her answer. Her flat green stare as she wriggled into her slip. She was a strange, violent woman, this Shannon.

"Of course," she said. "Where to, darling?"

We drove for a frantic hour, taking dark side streets to Kramer's house, to Bullock's. I made quick phone calls, and neither Kramer nor Bullock were at home or at their offices. I had to find them, and swiftly. We could still salvage a few thousand dollars from the ruins. Bullock would jump at the chance to get that manila envelope. And after that, there was one final thing to do before we left town. I was going to find Murdoch and kill him.

By seven o'clock I was desperate. On impulse I drove to Murdoch's house, and there was Bullock's car sitting in the driveway. I parked in back of it and got out. "Wait here," I told Shannon, kissing her. "Be back in ten minutes."

Murdoch answered the door chimes. "Good evening, Norman." His eyes were mocking as he ushered me into the living room. "It seems we have a crisis."

Kramer and Bullock stood bleakly by the fireplace. They glared at me as we came in. It was too late for my kind of deal. They already knew.

"So you couldn't wait," I snarled at Murdoch. "You had to tell them! Tear the town apart just to get me—"

"Matt's escaped," Bullock said harshly.

"Matt?" I didn't get it. My thoughts refused to focus. I sat down, weakly.

"This afternoon," Bullock said. "He stuck a gun in the orderly's face, walked right out of the sanitarium. We're through. Even if we could find him, it's too late. He'll run straight to the county attorney." He splashed brandy into his glass and gulped it like water. "Your imported hoods, your goddamn bright ideas!" He started toward the door. "I'm resigning right now, taking a trip upstate."

So Matt and Laurie had crossed me. They had promised to wait until Tuesday afternoon. I moistened my lips. "Hold on, Tom. I can find Matt. I'll keep him in line."

Murdoch and Kramer looked at me, their faces white and strained. Now they were staring *past* me. I turned, gingerly. Shannon stood in the doorway, very pale. She moved slowly into the room. Behind her was Kroll.

"Go on," said Kroll wearily, prodding her with the gun. "Get over there, you bitch, with the rest of them."

He stood in the doorway, weaving slightly, smiling. He was blind, deadly drunk. "I knew you'd wind up here. I've been waiting. All the serpents together in their nest."

"Don't be foolish," Murdoch snapped. "I'm here, Bernard, your friend Clem. Put that thing away."

Kroll was deaf. He took four wavering steps into the room. He looked at Kramer, then at me. The gun lifted slowly, steadied.

"Cuckold," Kroll whispered. "A martyred cuckold to boot. Real funny, wasn't it?" He turned to Shannon. "How you must have laughed! Take away his money first, then his pride. Then his honor. Kroll, the patsy!" The gun came up, swiveled toward her. His finger whitened on the trigger.

My yell was lost in the racket of gunfire and Shannon's screams. Bullock knelt by the fireplace, flame roaring from his gun, as Shannon crumpled to the carpet. Kroll moved very fast, skipping backwards with a crazed grin as he traded shots with Bullock. I dove, and tackled Kroll around his knees. He was down, prostrate, as I grappled for the gun. It came away easily and I brought the barrel down to smash his skull. But he lay motionless. His eyes were blank and a red stain was creeping across his shirt.

Bullock's voice was ragged. "Is he ..."

"Nice shooting," I said.

Kramer was vomiting in the fireplace. Murdoch leaned against the couch, his face gray. He was smiling.

I bent over Shannon. Her hair was spread out like fine strands of gold wire, and her skin was waxen. I touched her fingers. They were cold. There was a tearing sense of loss as I explored her body, looking for the wound. She moaned, stirred.

"She only fainted," Murdoch said. His tired voice seemed to fill the room. "I've made another error in judgment, Norman. I miscalculated the extent of Bernard's passion." He coughed rackingly. "One pays for errors. Ironic that he should have missed her and gotten me."

He tottered, slumped. It was incredible, seeing the blood trickle from the corner of his mouth. It was like seeing a machine cry, a statue bleed. "Not much point in depositing Bernard's earnest money now, is there?" He chuckled. "Quite a savings, gentlemen."

His eyes blinked, opened wide. They focused on me, glazing. "You'll destroy each other, you and her. At least I'm costing you, Norman. Fifty thousand dollars," he said, and died.

19

"I'm getting out of here," Kramer yelled, and bolted for the door.

"Hold on!" I shoved him back against the couch.

He looked horrified. "If you're under the impression we'll be a party to—"

"Shut up," I said savagely, "and put that gun away, Tom. The whole setup's tailor-made!" I started talking fast, explaining the way it had to be.

Kramer swallowed. "He's crazy, Tom. Look at his face."

"Not so crazy," Tom said slowly. "If we can find the bullets from my gun ..."

It took us an hour to find them—peering at the walls, digging into the woodwork with penknives. Three ugly, flattened lumps of lead. I put them in my pocket, grinning at Shannon as I took out a handkerchief and picked up Kroll's gun. I carefully shot him in the chest. Shannon almost fainted again.

"For powder burns," I explained, locking Kroll's fingers about the gun. "Murder and suicide. We've got motivation, circumstance, everything. Murdoch's editorials in the *Clarion* exposed Kroll as a grafting contractor. He's already confessed to that in court. He came here drunk, out for revenge. He shot Murdoch, then himself. Ballistics will prove the same gun killed both parties. Kramer and Bullock were innocent bystanders."

"But he was shot twice," Shannon whispered.

"Powder burns cover the same area," Bullock said, picking up the phone. "They'll find a slug from the same gun underneath him. The M.E.'ll make it open-and-shut."

He called police headquarters, lips pursed. Afterwards he said, "Actually, it's better this way. I was getting afraid of Clem. You'd better leave before the meat wagon gets here."

I took Shannon's arm and steered her toward the door. She moved like a somnambulist. "Make sure your stories jibe," I warned Kramer. "Let Bullock do all the talking."

Kramer was mush, palsied and quivering. "Whatever you say." Recollection stirred, and his mouth opened. "But Matt's still free—"

"I'll take care of Matt. See you at City Hall tomorrow, gentlemen."

"It's going to come off," Bullock said. "I can feel it." He glanced at me queerly. "I was just thinking."

"What's that?"

"You're beginning to look like Clem already."

We drove down Imperial. Shannon sat back lifelessly, eyes closed. She was spent.

"Norm, I've got to get drunk with you. Tonight. Good and drunk. You know what I mean?"

"We'll see."

As we rounded the corner, the squad car passed us from the opposite direction, sirens whining.

Neither of us spoke until I pulled up in front of Laurie's apartment. I patted Shannon's knee. "Sit tight. Be just a minute."

She didn't move, didn't open her eyes.

I reached the top step and pressed the buzzer, then leaned on it hard. Laurie's voice was wary, frightened. "Who is it?"

"Norm. Alone. Open up."

The door opened and I stepped inside.

"He's not here," Laurie said. "He just left."

I went into the bedroom. It was empty, as was the closet. On the table there were two half-filled coffee cups, still warm.

"So he left," I said harshly. "He's going to drive all the way to the county seat with one arm in a cast? Didn't we make a deal about Tuesday night? Bullock's troopers are combing the town for him right now."

Laurie's eyes were steady. "He can sue the city for false arrest."

I laughed. "We've got a dozen witnesses to swear he was drunk and disorderly, that he resisted arrest. My plans have changed. I'm not leaving town. Look, tell Matt when you see him that I'll give him five thousand dollars to forget all about that manila envelope."

"I'll tell him." Her voice was toneless. "But I know what his answer will be."

"All right." My patience was going. "Then he gets framed for that utilities shortage, tomorrow! Good night, Laurie."

I was halfway down the steps when she caught up with me. She was on the verge of tears.

"Please, Norm." She put one hand on my arm. "Don't do it to him. I'm begging you."

Shannon watched us from the Lincoln. Laurie gave her a long, searching look. "So she's the reason."

"Talk to Matt," I said. "Tell him he needs that envelope to substantiate any accusations. Tell him he's in no spot to bargain."

"All right." Laurie's lip trembled. "I'll call you later."

I slid behind the wheel of the Lincoln. "She seemed to have quite an affinity for you," Shannon said bitingly. "She's pretty."

"She hates my guts."

"Love and hate are both sides of the same coin. Don't lie to Shannon."

"I've got work to do tonight," I said irritably. "Our party will have to wait."

The quick intake of breath, the green eyes glowing. "What kind of work?"

"I've got to figure out how to dump Angelo tomorrow. And make a deal with my maniac brother."

"Then you won't mind if I take the car. The supermarket's open, and I've got shopping to do."

"Of course not. God, you're suspicious."

She dropped me at my apartment, and for just one moment her lean face was incredibly wistful as she kissed me good night. Her long body pressed against mine and her fingernails dug into the back of my neck. "It had better be business," she whispered fiercely. "I wanted you very badly tonight."

"There'll be other nights."

She smiled sweetly. Too sweetly.

The first thing I did was take a hot shower. Then I put on a bathrobe and slippers and poured myself a drink. For the next hour I planned.

Tomorrow I would have Bullock liquidate Angelo. There would be some repercussions—perhaps a county probe—but that could all be handled. The important thing was to close down the poker parlors immediately, the cribs. Until after election. Oddly enough, I wasn't too worried about Matt. Laurie could reason with him. We would work out a deal.

The doorbell rang. Angelo?

I took Shannon's little automatic from my coat and slid the safety catch off. "Who is it?"

"Laurie. Alone." This was password night.

I opened the door. "Come in. Have a drink. Is he going to be reasonable?"

Laurie stepped inside. She wore a tan polo coat, and she was shivering.

"Soda, water, or neat?"

"No thanks." Her eyes darted about the room, taking in the blue leather couch, the gray carpeting. "Nice."

"You didn't come here to compliment me upon my interior decorating ability," I said dryly. "He's still stubborn?"

She nodded mutely. The lamplight struck sparks from her red-gold hair as she took off her coat. I caught my breath. Her breasts looked full and defiant through the sheer dress.

"Nice outfit."

"I thought you'd like it."

Struck by a dark suspicion, I went to the window, peered down at Laurie's little yellow convertible sitting by the curb. It was empty. Her voice was tired, tinged with contempt. "Don't worry, I came alone."

"To tell me Matt's still going to play the fool?"

"To beg."

I stared at the proud gray eyes, the perfect body tensed and waiting.

I snickered. "Why do women think that's the ultimate solution? If all else fails, the bed is the last resort,"

Laurie's face was pink. "Go home," I said. "It's a nice try, but it didn't come off."

The phone rang. It was Shannon.

"Darling, I can't sleep."

"You're not just checking?" I growled.

"Let me come over. Please. I bought some champagne—"

"Dammit, I'm busy."

Deliberately, Laurie laughed. Full throaty laughter tinged with malicious bitchery.

"Who's that?" Shannon asked tightly.

"It's just the radio. What's the matter with you?"

"I'm possessive."

The humming emptiness of the wire. I glared at Laurie.

"Tell me you're alone, darling. It's important to me."

"I'm alone."

"Good night," she said.

I hung up. "Damn you, Laurie. What were you trying to do?"

"She seems rather jealous," Laurie said thoughtfully.

"She's all woman. We're a team, partners in everything. And," I added brutally, "she's better in bed than you ever thought of being. Beat it."

Her head went back as if I'd slapped her, but the remark did not have the desired effect. She crossed to the sideboard and poured herself a stiff three fingers of rye. "You did offer me a drink?"

"Help yourself." I was getting nervous. I wanted her to leave.

"You're really going through with it, Norm? You're framing him?"

"No choice. He's a fanatic. Finish your drink and go home," I said, starting into the kitchen. I took my time putting a pot of coffee on the stove. There was silence from the living room. Then Laurie's voice.

"Perhaps I came here to prove something."

There was a silken rustling. I came out of the kitchen and stood transfixed.

Laurie was unbuttoning her blouse, shrugging it off her creamy shoulders, letting it drop to the rug. The skirt was next. Her gray eyes were enigmatic as she pulled her slip over her head. She stood wearing only black lace panties, bra, high heels and sheer hose. Desire smashed a velvet fist along my loins.

"To prove what?" My voice sounded thick.

"You said she was better."

Laurie calmly unhooked her bra, let it fall. There was a challenge in her face as she turned toward the bedroom. My throat was dry, my face hot.

I followed her.

"You're trying to prove—"

"Don't talk," she said. "Don't say a word."

I put my hands on her shoulders, let them slide down to her hips. She was rigid as stone, eyes closed. Her arms came up and slid around my neck. I kissed her. Her lips were cold.

Then I heard the sound. The metallic click of a doorlatch sliding into place. Someone was in my apartment!

Laurie smiled. Her eyes opened and there was no passion there, only cold purpose.

"Who is it?" she called.

The sound of a door closing. Footsteps clicking hurriedly down the hall stairs.

I ran into the living room. It was empty. I threw open the door. The stairs were dark and deserted. From outside there was the cough of a motor, the scream of anguished tires clawing down the street. I got to the window just in time to see the Lincoln disappearing around the corner.

Laurie was dressing. I grabbed the telephone and frantically dialed Shannon's number. No answer. I hung up, then dialed again, waiting in an agony of suspense; then the slow, sick realization as I stared at Laurie's curling smile.

"You gambled," I said.

"I won."

"You would have gone through with it? Just on the chance she'd find us together?"

"She did find us together," Laurie said dreamily, "with my clothes scattered all over your living room."

I stared at her, slowly getting it.

Laurie was at the door. Something very close to pity was in her smile. "You see, Norm, I love Matt more than I hate you. And I hate you very much. It makes the difference."

She was gone. I started dialing again, counting the rings. I don't know how long I kept dialing.

20

The alarm went off at seven. I lurched out of bed, head splitting, fumbling blindly for the button, whimpering little curses as the clock kept ringing. I smashed it against the floor and it was still.

Three cups of hot black coffee. Three cigarettes, brooding. The cold sting of the razor, the gray, nervous face in the mirror, the twitching mouth. *Why* had she stopped by last night? What if she went to Angelo, told him everything? For a moment I couldn't breathe.

I finished dressing and slipped Shannon's automatic into my coat pocket. I had to explain. She had to believe me. Shannon still had the Lincoln. I'd have to walk.

Ten blocks over to Olive Street. Ten blocks of feverish panting—the sweat running into my eyes—trying to think of some explanation that would satisfy her.

I unlocked Shannon's front door quietly with the duplicate key she'd given me. "Shannon," I called. "Honey, it's Norm!" Her bedroom was cold and still. The bed had not been slept in. I stared at it, empty and shaking.

I walked down Main and turned right on Center Street, past the closed bars, gray and ugly in the morning sunlight. I finally spotted the Lincoln, parked in front of the Golden Wheel. Angelo's hotel.

Rage pumped scaldingly into my throat. My fingers curled around the handle of the gun in my coat pocket.

She was in the back casino, at one of the crap tables. Her laughter was feverishly shrill as she threw the dice. She laughed wildly, blonde hair tossing, as the tired stickman placed more chips in front of her.

Angelo sat in a booth across the room, drinking coffee. He watched Shannon like a cat.

Shannon left the game, picked up her drink and wavered over to Angelo's table. Now they were talking. I walked toward them. Angelo's face was darkly impassive as he saw me. Shannon looked up with a distorted smile.

"Good morning, darling. Work hard last night?"

I caught her by the wrist, jerked her to her feet. I slapped her openhanded, wanting to kill her.

"So we like to play," I said through my teeth. "Come on, you tramp, we're going home."

"Wait a minute." Angelo's cruel smile was etched with strain. "I got something to say."

"Say it!"

"You say Robin's okay?"

"That's right."

"Then you won't mind bringing me a letter from her? Today. Telling me how good she feels. You won't mind that?"

"No," I said, feeling the blood go out of my face.

"This afternoon, maybe? About four?"

"Sure," I said.

I dragged Shannon out through the lobby and threw her into the Lincoln. She was quiet, sullen. I drove in a cold rage, my thoughts spinning. Shannon nursed her wrist, swearing softly; then all at once she crumpled like a little girl and broke into a storm of weeping.

I pulled into her driveway and let her cry it out on my shoulder.

"Stop it," I said, putting an arm around her. "You won't believe this, but it's true. Listen."

I told her about Laurie, exactly the way it happened. She nodded dully, but she didn't believe me. She would never believe me in a thousand years.

"When I saw her clothes in the living room I could have killed you," she breathed. "I went straight home and got some money. I felt hopped up, crazy. I gambled all night."

"What did you tell Angelo?'

"N-nothing," she sniffled. "He only asked me if Robin was all right. I played innocent, dumb."

Real dumb. Sure. I pictured the whispered hint to Angelo, the silken noose tightening about my throat. "We're leaving town," I told her. "Tonight. Get some sleep. Then get packed. How much you got left ... two thousand, three?"

"I lost it all." Her eyes slid away from mine. "All of it, this morning. Does it matter, darling?"

I made myself kiss her. Under her tearful mask I could sense the squirming hate, the bitterness. Perhaps she did believe me. It didn't matter. Fear is the catalyst that turns love into hate, and I was very much afraid of her. There was no telling how much she had spilled to Angelo.

It was nine-thirty. The banks opened at ten. First I made myself stop at a downtown cafe and eat breakfast. The eggs felt slimy in my mouth and the coffee was like lye, but I got it down. By the time I reached the bank my nerves were screaming.

I drew out my entire account. Six thousand dollars. I tried to think of it as a real stake, a shining windfall for the poor slob who had hit town flat-broke less than a year ago, but it was nothing compared with what I might have in six months—if I stayed alive.

Driving to City Hall, I felt as if small, wild eyes were watching me. I kept searching the traffic for that prowling tan Mercury. I parked the Lincoln behind City Hall and went up to see Bullock.

"Any repercussions from last night?"

"Open and shut," Bullock said happily. "What's with Matt?"

"We'll have to smear him. Tell Kramer to wrap up Matt's ledger discrepancies this afternoon and get out a warrant. Alert the county attorney. Tell him Matt might make some wild accusations."

"Good idea. If we can just keep Angelo in line until after election ..."

I laughed. The sound was indescribably vicious. It reminded me of Murdoch's laughter, ice splintering, things tearing apart. I began talking.

"You're raving!" Bullock whispered hoarsely. "You're demented, Sands. This town's ready to pop, right this minute. We don't dare smash Angelo yet—it'd be just what the opposition needs! They'd cry gang war, and they'd be right!"

"All right." I started for the door. "So long."

He sat frozen. "What are you going to do?"

"See the district attorney. A real fearless district attorney who eats crooked politicians for breakfast. I'll give him some reading matter. This afternoon he'll hit this town like a tornado. You might get off with five years, Tom."

"Goddammit," he yelled, "you're nuts! You're worse than Clem ever was. You're a stark, raving mad-dog crazy—"

I yanked him out of his chair and shook him till his teeth rattled. "You small-time yellow-livered bastard, by tonight Angelo will know I've crossed him. He'll tear this town apart! We've got to get him first. Angelo's mainstays are Froggy Martin and Spinelli. With the three of them gone, the rest will scatter like rats. I'll finger him for you, fair enough?"

All the fight was gone out of him. He took a deep breath and nodded. "All right. Where and when?"

I went over it with him for half an hour. The important part of it was timing.

An hour later I called Angelo at his hotel. "You'll get your letter this afternoon." I gave him Shannon's address. "See you at four o'clock sharp."

"She's all right? You haven't done nothing to her?"

"Oh, we cut off a few fingers to keep her in line—" His frenzied roar again. I grinned into the mouthpiece, said, "Four sharp," and hung up.

Just enough to worry him. Enough to build up his strain to a howling crescendo of fear and worry. He was not yet sure if Robin was dead. Shannon was too smart to have given him more than a few bitter hints this morning. I could imagine the torment that was driving him mad right this minute.

I called Shannon.

"Norm, I'm worried."

"Don't be," I crooned into the phone. "I've stalled Angelo until midnight. But by then, honey, we'll be far away."

Even over the wire her contrition sounded real. "Darling, I'm sorry about this morning. Something bad's going to happen. I can feel it."

"I've got a few loose ends to tidy up," I said. "I'll pick you up at five sharp. I'll have twelve grand in my jeans."

The money, of course, was the bait. She'd wait for me all afternoon. But she'd get—Angelo.

The shock would snap Shannon into a hysterical confession. Angelo would probably kill her. At ten minutes after four Bullock's troopers would arrive in a prowl car. Angelo would be killed resisting arrest. Everything dovetailed. No loose ends.

The warrant for Matt was already out. By midnight he'd be behind bars. I felt like a heel, but what the hell, I told myself, it was his own stubborn fault.

It was twelve-thirty when I drove out of the service station. The Lincoln was oiled and gassed. The motor purred eagerly as I passed Orange Street and hit the main highway. The speedometer shot up to eighty and hung there quivering. Five miles then ten toward the coast and Highway 101. At first I kept glancing into the rearview mirror, but there was no sign of that tan Mercury and the highway was a smoking white ribbon of empty concrete. I leaned back and lit a cigarette. The relief was invigorating. Tonight I'd phone Bullock from Los Angeles, perhaps even Vegas, to find out how things had gone. In any case, I'd take a two-week vacation. Perhaps Catalina. Fishing, sleeping in the sun. I had six thousand dollars, and after election there would be more, much more. I began whistling.

It was too bad about Shannon. I would have a few bad nights, but I was used to bad nights. Thirty miles, forty. The jeweled beach towns rushing past; Dana Point, Newport, Laguna. A wicked little thought nibbled at my brain. I had forgotten something …

I was coming into Laguna when the thought suddenly uncoiled. I slammed on the brakes and sat fighting panic, coldly weighing my chances.

It was only one-fifteen. There was still time. Time enough to make a squealing U-turn, to roar back along the highway, doing ninety now and slowing down to sixty for the beach towns, swearing at the red lights. Just the other side of Dana Point I ran a stop sign, and there was the strident blare of a siren. He pulled me over to the side of the road and took an eternity getting off his motorcycle, the way they always do.

"Kind of hitting it up back there, weren't you?"

"Look, write it up and spare the sermon," I snapped. "I haven't got all day."

That was a mistake. His youngish face hardened. "Operator's license!"

He took ten whole minutes to write that ticket. All the time I sat fuming, trying to keep from letting the rage show. Calling myself nineteen kinds of a fool for not remembering that manila envelope in Shannon's refrigerator. Sweat broke out on my face as the picture unfolded: Shannon realizing she'd been set up for the patsy; Angelo going berserk with fury; Shannon offering him the records, trying to make a deal, telling him everything. Angelo would kill her anyway—I knew that. But now he'd have the records. And he'd know how to use them.

When I finally drove away, that cop followed me. He followed me for five miles. Carefully, I kept it under forty, raging inside, feeling that gun in my coat, wanting to use it.

Finally, when I turned left on the inland route, he kept going and didn't turn off after me. I made the next twenty miles in twelve minutes flat. It was ten after three when I careened into Shannon's driveway. I ran up the steps and threw open the front door.

"Come in," Matt said. He held the gun pointed carefully at my navel. "We've been waiting."

21

Matt stood in the middle of the living room, smiling crookedly. His left arm was still in the plaster cast, but the gun in his right hand was steady. Shannon sat limply on the sofa. "He's crazy," she whispered. "He keeps asking for—"

"The records," Matt broke in. "Where are they?"

I walked toward him confidently, my hand outstretched. "Give it here, Galahad. It's not loaded, remember?"

"I'm warning you, Norm."

I threw back my head to laugh and Matt pistol-whipped me across the jaw. The pain was blinding. My brother Matt? For a second I couldn't believe it. It was like being attacked by a rabbit. Then rage choked me and I went for him. This time the barrel smashed against my temple.

"You bastard," I said incredulously. I was on hands and knees, watching my blood drip down in tiny red spots on the carpet. I got up slowly.

Matt's face was contorted with emotion. "I'm not your brother anymore. Just a stranger who's going to kill you. Unless you deliver, right this minute."

I touched my cheek and stared at my red fingers. This wasn't really happening! I said, dreamily, "They're in a safe-deposit box."

"Where's the key?"

"I don't have it with me."

The gun smashed into my mouth this time. I stood reeling, tasting iron and salty blood. Shannon flew at him with a wordless cry and Matt shoved her hard against the piano. I shivered with fury as I reached in my coat pocket, but I made it look like I was trembling with fear.

"Here," I muttered. "Take it." My fingers touched the cold steel of Shannon's automatic. "How was I to know you meant bus—"

My right hand was a snake striking, and there was the ugly crunch of metal on bone. Matt's gun thumped on the carpet. He stared stupidly at his numb wrist, at me.

"Now," I said grinning, "you're going to—"

Agony exploded whitely in my groin and flared up to the top of my skull. I lay on my side, huddled into a moaning ball of pain. He had given me the knee! His own brother! I was clawing for the gun, and Matt's shoe was swinging at my face. Then the last fragments of light splintered into darkness.

"Darling? Oh Norm, are you all right?"

The genuine misery in her voice. The cold cloth on my forehead.

"Where is he?" I mumbled through puffed lips.

"Lie quietly, darling, please." She was crying, kneeling over me with a wet washcloth, and crying. "He's gone. I gave them to him, those damned records. He would have killed you."

"You gave them to him?" I struggled to my feet, shaking. The room spun. I wanted to hit her, but I was too weak. I slumped to my knees. "What time is it?" I croaked.

"Three forty-five." Her voice shook. "Oh sweetheart—"

"Oh sweetheart," I mimicked spitefully. "I'm a jealous woman, but I love you. I love you so much I'll give Matt the ammunition to kill you. I'll tell Angelo that Robin's dead, darling, just to teach you not to sleep with another woman!" Hatred throttled me as I tried to rise. At last I lay, cursing her weakly. "Got to get out of here," I said. "Help me up."

As she helped me to the sofa, there was the grinding of brakes outside. Then, heavy feet coming up the walk.

"Who's there?" Shannon called.

"Shut up," I whispered. I got to my feet. Nausea stirred blackly in my stomach. The tiny automatic lay in a corner. As I picked it up, the knocking at the door became loud, angry.

"Stall him," I whispered. "No matter what happens, stall him! You got that?"

She was breathless with panic, but she nodded. I took her gently by the shoulders, pulled her against me. The knocking was thunder. "I love you," I said, meaning it. "If we come out of this I'll make it up to you." I kissed her. "Answer it."

I made it to the bedroom closet just as the front door opened.

"We're a little early." Angelo's bass rumble. "I got impatient. You mind?"

Shannon's frightened "no."

It was dark and close in the closet. Silk things rustled as I moved. Silk things that whispered of Shannon, that smelled of her—a clean, April-rain freshness. Realization came over me in a burst of grief and bitterness. *God help me, I loved her.*

I opened the closet door just a hair. I could see Angelo's knees in the angle the hall made with the living room.

"... some coffee?" Shannon was saying.

"Sure." Froggy Martin's thin voice. "Don't mind if we do."

"No coffee," Angelo said. "This ain't a social call. When's he coming?"

Shannon, brightly, "Norm? Oh, he'll be hours."

"He better be minutes. Where's Robin?"

"I—don't know."

The seconds dragged by like years. My insides felt smashed. I wondered if Matt had continued kicking me when I was out. Sir Galahad with a gun. I felt a queer, perverse pride in him.

"It's four o'clock." Spinelli's voice.

"Give him time," Angelo said.

I breathed shallowly.

"I'll make some coffee," Shannon said.

"You just sit." Angelo's voice was animal now, the thin veneer of civilization peeling away as the minutes passed.

It must be four-ten by now, I thought. Bullock would come soon. He had to come!

Silence from the living room. Then Froggy's nasal whine. "He's not coming! Look at her, Angelo, look how white she is. He's not coming and you been played for a sucker. It's some kind of trap, I can feel it!"

Suddenly Angelo went mad. "Damn you," he blazed. "When's he coming? Is this another of his stinking blind alleys? Is it?"

Shannon sounded hysterical. "He'll be here later—"

The sound of a slap. Her muffled sob.

"You were in on that snatch," Angelo grated. "Where is she?"

"Honestly, I don't kn—"

The slaps continued. Angelo's laughter, merciless as flint. Goddamn him, if he hit her again, I'd blow his brains through the back of his head! *Where was Bullock?*

I ground my fists into my ears, breathing over and over like a litany, *"I'll make it up to you,"* but I could still hear those sounds. Sounds of a dress tearing. The creaking of sofa springs. Shannon's little cries. Spinelli's lascivious titter. *"Stall them,"* I had told her. She'd stall them with her body, with death if necessary. Because she loved me. The thought was a searing coal.

"I'll show you," Shannon said in a tortured whisper. "Please stop. I'll show you where she is."

"That's better. Real better. Let's go."

I couldn't take it anymore. A tiny corner of my mind was cold, infinitely scornful, telling me I couldn't afford luxuries like passion or revenge. Just wait. Let them go for the time being.

But I slid the closet door open and sighted on Angelo's right knee, all that was visible of him. I pressed the trigger.

The spiteful crack of the .22 in the closet was deafening. Angelo went down like an eyelid and Froggy dived for the protection of the sofa. I reached the hall door firing wildly.

Shep Spinelli was crouched in the center of the room, shooting into the hallway. Wood fragments dissolved next to my cheek as I fired two quick shots at him. His hands flew to his throat. He was flopping on the carpet as I stepped full into the living room, a perfect target. I shot at Angelo three times. He rolled frantically for cover as my bullets hit the carpet next to him.

Froggy's white face was a blur behind the sofa. I wheeled toward him as a firecracker went off in my chest. The room tilted crazily and the carpet jumped up to hit me in the face.

Stillness. I coughed, feeling the blood in my throat, thick and warm.

Froggy stood up, spraddle-legged. His eyes were bright. He took careful aim at my head. Angelo's bellow stopped him.

"I want him alive." Angelo's voice was thick with agony. "God, my knee. I think he smashed the kneecap."

Shannon lay half-across the sofa. Her eyes were closed. A crimson line trickled down from the corner of her mouth.

"Where's Robin?" Angelo said.

"She's dead," I answered dully.

"You're a liar!" He wouldn't believe it. He hobbled to his feet, swaying. "Ask the girl, Froggy."

Froggy was shaking her. She whimpered. Her fingers moved. "Norm," she murmured.

I crawled across the carpet toward her.

"Where's Robin?" Froggy said.

Shannon's lips moved. "Norm?" she breathed. "Darling?"

"Right here." I cradled her head in my arms. "Tell them about Robin, honey."

"She's fine." Shannon's smile was drowsy. "Isn't that right, darling? Is it over at last, darling, all over? Can we go now? Can we see Paris?"

"We'll see Paris." My eyes were stinging. It was hard to see.

"Just us," she said. "The Riviera ..."

Her head drooped sideways. She was smiling, but she wasn't breathing.

"Take him," Angelo said.

Froggy threw my right arm over his shoulder. They took me outside, put me in the back seat of the Buick. My chest hurt. I kept coughing, a bubbling cough. I tried to tell them about Robin.

Angelo's laughter was insane. "She said Robin was fine. I *heard* her say it. The last thing she said. You'll show us where Robin is."

"We got ways," Froggy said.

I tried to laugh, and it came out a sob.

The snarl of the siren behind us. Angelo swore and gunned the Buick. The squad car came hurtling alongside the Buick, forcing it toward the curb. Angelo was fighting the wheel, cursing gutturally. I tried to yell at the squad car, to tell Bullock he was too late, and a bullet frosted the window, spraying my face with glass.

The whole squad car was squirting flame. Froggy was leaning past Angelo, firing; then all at once his face seemed to dissolve in a red smear. He disappeared behind the front seat. As we careened around the corner, the Buick swerved into the squad car and I slammed hard against the left door. The squad car teetered sideways and smashed into a telephone pole in a jumble of glass and sound. My chest was ripping apart. The last thing I heard was Angelo's metallic laughter.

22

An eternity of pain-racked blackness.

Blackness and time and agony.

The room was small, incredibly dirty. Leprous patches of plaster flaked the walls and ceiling. A grimy window showed pale daylight outside. I moved my head and saw the battered table, the rickety chair. Angelo was slumped over the table, his head buried in his arms.

I tried to move. My straw pallet rustled beneath me. Angelo's head lifted. His face was something out of a sick dream—the grinning mouth, the black eyes sunken and mad. He reeled to his feet, clutching the table for support.

"Where are we?" My chest throbbed horribly. It hurt to talk.

"Holed up on Orange Street," Angelo said. "This is the third day." He lit a cigarette. "You're tough, baby. That's good. Where's Robin?" I tried to tell him, but he wouldn't believe me. He would never believe me. He had an obsession that Robin was alive and safe.

He told me the news, leering. How the whole town had gone smash. The mayor and half the city council had resigned. The county attorney's boys had closed down the cribs and most of the bars. Bullock had been killed in the squad car smashup. Angelo's boys had all fled.

"Rats," Angelo said, "deserting a sinking ship. They wanted me to come, too. They wouldn't help me find Robin. But you'll help me, baby. Where is she? Where's Robin?"

"She's dead."

"Come off it." The black eyes gleamed with a cunning madness. "You got a price, I got money. I got something else, too."

Angelo hobbled over to me. Deliberately, he snuffed out his cigarette on my cheek. I tried to scream and my chest was a crater of red fire. I passed out.

Voices penetrated the pain. A strange voice, dignified and tired. "*Señor*, I cannot be responsible. You must have an operation immediately. Your leg—"

"Never mind my leg. You get paid to answer questions and keep your mouth shut. What about him?"

The doctor leaned over me. He had kind brown eyes and a straggly white goatee. His fingers probed. "Shock. Loss of blood. As I told you yesterday, he needs plasma. But I think you, my friend, have gangrene."

"It's just a scratch. You croakers are all alike." Angelo's grin was feverish. He hobbled to the table, ripped open the sack of hamburgers and fries, began to wolf them down. "Only trouble is, it stinks. Better leave some more iodine."

I saw his leg, the trouser ripped away from it at the knee. The makeshift bandage, caked with blood and filthy. The ugly purple-green swelling. The smell.

"Same time tomorrow, doc?"

"As you wish." The doctor folded his stethoscope precisely and picked up his black bag with a shrug of resignation. Angelo came over to my pallet, his grin hungry, expectant. "He's well enough to talk?"

"He has the constitution of a bull, that one. He will live to be ninety."

Angelo threw back his head and laughed.

THE END

89800007R00186

Made in the USA
San Bernardino, CA
02 October 2018